Laurie L. Bolanos

PRINCE

of Conjurers

Nicobar Press

Laurie L. Bolanos/Nicobar Press
http://www.nicobarpress.com/

Publisher's Note: This is a work of fiction. Names, characters, places, and incidents are a product of the author's imagination. Locales and public names are sometimes used for atmospheric purposes. Any resemblance to actual people, living or dead, or to businesses, companies, events, institutions, or locales is completely coincidental.

Book Layout © 2014 BookDesignTemplates.com

Prince of Conjurers/ Laurie L. Bolanos. – 1st ed.
ISBN 978-1-938125-26-3

In memory of my soul-friend

Kellee Ann Olasin Chauvin

12/03/1970 -12/29/2001

and

Llewelyn Powys

whose life gave me inspiration

8/13/1884 - 12/2/1939

❧ ACKNOWLEDGEMENTS ❧

My critique group: Margaret Hauck, Farrah Rochon, Rosalind Green-Holmes, and Shauna Roberts for helping me turn straw into gold. You have my love and my thanks.

My thanks to Barry and Trudy Lacour for your suggestions and your support. Most of all for giving me life and a love of reading.

My thanks to Gilton and Amanda Bolanos for cheering me on along the way.

My thanks to Alexander Bolanos for your opinions and insightful advice.

My thanks to Cathy Peterson for your unwavering encouragement and always challenging me to push the envelope.

My thanks to Jack Chance for all the trips to the French Quarter, your confidence in me, and telling every person we met, "My cousin is an author. She's writing a book." Thanks also for the photo shoot.

My thanks to Christy Nichols for your assistance and advice, formatting Prince, and trusting the soul-process.

My thanks to Candice Detillier Huber for helping me with the finishing touches.

My thanks to Karen Muller Albert and Jennifer Pierce for proofreading Prince. Your time and energy is appreciated more than you know.

My thanks to Shehnaz Umrigar for always asking to read the next chapter.

My thanks to Nikola Bilbao, Iñaki Uzkudun, and Metxu from Basauri, who gave me the Basque translations.

My thanks to William Hammett for saying just the right thing at just the right time. Namaste.

My thanks to Raymond Forrester, Richard Mistretta, Francisco Ochoa, Corey Schouest, Brian Shamas, and David Trentadue for your honesty and insight into the male perspective.

My thanks to Andres De La Puente for encouraging me to finish my dream by making his own dream a reality with the launch of Groundstoground.com.

My thanks to the Elmwood Starbucks' baristas for taking good care of me.

My thanks to Joseph B Dunn (Joe B) and Niall Doherty of Disrupting the Rabblement for lending their names.

My thanks to Penny Nichols-Barthe, Angie Granier, and Stacy Hohman for being there for me when I needed to talk.

My thanks to Fiona Jayde Media for such a beautiful book cover.

❧ FOREWORD ❧

I was introduced to *Phantom of the Opera* in 1989 when given the role of understudy for Christine in a college dance production. Not long after, I purchased *Phantom of the Opera* on CD and immersed myself in the musical. I did not get the opportunity to see Sir Andrew Lloyd Webber's play until 1995. I found his adaptation awe-inspiring. The music lends itself to the emotional angst of the characters and captures the good, the bad, and the ugly of Erik as the Opera Ghost. Sitting in the historic Saenger theatre all those years ago, mesmerized by the production, I was hooked. I wanted more.

I read Gaston Leroux's book, *Phantom of the Opera*, since the play is based on his story. There were differences, and I had the opportunity to learn more about Erik. However, between the play and the book, I felt Erik deserved a better resolution. I chose to start *Prince of Conjurers* where Gaston Leroux ended, so I refer to his version of events.

Many other sequels have been written to keep Erik's story going, but *Prince of Conjurers* is the story that I envisioned and one that took me six years to write. Every day I pushed onward, telling myself that it didn't matter how long it took me to finish. As long as my story touched just one person, it would be worth all the time and effort. Not long after I wrote the last sentence, I realized that *I* was that one person. I have been changed by the experience. So, if you should also feel moved by the words, then as we say in South Louisiana, it's lagniappe.

❧ EPIGRAPH ❧

But I advise you, and in no uncertain terms, to value as you value your life, such friendships as may be possible for you in your own day: for as you grow older, you will find that wealth, power, fame, even your own honest achievements, seem unimportant; but you can never lose the splendor of having loved and having been loved by a few great spirits.

-Llewelyn Powys-

❦ TABLE OF CONTENTS ❦

PROLOGUE
Death of a Phantom

Paris, France 1898

I remember vividly the night I died; the night I killed the Phantom.

The scene was set. My coffin was center stage, haloed by a semicircle of lit candles in brass candelabras. Red bolts of silk draped artfully from floor to ceiling. The flickering candlelight's amber hue against the red created a somber mood. It was perfection.

It was most unfortunate for Georges, the man I had cast as my understudy. I did not choose him because he was special, but because he wasn't. He was unremarkable. What he did possess was bone structure and height similar to my own. And for that, he paid with his life to play the role of the century.

I performed a requiem in honor of his sacrifice.

I had several candidates, mind you. The physical attributes were easy to find. But there were other considerations that factored into my decision, making Georges the ideal choice. Every night he slept in the same dank alley. He had no kin. He was forgettable.

He was me.

Don't feel too badly for him. I fed him a meal fit for royalty and soused him with wine. A generous end to a non-descript life, don't you agree? As a sign of respect, I stared into his dull eyes as he futilely attempted to pry my fingers away from his throat. With each clumsy strike he made, his life ebbed away between the grasp of my hands. I looked deeply and found no spark within him to extinguish. That man had been dead for years already. In fact, you could say I was of great service to him.

I find people see what they want to believe. Don't you? That is, if you can create the right illusion, of course. I was successful the last time I faked my death. I have no reason to believe I won't succeed again.

Christine Daaé.

She accepted my proposal of her own free will. She had allowed me to kiss her. I made contact with her warm, soft skin to kiss her forehead. Imagine my surprise when she did not withdraw from me. I can still feel the pressure on my lips. For that briefest moment, I had felt a taste of all the happiness the world could offer.

As tears fell from my eyes, I bared my very soul to her.

No illusions.

My tears were real.

My pain still is.

She looked directly into my eyes, without fear, without abhorrence. All I saw reflected there was sympathy and love. It was not how she looked at Raoul, but it was love of some measure. She had been willing to give up everything to be my living wife.

Between you and me, at that moment, the small strain of humanity that runs in my soul overpowered my own wants and desires. Her happiness mattered more than my own. And I let her go.

Christine.

When I set her free, I meant it. I had wanted to die. However, it did not take long for bitterness to take root in my heart. Die for love of her? I think not! She is mine. The life I wanted was disappearing with the golden-haired, perfect-featured vicomte.

I waited in the shadows as Christine and Raoul crossed the river to my lake house. I was not far behind when they entered the Louis-Philippe room. Christine gasped when she saw my stiff, emaciated body lying in my casket.

As always, my work was meticulous. White wax, paste, and the mask—my prison and my salvation—transformed Georges into "The Phantom." I am not surprised Christine and Raoul have been fooled. I watch them steal glances at me, their noses covered with cloth. Pitiable Georges was quite odorous before he died and now, he bothers even me.

I know Raoul loves her.

What other man would drag my body to entomb me deep within the bowels of the Paris Opera House? That was my request of her: to bury me in the most deserted part of the Opera, the furthest dungeon below the fifth cellar where no one ever goes.

What does that say of her? She follows my wishes and has him place me there. I watch her touch my dead, rotting flesh and place the plain gold band on my littlest finger. The gold ring that once graced hers. I know there will always be something between us—a soul connection.

It angers me how they rejoice in my timely departure. The relief in their embrace. The passion of their kisses revolts me. I want to kill them both!

But, I am a patient man.

I rest my head against the damp stone wall of the dungeon and listen to Raoul and Christine whisper through the narrow cellar hallways. Why they whisper, I do not know.

"Leave Paris," their soft voices agree. Start their lives over, sail away. Passage to La Nouvelle-Orléans. I hear the word faintly as they believe they leave me to my endless slumber

La Nouvelle-Orléans.

Of course they cannot live here with the suspicion of Comte Philippe's death on Raoul's head, a death that weighs on my shoulders. Let them go and let them be blissfully unaware. Much planning must be done before I can follow. But follow them I shall.

I will remain a man of my word.

Raoul may continue to have her heart, but I will have her immortal soul.

I will collect what is mine.

It belongs to me…

I am the Prince of Conjurers.

CHAPTER ONE

New Orleans, Louisiana, 2009

Julie blew a wisp of hair from her face and raised the sledgehammer to strike again. At impact, pieces of plaster sprayed into the air and fell to the floor. Renovating was easier than she thought it would be and more therapeutic than the $150/hour she had paid for counseling over the last year. She raised her arms again, the hammer feeling lighter with each blow.

"You low-down dirty dog!" Julie yelled. The wall opened from the blow to the exact spot she had pictured her husband's face. Her ex-husband, Simon.

She didn't show mercy to her ex-best friend, Monika, either. Swing after swing, she felt the pent-up rage escaping until she became weak. Her anger gave way to grief, a grief that no longer had tears.

Her love for Simon had blinded her. He had seduced her and made her feel as if she were the most beautiful woman in the world. That's when she learned words could be powerful even if they were empty.

"You have the most mesmerizing eyes; so green, so alluring, so cat-like. Your brown hair, soft as silk. Your alabaster skin, flawless." She could hear his deep voice and French accent in her mind. She had believed him, all the flattery, all the love talk, everything out of his mouth, even though he had spewed nothing but lies. Married barely a year, Julie had given herself wholeheartedly to this man only to have her life as she knew it completely destroyed. Anger rose in her again when she thought about Monika.

She had been Julie's best friend since high school. And Monika, of all people, knew how hard it was for Julie to trust and love someone. She knew Julie's fear of losing the people she loved since it had happened to her throughout her life. Because of this, Monika's betrayal hurt more than anything.

She couldn't stop the memories from resurfacing. Her stomach churned at the recalling Marvin Gaye's seductive voice drifting down the stairs from their bedroom. Marvin Gaye had always been a sign that her husband wanted her. She had assumed Simon must have called her office and found she had left for the day earlier than usual.

With her pulse racing, Julie climbed up the stairs, kicking off her shoes. It had been at least two weeks since they had made love. She pictured him waiting in bed for her as she took off her belt and headed for their bedroom.

"Hello, Baby." She pushed open the ajar door, posing seductively.

The rest of the memory came as snapshots. Messed up bed. Sheets hanging over the edge. Two wine glasses on the nightstand. Empty bottle lying on its side. Two sets of clothing crumpled on the floor. Running water in the bathroom. Muffled laughter. Her heart racing. Difficulty breathing. Dread crushing her soul. Marvin Gaye singing on and on.

She can see her hand pulling back the shower curtain. Remember the feeling of her eyes widening in disbelief. Her cries, soundless to her ears now. Simon turned to face her, his blonde hair, dark and flattened to his head. Water dripped down his naked body as he held a blushing Monika in his arms. He stood there unapologetically, shrugging his shoulders. "I love Monika."

Simple as that. No explanation. No repentance. Nothing.

She couldn't remember much else past that point. The world revolved around her in slow motion while she remained on real time. Both of their voices droned on without making any sense to her. Simon's French accent, once charming, sounded hollow to her now. She flew from the room. They followed behind her saying words she could not decipher.

The trauma of that moment was the last straw in a series of traumas, breaking her already fragile psyche and earning her a diagnosis of Post Traumatic Stress Disorder from her esteemed psychiatrist, Dr. Rotel.

"Let's give it another year," he had told her. "Depending on your progress, you should be able to stop the Prozac by then."

A few years later, with little to show for it, she still took her pills faithfully every day. Except, of course, when she drank. Her temporary break with reality was the reason she was unemployed and collected social security disability. And, since Simon was the cheating spouse, Julie walked out of the marriage as the financial victor. A sad smile pulled at her lips at the small consolation. At least the whole experience wasn't a total loss.

She bought a historic shotgun house in the French Quarter on St. Peter's Street. Besides rebuilding her own life, it made her feel good to play a part in rebuilding New Orleans. Others saw Katrina as a disaster. For her, Katrina was a salvation. It had destroyed the home she'd shared with Simon. It had washed away all the ugliness and had given her a new start. And it had played a significant part in relocating Simon and Monika to Georgia, far away from her.

Goodbye and good riddance, Julie thought, tossing Simon and Monika from her mind. It was back to the business at hand, remodeling her house.

She scrutinized the wall more closely. It was a little too late now, had she been wrong, but the wall did not seem to be a weight-bearing one. She did not see any electrical wiring behind the wooden slats that held the plaster. She had dodged a bullet with that.

Stepping into the hallway, she looked between the two rooms. She could easily envision the smaller one as a nice sitting area for her bedroom. It was something to look forward to, and doing projects herself kept her body, if not her mind busy.

She walked back into her bedroom, pushed the button on her ionized air purifier, and picked up the larger chunks of plaster, tossing all the pieces into a black Hefty bag. She'd work on the wall a little bit each day and take her time, but she had made enough progress for now. Julie sat on the floor and sipped from her glass of Cabernet Sauvignon, admiring her work. The smooth, dry liquid felt good sliding down her throat.

Bam! Bam!

Julie placed the wine glass down, running to the front door as the kicking and banging continued.

"Semaj, I've asked you to stop kicking my door! Once I get it replaced, you'll ruin the new one out of habit."

With his arms full of groceries, Semaj pushed past her into the house, heading toward the kitchen. "It's all good," he twanged with his born-and-bred Texas accent. "I need to keep some of my food here for a while. My fridge is on the fritz."

"Great..." Julie mumbled under her breath while double-locking the door. "What are neighbors for?" she yelled back to him. Ever since Semaj had rented the house next to hers, he was pretty much over all the time for something or the other.

James, as he was formerly known, insisted he be called Semaj since pronouncing his name backwards sounded exotic. The 6'2" bear of a man had retired early from the Marines a few years back due to psychological issues of his own, one being he had difficulty holding a serious conversation. "It's all good," was his reply to everything whether the situation was bad or good.

They shared the same psychiatrist, Dr. Rotel, and had met at an outpatient clinic group meeting. She had shared some of her problems with the group and Semaj shared his, too. One of his main issues was an addiction to sex, which affected his ability to discriminate between appropriate and inappropriate partners.

His current flavor of the month, Armando, became a problem for Julie when she had caught him helping himself to her silverware. Semaj had promised never to bring him back again, but Semaj's other problem was keeping promises, so she wasn't holding her breath on that.

"What's up with you, Dawlin'?" Semaj asked. She had already told him three times that she was going to knock down the wall today, but most things she said seemed to go in one of his ears and out the other. Unless it was sexual or had to do with men and, preferably, both at the same time.

"Come see," she told him. He lumbered behind her, looking in all the rooms as he passed them. She waved her hand toward the wall. "I'm doing a little bit of remodeling. Remember, I told you yesterday."

Semaj glanced at the wall and the small sledge hammer resting on top of the plaster-filled garbage bag. "Oh, so that's the source of the pounding I heard earlier. I thought you were having wild jungle sex in here, but I guess I knew better than that since hell hadn't frozen over." He chortled at his own joke and smiled at her with bleached white teeth.

"Here," he said, picking up the sledgehammer, "let me help."

The thundering crash mingled with her protest of "No, thank you."

The middle portion of the wall collapsed to the floor. Pieces of plaster flew in every direction. Dust fell on her furniture. It reminded her of a snow globe whose contents were just beginning to settle. It was then she noticed a chunk of plaster had tipped over her glass of wine. She froze and watched as the red liquid spread across her floor, reminding her of another time she had seen a pool of red.

"No need to thank me," Semaj turned to her with a smile that faded at seeing the spill.

"Oh, Dawlin'," he said as he watched her look at the floor, wiping tears from her eyes and unable to speak. "It's all good," he said, helping her to sit on the bed, then grabbing some dirty clothes strewn about her room to wipe the mess off the floor.

When he finished, he kicked the wet clothes into a corner and gave Julie a hug of apology before leaving. Semaj was a pain in the ass, but he sure could give a good hug when she needed it most.

Julie surveyed the chunks of plaster and dust from the edge of her bed. She refused to look at her wine-soaked clothes, knowing they were probably ruined. There was only one thing that would relieve the anxiety building in her: alcohol and plenty of it.

Realizing that her last bottle of wine was now gone, this called for a trip out of the house. She grabbed her keys, put her license in her pocket along with a handful of cash, and headed out the door. Bourbon Street was just around the corner. She would find all the relief she needed there.

The sun had almost set, but the heat and humidity lingered on, which was common for October. Julie felt the hotness absorbed by the red bricked sidewalk penetrating through her thin sandals. Hopefully the cooler north winds would blow in later as the news had predicted, bringing it to a comfortable 60 degrees.

As she moved closer to the Quarter, Julie noticed a tall man with black hair sticking out from under his baseball cap leaning against a wall playing a harmonica, a walking stick lay beside him. At his feet sat an old cigar box filled with change. She listened for a minute, not recognizing the tune, but he played well, so she tossed a dollar into his box.

He lowered the harmonica and flashed her a brilliant smile. "Thanks."

She smiled back and continued on.

Not one block later, a feminine voice called out from the shadow of an alleyway. "Read your fortune!"

"No thanks, Star," Julie replied.

Before Julie had met Star, she questioned the unusualness of her name. However, once meeting her, Julie could see there had never been a name that fit anyone so perfectly. Star was petite with jaw-length hair so blonde it almost looked white. Her almond-shaped sea-green eyes sat in a long face. No one knew where Star lived or where she came from, but every evening, she came out just at dusk, and you could find her on the streets to give readings.

Semaj had warned Julie about the local palmist and voodoo practitioner shortly after they met. "She's probably harmless, but I'd stay clear of her if I were you. Because well, you know," he said with a trademark toss of his head, "Star spelled backward is Rats, so I don't trust her."

"It won't take long," Star urged.

Julie smiled, unmoved. "You know I don't believe in that stuff."

"One day you might." Julie heard Star's voice behind her. "You know where to find me if you should change your mind."

Julie waved a dismissive hand without turning around. The only thing she needed to find was the sweet comfort that alcohol would provide. Anyway, only a fool would believe one could find answers written in the stars or from this Star.

CHAPTER TWO

La Nouvelle-Orléans Louisiana, 1898
Christine.

Erik's thoughts never strayed from his ultimate mission. Not when dressed in his finest, not as he exchanged pleasantries with other patrons, not even when he received admiring glances from other females. He was out this evening for one reason and one reason only...

Erik surveyed the Greek Revival building with an expert eye as he entered the French Opera House for the first time. Overall, the red-and-white elliptical auditorium was well-designed and constructed. He would do very little to improve upon its appearance. James Gallier, Jr, the man who created this masterpiece, invited Erik here as his special guest, believing him to be a fellow architect.

Erik did not accept James' invitation solely to appreciate this engineering marvel. Tonight was the first night of opera season, which meant the opening of the social season and an opportunity to mingle with the upper echelon. And Erik counted on seeing one person in particular.

"Monsieur de la Croix, may I introduce my cousin, Jane Tyler?" James Gallier, Jr. stood before Erik, a plump woman at his side. She favored James, having the same dark brown hair and striking brown eyes. Erik took her gloved hand and barely brushed it with his lips, careful not to transfer the wax and paste that hid his scarred face.

"My pleasure," he answered. Jane blushed, averting her eyes. Erik felt a modicum of forbearance for the spinster. He knew meeting her, flattering her with words he did not feel, was a price he had to pay for the invitation to tonight's sold-out performance of Berlioz's "La Damnation de Faust."

He expected many more such introductions in the future. Erik had established himself in New Orleans with letters of recommendation from fictitious French companies. Presented with a wealthy, respected French architect and developer, what respectable man would not want to forge an association for their cousin or any other female relative for that matter? Erik's new persona, Monsieur David de la Croix, had been accepted in his new country with open arms.

James looked at the ceiling as the lights of the opera house dimmed and brightened several times. "The opera is about to begin."

Erik offered Jane his arm and escorted her to their box seats. Ironically, box five. The same seat reserved for him in Paris. He could not feel more at home in New Orleans with such a grand gesture from the fates. After Jane was comfortably seated, Erik took his place in the chair behind her. His eyes adjusted to the dark theater just as the curtain opened and Madame Rossini, the opera's prima donna, began to sing. Erik closed his eyes and imagined his Christine singing instead, though he needn't have, for just as he had hoped, there she sat.

Third row.

Center stage.

Her dark hair swept back, her earrings dangling against her bare neck and her forget-me-not eyes closed, drawing attention to her rosy cheeks. He drank in her profile as he watched her lips silently move to the words.

Yes, Christine. Remember the gift of music, my songbird.

"Sing for me," he whispered, projecting his voice to her ear, a skill mastered many years ago. Her eyes fluttered open. He fluidly sat back into his seat. She looked around nervously, put one hand on her ear, and the other on the gentleman's arm to her right.

Raoul.

The very sight of the vicomte left Erik feeling cold. He grimaced. For now her hand would seek Raoul for comfort. For now. Soon enough, it would be Raoul living a life of emptiness.

♀

Erik hung back in the shadows, a natural act for him. He had been watching Monsieur and Madame de Marigny for weeks, learning their routines, watching for patterns in their schedules. The time was not right to move. But, when it was, he would be prepared as always.

He closed his eyes as they passed by on the empty street. Their footsteps echoed—Raoul's heavy and slow; Christine's light and brisk. He could pick her out of a crowded room by that sound alone, like a single repeating note.

Erik sighed.

Almost as if she had heard him, she stopped, her arm pulling her husband to a halt. Under the dim light cast by the street lamp, Christine's eyes were wide and her lips quivered just before she began to speak in their native French.

"Raoul, I know that Erik died, forever gone from our lives." She fidgeted with her clutch, looking over her shoulder in Erik's direction.

"But I...sometimes I feel him near me. All around me, as though he still lives."

Raoul looked frustrated. He clenched his hands, then opened them again. "Christine, you must put him from your thoughts. Do not forget that we buried him ourselves." He placed his hands on her shoulders—the ownership in the gesture irritated Erik—then Raoul turned her squarely to face him. "For the sake of argument, if by some magic he lives, he would never find us. My cousin's family has given us refuge here, we have changed our surnames to theirs, we cannot be found by anyone or anything. You are free, Christine. You must believe that as I do. Do not let him control you from the grave."

She held her husband's gaze for a minute, taking a deep breath. "Of course. I don't know what has come over me." She placed her hand over the front of her waistline. "I must start my confinement soon and my nerves stir my imagination."

Confinement.

The word pierced his soul with a sharp pang of disbelief. A surge of anger swelled in his chest. He took deep breaths to control the rage building within him. He was no fool. He knew what Raoul had done with his Christine to bring about this confinement. Her pregnancy complicated things greatly. He had not once factored in the possibility of a child.

"The season has only just started, yet tonight, it ends for me. I dread having to stay indoors for so long. It brings back memories I'd rather forget." She shuddered.

Erik knew the exact memories she was referring to—weeks sequestered with him in the bowels of the opera house. Weeks that brought him such joy, yet only made endurable for her by her own fortitude. His new plan would make up for those unbearable days.

Raoul put his arms around his wife and gave her a light squeeze. They began walking again, hand in hand, toward their Uptown home. A heavy fog drifted off the river and over the levee to dance around Erik's feet. He watched the retreating couple as they disappeared within it.

He stared hard into the fog after the de Marignys, thinking. *Her confinement is only a delay*, he placated himself.

A man emerged from a cross-street, rapping the flagstones with his walking stick. A top hat covered his black hair. The light from a passing streetlamp fluttered across his face, dancing over finely sculptured bones and shadowed eyes. He paused to spare Erik a glance, tossing him a brilliant smile as he tipped his hat.

"Good evening," the stranger said.

Erik stiffened, ducking his head. The last thing he wanted to do was draw attention to himself. "Good evening," he mumbled, walking away. He avoided the street lamps on his way home, remaining in the shadows. He didn't have far to go. He and the de Marignys lived in the same neighborhood, although on opposite ends.

Everything could still go as planned. In fact, this postponement could work in his favor. It would give him time to perfect his home for its new guest. Maybe even replicate parts of the Louis-Philippe room from his lake house, their lake house. And the matter of Christine's replacement had not been resolved. Once he conjured her soul, he needed an acceptable host to put it. As of yet, he hadn't found anyone who suited his taste. Because he'd have to live with his choice for a long time, he must not rush into making a decision.

He pushed the iron gate open and walked toward the tall, imposing 1820's house at 1319 St. Charles Ave. His new home. At one time it had been painted white. Now, it peeled in several places and vines crept up the foundation. As he reached the steps, he could barely see the large white columns and hand-carved trim work through the fog.

Erik had practically stolen the property. The house had been abandoned some years ago under rumors the Devil once lived there with his mistress. The locals continued to avoid it, disturbed by the odd silence and strange sense of being watched.

"The Devil's mansion," he muttered. "Proof that people will believe what they want to believe."

The sale had been completed by correspondence before he had even crossed the Atlantic. It was all too easy; purchasing the home, transferring his funds, establishing an identity, traveling to New Orleans, and the crux of his plan, buying parcels of land on the North Shore of Lake Pontchartrain. He had been negotiating with the de Marigny family to develop it on the condition that Raoul de Marigny would be placed in charge to oversee the construction.

His plan was genius.

Christine would be left alone most of the time, without anyone around to interfere. Nothing prevented him from his greatest, most magnificent endeavor, as if for once in his wretched existence, he was accepted into the greater design of life and it approved of his intentions. The way was being made clear for him with very little effort. He could not ask for more.

Well, maybe just a little...

CHAPTER THREE

New Orleans, Louisiana, 2009

"My p-p-poker face," Julie howled into the microphone. She swayed off beat. "Can't read my poker face," she sang to the crowd. Semaj, Armando, and another one of their friends waved from the audience, coaxing her on. She waved back.

She knew her performance was a direct result of several shots of Patron Gold. By day, she could not sing a note in tune. By night, under the flashing stage lights at the Cat's Meow Karaoke Bar, emboldened by alcohol, she just didn't care.

"P-p-poker face," she hollered amid clapping and whistles from the crowd as the music ended. The emcee jumped on the stage, taking the microphone from her hand.

"Let's give a hand to the talented Juliana François!" he said. Julie bowed amid more claps and whistles. "Now, Cassie Johnson, get up here and show us what you got!" A chick with multiple facial piercings brushed past Julie, as she climbed down the stage.

Julie was grateful that Semaj sat at one of the stools closest to the door; the breeze drifting in provided a respite from the crowded heat. On his left, sat a modern-day Grace Kelly, and Julie recognized the other woman to his right as Armando. Tonight Armando was all tricked out as Jennifer Lopez. Julie shook her head in resigned acceptance of Semaj's "friend" and plunked down on the next available stool.

"So," she hollered over the first bars of music. "How was I? Did I sound good up there?"

"It's all good." Semaj exhaled a trail of smoke toward the ceiling.

"No, not 'all good'." Armando leaned in to take a drag from Semaj's cigarette. "You sounded like a pig going to slaughter."

"Tell me how you *really* feel," she replied.

"I thought I just did," Armando answered with a smirk.

"Highly entertaining though," Semaj said, patting her knee. Julie gave Semaj a grateful smile then leaned closer to the mysterious Grace Kelly.

"I don't think we were introduced. I'm Julie." Julie shook the limp manicured hand extended out to her.

"Oh, girlfriend," the woman replied, her voice harboring a hint of falsetto as she turned Julie's hand over to examine it. "Your nails are Gawd-awful. You *must* come by and let me fix them." She pulled a business card from her bra and handed it to Julie.

Le-a
Nails Extraordinaire
504-555-4040

"Leah, Leigha, Leeah?" Julie tried to pronounce the name.

"No, no, no...the hyphen is not silent." She spoke as if Julie should know. "My name is pronounced LeDasha."

While Julie stared at the name on the card, something clicked in her mind. Perfect make-up, perfect clothes, perfect nails, and Semaj's friend, Le-a was not the woman she appeared to be. She was a woman wannabe. And one, who quite frankly, could put real women to shame.

Sighing, Julie turned her head away and gave into her self-depreciating thoughts. *I'm sitting by a man who looks better than I do and I feel way too sober to deal with it. I believe another drink is in order.* She pulled out some cash and tapped on the counter.

"I've got this." Julie shivered with warm tingles from the rich-timbered voice that spoke close to her ear. "Put your money away."

She swung around, facing the owner of the voice, a man who was signaling to the bartender. He was tall, thirty-something with just the right amount of muscles, and his black hair was buzzed close to his head. His light-brown eyes framed with black lashes stood out against his café-au-lait skin. He could have been any of the guys filling the French Quarter on a good night, but somehow he was more eye-catching than most.

"What are you having?" The stranger motioned to all four of them.

"Sex on the Beach," Le-a answered.

"Fuzzy Navel," Armando spoke while staring at the man's shirt where it clung to his finely sculpted abs. Julie rolled her eyes, irritated by Armando's tactlessness.

"Corona, light." Semaj ordered as he mashed his cigarette on the floor with his foot.

"Rum and Coke," Julie answered, slanting a look his way unable to help appreciating the view.

Julie could hear the bartender grabbing glasses to fill their drink order as she noticed the stranger moving his gaze from her, focusing on Armando.

Unbelievable. Julie shook her head. *All the good-looking men are either married or gay.*

The man hesitated a moment then stepped closer to Armando, extending his hand. "My name is Heath."

Armando eagerly grabbed the man's hand, the multiple gaudy bracelets on his wrist jingled as they shook. "Charmed, I'm sure."

"I couldn't help but admire your bracelet," Heath said, releasing Armando's hand.

Armando stretched his arm out, turning his wrist up. "You like?"

Curious, Julie leaned over to get a look. Sure enough, among the many tacky pieces of gold costume jewelry was a dull silver bracelet with small silver balls and a silver charm. On the face of the charm was a complicated braided pattern of silk-like material in dark and light browns.

"Se-ma-j," Julie bit through clenched teeth, her voice elevating with each syllable. "What is *he* doing with *my* bracelet?"

Heath stepped back from Armando, resting his eyes on Julie. Julie could feel her face flushing and her jugular veins rising along her neck. She was going to blow and she didn't care who watched her. In one swift movement, Semaj unlatched the bracelet from Armando's wrist.

"It's all good?" He raised his eyebrows as he handed it to Julie, mouthing the words, "I'm sorry."

"It's not 'all good.'" Julie could barely contain her fury while making imaginary quotation marks in the air. Sorry was not going to cut it this time.

"Calm down, Chica. I only borrowed it. I was gonna bring it back," Armando said, waving his hand.

Julie stood.

So did Armando.

She pointed at Armando while looking at Semaj. "I don't want him near me, my house, or my things again. Is that understood?" Semaj avoided her gaze as he lit another cigarette and nodded. Another problem Semaj had was difficulty with confrontations.

"Don't be puttin' your finger in my face, Gringa." Armando moved closer to Julie. "I might be a lady, but I can fight like a man."

When he stepped into her personal space, Julie saw red. He was a small man, about her size. She was sure she could take him down if needed.

"I wouldn't have to point at you if you weren't a kleptomaniac!" she retorted.

"A kleptomaniac?" he gasped. "Whatever! At least I don't sit around all day collecting a nut check, you crazy, Prozac-poppin' Hag."

Julie fumed. She hated that term. "Well, at least I don't bend over for every Tom, Dick, and Harry. Did I mention Dick?"

Armando stepped back with a snort and flipped his long, brunette wig. "That might be true, but I'd rather be a whore any day than a dried-up old maid."

"What did you say?" Julie gasped with her fists clenched as she stood almost nose-to-nose with the transvestite. Even though the words came from Armando, they hurt like a blow to the chest. He might be right, but she would be willing to live with that fact if she could just punch the look off his face. She bent her arm about to strike when Semaj finally moved to action and grabbed Armando, dragging him back as he eyed Julie's shaking fists.

"No man will ever want you," Armando hollered as he struggled in Semaj's firm grasp.

"Don't listen to him, Julie," Semaj grunted.

"I'll have you know," she answered, fueled by her anger and hurt, "I'm so good, all the men want more!"

Did she really just say that?

Armando laughed as Semaj pulled him toward the restroom. Even over the music, the bar seemed unusually quiet. Julie turned her head. Several of the men standing nearby sized her up. One tried to give her his number. Shaking her head, she pushed her way out of the building.

She leaned her shoulder against the cool iron lamppost just outside the Cat's Meow. Julie trembled with the sudden adrenalin rush from the moment before. She put her hand on her forehead.

How could I have lost control like that? I must really be out of my mind!

From behind her, she heard a man clear his throat.

"Excuse me."

"No, I *do not* want your number," Julie said without turning around.

"I certainly hope that's not the case," the man said, walking around to face her. It was the guy who had just bought everyone a drink. Julie pictured the Rum and Coke that sat untouched at the bar.

"Sorry about that little performance in there." She nodded toward the bar, shifting uncomfortably. "Not one of my better moments."

"It was pretty clear that you were provoked." His words elicited a warm feeling inside her. It felt good to have someone on her side.

"Heath, isn't it?"

He nodded. "And you are Juliana, yes?"

"My friends call me Julie."

Heath's brown eyes softened as he stared at her, but he stood in silence.

Julie sighed inwardly. Her evening had been unusual enough without having to remain outside with a handsome, but albeit strange, gay man staring at her.

"Well, Heath, thank you for the drink, but I think I'm going to call it a night." She didn't wait for an answer but walked past him, headed directly for home.

"Wait!" he called out, apparently finding his voice as he caught up to her and matched her stride. "I would really like to talk to you."

"Yeah?" she continued to walk. "About what?" He touched her arm, sending a cascade of warm tingles down her spine, stopping her in her tracks. Julie looked at Heath more closely. Who was this man that he could cause such a physical reaction in her?

"I'd like to talk to you about the bracelet."

"Oh," Julie lifted her right hand up, "this." She had forgotten that she still clutched it.

"Yes, that would be the one. I'm an antiquities dealer. I buy and sell collectables."

"Oh," Julie repeated.

Oh..., she thought, realizing Heath didn't like Armando after all. *He was interested in the bracelet.*

"I would love to have a look at that bracelet, if you don't mind." Heath smiled. He had a really great smile. Deep creases appeared on each side of his broad grin. Not quite dimples, but very attractive all the same.

"Knock yourself out." Julie handed it to him.

His eyes glistened in the weak light of the streetlamp, and he held the bracelet as if it were the crown jewels. "Would you mind bringing this to my shop so I can examine it more thoroughly? I believe it is an important historical piece worth a great deal."

"I guess I could do that."

He handed the bracelet back to her and they walked again in silence.

Worth a great deal? I wonder how much money he's talking about? Could I pay off the rest of the house, make some investments? Maybe live off the dividends?

Heath interrupted her thoughts. "How did you obtain the bracelet?"

She scrunched her nose. "You would think by the way I behaved it was a priceless heirloom, but it's not. I found it not too long after I moved into my house." She pointed to the building on their left. "I notified my Realtor, who contacted the previous owner. The family informed her that they didn't want it. I was told to keep it with their compliments. But then that asshole stole it from me." She stopped walking and turned to Heath. "Excuse my language." She looked up at him. "There is nothing I hate more than a thief. The bracelet has no personal meaning for me, but it's the principle, you know?"

"I can understand that." He glanced at her house then turned back to her, searching her face. Curiosity rose in Julie. Could he be interested in more than just the bracelet? She pushed the thought from her head.

"So, where is your office located?"

Heath continued to stare.

Julie held up her hand. "To bring the bracelet, remember?"

"Of course, yes." He pulled out his wallet and handed her his card, his hand shaking slightly. A quizzical smile pulled at her lips. Did she make him nervous?

Montgomery H. Smith's Antiquities
Restorations, Appraisals, Auctions
622½ Pirates Alley
504-555-7227
By appointment only

"Montgomery? She questioned.

"Yes, it's a family name, but I have been called by my middle name since birth."

"Heath."

He nodded, pointing to the card where it said "By appointment only." "Be sure to call first. I'm not always there so it would be best not to just show up. I keep my own hours."

"Okay," Julie answered. She tucked the card into her jean pocket and walked to her front door.

"I'll wait to hear from you then," he called to her just as she was about to step inside.

She smiled back at him. "You do that."

After Julie turned the lock, she peeked out the window to watch Heath walk away. She couldn't tell for sure, but it seemed as if he had a little bounce in his step. She leaned against the door and wondered.

Was there something rotten in the state of Denmark, or could this be the beginning of something new and wonderful?

CHAPTER FOUR

La Nouvelle-Orléans, Louisiana, 1898

The interior of Erik's house, "The Devil's mansion," reflected its rumored history. Not one room was on the same level as another. A series of steps up or down linked the spaces on each floor, so the Devil would never have to walk on level ground.

It had taken Erik weeks to construct Christine's home inside the house. He had left the foyer, parlor, dining room, and kitchen intact with false doors that looked real, but didn't open. Should he have guests, nothing would seem out of the ordinary to them.

Behind the scenes he had created trap doors, secret passageways, and the torture chamber, an exact replica of the one at his lake house. He wanted a failsafe to deal with Raoul or any other fool who tried to interfere. This time if Raoul entered, he would not leave alive.

Once done with the necessities, Erik had built a suite of rooms with Christine's comfort in mind. He crafted a four-poster mahogany bed draped with white netting that cascaded elegantly over the sides for privacy. The dark silk bedding matched the hue of her eyes, and the walls were painted in robin's egg blue.

Next to her bed, French doors opened to a faux courtyard. To accomplish this architectural feat, Erik had bricked the house walls, put flagstone over the wood floor, and installed a running fountain in the center. He had added potted bromeliads, twining jasmine, miniature date palms, true aloe, a potted orange tree, and a weathered stone carving of two lovers embracing. He wanted Christine to feel as if she were truly outside even though she would still be within the confines of the home.

The domed ceiling lights of the courtyard were like the ones in his torture chamber, but set to a comfortable twenty-one centigrade, or as these New Orleanians would say, seventy degrees. A timed projection of the sun would cross the ceiling and set each night. A device hidden in the shrubbery would sense the darkness, activating the small star-light holes in the ceiling and the gas lamps on the wall. Every morning and evening was balmy with a gentle breeze courtesy of the mechanism he created to replicate the wind.

From hardwood floors in the bedroom to warmed Italian marble in the bathroom where Christine would soak in a porcelain claw-foot tub with gold-dipped cast iron pipes, he had spared no expense. No one could ever claim he did not pay attention to details and that particular detail had been very tricky indeed.

Erik had broken into Jean Lafitte's old blacksmith shop a few times and worked the metal himself. That was also where he discovered the lover's statue. It was supposedly, etched into likenesses of Lafitte and his true love. The dead pirate had no further use for it, and it was a perfect reflection of him and Christine.

Back inside the bedroom, he had created an intimate dining area with a small table for two. It faced a large stained glass window on which he had painstakingly replicated the Paris opera house stage. If Christine so chose, she could stand in front of it and sing while he played for her from the upright piano nearby.

As he reveled in the finished product, Erik rolled a delicate silver bracelet in his hand–Christine's welcome-home gift. The charm would have to be changed, of course. The golden woven bands would have to be removed and replaced. But that would be an easy fix once Christine was with him again. He turned the locket to look at the inscription and traced his finger over the only word, *Nightingale*.

How fitting that the bracelet would pass from one Nightingale to another. The previous owner had retraced her steps in desperation and searched the Opera de Paris for her treasured possession in vain. From behind the stage curtain, he had watched her weep with grief over its loss as she told the theatre managers that it had belonged to her deceased mother.

Her tears had brought him no remorse. When he saw the delicate jewelry, he knew in an instant that it belonged to Christine. The bracelet was made especially for a composer to give to his songbird. Erik did not hesitate to slip it off the woman's wrist. It was more than a lucky chance that their paths had crossed just before he was to leave for La Nouvelle-Orléans.

He placed the heirloom on the fireplace mantelpiece. There it would wait until he conjured Christine into her new body. He only hoped that once she accepted the idea of being with him again, she would appreciate all his thoughtful handiwork. He closed the door to her suite as he left to find his little songbird. Just seeing her was a reminder to him that all of his efforts were not in vain.

♀

Erik was drenched. Heavy rain droplets ran into his eyes, forcing him to take one hand off the steel pipe to wipe his face. He gripped the cold metal and leaned over again to look through the second-floor window. As Monsieur de la Croix, he had sent a congratulatory gift to Madame de Marigny on the birth of her son. He could see the hand-crafted rocking chair in the corner of the nursery.

Christine crossed the room, sat in his chair, and rocked the tiny bundle she held in her arms. Her long chestnut hair cascaded down her shoulders, and her cheeks glowed from the fire blazing in the grate. She held the baby close to her and began to sing.

Erik closed his eyes. Her celestial voice still had the ability to stir his soul, and his longing for her burned bright. She was so close and still so far away, separated by a thin glass barrier and a marriage. He placed his hand on the window, reaching out to her. The window creaked under the pressure of his touch.

Instantly, he pulled away, swung to the other side of the drain pipe, and flattened himself against the wall, his cape billowing behind him in the wind. He was getting too careless. He could hear her steps as she walked toward the window. She stood for a while and didn't move again until he heard the child crying.

"Maman is here," she cooed.

After a moment, he heard the rolling of the chair on the wood floor and he dared to look once more. Christine sang again and the child quieted. No illustrious Italian opera came from her lips, only a simple lullaby to comfort the boy.

Envy toward the child stewed inside Erik.

The child who lay in Christine's arms.

The child who had the love of a mother.

Love he had never known.

Ellendora, the woman who gave him life, had been cold and distant. There had been no comfort or caring in her voice. It had been rare for her to speak to him, let alone sing him a lullaby. She barely looked at her own son—he, who had adored her from behind the cloth that hid a face disfigured by her very hand.

Long before he had learned to speak, he had sensed something was not right with her. As he grew, he became good at not being seen or heard, and he caught whispers from people who called her mad and deranged. Sometimes those same people would take her away for months at a time to rest and get well. During those periods, he had been left to fend for himself because no one but his mother knew of his existence.

He knew deep in his soul why his mother turned her back on him. He knew why the cloth covered his entire face with only holes for eyes and a slit for a mouth. Hiding his deformity and her cruelty had been a given, but the parts of him without blemish, those were covered so she could forget the father he never knew. With a broken heart, he also knew that she would only find peace if he were to leave. And so he did.

On occasion, curiosity would overcome him and he would pass outside his childhood home to peer through the window and watch the mother who never wanted him. She eventually remarried and had other children. He had seen her smile during one of his undetected visits. She was a beautiful woman when she smiled.

If only she had smiled for him.

The last time he saw her was more than a decade ago when he once again had peered through the window. She had been dressed in her finest clothes lying in a simple pine box in the parlor. In one hand, someone had placed a cross. In the other, she held a ragged cloth. Erik had recognized it as the shroud he had worn over his face. Tender pain had crushed his heart at the sight of it in her hands.

She remembered him.

It didn't matter whether she only thought of him out of remorse for her sins. He didn't dare believe that she could possibly have longed for her lost child. It would be hoping too much. Whatever the reason, the only thing that mattered was that she thought of him at all. That small gesture was the closest thing that had ever felt like love from her.

His eyes glistened with tears thinking about it.

But this child, he stared at the boy sleeping in Christine's arms. *This child will have the love of a mother even if it is not his own. He will turn out fine.* "I did," he said out loud, "and I did not have the love of a mother at all."

♀

One more part of the plan.

Erik knocked on the door of the modest Creole house with his gloved hand. The hour was very late and he was still damp from the brief downpour. His breath hung in the chilled air, but he did not feel cold or wet. All he felt was the fire burning in his mind.

...Christine...

Impatient, he knocked again then heard footsteps echo through the thin-walled house. A short, dark-skinned woman opened the door a crack.

"It's late. Go home. Come back tomorrow," she said, trying to close the door. Erik put his hand on the edge of the door, preventing the woman from shutting it.

"Precisely why I am here. I desire to see your mistress privately."

"No. No." She shook her head. "Mamzelle will see no one now." She tried to shut the door, but the woman was no match for him. Erik pushed the door forward and stepped over the threshold where the light in the room illuminated his face.

The wax and white paste had been washed away by the rain. Erik saw his grotesque reflection in her eyes and her face held the look of horror he had seen time and again in many others. He found fear to be an effective tool for getting what he wanted.

"Your mistress *will* see me. I have an open invitation." With a cold, twisted grin he bowed, toying with the woman.

She darted to the back of the house, shrieking. "Mamzelle! Mamzelle! The Devil has come!"

Erik stepped further inside and closed the door, locking it behind him. He sat down in the chair closest to the fire, gazing into its depths while he waited.

"Who *dares* disturb me at this hour?" A female voice demanded. "I know the Devil and you, sir, are not him."

Erik turned his head toward her. She was a strikingly tall woman wearing a flowing red robe. The firelight shimmered on the light-brown skin of her arms and danced in her flashing dark eyes. She wore a bright yellow tignon knotted seven times around her head, and gold-hooped earrings swung from her ears as she shook her head with displeasure. When Erik stood, they were almost eye level—he being the taller of the two.

So, this is the infamous Voodoo Queen of New Orleans.

"Marie Laveau?"

She tilted her head when he addressed her. Her eyes lit in recognition as she looked at him. "Ah, Monsieur de la Croix, I was wondering when we would meet."

Erik was unimpressed that she would know his name. He knew she got her information from gossipmongers and hearsay. It was no surprise to him there would be gossip at the arrival of an eligible foreigner.

"Do not tell me what brings you to me. I will read your intentions on my own." She left the room, returning with a bag. "Here," she said, handing it to him. "Open the bag and throw the contents on the floor."

He held the bag, giving her a pointed look. Was this a ruse of some kind? Erik didn't like to play games. He was aware Marie had skills with herbology and the darker side of humanity, but she basically utilized illusion. If she had trickery on her mind, no lotion or powder could penetrate through his gloved hands, so he would play her game for the moment until his patience wore thin. He shook the bag, and a collection of dried bones fell out, scattering across the floor. Marie gyrated around them, chanting then stopped. She closed her eyes before she spoke.

"You are here because you are seeking your heart's desire."

"Does not every person come seeking such?" he questioned.

She ignored him as she continued. "You seek redemption from a brown-haired angel." Marie's eyes fluttered open and she walked a circle around Erik, taking him in. "You plan to claim her."

He had to admit, he was intrigued. How could she know this?

She stared at his raw and scarred face without flinching. "You want her Ache. Her Life-force," she paused. "You want her soul."

Erik's heart began to thump wildly in his chest with a mixture of rage, fear, and excitement. Somehow the advantage had turned in Marie's favor. He had thought he would come here, intimidate her and insist that she do as he bid, but now he found himself exposed and vulnerable.

"You know what to do," she continued, "but you are missing a piece to the puzzle. You believe I can supply the missing piece. That is why you are here."

"Yes," Erik answered softly, wondering whether she truly could see his intentions in the bones.

"Some magic is real," she said as if she could read his thoughts. She picked up the bones and replaced them in the bag. "You have the mark on you. Not here," she pointed to his blemished face, "but here." She pointed to his chest. "You are capable of greatness, whether it be good or evil."

"Good or evil," Erik repeated. "That is only measured by the perspective of each individual, is it not? My good could be your evil and my evil, your good."

"Nay, you can exact from the gray domain all you wish, but you cannot bend dark or light. They are what they are. You should know that," she said, pausing. "Erik."

At the mention of his true name, rage flamed through him and in two steps he grabbed her by the arms and shook her with violence he normally reserved for the male sex.

"How do you know my name?"

With her chin raised, she answered, "I commune with the Loa. As I said before, I knew we would meet. I expected you to come eventually." Her haughtiness only fueled his anger and he gripped her slender neck with his right hand, squeezing hard. Unfazed by his actions, she only gave a hoarse laugh in response.

"You are but a prince. Prince of Conjurers, yes?"

Stunned, he released her.

"But I am a *Queen*." Her face flushed with anger and she stepped closer to him with her head held high. "You will do well to remember that."

Erik regained himself and returned her hard gaze. Neither one blinked nor bent to the other's will. The clock over the fireplace ticked rhythmically until a whistle emanated from the kitchen and jarred them from the moment.

"Tea?" she asked with insincere sweetness.

"I would rather not," Erik replied with a cold smile in return.

"I thought as much." She turned and walked toward the back and stopped under the doorway. "I am tired, Prince Erik. Ask what you came here to ask."

"You know the ways of a Bokor. I need you to make me the Zombie potion."

She exhaled in consideration. "That is very dark magic. It would take time to get the necessary ingredients. I have to call upon the Petro to do it and that drains me."

"I doubt it will take as much effort from you as you claim."

She turned to face him. "Why do you presume that?"

"As for your ways and beliefs, I am ignorant. I know not the Petro you call upon, but there is a heaviness about you that I recognize. It is the very same heaviness that I see in myself. Darkness surrounds you already." He sniffed with disdain. "You are not the benevolent woman that this city knew your mother to be. Heaven will probably never welcome us, you and I. We are the kind of people who are capable of making our own heaven here on earth. Now, give me what I ask."

Ignoring his little tirade, she sashayed back toward him. "You will succeed in due course. The bones do not lie. You will catch your tarnished angel." She ran her hand down his arm. "I will do as you wish, but you must do something for me in exchange. My service to you is not free."

"I have more money than God Himself," Erik said coolly. "Name your price."

She laughed.

"I don't want your money, little prince. I want power. I want respect." She pushed a finger in his chest. "And you will get it for me."

"How so?"

She smiled at him with dark eyes.

"There is a son of a very prominent French official who transgressed upon a girl of modest station. Even though his family is politically connected and her rank is far below his, he cannot buy his way out of certain incarceration. The evidence is overwhelming and he will be convicted by the courts. His father came to me requesting that I reverse this inevitable misfortune. *He* will pay me handsomely for my trouble."

Irritated by her veiled explanation, Erik asked, "What does this have to do with me?"

"Everything. You must do this—you—the creature of the night. Be the voice that whispers in the magistrate's ear. Be the apparition that strikes fear into each juror's heart. Tell them they will be cursed to hell if the boy is found guilty. I want them to set him free." Her voice rose.

Composing herself, she spoke more softly. "You will know who to visit. I will leave a talisman outside the door of every juror, magistrate, and judge associated with the case." She held up a red bag filled with herbs for Erik to make note of. "They will recognize it as my mark. You will recognize it as who to target."

Erik interrupted. "What of the girl? Does she not deserve justice for being violated?"

"Forget the girl. She plays no part in this bargain between us." Erik felt his lips thinning as the muscles in his face tightened. He would not forget. He would put this boy on his list of unfinished business and pay him a visit once he had time to attend to it. The girl deserved revenge and he would give it to her.

"I know what you are capable of doing. Make this happen and I will give you what you ask."

"Consider it done," he answered grimly.

It would not bring him pleasure to become the Phantom of Fear again, but he would do whatever it took to have Christine back. He was almost out the door when Marie called to him.

"One more thing before you leave. Consider this plan of yours very carefully, Erik. There is a spiritual cost to anything you do," she warned.

Without hesitation he found himself replying to her. "There is no price I would not pay."

CHAPTER FIVE

New Orleans, Louisiana, 2009

Julie opened heavy eyes to the late afternoon sun that dared inch around the edges of her closed shades. She dragged herself out of bed and into the shower. She hated sleeping the day away, feeling so unproductive when she did. It was just one of the many character flaws she was working on with Dr. Rotel. Also, another reason for remodeling the house on her own. Productivity reduces depression.

Revived as she stood under the warm water, her thoughts turned to Heath, his muscular body, brown eyes, and bright smile. She couldn't get him out of her mind, which surprised her. He wasn't even her type. Why was she obsessing over a man she hardly knew? And hadn't she decided that all men were lost causes?

She checked her appearance in the mirror as she removed the wet towel from her head. Her brown hair flopped just to her shoulders. She ran her fingers through the tangled mess. Since the divorce, she hadn't given much consideration to her appearance. She would let her hair air dry without putting a brush through it. Apparently, a decreased interest in self-care was also a sign of depression. She was a walking textbook. Maybe it was time to make some changes?

Julie hopped up and down, struggling to get her jeans on over her hips and snapped closed. She turned sideways and looked in the full-length mirror again. About an inch of her stomach hung over the waistband of her size seven jeans. When the hell did this happen? She stared at her reflection in disbelief. She couldn't remember the last time she had worn jeans.

She tried sucking her gut in. Much better. With a loud sigh, she let it back out again. Keeping it in would take too much effort. She would have to add sit-ups to her daily routine.

The smell of fresh-brewed coffee permeated the house. She shuffled to the kitchen grateful she had remembered to set the machine to brew. She fixed herself a cup, still feeling tired. After returning home last night, she had stayed up until 3:00 am cleaning up the mess Semaj had created. She had to admit, begrudgingly, that this time he had been of some help. She now had a jagged archway where the wall once had been, and it wouldn't take as long for her to knock the rest down.

Maybe it was the idea of the caffeine that made her more alert because after only a few sips, she felt energized. Reading the morning paper, Julie saw the words, but could not absorb the content.

When did I stop caring about the way I look? Once, I wouldn't have dreamed of stepping foot out my door without make-up, my hair fixed, or my nails done. How did I let myself go like this? And why am I suddenly realizing this now?

Deep inside, she knew the answer. She wanted to make a good impression on Heath. He was the first man she had felt any interest in since Simon.

Being interested in Heath felt both exciting and awful, as it awakened the fear of being vulnerable to someone again and the possibility that her interest wouldn't be returned. Somehow, she had lost herself somewhere between the divorce and this moment. She had been sleep-walking through life. Meeting Heath was a wake-up call, a reminder she was still alive and should be living her life more fully.

Julie flipped Heath's business card between her fingers. 622½ Pirates Alley. She searched her memory. She'd been on Pirate's Alley hundreds of times and had never seen it. Was it all a scam? Was there something else behind his intentions? The bracelet was unusual and old to be sure, but there was nothing obviously valuable about it, no diamonds or rubies.

She would just have to make a casual pass down Pirates Alley, discreetly looking to see whether there was an antiques shop there or not. She had every right to be in that area after all. Say, for instance, if she were to go to Café du Monde and get beignets. Maybe she had overlooked his shop on previous occasions. Maybe his shop was really there.

No time like the present. Julie slipped on her sandals, located her brush, and tamed her hair into a ponytail.

"Damn!" she cursed when she looked closer in the mirror at her almost uni-brow. She couldn't leave until she'd managed to shape her man brows and pull all the unwanted chin invaders that glared back at her from her reflection. Finally feeling half-way decent, she headed out the front door.

Semaj sat on his two-stepped stoop, a cigarette hanging loosely between his lips. He stretched out his long legs and leaned back on both elbows, giving her a pleasant nod. "Hey Dawlin'."

"Hey, Semaj," she said. "Look, I want to apologize for last night. I didn't mean to make a scene and all. I know Armando is your…your…" Julie paused as she thought about how to say it "…was your date last night and I know you really like him, so I am willing to put aside my reservations and make an effort, for your sake, to be nice to him. I trust you to use the spare key to my house as you need to, but I don't want Armando in my house. *Him* I don't trust. He did steal my bracelet and God knows what else." She whispered the last part when she heard someone inside Semaj's house walking toward the ajar door.

"I know," he mumbled, the cigarette jiggling. He sat up, discarded the burning butt and crushed it with the heel of his shoe. "That's why I dumped his ass last night."

"You're kidding!" Julie was blindsided. "Then who…"

The door swung open.

"Semaj, brunch is ready!" Le-a said in her melodic falsetto voice. She stood in the doorway looking like Doris Day, wearing a frilly apron over a fitted below-the-knee dress. She glanced at Julie, winking. "I made plenty. Come on in and eat if you're hungry." She turned around, her heels clacking on the wood floor as she walked away.

Julie raised her newly plucked eyebrows at Semaj.

Semaj smiled at her. "It's all good, emphasis on the *all*, Dawlin'."

"Tell Le-a thanks for the offer. I have to pass on it this time."

"Where ya off to?"

She hesitated, not sure if she wanted to tell him.

"I saw you leave with that guy last night. Is there anything I should know about?" He gave her a pointed look. "You know, like a little Jungle Fever? Don't think I don't notice your hair and make-up."

"No," she lied. "It's nothing like that. He was interested in the bracelet."

"Really?"

"Yes, really," she said, trying to conceal her inner hope from him as she turned, walking away.

"And what are you interested in?" Semaj called after her.

"Just interested in taking a walk." Julie glanced back and winked. "For now."

♀

As she got closer to Pirates Alley, the longer each step seemed to take. *Ok, right foot, left foot.* Julie forced herself to move onward while the anxiety built up. She held a desperate wish that the shop was there. Taking a deep breath, she turned right onto Pirates Alley.

Julie read the names under her breath as she meandered past all the storefronts; Old Fleur de Paris hat shop, Faulkner House bookstore, and Pirates Alley Café and Absinthe House. To one side lay another alley and the fortress-like back wall of the Cabildo. On the other side, was St. Anthony's garden behind the St. Louis Cathedral. No antiques shop. Her heart dropped.

Even though she had checked for Health's store, she retraced her steps along the alley again to make absolutely sure she wasn't mistaken. Back of building, alleyway, café, book store, and hat shop. Disappointment crushed her.

She looked at Heath's card. Had she called, he probably would have suggested they meet somewhere other than the shop that did not exist, and then he would have pulled whatever scam he had planned. She had convinced herself that he was genuine and down to earth. *How could she have been so foolish? How could she have thought it possible to open her heart to someone again?*

The Pirates Alley Café and Absinthe House mocked her with the numbers 622 emblazoned on the glass window of the doors. There was no need to stand there any longer with dashed hopes. The side alley opened up to St. Peters Street. She would cut through there and make the straight shot home. As she pushed through the throng of tourists, she thought about stopping at the ice cream shop on the corner. Nothing like a scoop of double fudge chocolate to ease the disappointment.

"Excuse me, Ma'am." A girl wearing an Ohio State shirt touched her arm. "I was wondering whether you could take our picture?" She indicated herself and a glassy-eyed guy next to her.

"Sure." Julie took the digital camera and located the couple in the view finder. "Say cheese." She pressed the shutter release and then looked at the LCD screen. They both had their eyes half-closed and were making peace signs. "It looks great," she lied, handing the camera back.

"Thanks," the girl said, and she and her companion walked off. Julie could hear her remark to the guy how friendly everyone was in New Orleans. It was then that Julie noticed the spot where they had been standing. The sound of her heart pounded in her ears. She felt her mouth gape open.

"Oh-My-God." She could barely breathe.

There before her was a small bay window painted with the words *Montgomery H. Smith's Antiquities, 622½ Pirates Alley.* The shop measured about 15 feet across, if that. It was attached to the back of the café. In the display sat an old clock, spectacles, a telegraph machine, and smaller collectable items.

She didn't know whether to laugh, cry, or both. It was real. He was real. And he was there, inside, looking back at her, motioning for her to come in. *Jesus, Mary, and Joseph*, she hadn't expected that. She would have to wing it. The bell atop the door chimed as she walked in.

"Juliana." Heath's face lit up. Her spirit soared at his reaction.

"Hi, Heath, I was just passing by." The cathedral bells began to toll, and she used that fact to support the lie that came so easily. "I'm on my way home from mass."

"I'm glad you came. I was thinking about you." He closed his laptop and placed it under the counter.

"You were?" Dare she hope he was interested in her?

"Did you bring the bracelet?"

She masked her disappointment. Not her. It *was* the bracelet. "No, as I said, I was just passing by."

Heath stood, placing his hands in his pockets. "No matter. I was just about to leave for a quick bite. Have you eaten yet?"

She shook her head no.

"Why don't we go grab something? My treat."

"Sure, why not?" she answered casually. Now he wanted to have lunch with her? Did this man like her or not?

"Hang on while I get my wallet." He ran up the narrow stairs located at the side of the corridor, two steps at a time.

Julie gazed around the tiny store. Heath's stock included old hair pins, brushes, mirrors, shavers, radios, and jewelry. Some items sat on open shelves, and others were locked inside glass cases. Most items she couldn't readily identify, such as a neatly laid row of short handles made of everything from ivory to thin, stamped metal, each with a small hook on the end.

She lingered over an antique frame with a black-and-white picture so old, it was yellowed. The man and woman in it were masked, dressed in what appeared to be Egyptian costumes. The details were hard to make out, but something about them captivated her attention. Perhaps it was the way the man rested a possessive hand on the woman's arm or the way her head tilted toward him.

"That's one of my favorite pictures." Heath broke the silence.

Julie jumped at the sound of his voice. She hadn't even heard him come back down.

"Every item in this shop has its own story." He cleared his throat, looking at the picture she had been admiring. "Maybe I will tell you the story behind that photo one day. There is a rich history behind my collection. What was it about that photo that caught your attention?"

"Oh." Julie glanced back at the picture. "I'm not sure. Moments like these captured from so long ago are interesting. Where do you suppose they were going?"

He gave her a curious stare. "A masquerade ball here in New Orleans. The information is scribbled on the back. I have more pictures and other items in my apartment upstairs. Maybe you'd like to see them one day?" His brown eyes sparkled, his passion for his collection shining through.

Nothing stirred her with such enthusiasm. Even renovating her house was a chore, not something she did for the joy of it. How sad. Maybe Heath was here to motivate her. Whether it was to arouse her passion for life or to arouse just plain old physical passion. Either would work.

"Yes, I think I would like that." She felt motivated already. His apartment would have a bed. Maybe they could make their own history? *Jesus, Mary, and Joseph! What was she thinking?* She looked around the room for any excuse to change the subject, and she spotted a picture in mosaic tile.

She drew closer to the tile, intrigued by the scene it portrayed. A woman stood on bright white stone with her back to Julie, her long red hair streamed in tangles, whipped by the wind. Churning water stretched out before the statuesque woman. Sunlight rested on her shoulders, surrounding her body with a soft glow.

"Where did you find this?" She reached her hand out, fingertips just hovering over the surface. She couldn't seem to tear her gaze away from the image.

"I made it many years ago." Heath picked up the heavy picture and placed it behind the counter. "I just recently repaired a cracked tile and it's still drying. Otherwise, it wouldn't be out."

"You made that? It's amazing! I almost felt..." Julie couldn't quite describe the emotions the image stirred. It was like a word on the tip of her tongue that she couldn't fully recall.

"What? You almost felt what?" he asked.

"I'm not sure. Really, it's just beautiful. The colors are just so vibrant. It kind of makes you feel like you are there."

Heath nodded, but didn't say anything.

"How much would you charge for something like that?"

"The mosaic is not for sale." He swallowed.

She smiled. "I probably couldn't afford it if it were."

"Come on." He grabbed her by the hand, pulling her out the store. "You can see more of my collection another day. I'm famished."

Julie looked at his hand, holding hers.

Warm tingles shimmered up her arm, making her heart flutter.
Was she the only one feeling something?

CHAPTER SIX

La Nouvelle-Orléans, Louisiana, 1898

"Welcome." The madam ushered Erik into her marbled foyer. Lulu White was a stout woman with hair so fiercely red that it could only be a wig. She dressed fashionably, but was overly draped in jewelry that sparkled against her light-brown skin. "Is this your first time to the Mahogany Hall?" she asked without giving Erik a chance to respond as she removed his hat then his cloak and bustled off to hang them up.

A copy of the *Daily Picayune* lay on the parlor credenza. The headline splashed across the front page declared: MATHEW MAGINNIS EXONERATED! Under the declaration, the accompanying picture showed a young aristocrat on the courthouse steps with a broad, arrogant smile on his face.

Erik smirked. *So this was the boy freed by his handiwork.* Now he had a face to go with the name. The blue blood wouldn't be smug for much longer, not once Erik paid him a visit.

"Well," Lulu said upon her return. "Let me tell you a little bit about my place. I have fifteen rooms. All with attached baths. Hot and cold water available, too. Oh, yes, nothing but the finest of everything here at Mahogany Hall." She held up her hand with fingers spread. "We have five parlors. None like you'll find anywhere else in Storyville, I tell you. Each parlor has a theme and all the girls know how to help you celebrate. A discriminating gentleman such as yourself is sure to find something to your liking."

She flicked her gaze down to Erik's hands.

"Ah, you have the Blue Book!" she exclaimed, yanking the booklet from his grip and flipping it open. "Here, look." She pointed. "My bordello is the most highly recommended. And here, on page eleven, all my girls are listed. I have forty-five octoroons, sir. I have more octoroons than any other place in The District.

"Mind you, all my nieces are very good fellows, but Izzie Dupre might just be the type of girl for you." She pointed to a picture of a nude woman facing a mirror with her head turned slightly toward the camera. "She is a favorite among my visitors. There is nothing too fun or too adventurous for her." She lowered her voice to a confidential whisper. "I have heard some of my regular callers say that one visit with Izzie can teach more than words can describe. If you know what I mean." She nudged him with her elbow, a suggestive smile on her face.

Erik snatched the book back and stuffed it into his pocket. "I am quite capable of deciding that for myself." He brushed past her farther into the house.

"Just a minute, sir," Lulu called to him. "It is five dollars for the evening."

Erik turned on his heel, flicking a twenty dollar gold coin at the astonished woman.

"I prefer, 'Madam,'" he said, without hiding his contempt, "the privacy of perusing your home on my own. See to it that no person try to attend to me." He didn't want anyone hovering around him while he searched for a suitable host for Christine's soul, so he reiterated his demand, making sure Lulu understood. "I wish to be left in peace to see just what you have to offer." She nodded while pocketing the twenty dollars.

"Oh sir!" she called out again. He stopped without turning back to her. "We have several gentlemen who visit the hall and prefer only to watch. The circus act tends to be most entertaining for them. Might I recommend going directly to the fourth floor? The elevator is down the hallway to your left."

His hand tightened around the cat's gut rope stuffed deep in his pocket. He pictured it around Lulu's neck, struggling with the urge to shut her up permanently. *You must not become distracted*, he reminded himself, walking away from her without responding.

The first parlor shimmered with hazy smoke. Erik breathed in deeply. The scent held more than Southern-grown tobacco. Several people milled around and swayed to the rhythmic music that floated down from upstairs. The partially dressed women wore masks. Their naked bodies reflected in mirrors that surrounded the room. They casually rubbed against their prospective partners, allowing them to touch their exposed skin.

A younger girl, unmasked, about fourteen, entered the room. She was draped in a loosely fitted linen tunic that hung down to her bare feet. She carried a tray with crystal glasses, red liquid slopping against the sides; likely the fine wine Lulu advertised in the infamous *Blue Book*. Erik scrutinized all the women in the room. Even masked, he could tell none were acceptable. Not just anyone would do to house

Christine's soul. He headed toward the stairs to view the rest of the inventory.

The second floor foyer was painted black. A wall plaque advertised it as *The Dungeon*. The men here played victim, some tied to iron frames against the walls, others restrained on tables while being struck and berated. Nude women in sharp-heeled boots stalked among them, brandishing whips and riding crops. These women were not what he wanted.

On the third floor, he discovered the source of the music, a pianist and several brass players. Potted ferns and palms flanked the edges of the room, an opulent chandelier hung from the ceiling, and oil paintings decorated the walls. The ladies were dressed in rich silks, their fingers and necks adorned with jewels, and their hair swept up in elegant styles.

At first glance, these women gave the appearance of fine, moral citizens, but the illusion failed when they stumbled off towards the bedroom with no need for persuasion from the men on their arms. A very tall man with black hair and a brilliant smile pulled one of Lulu's nieces into a corner. She moaned as he kissed her neck. Not one among these women would do.

Running out of options, he had low expectations for finding a woman on the fourth floor, either. His search gave rise to bitter disappointment. Last night, he had systematically discounted Josie Arlington's "nieces" just as he had Mrs. Hamilton's and Mrs. Townsend's the previous nights. And the twenty-five cent whores, who carried their beds on their backs, were not even an option, no matter how easily they could disappear.

At the last grand foyer, candles provided light for the circus. Erik sat in one of the many plush chairs assembled for viewing the live show. One woman crawled seductively across the floor dressed in a cat's ears and tail. Another had an elephant's nose and ears, splattering water on herself. While a third woman scantily costumed as a monkey gyrated wildly, groping at the man closest to her. To the side, a "stretch woman" flexed into contorted positions, completely nude.

Tasteless.

Erik looked up at the ceiling, wondering at the absurdity of it all. The band below started to play twelve-bar blues and the faint music sounded discordant against this freakish performance. Bored with the exhibition, Erik gazed around the room in one last hope.

He hadn't noticed before but in the far left corner sat a cage. Inside was a pitiable woman with an open gap that extended from her nose to her mouth. The hand that grasped the bar of her prison had three fingers webbed together; where the other hand should be was a smooth stump. Above her cage, the sign read, "TAKE A TURN WITH THE FOUR DOLLAR FREAK."

Erik remembered the jeers and taunts he, himself, once had experienced while he looked out from such a cage, and his vision turned black with rage. He could still hear the scratchy voice of his jailor calling out, "See the freak! See the freak boy! Son of the Devil, he is!"

Erik touched his scarred face, now disguised. He felt murderous. First, he would set the girl free, and kill all the men, then burn down the building with all those who remained inside. He reached for his rope when a siren's song stopped him in mid-motion, his plans of destruction forgotten as her voice called to his soul.

"Hmmm...Hmmm.....Hmmm..."

The woman hummed to the music from the third floor.

"Hmmm...light and rain. Hmmm...hope will remain." The sultry voice sang low, inaudible to anyone else but Erik's sensitive ear. Her voice held a subtle, ripe sweetness.

Turning slowly toward the voice, Erik noticed a woman behind him down the hall. She was dressed in the same white linen as the girl downstairs and, instead of delivering drinks, she was picking up empty plates and glasses lined up outside the bedroom doors and placing them on her tray.

Her back remained toward him. When he touched her warm shoulder, she spun around, dropping one of the long-stemmed glasses onto the floor. It shattered into pieces. Gasping, she stiffened, keeping her eyes lowered. The ends of her curly, honey-brown hair grazed past her cinnamon-skinned shoulders as she trembled, staring down at her costly mistake.

Erik gazed at her. Her tunic-dress clung to her body and revealed full, rounded breasts, a narrow waist, and full hips. He put his hand under her chin and raised her face up to look at him. Her skin was beautiful and unblemished, light golden eyes framed by dark lashes.

His heart beat against his chest and blood pounded in his ears. She could very well be the perfect vessel for his Christine.

He spoke as kindly as he could muster. "Do not worry my angel. I will reimburse your mistress ten-fold its worth."

A breath of relief escaped her lips.

He smiled at her. "Tell me, what is your name?"

"Naomi," she replied, her eyes wide with innocence. Eyes that reminded him of Christine's doe-eyed gaze.

He burned inside with the light of a million suns.
Yes, she would do quite nicely.

CHAPTER SEVEN

New Orleans, Louisiana 2009

Heath released Julie's hand to lock the door of his store.

Julie gasped inwardly as she felt the loss of his touch. *This cannot be right. I barely know this man. I've got to call Dr. Rotel and get my Prozac levels tested. I must be overmedicated,* she thought, shoving her hand into her jeans pocket.

"You know, last night when I left your house, I was approached by an unusual woman. I think her name was Saturn or something. She read my palm."

"Her name is Star," Julie said, surprised that Heath had a reading. "If you don't mind my asking, what did she tell you?"

Health smiled at her, crease lines by his mouth deepening. "Not at all. She told me that my life-line was long. She said that I've been waiting for the right woman."

"Is that true? Have you been waiting for the right woman?" Julie asked. She cringed, realizing she had spoken out loud what she had been thinking. *Cancel that. Maybe I am undermedicated. Got to call Dr. Rotel and have my dosage upped.*

If it was at all possible, his smile deepened. "The right person is always worth the wait, don't you think?"

"Uh, yeah," she gulped, fighting the thought that shot through her head unbidden, *Let it be me.* Jolting to her senses, she cried internally, *Wait! I hardly know this man. Why am I feeling this way?*

"I'll have a great marriage, kids, grandkids. You know, all the typical things a palm reader says."

"Oh, so you think it might have been a bunch of bull?" Julie asked.

"Oddly, no. I have a good feeling that my luck is looking up." He stepped back so Julie could walk through the open door of the Pirates Alley Cafe and Absinthe House. He led her to a table for two near the window and handed Julie one of the menus wedged between the condiments.

"Let me know when you're ready to order," called the busy bartender.

Julie looked at the glossy pictures of sandwiches on the menu and her mouth watered.

Heath noticed her interest. "Their muffaletta sandwiches are really good here."

It did look good, but she was suddenly aware of the pressure of her jeans against her expanding girth and reluctantly chose something else. "I think I'll have the pita bread with hummus and a glass of water."

"Have you tried the absinthe?" he asked her.

"No, I haven't," Julie said without much interest. After all the alcohol she drank last night, she wasn't too keen on having any with lunch.

"Great, let me be the first to introduce you to it. I insist that at the very least you taste it. I think you'll like it. You can't try the original version since it was banned in the early 1900's, but the new version is pretty good." Health placed the menu back between the condiments.

"Really? Why?" Julie asked now determined not to let a drop pass her lips.

"Back then it was made from wormwood and many other herbs. The wormwood contains thujone, which is poisonous in high dosages. The government regulates the amount of wormwood used now, so you needn't be worried. By the way, they say absinthe had an aphrodisiac effect. Some say it still does." He winked at her.

Oh, great. Just what I need—an aphrodisiac to mess with me when I'm already attracted to this man. She gave him a crooked smile, glad he couldn't read her thoughts.

Heath got up and placed their order while Julie looked around. It was her first time at the cafe. All the tables and chairs were made of thick, heavy wood. The interior looked typical for the Quarter with glimpses of brick showing through stucco. The cafe's only employee, the bartender, talked and laughed with the patrons at the bar.

When Heath returned to the table, Julie thought she'd try to direct the conversation to a subject that would distract her from the way his jeans accentuated his firm-looking thighs.

"So," she started. "Where are you from? Not New Orleans, right?"

He raised his eyebrow. "Is it that obvious? What gave me away?"

"No accent."

"Well, you are correct. I am a Texas transplant, but I have traveled most of my life. That's why you don't hear an accent. I moved here not too long ago."

"What brings you to New Orleans then?"

Heath leaned back and relaxed into his chair, giving her a thoughtful look. "I came here to bring history to life and make some history of my own."

"What?" Julie asked.

"My antiques store..."

"Oh, right." All Julie heard was Heath's voice repeating, *make some history of my own.* And her under-medicated head thought, *Let it be with me.*

"Is this a family business? Did your father deal with antiques, too?"

"My father died many years ago," he answered without ceremony.

Julie stiffened, hoping she hadn't touched on a sensitive subject. "I'm sorry."

"It's okay. He was an old man when he passed. I was a surprise baby, born when he was in his fifties. But to answer your question, he was in the oil industry."

"So, why antiquities and not oil?"

Heath hesitated before answering. "I never had a desire to carry on my father's business. My interest lies in anthropology and history. I double-majored in college and later got my Masters. I began researching and collecting after that."

Julie didn't feel Heath said any of this to boast. Even so, uncertainty encroached on her mind. It didn't seem as if they would have much in common. She, after all, was a college drop-out.

"Enough about me. Tell me something about you." He interrupted her musing.

Talk about myself? His interest took her by surprise. Simon had been so self-absorbed, he never inquired about her day or her interests.

I don't usually like to talk about myself." She squirmed in her seat. Besides, she wasn't finished asking questions yet. He hadn't said anything about his mother, how old he was, when his birthday was or his favorite color. More importantly, was he single? His left finger was bare. That was a good sign, at least, but didn't mean there wasn't a girlfriend waiting somewhere in the wings.

The bartender arrived with their waters and two glasses filled with a cloudy drink that smelled like licorice. "I should have your order ready in about fifteen minutes."

"Thanks." Heath answered.

Julie picked up the absinthe to take a sip. Somehow having a little alcohol didn't seem like such a bad idea anymore. With an expectant look, Heath watched her. She felt her eyes open wide for a second after she swallowed. It was very strong. A warmth surged through her body, and for a moment, she felt a little light-headed.

"It is good," she agreed.

Heath, pleased with her response, took a sip of his own. "Now, *tell me* about you." The words "tell me" hovered in her ears and echoed in her mind. Her curiosity about him forgotten, she suddenly felt she could be open with Heath about her most innermost secrets even though they had known each other less than a day.

"I am an only child. In fact, I was adopted by my parents at the age of two. And, no. I've never had the desire to know anything about my birth parents. When I came along, my adoptive parents had already established their medical practices at LSU Medical Center," she said proudly. "They were nationally recognized surgeons."

"Were?" he asked.

Julie took a deep breath. It was rare for her to speak about her parents to anyone except Dr. Rotel. But as Heath's understanding eyes watched her face unwaveringly, she felt her normal defenses fall, and for some reason, she wanted to share her story with him.

"I was a freshman in college. It was my first semester. And I was more interested in playing around than studying. My mom and dad didn't approve, of course. I had happened to overhear them discussing my 'outlandish behavior.' They were going to let me get it out of my system, but had intended to put an end to it come spring. They only wanted the best for me. I know that now. Hindsight is twenty-twenty or so they say. Anyway, knowing what they had planned, I had decided to milk my freedom for all it was worth."

Heath nodded for her to continue.

"That particular weekend, a group of my friends and I had decided to make our own Lollapalooza. We started Friday night, here in the Quarter, and made the rounds until early Sunday morning. It had been almost forty-eight hours since I had slept. My parents thought I was staying at my friend Monika's house and her parents thought she was at mine. I was expected home before midnight on Saturday so that I could go to mass with them Sunday morning. They trusted me to be there."

Julie took another sip of absinthe. Speaking the truth about this part of her life with Heath felt more freeing than her bi-monthly therapy.

"My parents went to bed at 10:00 pm sharp, every night, without fail. They never waited up for me. They trusted me," she repeated, clearing her throat. "I had stumbled into the house sometime after 4:00 am trying to get to my room without disturbing them. On my way, I slipped on something in the hall and tried to catch myself, but wound up knocking a picture off the wall. The noise was so loud, I knew there was no way they had slept through it. I stood there, cringing, waiting for them to come out fussing. Nothing. I managed to find the light switch and flicked it on."

Julie stopped, realizing she had just mimed turning on an imaginary light switch. She smiled weakly and placed her hand down on the table.

"All I saw was blood. Everywhere. On the walls. On the floor. I saw hand prints in blood with drag marks behind them. I don't know why I followed the trail. I just had to. My mother was lying on her stomach in the den. I'll never get the picture out of my mind how inhumanly distorted her body looked—like a twisted Voodoo doll. I knew she was dead. I turned around and started screaming for my dad and noticed the house had been ransacked. I followed another trail and found my father on the bathroom floor, his head smashed in. Later on, I found out they had been dead for hours."

Julie let out a breath. She had nothing further to say. Heath stared at her, the muscles in his face tight and his lips thin. He gripped the side of the table so hard his knuckles turned white, and his brown eyes looked black.

"The persons responsible," he said slowly, "were they caught?"

She gave a sad shake of her head. "The police have no leads, and it's been over ten years. My parents are some cold-case file long forgotten on a back shelf somewhere that is *if* all the documents weren't destroyed by Hurricane Katrina." She sipped the absinthe again, garnering strength from the elixir. "I'm told I have survivor's guilt. I have always wondered had I been home, would things have turned out differently?"

"Listen to me," Heath said in a gentle voice as he deliberately removed his hands from the table's edge. "You could not have done anything to change your parents' death. The only difference and likelihood is that you would have been killed alongside them."

How many people had told her that? Dr. Rotel, Monika, Simon, Semaj…And yet, not until this moment, did the truth finally set in, and she felt the door of the emotional prison she had locked herself in cracking open.

Heath ran his hand over his closely buzzed hair and locked serious eyes on her. "I know exactly how you feel, Juliana. I also lost someone I love to a brutal murder. I held her in my arms as she died. I have never felt so helpless, so alone, so torn."

A silence sat between them briefly. Julie wanted to reach out, touch his hand in a commiserating gesture of comfort, but felt she couldn't. She sat, transfixed, wondering if the "her" he spoke of was his mother or another woman that he had loved deeply?

"It took me some time to wrestle with the fact I couldn't change anything. It wasn't my life to change. During that time, I had an epiphany about the world. I realized that nothing is written in stone until we make the choice to manifest it. Our reality ebbs and flows by the decisions we make. I see life as a blank canvas. The artist already knows the general design, but we get input on the color, size, and clarity of the stroke." Julie nodded but she wasn't sure she understood precisely what he meant.

"Was her killer caught?"

He muttered something she couldn't quite understand.

"What?" she asked.

"Yes. And he paid dearly."

"Which one of you ordered the muffaletta?" the bartender asked, interrupting the weighted conversation. Julie pointed at Heath. "Enjoy," the woman said, depositing his plate on the table followed by Julie's hummus then returned to the bar.

"On a lighter note," Heath said while cutting his muffaletta in half, "why don't I tell you about your bracelet?"

CHAPTER EIGHT

La Nouvelle-Orléans, Louisiana, 1898

A freckled-faced scullery maid rushed into the room. "Madame, it's *him* again."

Lulu White, stress lines on her brow, maneuvered around her desk barking orders. "Call the police. Get Henry down here to help. And Evie, notify Tom Anderson."

"Yes ma'am" the wide-eyed girl replied, scampering from the room.

"Excuse me, Monsieur de la Croix," Lulu said, marching out the room behind the skittish maid.

Even from her office, Erik could hear raised voices coming from the kitchen. Annoyed, he tapped his foot. After months of planning and preparation, with Naomi just upstairs, he found it irksome to wait a minute longer. Rising from his chair, he left the room determined to resolve Lulu's problem for her. Within a few broad strides he passed the mirrored parlor and pushed open the kitchen door.

"I want to see her," a deep voice demanded.

"You'll do no such thing," Lulu hissed. "She belongs here with us."

A burly, dark-skinned man stood in the back doorway. His large, beefy hands gripped the edge of the door, preventing Lulu from shutting it. The disgruntled man was taller than Erik, almost by a foot, and had a prominent chin and small, dark eyes.

"I am Alphonse Joseph Batiste," he bellowed, looking at each person as if his name should mean something.

Erik smirked. He could make easy work of this drunkard, but at the same time, he understood the longing a man could have for a woman. He would not interfere just yet. He was curious to see how this situation would unfold.

"I must see her!" Alphonse shouldered the door. Grunting, Lulu managed to hold it firm.

A chorus of male voices called out behind Alphonse, "Yeah! Us too! Let us in!" In the alley, a single line of dark-skinned men wrapped around the house, holding up dollar bills. They shifted and swayed to keep warm in the cold early hour of the morning.

"Shoo! Shoo!" Lulu pushed out with her free hand. "You know you aren't allowed in until the last patron leaves. And you," she directed to Alphonse, "I already know who you are. You needn't announce it to the whole world."

"Mimi!" Alphonse called out, leaning his head around Lulu. "Mimi, it's Joe B!" The cook staff stood ready with knives in their hands should he push his way farther in.

Mimi? Dawning realization made the hairs on the back of Erik's neck rise. *Did he mean Naomi?*

"You are not welcome here at all." Lulu continued to press the door back. "Just as you were told last Tuesday and the Tuesday before that. The police will arrive any minute. You haven't got much time. For your own sake, you must go." Anger flashed across the man's face at Lulu's rebuke.

In all fairness, Erik preferred to confirm his suspicions before killing the man, especially in front of so many witnesses. It was most fortunate he had other means at his disposal for diffusing the situation. Anger was a strong emotion to penetrate, but not impossible. He grabbed an opened bottle of wine on the counter—not absinthe, but it would have to suffice. He poured it into a glass goblet, stepping forward.

"Drink this," Erik handed the goblet to the man, looking into his fathomless, dark eyes.

Alphonse quieted and stared at the glass.

Lulu spun around, shocked. "Monsieur de la Croix, what are you doing?"

Erik ignored her, keeping eye contact with Alphonse who looked more suspicious now than angry. He accepted the drink, consuming it in one swallow. An uncomfortable silence filled the room and no one spoke. The onlookers glanced nervously between the man in the doorway and Erik.

Erik watched Alphonse's pupils dilate ever so slightly and said, "You feel better now."

Alphonse nodded his head.

"You will not worry about Mimi anymore tonight," Erik said in a low voice.

"I won't worry about her," he repeated.

"You will go home now and rest," Erik commanded, softer still.

Alphonse stepped back out of the doorway. He shook his head, his eyes clouded by confusion. He walked away, looking back at the house once with his brow creased. The cook took it upon herself to shut the door and lock it amid the protests of the remaining men waiting outside.

"What did you do?" Lulu asked Erik.

"I'm here!" A tall, scraggly boy rushed into the room, holding a board of wood in his hands ready for action.

This is the Henry that would have staved the man off? Erik wondered.

Distracted, Lulu fussed, "A whole lot of good that does me, Henry. We could have all been killed and chopped into pieces in the time it took you to get here! When I call for you, you will obey me immediately!"

"Yes, Ma'am!" Henry replied, clicking his heels together.

"Off you go!" She gave him a forgiving smile. He grabbed a red apple, took a bite, and left the room with the board in tow. Lulu faced Erik. "Whatever you did, thank you."

Erik didn't want her thanks.

"I'll be in your office. I expect not to wait very long." Lulu's smile faded as he strode out of the kitchen and back to her office. When he passed the foyer, he noticed the nervous girl, Evie, helping a short, robust man out of his coat. The suit he wore matched his dull brown hair and he sported a bushy mustache whose ends curled up to each pink cheek.

Erik returned to Lulu's office and sat in the stiff leather chair. If Lulu took too long, he would climb back up those stairs, toss Naomi over his shoulder, and carry her out of there, damn the consequences.

"Monsieur de la Croix, I presume?" the short man in the brown suit asked as he entered Lulu's office.

Erik replied with a curt nod.

The man extended his hand. "Tom Anderson."

Erik glanced at the stubby hand without accepting it. Instead, he turned his face to the opposite wall, pretending to examine an oil painting of a woman wearing a riding suit and hat as a horse grazed behind her in the distance. He was not here for pleasantries or for making friends. He wanted Naomi.

Out of the corner of his eye, Erik saw the man slowly withdraw his rejected hand, curl it into a fist, and bring it to his lips while making a small cough to clear his throat. Erik pulled out his pocket watch. Lulu had exactly thirty seconds.

"I'm the 'mayor' unofficially, so to speak, of The District. I'm here to conduct negotiations on behalf of Lulu White for Naomi Heming."

"Negotiations, is it?" Erik's interest was renewed.

Lulu bustled into the room. "Ah, Tom, sorry I'm late. That dreadful Batiste man showed up...again."

"Were the police called?" Tom inquired with concern. "I could get Stan McCullough over here and end this nonsense once and for all."

Lulu shook her head. "I don't think that will be necessary." She waved her hand toward Erik. "Monsieur de la Croix somehow convinced him to leave before the patrolman even arrived." She dropped her voice and leaned closer to Tom's ear. "And once Naomi is gone, he won't be our problem anymore."

Erik narrowed his eyes. *Alphonse* was *here for Naomi.* Stupid fools did not know he had a keen sense of hearing.

"Oh, what was I thinking?" She laughed, nervously misinterpreting his expression. Have you two gentlemen been properly introduced?" She sat back down behind her desk.

"Yes," they both answered—one tone jovial, the other cold.

"Let us begin." Lulu motioned for Tom to sit in an identical chair opposite Erik.

"Ahem." Tom cleared his throat again, put on his spectacles, and began to read from a sheet of paper he pulled out of his vest pocket. "Naomi Heming, age seventeen, parents Narcille and Clarence, deceased, raised by paternal cousins, Cora and Eugene Heming in Avoyelles Parish, State of Louisiana. Employed at Mahogany Hall for the duration of three months, family compensation recorded at fifty dollars." He looked at Lulu over his glasses. "And there has been another twenty dollars spent on clothing, and food and board, is that correct?"

"That is an accurate account," Lulu responded.

"There is also the matter of Mrs. White's compensation," Tom added.

"I see," said Erik. "And what might be a fair price to compensate Mrs. White?"

Tom and Lulu exchanged glances again, and Tom responded. "One thousand dollars should more than cover the expenses."

Erik set his jaw at the outlandish amount. Money was not an issue, but the steepness of her price placed him in the uncomfortable position of purchasing a human being.

"I believe slavery was abolished over thirty years ago, Mr. Anderson. I am confident the presiding mayor of New Orleans would be very interested in what you allow to take place in 'your' district."

"Oh, no!" Lulu emitted a nervous laugh. "It is not at all as you suggest. I mean, you must imagine it from my perspective, Monsieur de la Croix. Naomi has been in training these three months, sir. Many hours have been spent in teaching her how to speak properly and to carry herself like a lady. Her job at present, besides cleaning and bringing food and drink, has been to observe how the other doves perform their duties on each floor. My patrons all know that my servers will eventually be available to them and I've had many inquiries about Miss Heming. Interest in her is growing still– considering she is a dove that has never flown before, if you get my meaning."

Erik could not misinterpret Lulu's vulgar reference. She disgusted him.

"I've even had other madams interested in having her work at their homes. And, after her debut, I had planned to station her with my fetish specialists. I would have seen a considerable increase in profits once she began to work."

"Future earnings, loss of wages for Mrs. White," Tom clarified.

"And what of Miss Heming's welfare; is that of no concern to you?" Erik coolly inquired.

Of course, sir! I assure you it is," Tom answered. "And, I would like to point out, we cannot force the girl to go with you. Once the arrangements are settled, we will call her down here and get her feelings on the matter. So you see, there is no selling or buying occurring on the premises. We are simply coming to an understanding."

Erik sat back into the chair with his fingers intertwined, a cursory smile on his lips. He would not give in too easily to the greedy duo.

"With that said," Tom continued, "We need to discuss Miss Heming's living arrangements, as we are in every sense her current guardians. Will we be sending her to your St. Charles address?"

Erik unclasped his hands. "No. I have purchased a small home for Miss Heming on St. Peter Street. She will reside there with a maid and cook to tend to her needs. They are ready to receive her as we speak. If this 'arrangement' works out, I will transfer the house into her name."

"Very good, very good," Tom muttered, making notations on his paper. "I would also like to mention that Miss Heming will require some incidental monies as well for appropriate attire. The clothes Mrs. White provided are not acceptable for public display."

"Miss Heming will lack for nothing, I assure you. I will include additional money to procure a suitable day dress, shoes, and accessories. As for the rest of her wardrobe, I will see to that myself," he said, not revealing his irritation. "I have entertained these 'negotiations' long enough. Bring Miss Heming down so we can be done with this."

Lulu picked up a small hand bell on her desk and rang it. Within moments, Evie curtseyed in the doorway.

"Evie, Naomi Heming is either on the fourth floor or in the kitchen. Bring her to me." Evie acknowledged Lulu with another curtsey and left.

"While we're waiting, just to make sure we are in agreement, if Miss Heming accepts this proposal and my calculations are correct, you will make payment to Ms. White in the sum of..." Tom looked down at his notes. "One thousand one hundred dollars?"

"Before I confirm that, you must first inform me of the nature of the relationship between Miss Heming and Mr. Alphonse Joseph Batiste," Erik said, sweeping a condescending look over both of them.

"It's a reasonable question, Lulu," Tom piped up. "He deserves to know everything."

Lulu dropped her eyes. "Well, I only know what her family told me. He's from Marksville, as she is, and he's been infatuated with her since she was school-aged. They told me she never returned his affections and they certainly did not encourage her to." She looked up at Erik. "He comes from a less than desirable family if you know what I mean."

"I can imagine," Erik said dryly.

Tom elaborated. "This circumstance is not uncommon in The District. These girls come here from small towns and their men folk don't take kindly to having them come to work in an establishment such as this with any manner of man laying their hands on them in the Biblical sense, of course." He coughed. "We have a strict policy against any relationships outside the brothel. We prefer to avoid any possible confrontations. It is bad for business. Jealously can be very costly and unpleasant, so we frown upon the doves keeping ties with their past."

"I don't understand it," Lulu broke in. "Usually one good talking to does the trick and they don't return, but this one is stubborn as a mule. I tried to get Miss Heming to talk to him, reason with him. She refused. She claims she doesn't even know him. Maybe you'll have better luck at getting the story out of her."

"None the less." Tom gave Lulu a look as he cut her off. "You will not have to contend with him either. We will protect your privacy, and the only information he will receive *if* he should return is that Miss Heming left of her own accord to places unknown."

A soft knock on the door made Erik turn around. "Here's Miss Heming, Ma'am, as you asked." Evie curtseyed out of the room backwards. Naomi stood in the doorway, clenching her hands, her golden eyes apprehensive. Her gaze slowly swept the room resting on Tom, then Erik, her face softening and a shy smile appearing on her lips as she registered his presence.

"Come in, come in," Lulu said kindly. "And shut the door behind you, dearie."

♀

Erik leaned back in his carriage, hands behind his head with a satisfied grin that felt permanently etched on his face. The girl had accepted. For once, Lulu's propensity for endless chatter was beneficial. She had gone to great depths explaining to Naomi the benefits of such a liaison.

In three days' time, Naomi would move into her new home and he would call on her. In the meantime, he would send a seamstress over to Mahogany Hall to measure her and create an extensive wardrobe. Everything made for Naomi's use now would be in place for Christine. He had held up his end of the bargain, and it was only a matter of time before Marie would come through with the potion he had bartered for.

The carriage jolted to a halt in front of his home. He paid the driver handsomely, his generosity reflecting his pleasure. He stood on his walkway and breathed in the crisp morning air, enjoying the scent of the sweet olive bushes overgrown against the house. He remained immobile as the crest of the sun rose, watching the many subtle and lovely shades that could only be seen in early morning. It was a new dawn. It was beautiful. He lingered held in awe of something greater and more powerful than himself and for a moment, he permitted himself to bask in its rays.

"Buon giorno!" the iceman called out to one of Erik's neighbors as he passed down the street.

His reverie broken, Erik entered his house. Behind his closed door, he felt invigorated. The new day, the events of the past few hours, wiped away all fatigue. He ascended the stairs two at a time to his greenhouse on the roof. He wanted to work on his herbs. Marie's potion would have to be altered to suit his needs. He wasn't looking for a zombie, but a means to still the mind and body long enough to summon Christine's soul into it.

He dropped dried lion's tooth into his mortar and began to grind it into a fine powder with the pestle. He added king's cure, pilewort, and vanilla grass, repeating the same grinding technique. He poured the pulverized combination into a small walnut-colored glass jar and sealed the lid. Later on, with one-fourth of Marie's potion, he would simmer the ingredients in oil, infusing it. He pictured Naomi's beautiful cinnamon skin, imagining the moment when he would anoint her with the oil that would absorb through her every pore and allow him to call for his beloved.

CHAPTER NINE

New Orleans, Louisiana, 2009

"So tell me about the bracelet," Julie said after swallowing a bite of hummus.

Heath wiped his mouth with his napkin. "The inscription on the back, *Nightingale*, is what leads me to believe it is a precious heirloom."

Julie's eyes widened. "Yes, I've seen that inscription."

"Let's assume this is the original and not a reproduction. The bracelet was commissioned in 1849 in Paris, France, so it is quite old. Its history begins with Jenny Lind, one of the greatest opera singers in the world."

Julie scrunched her nose in recognition of the name. "Isn't that a brand of baby crib?"

"Yes," Heath replied. "Jenny was so famous, the businessmen of that era started branding products after her so people would buy them. Clothing, jewelry, baby furniture, you name it. It was like Beatlemania, or Jennymania, if you will."

Julie found that hard to believe. "Really? Over an opera singer?"

"Times were different then. People appreciated the arts. You have to remember there weren't televisions, telephones, or computers. Opera provided entertainment and a means to socialize. Besides, Jenny Lind had a natural talent. If she were alive today, her voice would still awe the masses. And she was considered a beautiful woman. Many men sought after her. Hans Christian Anderson for one."

Julie knew that author. "He wrote the 'Ugly Duckling'." It was one of her favorite childhood fairy tales because the story taught her that ugly wasn't necessarily ugly at all, just different and maybe even beautiful in its own way.

"Yes, he also wrote the story 'The Nightingale' which was inspired by Jenny Lind. She was his muse. This is where your bracelet comes in. There was another man, a man Jenny wanted to marry. Their relationship was rarely spoken of and very few people were aware of it, but they were madly in love. You may have heard of the composer, Frédéric Chopin?"

Julie nodded. She couldn't name a specific piece of his work, but her parents loved classical music and Chopin had been among their collection.

"Their affair lasted about a year until his death in 1849 from tuberculosis. Shortly before, Chopin had a bracelet made for Jenny, her very favorite type, hair jewelry."

"What?" Her jaw dropped. "People actually make jewelry out of hair?"

"Yes, it was very popular. Didn't you see the woven hair in the charm?"

"I did," she gasped. "But I didn't know it was *hair*. I thought it was silk or some other kind of thread."

"Chopin had his hair and Jenny's intertwined and placed in the charm on the bracelet, with a single word, *Nightingale*, inscribed on the back. It is a timeless piece of history. And it looks as if it is in excellent condition as well."

Julie still couldn't get past the part about the hair. She found the idea somehow revolting and romantic at the same time. "How did the bracelet get to New Orleans?"

"That's the million dollar question. It has been missing for over a hundred years. Jenny passed the bracelet on to her daughter, also named Jenny. The daughter made an entry in her diary and noted in a letter to a family friend that she lost it in the Paris Opera House in 1898. What happened between then and now is a mystery."

Julie pictured the silver bracelet and its charm of woven hair, once discounted by her, and it now felt more significant. "Well, at least we know they were brunettes," she mused out loud.

"No," Heath corrected. "They were both blondes."

"Can blonde hair change with age and turn brown?" she asked. "Because the hair in my charm is most definitely brown."

"I have never seen that happen before. Once I examine the bracelet closely, I might have some answers for you."

"Would you mind appraising the bracelet for me?"

"I'm so glad you finally asked," he said, smiling and revealing his sexy laugh lines. "I'll be right back. Let me settle the bill."

"Okay," she said, slanting a glance at Heath's firm butt as he walked off to pay the bartender. She gulped down the rest of her water, hoping it would cool the flush she felt creeping up her face.

"How about I walk you home?" he asked when he returned to the table.

"Sure," she said, a little disappointed that their time together was drawing to an end.

They walked outside the café doors into a welcome breeze. It was a nice contrast to the warm humidity from earlier. As they approached the cross-street, Julie saw Armando farther down on St Peter, heading their direction.

"No," Julie said, pulling Heath right onto Royal. "Let's not go back that way. Let's take St. Phillip to Bourbon. I just saw Armando and I'd like to avoid him after last night."

"I don't blame you," Heath agreed.

"So how long have you been in New Orleans?" Julie asked, changing the subject.

"A few weeks."

"Have you been to the Aquarium of the Americas or Audubon Zoo yet?"

"I haven't had a chance. I've been working on a project."

"Well, maybe you can let me show you around this great city of ours?" Julie asked casually, hoping Heath would say yes.

"I'd like that," he said, a muscle twitching in his cheek as he glanced away with a bashful hesitation that Julie found intriguing.

Julie smiled inwardly. *Okay, so maybe he is interested in the bracelet and me?*

"Heath! Yo, Heath!" a coarse voice called out followed by a rapid succession of coughing.

"Smooth, how are you doing?" Heath crossed the street, slapping the man's open palm. Smooth was a thin, tall man with coal-black skin and dusky patches under his bloodshot eyes.

"Haven't seen you in a few days," he croaked.

"Yes." Heath nodded. "I know. I've been busy lately."

"Who's this beautiful lady?" Smooth reached a calloused hand out to Julie.

She shook his hand. "I'm Julie."

"Well, Julie," Smooth said. "I've been trying to convince Heath to come back and pick up the mic. Have you ever heard this man sing?"

"I don't believe I have," she said, giving Heath a surprised stare.

"Not tonight, Smooth. Maybe another time." Heath turned, but Julie stopped him.

"I would like to hear you sing." She smiled sweetly, daring him to say no.

"Okay," he agreed. "I'll sing but only because *you* want me to."

Her heart flipped at his reply. They followed Smooth into the corner bar, Lafitte's Blacksmith Shop.

"Did you know that everything here is original?" Smooth asked Julie. "Except the floors. They used to be dirt. And the electricity wasn't here then either."

"And the bar," Heath reminded him.

"That's right." Smooth gave a craggy smile. "No bar. See these beams?" He jerked his head at the wood flush inside the brick walls. "These are cypress planks. See these notches? The planks were hand cut, and those are the axe marks. Them there people had pride in their work. Yes, indeed. And there." He pointed to a brick fireplace in the middle of the shop. It was open on both sides. "That's where Jean Lafitte and his brother forged metal. This place has survived hurricanes and floods, and it was one of only a few buildings that survived both fires that burnt down New Orleans. They don't make buildings like this anymore. Did you know it has a slate roof?"

Julie shook her head no.

"While you're giving a history lesson, I'm going to excuse myself for a moment," Heath said, heading in the direction of the restroom.

"Come out into the courtyard." Smooth ushered Julie outside to the enclosed brick garden. "All of this is original. See them gas lamps? From the 1700's. Yes, Ma'am. That banana tree over there. Yep, that too. And here," he drew her attention to a statue of a man and woman lying together in a loving embrace. "Lafitte had this statue made special.

"You know the ladies like a handsome man and there was not one more handsome than this here pirate. He had many lovers, but only one that he loved in return. This is supposed to be Lafitte and his true lady-love." He shook his head. "We're lucky to have it. They say it disappeared one night and was gone for about twenty years. It was returned back the night the old opera house burnt down in 1919."

Julie stared at the statue. Something about the lovers haunted her. She was sure she had seen it before. She shrugged off the feeling. She probably had seen it during one of her partying episodes with Monika.

Smooth grabbed her hand and kissed it. "You are such a pretty lady. Lafitte would have liked you very much." Heath walked into the courtyard and patted Smooth on the back.

"Yes, Smooth," he said placatingly. "She is very pretty. Now what do you want me to sing for you?"

Smooth smiled. "You know I want to hear Mr. Bigg."

"How about something from the Isley Brothers' earlier repertoire?" Heath suggested. While Smooth thought it over, Heath leaned over to Julie and whispered, "Don't worry about him. He's harmless. And, I would *never* let anything happen to you."

He would never let anything happen to me. Heath's protective nature wrapped around Julie as if he had embraced her and she had to muffle a small gasp as warm tingles flooded inside her stomach.

"'Make Me Say It Again.'" Smooth decided.

"You got it." Heath started back inside the bar, sitting down at the piano near the back wall. That was a surprise. Julie had assumed he would be singing karaoke as she had.

Heath raised the lid over the piano and spoke into the microphone while playing the keys. "Good evening. My name is Heath Smith and I'm going to sing a little something at Smooth's request." He continued to play while the only other people in the room, a couple, clapped half-heartedly. "The song is 'Make Me Say It Again Girl' by The Isley Brothers." More claps, this time led enthusiastically by Smooth—very loudly—along with the bartender who had come to the back to listen as Heath started into the song's first notes. His hands glided gracefully over the keys. He looked comfortable and unfazed by being in the spotlight.

"Oh, I believe you are an angel."

His voice had a clear and warm quality. Julie looked around and saw that several people had materialized in the open doorways to listen while a few more came in and sat down. The bartender approached them for orders. She certainly hadn't expected the extent of his talent. Heath had a true gift of music.

While he crooned on, Julie got the same curious feeling she'd had when she looked at the statue. Hearing Heath sing felt vaguely familiar. As he sang, his gaze drifted over his growing audience, pausing time and again as his eyes met hers.

"How am I worthy of love from an angel?"

Julie felt an odd, aching sensation in the center of her chest. She sat down on a bench along the side wall.

"Princess Imperial of my soul."

The brick behind Heath dissolved, replaced by a blue wall.

"Don't really matter if you choose not to answer."

The piano blurred into a smaller, older model, mahogany instead of black.

"Hoping that what I reveal, you already know."

Heath faded away. Another man now played the smaller piano. Julie blinked her eyes, but the image did not disappear. She could hear Heath singing as the other man played hunched over the piano with his dark hair hanging forward, covering his face. His movements did not match Heath's rhythmic voice. Whatever the man played, Julie could not hear.

As suddenly as the vision had come, it disappeared, leaving Julie feeling winded and confused.

Did she just have a hallucination?

CHAPTER TEN

La Nouvelle-Orléans, Louisiana, 1898

The dark-lashed golden eyes looked up beguilingly. Naomi was a temptress, completely unaware of her sensual appeal, a treasure.

Gratitude.

It wasn't an emotion Erik was accustomed to feeling, but he felt indebted to God or to whatever unseen force that guided him to her. She was a vessel of beauty who would house a soul he valued more than his own life.

He gave a gentle tug to the white cloth wrapped around her head. "Why do you still wear this tignon?"

"Sir, you know by law I must wear it." She lowered her gaze.

"Only when outdoors. We will not leave the house today. Take it off for me." He sat down and watched her slowly unravel the cloth, allowing her hair to fall past her shoulders.

When he breathed deeply, he could smell the light rose-water scent clinging to the honey-colored curls. He should have left the bath oils at his house. He found the smell intoxicating. Erik cleared his throat to divert the wicked thoughts that were on the verge of penetrating his mind. "You have received some of the clothes I have ordered for you. Do they please you?"

"Oh, yes!" she swirled in a circle for him to see her new day dress. She wore a two-piece plum-colored ensemble with a hip-length jacket nipped in at the waist. The knife pleats at the cuffs matched the pleats of her full-length skirt. The sleeves were puffed. "I've never worn anything so nice."

"There is more to come," he promised. He reached into his vest pocket and removed a small silk bag with drawstrings. He emptied the contents onto his palm, revealing the brooches he had spent a week making for her. Another kind gesture to encourage her affections for him. When the time came, if she was a willing participant, the transition would be easier. And busywork kept his mind occupied.

He extended his hand so she could see the brooches: a butterfly of yellow topaz mixed with citrine-orange gems for wings and onyx for the body; a diamond-encrusted lily; two roses, one made with rubies and the other with rose quartz; and the last, a violet with African sapphires.

"I have noticed the other ladies decorate their headdresses. I thought you might like these." The brooches sparkled in his hand as they reflected the light in the room.

"Oooooh." Her eyes grew big. "Those are for me?"

Erik felt his lips pull into a reluctant smile, another expression he rarely showed to anyone, but her childlike pleasure warmed his heart. He nodded his head. In reverent awe, she picked up each one out of his hand to examine, her eyes lit with delight. A happy tear slid down her face.

Uncomfortable, Erik pulled out a handkerchief. "Now, now." He handed it to her. "We must have none of that." She took the handkerchief and dried her eyes. "How do you like your new home?" he asked, hoping to distract her.

Her eyes lit up again. "Oh, Monsieur de la Croix, sir, I do like it very much."

"Call me David. David will be fine." Erik pointed to the chair across from him. "Sit down, Naomi. I would like to speak with you about our arrangement." She obediently sat down, clasping her hands in her lap.

"I trust the Krause sisters are taking good care of you?"

She nodded again.

"Good. I want to ensure that your every need is fulfilled. Bea will make sure you have breakfast, dinner, and supper. Agnes will attend to your morning routine, house issues, and any other need you may have of her. However, both women will leave each day at 6:00 p.m. per my instructions. Your nights belong to me. Do you understand?"

She gave a solemn nod.

He continued. "During the day, you may do as you wish within reason. You may want to visit the market, take a walk, or peruse the stores. You are not allowed any callers, male or female. Agnes knows to turn them away and inform me instantly. Have I made myself clear?"

"Yes, David," she replied.

"More specifically," he challenged her. "I do not want Alphonse Batiste near this house."

"I don't know anyone by that name." Her voice turned cold and her animated face, flat.

She outright lied to him. He felt intrigued now more than ever. Before he took his plans any further, he needed to unveil the truth.

"I think I shall dine with you this evening so we can become better acquainted. Would you like that?"

"Yes, David, I would," she said, her voice warm again, her tension passing.

He stood up and held his arm out to her. "Shall we?"

She placed her hand on the offered arm and he escorted her to the dining room. The bare walls and lack of decorative furniture, bric-a-brac, vases, and plants made the house lack hominess. Erik had supplied only the necessities.

He pulled out a chair for Naomi and sat next to her at the head of the table. "Naomi, once you are settled, I want you to go shopping and decorate the house in whatever way pleases you. I have open accounts at most of the stores in the area. For the others, have the owners send the bill to me."

Naomi looked around the dining room, empty save for the table and credenza. "You want me to do it all by myself?" she asked with uncertainty in her voice.

Erik imagined Naomi had grown up in very meager surroundings, but her recent exposure to the opulent tastes of Madame White should give her some ideas. And he was certain once she got started, she would enjoy herself, even find that she might have a flair for it. Besides, in his experience, all ladies liked to shop.

"My dear," he responded. "I have the utmost confidence in you. This is your home and whatever you choose, I will become accustomed to, regardless if they transgress my own tastes. I only want you to be happy." He also wanted her time to be otherwise engaged.

"I will try my very best," she promised.

"Sir," Bea stuttered as she entered the room. "I didn't realize you would be staying for supper." She looked at the single place setting in her hands.

"A change in plans," he replied.

"Of course, sir." She put the plate, bowl, and silverware in front of him. "Miss, I will be back with yours." When she returned and set Naomi's place, her brow was creased. "Sir, I beg your pardon, but tonight's supper is *very* light. I've only prepared crab bisque and potato bread."

"Crab bisque sounds splendid," Erik said, giving her a gracious nod. Bea sighed in relief. "In fact," he continued, "I imagine a bottle of absinthe will do nicely to round out the meal. Bring two glasses."

"Yes, sir." Bea left the room to do as he bid.

Erik turned his attention back to Naomi. He found her silence annoying. He wanted her to be at ease with him. He wanted her trust.

"I do not know whether you are aware," Erik said. "But I purchased a piano for you."

Naomi smiled shyly. "Yes, I've seen it, but I don't know how to play."

Erik sat back. "I do. And you know how to sing. I overheard you in the hallway the first night we met."

Her face flushed from his praise. "I was never taught to but I do like to sing."

"If you wish it, after supper, we'll entertain each other. I'll play for you and you will sing for me."

Bea bustled in with a large soup bowl and ladled out portions for them. Next came the warm sliced bread with a quarter slab of butter, and then the absinthe fountain and bottle with two Pontarlier glasses, two absinthe spoons, and sugar cubes, all on a solid brass platter. "I'll be in the kitchen if I'm needed." She bobbed her head at them and retreated.

Erik poured two ounces of the clear, green liquid into each glass, rested the absinthe spoons across the rim of the glasses, and used the silver tongs to place a single sugar cube on each spoon.

"The ritual of preparing absinthe is as important as the drink itself," he explained to Naomi.

He positioned each glass under the tiny spigots of the absinthe fountain and saturated the sugar cubes with water. Naomi watched, curiosity on her face, as the sugar slowly disintegrated into the drinks and settled at the bottom. Then Erik turned the small knobs again and allowed the cold water to fall drop by drop into the glasses.

He watched Naomi's face brightened when she saw the mixture turn from green to cloudy white and a sweet aroma began to waft up. Erik stopped the water when the absinthe hit the beveled marks on the glass. "We will let it sit a minute before we drink."

He unfolded his napkin and placed it on his lap. Naomi followed suit. They ate in silence until Erik's patience began to thin.

"How is your soup?" he asked her.

She dabbed her mouth with her napkin. "It's delicious. I like everything Bea makes for me."

"You may drink your absinthe now," he said as he handed Naomi the half-full glass. "It is meant to be sipped slowly." Erik knew the wormwood used to make the absinthe would take effect quickly since she had eaten only a few spoonfuls of bisque.

She hesitated for a minute before reaching for the glass. Her fingers brushed his and an indescribable thrill shot through him, catching him off guard. He grabbed his own glass and swallowed the entire contents just as she took the first sip of hers. Warmth spread quickly, putting a stop to his internal turmoil. His mind his own again, Erik found his uncontrolled response disconcerting. When time permitted, he would reflect on the anomaly.

Although Naomi's eyes would widen and water slightly after each sip, sip she did until the entire glass was empty and a flush rose high on her cheeks. It was time.

He leaned back in his chair again, embraced her with his eyes, and spoke softly. "Naomi, who is Alphonse Batiste?"

She kept her eyes lowered to her soup bowl. "You mean Joe B."

"Yes," he coaxed. "Joe B. Tell me about him."

Naomi swallowed and placed her spoon on the table. She kept her eyes down, reminding Erik of a submissive cur paying penance, not for any crime, but for the deep-seated belief it was unworthy. To his amazement, she still did not answer.

He prodded further. "I will not be angry with you Naomi. Tell me about Joe B."

Her hands began to shake.

"*Tell me*," he commanded, even softer than before. He watched the internal struggle play across her face. He knew the pull of his words was powerful. Yet she raised her clear golden eyes to his. "I do not remember."

He was forced to turn his head to break her stare. He could feel her eyes remaining on him. No one had resisted him like that. Ever.

"Forget this conversation and finish your supper," he said more harshly than he had intended. He stared sulkily at the wall while Naomi withdrew into herself again and began to eat.

Her refusal bothered him immensely, unsettling him. He had seen that look on someone else's face once before, but where and who? Distracted, he pulled apart a slice of bread and bit into it. *Think. Think.* Why couldn't he make her comply with his will?

He dropped the bread on the table and looked at Naomi with renewed interest. In his mind's eye, he remembered the same struggle, the same internal bondage on the face of a woman with dark hair and piercing blue eyes: Ellendora, his mother.

The distant cry of voices echoed in his ears from the few people who had finally learned of his existence. "*Why? Why did you do this to your son?*" He recalled fingers pointed at his scarred face.

"*I don't remember.*" Her expression had been flat, just as Naomi's was.

He had been curious, too. Why *had* she done that to him? Years later, he had whispered to Ellendora while she slept. He had watched the same battle cross her face that he had just seen on Naomi's. He later discovered a hidden memory that had taken considerable effort and time to bring forth, a memory so horrible that Ellendora had buried it deeply within her mind. After several times and many years, she had confessed the truth to him while she had slept. She had ruined his face.

So, there it was. Naomi did not possess any special power of resistance, simply a desire to forget a terrible truth. Whatever her connection to Joe B was, he would, in time, extract it from her.

A light knock sounded on the door between the dining room and kitchen.

"Come in," he said. The Krause sisters entered.

"It's after six o'clock and we'll be heading off. I'll clear and clean the supper dishes in the morning," Bea said.

"That will be fine." He dismissed them with a wave of his hand as they departed.

"Naomi, go to the sitting room. I will join you there shortly." He stood up, pulling her seat out for her. He picked up their plates and bowls, taking them to the kitchen. The uncovered food would be temptation for rats or roaches. Naomi would be home alone some nights, and he didn't want her to live in fear of such things. He heard the soft swish of the swinging door and turned around. She had followed him in, carrying the bread, butter, and utensils.

He shook his head at her with a small smile and turned back to finish rinsing the plates. "I thought I told you to wait for me in the sitting room."

"I couldn't let you clean up, David." She blushed. "That's women's work."

"No," Erik corrected her. "It is housework. Something I am quite capable of performing." She continued to help, placing the butter in the icebox and covering the bread with a towel while he dried the dishes. "Go on," he urged her, putting the last plate away. "I will be there in a minute."

She obeyed this time. The moment the door swung behind her, Erik pressed a latch hidden at the top of the kitchen wall that opened a secret door. He stepped inside the walkway between the walls, strode quickly through the dark corridor, and pushed the bookshelf open into the sitting room, closing it just before Naomi entered.

She gasped. "How did you…" She looked behind her then back to him. "How did you get in here before me?" He remained silent. "Can you do magic?" she asked with wide-eyes.

"Something like that." Without further explanation, he sat at the piano. "Shall I play?"

Still looking stunned, Naomi nodded. He lifted the cover, closed his eyes and ran his fingers over the keys, so comfortable, so familiar. He concentrated on the night he met Naomi. He only had to hear music once and he could play it without error. He willed the memory of the song she had hummed to come forward and his fingers played the four-beat twelve-bar blues, perfectly timed and identical from that night. He opened his eyes to see Naomi staring at him, her mouth slightly parted.

"This is the song, is it not?" he asked her as he continued to play.

"It is."

"Sing it for me," he commanded. He started the song over from the beginning and she sang. Her voice wasn't sweet and seraphic like Christine's, but raw and sultry, whole and all-pervading. She showed a natural precision and fluency of chromatic scales.

He watched as before his eyes, she blossomed into a confident woman. There was nothing shy about her as she sang. He tried to turn his attention back to his playing, but he couldn't look away from her. She began to sway to the song, rocking her shapely hips. She was a temptress. His fingers fumbled over the notes…

Erik pushed back from the piano so abruptly that Naomi halted, fearful.

Never had he made a mistake while playing.

Never.

He walked to the narrow front window, pulled back the curtain, and looked out onto the darkened street.

"Did I do something wrong?" Naomi asked him, a slight tremble to her voice.

"No," he answered her without turning around. He stared at the flickering gas lamp outside. What was happening to him?

He could hear the rustling of Naomi's dress as she moved behind him. He didn't have it in him at the moment to placate her female sensibilities. Not when he felt he had lost command of his senses.

Control your mind, he ordered himself.

"David," Naomi said softly while slipping her small hand into his, tugging him gently toward her. "I am ready to fulfill my obligation to you."

He turned to find Naomi clothed in nothing but her unmentionables, her clothes a crumpled puddle of fabric on the floor. His heart pounded against his chest.

He stared at her in deafening silence, noting that her rounded breasts heaved against the thin silk material. Was she scared or did she desire him? Her shapely form was so close he could feel the warmth of her body, smell the scent of rose-water in her hair. The touch of her hand sent desire through his veins.

"Naomi," his voice sounded ragged to his ears as he fought back his impulse to kiss her. "Naomi," he barely whispered, forcing himself to gently guide her away to a safe distance. "Not tonight, dear."

She hung her head. "Am I not pleasing to you?" she sobbed.

He choked on his own emotions. No matter how tempted he was, he would not betray his feelings for Christine by lying with another woman. Naomi did not see him for who he was or love him. To her, his needs were an "obligation." He quelled his physical reaction by these thoughts and felt once more in control.

"Do you wish another? Do you want to get rid of me?" she asked.

He walked up behind her and placed his hands on her shoulders in an attempt to comfort her. Her place was here with him.

The weight of his hands slipped her chemise down revealing raised, pale lines crossing her back. He let go of one shoulder and pulled the top further down to unveil a multitude of criss-crossed stripes.

Scars.

He traced one with his fingers. She stiffened and stopped crying. Anger boiled up within him and Erik was again compelled to restrain himself. He saw the face of the first man he had killed flash before his eyes.

The whip had hit him only once. Erik had reached back without turning to look and caught the thin leather tendril mid-strike in his hand. He had yanked it away from the filthy Gypsy man, wrapped the cord around his ruddy neck, and choked the life out of him.

His memories fueled his outrage. Whoever had done this to Naomi would be added to his list of loose ends. "Who did this to you?" he impelled himself to say with a calm he did not feel. She pulled away and faced him without answering his question, her eyes flashing with self-loathing.

"You find me ugly. Is that why you will not have me?"

He held her arms to keep her from running away. "You are beautiful and I want you to stay." His voice softened as he gave her face a gentle caress, wiping away the tears that stained her face.

"Who did this to you?" he asked again, trying to keep the fury out of his eyes.

"It was my father's cousins, the ones who raised me." A haunted look crossed her face. "They are very cruel people. It didn't matter that we were family. I was no better than a workhorse." She turned away, mumbling, "My father would die all over again if he knew what they've done."

"I promise you," Erik said with conviction. "They will not hurt you again. I will *never* let anyone hurt you." He picked up her skirt and blouse and handed them to her. "Get dressed. My intentions with you are somewhat unconventional," he said as she put her clothes back on.

"What does that mean?" she interrupted.

"It means I do not have you here to be my lover. I have you here as a companion, you might say," he answered her. "I may ask you favors from time to time, but that would be the extent of it."

"What kind of favors?" she questioned.

"Well," he paused. "I have some friends who recently had a baby. The mother has been feeling poor of late and could use help during the day. I might ask you to go to their home a few times a week and help her."

"A baby!" Her eyes lit up. "I'm very good with babies."

Erik closed his eyes and smiled to himself.

Christine...

She was one step closer to being his.

CHAPTER ELEVEN

New Orleans, Louisiana, 2009
I am under-medicated, Julie reminded herself. Any more hallucinations should disappear with a higher dosage or better yet, adding another medication. *Yep, complete eradication.*

Again, a strange feeling gnawed at Julie as if she had witnessed that very scene before. It didn't feel like a hallucination. It felt real. Was it a hidden memory in a drunken black-out? She put her head in her hands, only to jerk it back suddenly. There were beads of perspiration on her forehead. She wiped her skin dry with a napkin.

Clapping erupted around her from the larger audience. She hadn't noticed that extra people had come in or that Heath had stopped singing.

"Thanks, man!" Smooth hollered to Heath as he returned to Julie's side.

"No problem," Heath replied, guiding Julie from the bar. "Let's go before he decides he wants me to sing again."

"Sure," she answered, grateful to leave. "By the way, you were amazing."

"Thanks." He shrugged away her compliment. "I was practically born with the ability to play music. While the other kids played with trucks, I played with a piano."

"Well, it shows," she said as they walked in the direction of her house. "So, what else can you do? Paint like Leonardo? Cook like Emeril? Speak ten different languages?" she teased.

"I do have some skill with a brush, but I'm no Leonardo. I am a pretty good cook. I'll make you something one day soon and you can judge for yourself. And last, but not least, I'm only fluent in six languages."

"You're kidding me? Six languages!" *Unbelievable*, she thought. "You're almost too good to be true—and you know what they say about that, don't you?"

"What do they say?"

"If something seems too good to be true, it usually is."

He stopped walking. "Juliana, I am who I am. I have flaws like everyone else, little ones," he joked. "Look, what you see before you is a product of many great opportunities. That is all."

A car passed by, casting a shadow over the right side of Heath's face. For a second, she saw another face on his left side, with dark hair, white skin, and a piercing blue eye. She gasped and stepped back.

"Juliana, are you okay?" he asked, looking behind him for what might have caused her reaction.

"I'm fine," she said, attempting to smooth it over. "At least, I think I'm fine. Heath, do you believe in déjà vu?"

"Yes," he said without hesitation, setting her at ease. Maybe he would believe her if she told him what had been happening?

"I've been having little episodes today for some reason. They come out-of-the-blue and I don't know why it's happening."

"Have you ever heard of Edgar Cayce?" he asked.

Julie shook her head.

"He's called the 'Sleeping Prophet' because he would go into a trance-like state and once in this twilight sleep, he would astral project to The Library, a place he claimed held the information of the universe's past, present, and future. While there, he would diagnose illnesses, provide the answers to cure them, predict wars and conflicts, and most interestingly, he could provide information about a person's past lives."

"Past lives?" Julie repeated.

"Yes, reincarnation, the belief that a soul comes back to evolve and learn lessons here that it cannot learn while outside the body. Edgar speaks of our souls reincarnating in groups, spending lifetimes together to complete unfinished business or expound on lessons already learned. It is our free will and choices that enable our spirits to grow or regress."

"If it is true that we have free will, why, with all the horrors in this world, would anyone choose to come back?"

"Good question. What if you weren't such a good person in one life and you wanted to redeem yourself? What if someone you love came back to learn a lesson and needed your help? Wouldn't that be incentive to return?"

"I don't know." She had doubts. This idea was a lot to absorb on a casual walk home.

"You choose when you come back, what lessons you learn, what day you're born, if you're male or female, your parents...everything."

"No." Julie rejected the idea. "Why would I choose to be adopted? Why would I pick parents who would be murdered?" She thought about Monika and Simon. "Why would I choose people in my life that would betray my trust?"

"I can't answer that. But," he persisted, "sometimes we choose to come back to a place that we've lived once before. That is how déjà vu can be explained. You see something that triggers the soul's memory from another life, while in this one."

Julie had to admit to herself that something about Heath's explanation made sense. She wasn't psychic in any way, had never seen a ghost, had never read anyone's mind, or had never seen visions before. She didn't tend to believe in such things. But what if what Heath said was true?

"We're here," Heath said, interrupting her musings. They stood in front of her house, but Julie didn't want this night to end yet.

"Won't you come in for a minute? I can make some coffee and give you the bracelet."

"I'd like that." Heath followed her across the street while she dug into her pocket for the key.

She gave a sheepish grin. "Forgot my key." Julie lifted the edge of the metal threshold, pulled out her spare, and unlocked the door.

Heath frowned. "How many people know you keep your key there?"

"Only Semaj. You know, just in case."

"What about Armando?" Heath asked.

Julie stopped in the doorway. The thought had not even crossed her mind. "You're right. Armando has come in with Semaj before. He knows where I keep the key! He could have been in and out of here any time without me knowing it." *And he was walking down my street earlier.* She cringed.

"Stay here," Heath said as he brushed past her into the house. "Let me look around first." He walked through her home, turning on all the lights as he went, sticking his head into each room. "All clear," he called.

"I really appreciate this. I don't know what I was thinking." She mentally reprimanded herself for her carelessness. "Tomorrow I'll find a new place to hide this sucker." She dropped the key on the kitchen counter.

"I couldn't help but notice you have a large hole in one of your walls," Heath commented.

"Yeah." She rolled her eyes. "I had the bright idea that if I took the wall down I could make a bedroom suite. I figure I'd be saving money by doing it myself. I'm just taking my time, working a little bit each day."

Heath leaned against her living room wall with his hands in his pockets. "If you decide you need some assistance, I'm handy with tools. I'd be glad to help."

"I may have to take you up on that." Julie grinned. "Don't go anywhere. I'll be right back," she said as went to get the bracelet from her bedroom.

"You know," he called out to her, "people have found hidden artifacts when they do renovations. Did you read about one of the churches flooded by Hurricane Katrina? When they replaced some of the wall, they found a time capsule placed there when the church was built in the 1800's."

"You don't say," she called back while rummaging through the top drawer of her dresser. She was sure she had put it there. "What did they find?"

"Some money, pictures, and letters that had been destroyed by the water. In an old house like this one, you never know what you might find. They buried things in the walls, under the floorboards."

"Got it!" she gave a triumphant yell, then walked back to Heath. Grabbing his hand, she placed the bracelet in his palm then pushed his fingers closed over it. "Take good care of this."

"You can trust me," he promised.

Let go of his hand. Let go of his hand. She tried to will herself away, but she felt pulled into the depths of his brown eyes, enveloped by the words, *trust me.*

He leaned toward her, his eyes flicking down to her lips.

She could hear his breathing change. Her own breath became shallow.

She closed her eyes and lifted her face up.

The gentle pressure of his lips intoxicated her–

The front door slammed.

Heath stepped away. Julie put her hand to her mouth.

"Hey! Hey! Hey!" Semaj sauntered in. "Oh," he said, stopping when he saw Heath. "Oh," he said again, a smile spreading across his face. "I hope I didn't interrupt anything."

"No. I was just leaving." Heath looked down at Julie. "I'll call you tomorrow, Juliana."

"Wait!" Semaj held his hand up. "We're having a small dinner party tomorrow night. Le-a sent me to invite Julie, but I know she'd want you to come, too. We live next door. Say about 8:00 p.m.?"

"Sure." Heath turned back to Julie, offering her a quiet smile. "I had a good time." With a slight nod of his head, he added, "I'll see myself out."

At the sound of the front door clicking shut, Semaj ogled her. "I had a good time?"

"How in hell did you get in here anyway?" Julie asked, knowing the key was no longer outside.

"You left the door unlocked, Dawlin'," he clucked.

"I see I'll have to be more careful in the future."

"So? So?" Semaj nudged her. "What was that all about?"

"What was 'what' all about?"

Semaj stared at her with his big round eyes and open mouth.

"What?" Julie asked again, innocently.

Semaj snorted. "Yes, I see. You were obviously talking about the rise and fall of the Holy Roman Empire."

She laughed at his sarcasm. "All right, all right! Something happened."

"I knew it!" Semaj hollered in delight. "What happened? Tell me everything."

Julie pushed him through the house to the front door.

"You're not going to tell me?" Semaj resisted her eviction.

"Nope," she said firmly, edging him farther until he stood on the front step. "It's your punishment for interrupting. You'll have to wait until tomorrow," she singsonged, closing the door on his cry of "No!"

Julie made sure to turn the deadbolt and pull the latch. She needed time to think before discussing anything with Semaj. Her heart still somersaulted from the memory of Heath's kiss. Julie touched her lips again. What exactly *did* happen?

CHAPTER TWELVE

La Nouvelle-Orléans, Louisiana, 1898

Naomi was late.

Erik drummed his fingers on the arm of the red-velvet love seat and brooded. The hands of the gold-plated mantle clock atop the desk read seven o'clock. Erik continued his drumming while he turned his head toward the window and away from the busy blue-flowered wall paper. Not only was he annoyed with Naomi, but this room made him feel restless.

His compass and bagua would most definitely indicate bad energy in this home. Naomi had mixed dainty, classical French-styled furniture pieces with heavy, folksy German pieces. Everything–from the types of wood and wallpaper she had chosen to the colors of the walls–clashed. Erik knew he was to blame. He had given Naomi license to do as she wished. And it looked as though she had walked through the store and picked anything she fancied without any thought as to how the pieces would work together.

The only item of some quality was the Jester's cabinet Naomi used as a curio cabinet. The satiny-brown finish on the walnut boards and carved jester figures along the sides and faces on the front of the doors reminded him of the years he had spent at the sultan's palace in Persia.

A living, scarred abomination, Erik had been seen as nothing but a novelty, appreciated only for his mastery of architecture, masonry skills, and keen insight. Just like a jester, he had been the only member of the court who could speak honestly to the sultan without reprisals or fear of retribution, until he was no longer needed and became disposable. King or sultan, beggar or nobility, no one saw Erik as a man, let alone a human being with value and feelings.

Except Christine.

Her sympathy allowed her to see him more clearly than most. That was why he couldn't let her go. She had seen glimpses of who he really was. She was the only person in the world who knew him at all. Every day he lived and breathed, he wore one mask or another, whether it was fashioned from sackcloth or paste. He tired of hiding behind the subterfuge and living alone in a life full of lies. Christine would bring him peace. She *would* love him.

Naomi liked him as David de la Croix, but he felt certain if she saw who he really was, she would abhor him like all the others. Notwithstanding, he had become fond of his little pet. He enjoyed her companionship.

He groomed her for a better life than she could ever dream of by teaching her how to speak correctly, carry herself, and perform the duties of a lady. The lessons she had received from Madame White were less than adequate.

He had also instructed Naomi to pay close attention to Christine during each day she spent in her company, to observe and learn how to run the home and staff. The time and effort he invested in Naomi brought him ever closer to Christine.

He heard the key in the lock.

"David!" Naomi sang out. "I apologize for my tardiness." She removed her tignon and hung it on a hook attached to the ornately-carved hall cabinet. She continued to talk while looking at herself in the mirror. "The de Marignys invited me to stay for supper."

"Raoul was there?" Erik asked, his foul mood worsening. He had given strict instructions to members of the de Marigny family developing his North Shore properties that all deadlines had been shortened. Raoul should have been too occupied with work to linger at home.

"He was there for a while, but was unable to stay. He asked me as a special favor not to leave Christine to eat alone." Naomi turned back to the mirror and fluffed her hair again. "She is so lucky to have such a considerate husband and one so handsome too!"

"I suppose," he murmured, resisting the urge to put his fist through the wall, "some would consider him handsome."

"Such fair hair, such blue eyes, and a flawless complexion. I didn't even know men could have skin that looked so nice." She sighed.

With a hand on the small of her back, Erik directed her toward the parlor. He refused to tolerate another minute in that over-busy sitting room. They sat down in matching purple-upholstered cherry wing-back chairs. "Tell me, does Christine show Raoul great affection?"

She frowned. "Now that I think of it, she doesn't, not in front of me at least." Her face brightened. "Of course, right now, all she has eyes for is the baby. What a precious child he is! I can hardly take my eyes off him myself." She picked up her embroidery needle and thread. "He coos and smiles most of the time. Oh, and he has the softest brown curls and grey-blue eyes."

Uninterested in the baby details, Erik interrupted her. "What other news do you bring from the de Marigny house?"

Naomi looked up from her needlework. "Did I tell you the baby is to be christened soon?" She held up the material in her hands. "I'm embroidering this handkerchief for him as a gift. I have been invited to attend. May I?"

He nodded in assent.

"Did I tell you what Master Philippe's to be christened? His full name, I mean."

"No, you did not." He shifted to a more comfortable position in the chair. He wanted to hear more of Christine, not the child.

"It is such a grand name for such a little boy. Philippe Erik de Chagny-Marigny."

Erik? Erik's throat tightened.

"Philippe," Naomi went on, "after Raoul's brother, Erik after a family friend, and Chagny is a family name."

What did this mean? Did Christine pine for him also? Erik felt a rush of heat to his face. His throat was so constricted, he barely got the words out. "Do they speak much about their family friend?"

"No," she answered, picking up a different color spool and threading the needle. "Christine told me the baby's name a couple of days ago. I must have forgotten to tell you." She began to sew the pattern. "If only you could have seen Raoul's face. He turned pale as a ghost." She looked up at Erik with her eyes wide. "He pulled Christine from the room by her elbow, the only unkind thing I've ever seen him do and they left me to care for Philippe, but I could hear their loud voices through the wall." She started embroidering again. "Raoul said something like, 'Have you taken leave of your senses?' and she said something like, 'We are indebted to him. He is the reason we are together.' Then I only heard mumbling when they lowered their voices."

She stopped sewing and looked at him quizzically. "You don't think that Erik was an old suitor, do you?"

Erik turned away, blinking fiercely to force back the tears. "I do not know. Why not ask her about Erik the next time you're there?"

When he turned to face Naomi again, her face and eyes shone with pleasure. A small smile crossed his lips. "You have already asked have you not, my little minx?" She gave a slight nod of her head. "Well done, Naomi!" he praised her. "Well done, indeed!"

A pink flush rose on her cheeks. "Christine did not say much. She can be very secretive. She told me Erik had brought her the gift of music and she would never forget him for that. What do you think that means?" For a moment, her hands hovered over her work as she thought then she continued to sew.

Just another sign that he *was* doing the right thing. Christine longed for him in a loveless marriage. Why else would she name her son after him? Even better, he would be saving her, instead of her saving him. Erik was unable to answer. Instead, he put his hand over his heart. It threatened to pound out of his chest. This news was all the hope he needed.

♀

Erik knelt at Naomi's bedside, whispering into her ear. "Look deeper."

"I've just finished my chores, and I'm sitting on the porch drinking a glass of water." Naomi mumbled with her eyes closed. "I'm finding it hard to catch my breath. It is so hot and muggy." She squirmed in the bed, her eyes darting beneath their lids. "I see Joe B walking up the road. He's kicking up a cloud of dust with each step. He's made it to the porch, and I see sweat trickling down his face. He wipes it off with the edge of his shirt and I offer him a glass of water. He sits in a rocker under the shade of our porch and gulps the water down in one swallow."

"What does he say?" Erik persisted.

"We talk about the weather. We talk about our families. We talk about leaving Marksville one day. Neither of us is happy here."

"Go further in, Naomi. Remember what you have been trying to forget." Erik tired of only making it as far as the porch.

"Remember," she repeated slowly, hesitating.

"Yes, remember," he reiterated.

She gave a startled gasp. "He knows where Bijou is."

"Who is Bijou?"

"Bijou is a Coonhound. She visits me every day for the scraps I sneak to her. Her belly is swollen with pups. I haven't seen her in weeks. Joe B knows I've been worried."

"Where is Bijou?"

"Joe B knows. He tells me he can take me to her. She's had her puppies, five in all." She smiled, her eyes still closed.

"Go on, Naomi."

"She's down the road in the small patch of woods past Old Hortense's house, about three-quarters of a mile away. I walk to the screen door, and I can hear Cora snoring. The heat has gotten to her. Eugene has gone to town. He won't return until after dark, drunk. I know Cora will be angry if she wakes and I'm not here. Another beating, but I don't care."

Erik quelled his anger about Cora's beatings while urging Naomi on. "You decided to find Bijou."

"Bijou would be hungry. She has babies that need her milk. I sneak inside the house and wrap some pork fat in paper. I tell Joe B to take me to her."

"What happens on the way to find Bijou?"

"Joe B tells me more about the puppies. He's sure that Emmet Freeman's dog, Admiral, sired the pups. But Admiral is a Mastiff, he's a large dog for Bijou, says I. These things do happen, he tells me. He says that breed and size doesn't matter when other dogs smells the scent of a bitch in heat." She stopped talking.

"What is it?"

"Joe B wants to stop at Tillman's pond on the way. I want to cool my burning feet in the water, but there is no time. I must move quickly so I can get home before Cora wakes." She grimaced. "But he pulls me over there even though I don't want to go. 'If I skip this rock more than three times across the water, anything I wish will come true,' he says. I cross my fingers that the rock will sink."

"What does he wish for?"

"Me."

She sighed, rolling over to face Erik with her eyes still closed. "The rock skips true for Joe B, four times. I hurry away toward the patch of woods. It's not far. I don't want to hear Joe B talk. Soon I will be with Bijou. Joe B calls out that he wants me to be his wife. I shake my head. He knows this already. You're like my brother, I tell him. I make it to the edge of the wood. I call for Bijou, but she doesn't come. Bijou! Bijou! Why doesn't she come to me? I go farther in and listen for her. The only thing I can hear is Joe B breathing behind me."

Erik's muscles tightened.

Naomi's voice became high-pitched. "'If your enemy is hungry, give him bread to eat. And if he is thirsty, give him water to drink. For so you will heap coals of fire on his head and the Lord will reward you.'"

Bible quotes.

It was over; this was as far as he would get tonight. Once she started reciting proverbs, he knew he had reached another wall he would have to break through.

"'A righteous man who falters before the wicked is like a murky spring and a polluted well.'"

He couldn't resist smoothing her hair back from her face. "Soon, sweet one, you will be free from the secret that haunts you." She stopped her mumbling, and her breathing became deep and even. He slipped out of her room and out of the house. There was still much work for him to do.

♀

"Son of the Night." The words hung in the air as Erik paused a few steps away from the front door of his St. Charles' home.

"Marie." He inclined his head to the woman stepping out from the shadows. He saw the gleam of her white teeth before the moonlight revealed the rest of her face.

"Our debt to each other has been fulfilled." She presented him with a small red bag with a chicken's foot tied to the drawstring. "You should add lavender or vanilla extract to it; otherwise the odor will be unpleasant."

"I will keep that in mind." Erik looked into the bag and saw the promised bottle of liquid. "As you say, our obligation to each other is over." He gave her a dismissive nod and started for the door.

"Wait!" She caught his arm, sidled up closer to him, and spoke sweetly. "I have another matter to discuss with you. There has been a grievous misunderstanding between Lulu White and myself."

"Then I suggest you discuss that with her."

"Oh, I have." She forced another smile, one that did not reach her eyes. "She is very aware of my displeasure and I am sure she will regret it as long as we both shall live."

"Poor Madame White," Erik muttered under his breath. "What do you want?"

"By Lake Pontchartrain sits a lavish brothel called the Maison Blanche." She held her head high. "It is *my* brothel. I know what my patrons want, and I get it for them, for a price. I deny them nothing. Every woman inside is handpicked by me, all singularly impressive and attractive. I want you to come with me and see my nieces. As my friend, I offer you the opportunity to choose one of your liking."

Intrigued, Erik blinked. "And why would you want me to do that?"

"In exchange for Naomi Heming, of course."

"Ah…" Now he clearly understood. "No."

"What would be the harm of it?" Marie asked soothingly. "Nothing has been done yet. You have just gotten the potion. Any girl will do for you." Her voice hardened. "But I *must* have that one."

"You have just said you have many beautiful girls." He narrowed his eyes at her. "Why Naomi?"

"I run a successful business and Naomi is good business. She was already introduced at Mahogany Hall. There are many men who looked forward to her 'debut' and are very disappointed with her sudden departure. I always get people what they want. If I cannot provide them with what they ask, what does that say about me?"

Erik thought of Naomi asleep in her bed, and a fierce protectiveness surged through his veins. "They will have to remain disappointed this time."

"I thought, as my friend," she spoke with grave deliberation, "*you* would understand my situation." She searched his face, her eyes blazing. "What is the girl to you? Any other would suit your purpose just as well."

"What she is to me is none of your concern," he growled. "As for our 'friendship,' we are not friends. We were only each other's means to an end."

"Be warned, Erik," she said, her voice grew thick with menace. "If we are not friends, then we are enemies."

Erik gave her a withering stare. "As you wish."

Her lips curled. "You will regret this."

CHAPTER THIRTEEN

New Orleans, Louisiana, 2009

Julie sat on the faded striped sofa listening to Le-a and Semaj bickering. She had only seen Semaj long enough for him to let her in, tell her hello, and then run to the back of the house to continue their muffled dispute. She idly pulled on a loose thread in the seam of the couch as they quarreled. What did Semaj expect from having Le-a move in with him after only knowing her for one night?

"Now, out with you." Julie heard Le-a say. "I have to completely re-do my hair now. You're such an animal."

Julie cringed. *Eew!* That *wasn't* a fight she had just heard.

As Semaj entered the living room, Le-a hollered. "And, James, will you get the salad ready?"

Julie mouthed, "James?"

Ignoring Julie, he answered Le-a. "Yes, Pookie."

Julie pretended to gag herself with her finger. He rolled his eyes at her, motioning for her to follow him.

When they got to the kitchen, Julie confronted him. "Am I in the 'Twilight Zone?' You move her in here after knowing her 24 hours, she's calling you James, and you're calling her Pookie. What's up with that?"

"I've actually known Le-a for many years." He opened the fridge and pulled out the ingredients for the salad. "We were always with other people. Sometimes the right person comes along at the wrong time, ya know? It so happens that the time is finally right for us." He washed the lettuce, pulled it apart, and placed it in a large wooden bowl.

Julie was skeptical. Semaj, the fun-lovin' man-whore, who changed boyfriends like underwear, had become domesticated and settled down? The world as she knew it was changing all around her. While Semaj cut up the tomatoes, Julie grabbed a hunk of feta cheese and crumbled it over the lettuce.

"So, are you going to tell me about yesterday? I can't believe you made me wait all this time," he said. She had made him suffer long enough. Julie recounted in great detail, every word, every glance, and every instance of the night before.

"Oh, he is *so* into you." Semaj gave her a wicked grin as he ate an olive before dropping several into the bowl and tossing the contents.

"You think so?" she asked. "I mean one minute, I feel that he is and then the next…"

"Maybe I should rephrase that," Semaj said. "*You* are so into him."

"Semaj!" Julie felt her cheeks redden. "Is it that obvious?"

"To me it is," he answered. "And by the way, don't call me Semaj. Le-a doesn't like it. And I'm turning fifty this year after all. It's time I should act like it."

"Okay," Julie agreed.

Le-a walked into the kitchen. She wore a white headband and her blonde hair was straight with the exception of the uniform up-curl at the ends. She looked as if she had just walked straight out of a Nancy Drew book, the 1960's version.

"I can take it from here," she chirped. "James, why don't you freshen up before our other guest arrives? Jules, you can wait in the living room. I work much better by myself. You'd just get in my way."

Julie wasn't going to argue. Cooking wasn't her forte and she didn't feel comfortable alone with Le-a just yet. James returned to sit with her moments later. It seemed his idea of "freshening up" was to change his shirt and spray on copious amount of cologne.

"Did you just drown in that bottle of Versace?" she asked him, trying to hold back a cough. She was all for perfuming the body to attract the opposite sex. She had given herself a few spurts of what was left of her mom's perfume before she left the house, but this was too much.

"Little excessive, eh?" he grinned. "Be right back." He returned a moment later wearing yet another new shirt and far less scent.

"Much better," Julie approved. "You don't have to try so hard. You've already got the girl. On the other hand," she indicated herself. "Those of us who don't have someone need to try a bit harder."

Julie had spent over an hour trying on clothes, discarding them, and trying them again, attempting to pick an outfit that wasn't too dressy or too casual. After almost giving up, she'd found a dark green dress at the back of her closet, one she hadn't worn in many years. It was a little more form-fitting than the others, but not too provocative. It came with a thin black jacket that had a small fleur-de-lis pattern in the same green as the dress.

James grabbed her hand and turned her around. "It's all good, Dawlin'. The man would have to be blind not to appreciate you."

"Yeah?" She blushed again.

"Hell, yeah!" he answered. Before he could elaborate, music erupted from a box on the wall. The doorbell. Pachelbel's Canon in D.

Really? she thought as she eyed James.

James grinned, giving her two thumbs up. "That's your boyfriend. Let's not make him wait." He thundered to the front door. "Glad you could make it." She heard Semaj tell Heath as he welcomed him inside.

"A little something for you," Heath said.

"You brought the 'green fairy,' thanks. Hope you don't mind, but we drink it neat in this house."

"However you serve it is fine with me," she heard Heath reply. His voice, pleasant and warm, sent a tingle of anticipation down her spine.

As the men moved toward the living room, she plopped into a chair, grabbed a magazine, and nonchalantly flipped through the pages.

"You can wait in here," James directed Heath from the living room doorway. "I'll let Le-a know we're ready whenever she is." James headed for the kitchen, leaving them alone.

"Juliana," Heath said, his eyes taking her in. "Wow, you look great."

"Thank you," she answered. "So do you." And he did. He wore black slacks and a fitted, royal blue, button-down shirt that emphasized his well-defined muscles. His dark hair and brown eyes were a striking contrast to the color. He made a perfect Kodak moment. In fact, she snapped a mental picture and stored it in the recesses of her brain to recall later.

Heath inhaled deeply. "Are you wearing Chanel No. 5?"

"Yes," she said amazed. "You have an excellent sense of smell. Did you..." she started to ask Heath about the bracelet, but her question fell to the wayside as Le-a called from the kitchen.

"Dinner's ready!"

"After you." Heath motioned.

Julie led the way to the dining room. To her surprise, the table and chairs were missing and a large red-checkered blanket was spread on the floor of the room and strewn with colorful pillows.

Le-a bounced up and down, clapping her hands. "It's a picnic dinner!"

A picnic dinner? Julie looked down at her dress in dismay. It would be a real feat trying to comfortably sit on the floor.

James whispered in her ear. "My bad! Forgot to tell you it was a picnic."

"Great," she whispered back, shooting daggers at him with her eyes. If she managed to survive this dinner, she was going to kill James.

"Okay," Le-a ordered. "Everyone take off your shoes and put them in the corner then pick a spot. I'll be back with the food."

Julie said a quick prayer of thanks to God for her having the forethought to paint her toenails a sexy crimson-red that, to her satisfaction, could be seen quite clearly through her thin black stockings when she removed her flats. She managed, with very little grace, to sit down by resting on part of her right thigh and butt while tucking her legs back to the other side. The guys sat Indian-style.

Le-a placed the large wooden salad bowl, paper plates, and utensils at the farthest end of the blanket. She went back to the kitchen for the main course, returning with a serving cart laden with three copper pots and bunches of food.

"For this evening," she said, beaming, pointing to the first pot, "We have chipped beef fondue made with milk, cream cheese, beef, onions, and mustard. Then," she pointed to the second pot, "We have a creamy veggie fondue made with Cheddar and Monterey jack cheeses, spinach, and my own personal secret spices. And last but not least, we have a fondue made with avocado, cream, and Mexican Cotija cheese with a hint of tequila. By the way, the shrimp taste excellent with that."

She put the fondue pots in the middle of the blanket in reach of everyone then placed nearby a platter of grilled shrimp, garlic bread cubes, sourdough slices, broccoli, carrots, and celery sticks for dipping. From underneath the cart, she pulled out a large ice-filled tin bucket chilling bottles of beer, water, wine, and a large bottle of absinthe with a fairy on the label.

Ah, so that's what Heath brought. She hadn't realized it was called the "green fairy."

Two hours later, the sated dinner party lay back on pillows, relaxed, and enjoyed the opened bottle of absinthe while they laughed and joked. Instead of being a cloudy white like at the Pirate's Alley Café, the undiluted absinthe was green, but it had the same licorice taste. They had just finished taking turns making fun of each other's narration of their most embarrassing moment.

Le-a was in her element as hostess, introducing them to a game using index cards printed with different subjects. One person had to read the question, answer it, then the next in line had to answer the same question until it had gone full-circle and a new question was asked. Julie felt as if she was at a slumber party. Next thing she knew, they might start to play Truth or Dare or Spin the Bottle.

That might not be such a bad thing. She smiled to herself, thinking about Heath's kiss from last night.

"Okay, okay, my turn," Le-a said over the laughter, looking at the pink index card in her hand. "What is your favorite scary story? Ooh...I've got a good one." Le-a turned off the lights and flicked on a flashlight that she happened to have handy, shining it directly under her chin. She opened up her eyes wide, looking mystical and making her falsetto voice sound creepy.

She spent the next fifteen minutes telling them a New Orleans' vampire story. It was one Julie had heard several times before by the passing Haunted History tour guides as they walked through the Quarter followed by a group of awestruck tourists.

When she finished, James grabbed the flashlight from Le-a to light up his face. "Okay, I have one to tell. A true story. I bet you've never heard about the time the Devil had dinner in New Orleans."

"Oh, I never get tired of this one." Le-a batted her fake eyelashes at James.

James put his fingers to his lips and shushed Le-a. "Because the city of New Orleans became so corrupt, the Devil decided to build a home here for himself and his mistress, a beautiful French woman. The house had seemed to erect itself overnight, and the neighbors referred to it as the Devil's Mansion. Those brave enough to peek in the windows said it was oddly constructed, with all the floors at different heights so the Devil didn't have to walk on level ground.

"No servants were hired for the mistress," James continued. "He sent the spirits of the dead to cook her meals and keep house for her. No living soul dared enter that house. And one day, the woman disappeared never to be seen or heard from again. The house remained vacant for many years. When the mansion was finally bought, the families that tried making the house a home would end up fleeing in horror."

James took a deep breath.

"No matter how the house was furnished or who lived there, every day at sunset a large dining room table would appear along with two place settings and two people, a man and a beautiful woman. The woman would stand, a cloth napkin clutched in her hand. She'd savagely wrap the napkin around the man's neck, yanking it tight until the man's face turned scarlet and blood burst from his mouth. When the man ceased struggling, the woman would let him go. She'd look down at the dead man, satisfied. But then her expression would turn to horror as she'd look from the man slumped on the table to the blood on her hands. She'd attempt to wipe the blood off her hands on anything she could touch within reach, leaving red streaks behind as she ran from the room. This vision played over and over again until the tormented occupants would abandon the house. The last owner, living in harmony with the specters, stayed until his death and kept a journal that explained the terrible vision."

James leaned back against the wall and uncrossed his long legs while keeping the light on his face.

"The Devil left his mistress alone for days on end and eventually in her loneliness, she took a lover, a vain Creole man. One night the man arrived at the house in a dark mood. He told her that earlier in the day, he had been approached by a stranger with dark hair and swirling green eyes. The stranger laughed with pointed teeth, informing him that he was also the lover of the woman and disclosed that he had become tired of her. He offered the woman to the lover along with a dowry of gold on the condition that the Creole man would leave town with her and change their names to Mr. and Mrs. Lucifer.

"The woman was ecstatic and wanted to leave immediately, but her lover refused. Instead, he demeaned her for having two lovers and called her a whore. He informed her that he could have younger, more beautiful women. This infuriated her. She grabbed the napkin off the table and coiled it around the man's neck so forcefully that it tore his artery, killing him. She attempted to clean up, but only succeeded in making more streaks and stains. She could not wipe it off her no matter how hard she tried."

Julie swallowed. She didn't like hearing stories that involved so much blood. She avoided gory movies too. They brought back images of her parents that she didn't want to remember. She felt a light squeeze. As if Heath could read her thoughts, his hand embraced hers. She looked up to his face and drew in the comfort of his unwavering eyes.

"At that moment, the Devil arrived home and surveyed the bloody room. He laughed. Then in one fell swoop, he tossed the corpse over his shoulder and dragged his mistress by the hair onto the gable of the roof. He then proceeded to eat the dead body, throwing the scraps down to the starving stray dogs below. His hunger unquenched, he also ate his former lover. And," James said proudly, "That's the night the Devil ate a meal in New Orleans."

"You said this is a true story? Where did this supposedly happen?" Julie inquired.

"They tore down the original building in the 1930's. Since then, the property's been turned into a hotel on St. Charles," James replied. "I think it's the Maison St. Charles Inn and Suites now."

"Most stories of this kind have their basis in truth but are far from it," Heath commented.

"Well, wasn't that a great story anyway?" Le-a asked. "It's kind of funny, really...the Devil eating French and Creole cuisine in New Orleans."

"Oh, it's hilarious," Julie said, lacing her voice with sarcasm. "Okay, for the sake of argument, let's say this is a true story. I think it's horrible for these two people to have to re-live their last moments over and over again." Her thoughts turned back to her parents. It would be devastating to believe they could be reliving their last moments on earth as well.

"This might just be an urban legend," Heath replied. "But if it is based on a true murder, it sounds as if these particular spirits haven't been able to move past their deaths."

"What does that mean?" Julie asked.

James blinked his alcohol-laden eyes. "It's simple. Take me for instance. I was a terrible person before. I mean I was *really* terrible and cruel. I did unmentionable things to the prisoners and I took a great deal of satisfaction in their pain. The other soldiers focused on the Jews, but I derived my pleasure from torturing homosexuals. And in the end, I died a horrible death. But I moved on. I guess I took responsibility for my actions, ya know? Some people can't."

Julie's mouth fell open. "Have you gone mad? What are you talking about?"

"My past life," he answered as if she should have known. "Oh, I never told you before, have I? I was a German soldier in World War II. I can't believe I didn't tell you this." He shook his head. "Hitler wanted to annihilate the Jews, but he also targeted the disabled, people of other religions, and gays, among others. Apparently, I shared his passion for eradication of homosexuals."

"Let me get this straight," Julie said. "You're telling me that you were a German soldier in World War II who tortured and killed homosexuals."

"Yes."

"If you hated homosexuals so much, why are you one now?" she asked, exasperated.

"I'm walking a mile, or a lifetime, in the shoes of the very people I discriminated against. Not under the same circumstances, thank God, but I get the idea all the same."

She looked at Le-a and Heath. "Do the two of you believe this?"

"I do!" Le-a answered. Heath didn't answer, but instead looked at James thoughtfully.

"Do you remember your name?" Heath asked him.

"Yeah, what *was* your name?" Julie added.

"Well, I only know my first name, Burkhart."

Heath blinked. "That's an unusual name. Do you know when you died?"

"Are you seriously entertaining this?" Julie asked Heath.

"I'm asking because I could do some research to see if his account is true," he answered her.

"I died in 1944."

"Did you remember this on your own?" Heath continued.

"God, no! I have no memory of this," James said.

"How did you find out then?" Julie whispered, thinking about her recent moments of déjà vu.

"I was told during a reading."

"Star did it," Le-a added. "She read us both."

"Star!" Julie cried out. "You told me she was a quack!"

"I didn't want to believe what she had told me. Since I've had time to digest it, I believe the account might be true. It feels right." James got up and turned the dining room light back on.

"She told me," Le-a chattered, "that I was a woman in my past life."

It didn't take a genius to figure that one out, Julie thought.

James placed his hand on Julie's knee. "It's okay if you don't believe. Maybe it's something you're not ready for. Maybe you're just one of those people who don't even need to know."

"Damn right!" she answered. "I can barely deal with this life, let alone worry about another one." Julie sighed, looking at Heath. "I suppose you've been reincarnated, too."

"I suppose I have," he said.

"Did Star give you a past life reading?"

"No, actually. I happened to sit next to a guy who 'had the sight' on one of my business trips."

"And do you know who you were?" she asked after gulping down the remaining absinthe in her glass.

Heath studied her, considering her question. He glanced at James and Le-a. After a long pause, he answered her.

"Why don't we leave that as a discussion for another day?"

CHAPTER FOURTEEN

La Nouvelle-Orléans, Louisiana, 1898

In the distance, a two-story white house stood alone on a stretch of flat, grassy land a few hundred feet from the shore of Lake Pontchartrain. Several people milled about on its wide porch, and many more walked on the grounds that surrounded it.

The nearby lake shimmered a deep purple as the sun sank beneath the western waves. Erik closed his eyes, tuning out everything around him. If he listened hard enough, very faint music wafted on the light breeze. He was certain the inhabitants of the Maison Blanche imagined themselves to be a merry party, but the party he had orchestrated was merrier still.

Agnes and Bea had chatted nonstop before leaving the house and Naomi had run round in a nervous flutter while the Krause sisters tried to get her ready. Although miscegenation was against the law in New Orleans, Erik didn't live his life by the laws of men. He wasn't concerned for Naomi. Most people turned a blind eye to inter-racial marriage and he had found a judge willing to perform the ceremony; a few gold bars remedied the man's objections.

He opened his eyes and looked at Naomi, who stared serenely at the portly man speaking before them. She wore a beaded dress that sparkled in the light as she moved. To the people standing across the clearing, he was sure she shone like a jewel.

Perfection.

He had purposefully arranged this ceremony to be in the line of sight of Marie's brothel. If Marie wanted a war, he would make the first move. Marriage was a good, strategic decision on his part. As a gentleman's wife, Naomi would no longer be prey to the mercies of others. She would have his protection and his name, which would transfer to Christine once it was she by his side.

The man cleared his throat. "Monsieur de la Croix." Naomi looked at him now with expectant eyes. "Monsieur de la Croix, the ring?" Erik reached in his pocket and pulled out a simple silver band. With his best attempt at a smile, he slipped the ring onto her slender finger. "I now pronounce you man and wife."

Naomi closed her eyes and tilted her face upward. Erik flicked his eyes over her full lips, but forced himself to kiss her forehead instead. Her new status as his wife did not mean he would take any liberties.

Bea and Agnes clapped their hands, congratulating Naomi with hugs, rearranging her dress and fussing over her. Erik glanced toward the bordello again. In the middle of the porch, a brightly dressed figure with a yellow tignon stood among the others, arms crossed, and even at this distance, he saw murder in her eyes. He had accomplished everything he had intended to do. His heart soared in triumph.

♀

Erik paced outside Naomi's bedroom door while she changed out of her wedding dress. Even though they had discussed the marriage was a formality only, he could not be sure she understood what that meant. And when she opened the door wearing a silky, form-fitting peignoir set, he knew he had been right to be concerned.

His mouth went dry.

She was his wife, his beautiful, sensual wife. He could give up his dream of Christine and start his life over with her. He could be a husband, live life like other men. He wrenched himself from the tempting thoughts. Naomi saw him as David, a successful business man. She didn't know he wasn't whole. She didn't know he was kept together by wax and paste. She would not make a life with him, but with a brilliant illusion.

And give up Christine? Never! His resolution grew stronger.

"Do you like it?" She leaned against the door. "Bea and Agnes gave it to me as a wedding gift. I thought I'd wear it in case..."

"I am not going to change my mind," he said firmly. "We must talk."

"Talk, talk, talk," she pouted. "All you ever want to do is talk."

He knew that must be how it seemed from her perspective. She had no idea how much was at stake for him. "Naomi, you must know by now, I am not like other men."

She nodded. "I've seen you appear in a room out of thin air."

"What if I told you I could give you a life far better than your imagination?"

She crinkled her forehead. "What do you mean?"

"What if you could have a life like Christine's? What if you could live in an expensive house, have a handsome husband who adored you, and a beautiful child to call you Momma? What if you could live like a lady in the city without a care in the world? What if you could *be* Christine? Would you?"

"How is that possible?"

"Would you want her life if you could have it?" he pressed.

"What about Christine? Would that mean she wouldn't have her life anymore?" He could see her mind whirring. "Besides, Raoul doesn't love me."

"I am offering you the chance to be Christine, in every way. You do not need to worry about her. I know the man you spoke of earlier, Erik. They knew each other before she ever met Raoul. Christine was engaged to Erik once and must know now that leaving him was a mistake."

"What?" Naomi walked to her bed and sat down.

"This cannot come as such a surprise to you. You told me yourself she said she would *never* forget Erik. Don't you see? They love each other and want to be together. You would be doing her a great service," he persisted.

"Even so," she said slowly, processing his words. "I look nothing like her. Raoul would not accept me as his wife."

"He will not know she is gone. You know her habits, her mannerisms, how to run her household. You will step in right where she left off."

"But I *do not* look like her."

"Oh, but you will, identical to her in every way."

"You can do that?"

Erik nodded.

"Will it hurt?"

"No," he said. "Do not ask me to explain how this can be. You must just accept the fact that I can do it."

With a pained expression, she asked, "What about you? You will be all alone?" She shook her head. "I couldn't leave you."

Her concern touched him, and he almost choked on his words. "You have no obligation to me. I will be fine. Knowing that Christine and Erik are reunited and that you are well cared for is all I need. Besides," he cupped her chin, "we will see each other out at dinners or parties, only you must not let on that you know me."

"Not know you! I couldn't do that! You have been the kindest man. How could I pretend not to know you?"

"You will find a way."

She gave him a little smile, reflecting a few moments more. "I will look exactly like her?"

"Yes, in every way; even her voice will be yours."

Naomi placed her hand to her throat. "Is that really possible?"

"It certainly is."

"Christine wants this?"

"More than even she knows. No, that is not correct," he amended. "She knows. Why else would she name her son after another man?" He could see Naomi considering his convincing argument.

Her brows furrowed in thought. "Raoul and Philippe will love me?"

"As much as they adore Christine," he promised. "You will have everything that I could give you and more. You will be a gentlewoman with the respect of your neighbors. You will *never* have to wear a tignon again."

Naomi ran her hand through her hair and squared her chin resolutely. "What do I have to do?"

"You will have to trust me. Can you do that?"

"I trust you with my life."

Startled by her sincere admission, he hesitated, only for a moment. "There is no time to waste. Put your traveling cloak on. We must to go to my house. Everything I need is there."

She obediently secured her cloak, the black wrap covering the length of her entire body like a shroud. By the cover of night, they stepped outside, and Erik signaled a coach. It pulled over and he assisted Naomi inside.

"Again, I ask you, do you trust me?" He needed to hear her say it once more.

"I do."

"When we get to my home, I will hand you a sachet. I want you to put it to your nose and breathe in deeply. It will put you to sleep. From there, I will do the rest. When you wake, you will be Christine."

With a muffled cry, she flung her arms around his neck. "I'm going to miss you, David."

He allowed her to hang onto him for a few minutes, surprised by her outburst. He could still stop this, turn the carriage around and have her as his wife. But stubborn will overcame his doubt and he gently pried her off. "I will miss you, too."

The carriage pulled up in front of his St. Charles house. Once they stepped on the front porch, Erik held out the Mazenderan-scented sachet, the sultana's favorite means for disabling her play-things. Naomi gingerly took it from him. Looking directly into his eyes, she raised her hands to her nose and inhaled. The effect was instant. She slumped into his arms, unconscious. The next time he met those eyes again, another woman would be staring back at him.

♀

He carried Naomi over the threshold of the front door, peering down at her tranquil face convinced that Raoul would be the man to soothe away all her past hurts and provide her with many years of happiness. He kept her in his arms as he tripped the first hidden latch that opened one of the many entryways into the lavish secret chamber he had made for Christine.

He laid Naomi down on the bed and removed her cloak and slippers, casting them aside. He lit a fire in the grate and threw a handful of sweet grass into the flames. He worked quickly, feeling as though an unseen force urged him on.

His life with the Gypsies, the Persians, and the Tonken pirates had yielded a wealth of knowledge in the mystical arts. He had a soul-knowledge of how the exchange should work and he was certain that his methodology was correct. Just as he knew if he wanted to beckon Christine to him, he had to use one of the oldest languages known to man.

He worked by the soft firelight, hands trembling with nervous excitement as he mixed the oil he had created with Marie's potion and poured it onto his gloved hands. He applied the fragrant oil to Naomi's feet, then moved to her small, delicate hands. He pulled back the top of her peignoir to smooth the oil on the expanse of bare skin just above her breasts.

Hands in mid-air, he hesitated before completing the last step. How was Christine going to react when she woke up here? What would she say? She would need time and his patience; he knew that. She would miss her son. He would assure her that as Naomi, she could visit Philippe without question once, of course, she was compliant with her new situation.

He placed his hand on the center of her forehead and rubbed the oil in. His voice, like silent thunder, heavy with longing and desire, filled the room as he commanded Christine to come to him.

"Entzun Nire Ahosta!"

CHAPTER FIFTEEN

New Orleans, Louisiana, 2009

Julie poured the last of the absinthe into her cup and drank it. Her muscles relaxed as the familiar rush crept through her. She stared into the empty glass before speaking.

"As crazy as it sounds," she said, "I do believe that *you* believe in reincarnation. For myself, I don't know. Maybe I'm scared to face the 'possible' truth about myself. What if I was told something horrible like James? What if I was an awful person? I don't think I'd want to know that."

"What you've got to see," James said, "is that it's not you, the you that you are today. I know I'm not that person. Hell, I don't remember one bit of it. But if I was that person, I can proudly look at myself today and know that even though I'm not perfect, I've certainly improved. What more can I ask for? We can't all be the good guy, ya know."

"Maybe one day, I don't know…maybe I'll ask. Besides, I haven't seen Star around anyway." Julie was glad Star had been missing in action. She didn't want her overzealous neighbors dragging her outside for a reading.

"Juliana, asking for a past life reading is a very personal decision and," Heath looked at the others, "one that should be done in private as well."

Julie smiled gratefully at him.

"James followed Star once," Le-a commented. "Tell them, Pookie."

"It's true. Drunk off my ass, I decided to see where she lives. I followed her as she entered the St. Louis No. 1 cemetery. Usually the gates are locked, but she pushed them open and walked through the long alleys of tombs, stopping in front of a crypt. I crouched behind another crypt so she wouldn't see me. A sound like a pop echoed off the headstones, so I stayed down for a minute. When I looked for her again, she was gone. I thought I had imagined the whole thing, but on the ground I saw the yellow sash that she had worn in her hair. When I picked it up, I noticed Star had been standing at Marie Laveau's tomb."

"Marie Laveau you say?" Heath asked.

"Star does claim to be a Voodoo priestess," Le-a added.

"I know I was three sheets to the wind, but I swear," James promised, placing a hand over his heart, "I never saw her leave. She was there one minute and gone the next. It's possible she went there to leave a token or mark an X as many people do, but…"

"I have a very busy day tomorrow," Heath interrupted as he glanced at his watch. "So I'm afraid I have to cut this night short. Dinner was perfection," he praised Le-a. "Thanks for inviting me. I had a great time." Turning to Julie, he gestured toward the door. "Juliana, may I see you home?"

Le-a scrunched her nose. "But she lives next door." James elbowed Le-a, tossing her a meaningful look to Julie's embarrassment.

"Uh, yeah," Le-a added, "you guys go ahead. James and I have everything under control here."

"Are you sure you don't need any help cleaning up?" Julie asked.

"Nah, it's all good." James smiled.

"Okay, if you're sure," Julie pressed.

"God," he commented to Le-a loud enough for them to hear. "Some people just don't know when to leave." He winked at Julie before closing the door behind them.

Julie and Heath walked the twenty steps to her door. In those few seconds, she wondered whether there would be a repeat of the kiss from the night before. Only she hoped this time it would be for a much longer time and then after, maybe something more…much more.

Julie went to the small garden box attached under her front window, moved the decorative stone lying in the dirt behind the flaming sword bromeliad, and removed her key from under it. She waved it at Heath with a smile. "Told you I'd find another spot for it."

"Good." He nodded in approval.

She opened the door and lingered for a moment. "Would you like to come in?"

Please say yes. Please say yes, she wished.

"I can't," Heath answered with regret. "Another time. Tomorrow, perhaps?"

Julie masked her disappointment with an animated smile. "Sure."

"I have a morning meeting in Baton Rouge. I'll call you when I get back. Maybe we'll rent a movie or something."

Or something, Julie smiled. "That would be nice."

"How about a thriller since tomorrow is Halloween?"

"Okay," she said with renewed hope, imagining herself clinging to him during a scary scene.

"Here." Heath pulled a small silk bag from his pocket and handed it to her. "It's the bracelet. I cleaned and polished it. I also tightened the clasp. I took several pictures I can use to complete the authentication."

"Thanks." She took the bag, hovering in her doorway. Would he at least kiss her?

"No problem." He smiled. "I hope to have confirmation very soon."

"There's no rush...whenever." Julie tried sounding unconcerned.

"Okay...so...I guess I'll see you tomorrow," he said, then walked away.

"I guess so," Julie said. *No kiss*. She stood in the doorway, watching him. He didn't turn around. Not once. And yet, she still stood there, feeling like a fool, until she couldn't see him any longer.

She sighed and shut the door. What was she doing? This whole Heath situation confused her. It felt right being with him–as if she'd known him for ages. And the kiss. She hadn't told James this part, but her toes had actually curled. She had read about this happening in romance novels and had found it hard to believe, yet when Heath's lips found hers...well...a woman could not forget this.

She went to her room and changed into a comfortable set of pajamas. Sitting on her bed, she opened the black bag and withdrew the bracelet that had started this whole mess. The silver gleamed brightly under the fluorescent ceiling-fan light.

As she looked closely, she could see the brown strands woven inside the charm were indeed hair. Who did the pieces of hair belong to? She put the bracelet on her left wrist and snapped the delicate clasp tight. She could feel a light sheen of oil on her fingertips and on parts of her wrist where the bracelet rested against her skin. Heath must have been a bit liberal when cleaning it.

Julie stretched out on her bed. In five minutes, she would make herself get up, scrub off her make-up, and wash her oily hand and wrist. She closed her eyes, listening to the night sounds of the Quarter...faded laughter, far-off horn-honking, and the fleeting sound of music. She pictured Heath walking home into the heart of the Quarter. She wished he had stayed. Again, Julie sighed, and listened.

Quiet.

Eerily quiet.

Julie sat up when she heard the clip-clop of horse's hooves on the street outside and muffled talking. She ran down the hall to the narrow front window, where daylight streamed through. *This is not right*, she thought, pulling back the curtain.

Several horse-drawn carriages—some open, others closed—were passing by. Men with hats and canes and turbaned women dressed in old-fashioned clothing scuttled across the dirt street outside the window. Julie's left hand and wrist tingled. She must be dreaming. She spun around to gain her bearings.

She cried out.

Her house was different. The chair-rail and the taupe walls were gone, replaced with floor-to-ceiling flowered wallpaper. The sofa was missing and a red-velvet Victorian loveseat and several carved armchairs were in the room instead.

Where before she could see straight into her kitchen, there was now a wall separating the rooms. As she tried to comprehend what was happening, the bracelet heated, becoming uncomfortably warm against her skin. She fumbled with the clasp and let the bracelet fall to the floor. She turned back to look out the window. It was night once again. The street was empty and all she heard was the faint pervading sound of music coming from the Cat's Meow.

She turned to face her living room, breathing a sigh of relief. As her eyes alighted on each familiar item, she felt more grounded and her panic subsided. Julie looked at her wrist. It still tingled. And where the bracelet had last touched her skin, a faint pinkish mark was visible.

Julie cautiously stepped around the innocent-looking heirloom lying on the floor, got a dish towel from the kitchen and used it to pick up the bracelet, being very careful not to let it touch her skin again. She kept her eyes averted from the offending object and walked back to her room where she dumped it back into the silk bag, pulled the drawstrings, and tossed the bag onto the top shelf in her closet. To her relief, it landed in the very back. Out of sight, out of mind.

Not likely.

She sat on the edge of her bed with her back to the closet door. She could sense the bracelet's presence behind her, and her mind's eye could see the black bag on the shelf. She focused her eyes straight ahead at the half-demolished wall. She would divert her mind from what had just happened with the bracelet by tearing down what remained of the wall.

♀

It was just after 2:00 am. She had banged, chiseled, and knocked away plaster until all that remained were five two-by-fours. She certainly didn't plan to stay awake and figure out how to remove the wood beams tonight. Fatigue had won the battle, and she finally let the hammer slip out of her hand to the floor.

The sound of the hammer smacking the newly exposed plank flooring roused Julie from her exhaustion. Out of the corner of her eye, she thought she saw the floor jostle when the hammer hit.

Instantly, she heard Heath's voice inside her head. *You know, many people have found hidden artifacts when they do renovations. In an old house like this one, you never know what you might find. They buried things in the walls, under the floorboards…*

She knelt down and grabbed a flat-head screwdriver from her open tool chest. With trembling hands, she wedged it between the strips of wood flooring that were once hidden under the wall. A thrill of anticipation rushed through her, as if she were watching ocean waves toss a bottle closer and closer to shore, wondering if it contained a message inside.

Julie lifted up the side of the small plank until she could grip it with her hand. She tossed the screwdriver, removed the wood, and peered into the hole. Inside the opening, she could see a small chest resting in a makeshift box anchored underneath the floor. With her heart racing, she reached in. The chest was hand-carved wood that looked old and rustic. It was about as long as a dollar bill and about half as wide. There was no lock.

She sat back for a minute to savor the moment. Imagining what was inside the box was almost as exciting as actually finding out. Could it be a stash of money, more heirlooms, or personal items of someone long dead?

The old lid protested with a cracking sound as Julie flipped it open. Inside, lay a scroll of yellow paper. She took it out and unrolled it, revealing a small walnut-colored vial. She held the vial up to the light and shook it. There was powder inside.

She put the vial down and spread out the paper. On the inside were a few sentences scribbled with childish handwriting in red ink. She had taken French in high school, but did not recognize anything about this language. Julie set the paper aside and it curled up as though it once again wrapped around the vial. One item remained in the small chest, a worn, leather-bound book only a little bigger than her hand.

Turning the pages of the book, she saw that it was filled with notations in the same red-scribbled handwriting. A few pages had diagrams of the vial with measurements of some sort. It was all written in the same indecipherable language. Disappointed, she felt along the inside of the empty chest to see whether it might have a false bottom.

Nope.

She turned it around, carefully inspecting it. She didn't recognize the wood, but the inside smelled like cedar. When she turned it upside down, she was surprised to see an inscription on the bottom of the chest, *Sinsetsi. 1898.*

Was it a family or company name? Puzzled, Julie put the box back down and looked at the paper again. Heath spoke several languages. Maybe he could identify it?

Julie replaced the slat of wood over the hole, put the vial back in the chest, and placed the chest on her dresser. She went into her living room and sat on the sofa close to her phone with the paper and book in hand. It would be hard waiting until morning. Once the clock turned to 8:00 am, she would dial Heath's number in the hope that he could translate it.

☥

Julie blinked opened heavy eyelids only to be blinded by the glare of light coming through the window. She moved, blocking the brightness when she remembered her plan.

"Jesus, Mary, and Joseph!" she yelled. Her clock blinked 10:00 am. She had fallen asleep. Her hands fumbled while dialing Heath's number. "Come on. Come on," she mumbled urgently as the phone rang. "Pick up."

By the eighth ring, she heard Heath's familiar voice. "You have reached Montgomery H. Smith's Antiques shop. No one is available to answer the phone. Please leave your name, number, date, and time you called along with a brief message, and I will get back to you as soon as possible."

Beep.

"Heath, if you're there, pick up the phone." Julie rushed the words and waited a second to see whether he would answer. "It's Julie. Look, I couldn't sleep last night...Oh, hell! I don't have time to explain. I found some papers hidden under the floor written in another language and I'm hoping you can tell me what it says. Call me as soon as you get this message." She hardly got the last word out when she heard the second beep indicating the phone had stopped recording.

"Damn!" Julie muttered as she remembered Heath had a meeting today. While she brushed her teeth, she wondered who else could decipher the writing. She held a possible treasure-trove of information in her hands and she wanted answers.

She contemplated going to the library to compare the scribble to every available foreign language book so at the very least, she could identify it when suddenly a possible solution popped into her mind. Julie barreled out of her house right to James' front door and pounded.

"Hang on! Hang on!" James hollered. She could hear his casual footsteps as he took his sweet time. He opened the door a crack, saw it was Julie, and flung it open wide. "Hey Dawlin'! Come to give me the scoop?" he asked.

James wore a too-small pink bathrobe whose belt barely tied around his spare tire. The rest of the material miraculously made it to his mid-thighs, preventing her from seeing anything other than his bird legs. He wore a matching pink scarf tied around his head to keep his hair out of his face which was covered in cold cream, and he held two cucumber slices in his hand.

"What *are* you doing?" she asked, distracted by his appearance.

"This?" he gestured from head-to-toe. "Le-a is exfoliating my face." He tossed his head. "What? You don't like it?"

"Oh, no," Julie mocked. "You make a beautiful Queen."

James struck a few exaggerated Madonna poses.

"Please, please don't move," Julie begged, her lips turning up at the corners. "I've no interest in accidentally seeing your goodies. It could scar me for life."

James began to do slow pelvic gyrations. "You mean you don't want me to do this?"

Julie laughed.

He started to shake his hips. "Or this?"

Julie threw her hands up in defeat, choking back another laugh. "Stop! I beg you." He kept it up. Julie stomped her foot. "I'm serious. Really. I've got something to tell you."

"It's all good." James stopped. "I can tell when my dancing isn't appreciated. What's up?" Julie told him about last night's discovery, leaving out the part of her paranormal experience with the bracelet.

"So, you see, I thought since you were in the military, maybe you know someone who could read it. You know, someone who did translation work."

James gave his chin a thoughtful rub then scrunched his face when he noticed the smudge of cream on his hand. "I might know someone who knows someone. Let me make a few calls and see what I can do."

"Thank you, thank you, thank you!" Julie bounced with excitement.

James held up a hand. "Don't thank me yet. I'm not promising anything. In the meantime, go make copies in case the originals are worth something. And," he looked at her miss-matched pajamas, "go change your clothes. I'm not going anywhere with you dressed like that. I have standards you know." James flashed a smile and tossed his head, causing a clump of cold cream to fall to the floor.

Julie looked at the white mess.

"Oh, yeah," she countered. "I can see that."

CHAPTER SIXTEEN

New Orleans, Louisiana, 2009

"Where are we going again?" Julie asked, breathless. She practically skipped to keep up with James' long strides.

"Right there." James pointed across the street to a Spanish-style building with reddish stucco and Paris green hurricane shutters. It was the Déjà Vu Restaurant and Bar.

You've got to be kidding me. How ironic, she thought as they entered.

She followed James to a booth where a scruffy, unshaven man sat eating an oyster po-boy. As they approached, James squared his shoulders, and his usual hip swagger was no longer noticeable.

"What's your vector, Victor?" James said in a much deeper voice.

A slow smile pulled at the man's lips. "James, what's up? How's life treating you?" They shook hands.

"Can't complain," James answered.

"Sit down." The man motioned to James and Julie. "What's your poison? I'm buying."

"I'll have one of those." James motioned to the mug of beer on the table.

Julie scooted in after him. "Nothing for me, thanks."

"I'm Vic." The man nodded at Julie, wiping his mouth with his napkin.

"This is my friend, Julie. The one I was telling you about," James told him.

Vic put his hand out. "Let's have a look see, shall we?" Julie almost reached out to shake his hand, but realized he meant the papers. She pulled the copies out of her purse, handing them to him. She also pulled out the vial.

"I found this with the papers."

Vic took the vial, looked at it, and stated the obvious. "It has powder in it." He put it down and pushed it back toward her. Squinting his eyes, he looked at the papers.

"I know the handwriting is hard to decipher. Do you think you can read it?" Julie asked.

Vic pulled out a pair of drugstore bifocals and examined the writing closely. "If I didn't know any better, I'd say this was written in Basque."

"Basque?" Julie looked at James, who shrugged his shoulders. "What is that? I've never heard of it before."

"It's a very old language. Not many people speak or write it." Vic flipped through the pages.

"Can you translate it?" Julie crossed her fingers under the table.

"Nah." Vic stared hard at the writing. "I was never much good at it. I only know a few words and it's been a long time, but I think I know a guy who can."

"Let's go see him then." Julie grabbed her purse, sliding out of the booth.

"No way," Vic motioned for her to sit down. "He's a paranoid son-of-a-bitch. But I'll take these to him when I leave. He might read them, he might not."

"That's all I can ask for," Julie said. She had copied the word *Sinsetsi* on a slip of paper that she also handed to Vic. "I don't know if this means anything, but the box I found had this inscribed on the back. I'm thinking it's a family name or a company."

Vic slowly raised his eyes from the paper. "No, it's not a name. This word I know."

"What does it say?" Julie and James said in unison.

"It says, believe," he answered.

"Believe," Julie repeated, baffled.

"I'll call you if my friend can tell you anything more. Give me till the end of the week."

Julie nodded.

"Hey," James touched her hand, "mind going home without me? I want to stay and catch up with Vic for a bit." He used his deep voice again.

"No problem." Julie smiled. Before leaving the bar, she turned back and saw Vic and James knock their mugs together. It looked as if those two were going to take a long walk down memory lane.

Julie dawdled on the short walk home, admiring the early Halloween costumers that were already reveling. As she meandered, she decided she would tell Heath everything tonight. Not only the discovery under her floor, but the strange occurrence with the bracelet. If anyone could help her make sense of everything, she believed he could. He seemed open-minded to metaphysical ideas.

"Read your fortune," a familiar voice called out. Julie raised her eyes. Star smiled at her from across the street. She leaned against a street pole. Her green eyes appraised Julie while a light wind blew a thin strand of white-blonde hair across her face.

The sun loomed red in the west, large and hanging low, but hadn't set yet. It was only just past four. "What are you doing out so early?" Julie called back to Star.

"Oh, I come out early on occasion. Would you like me to read your fortune?"

Julie paused, considering. For the past couple of days, experiencing déjà vu, she had felt as if she sat on the cusp of something. There was nothing to lose by listening to what Star had to say. Yes, she wanted to know.

Julie nodded before she lost her nerve. Her stomach twisted in knots as she crossed to the other side of the street. "How much does it cost?"

Star took Julie's right hand into her own and turned it palm up. "The first one is on the house," she answered. Star focused on Julie's hand. "That's interesting. You have a mark here." She pointed to the middle of Julie's palm. "It is very rare to see this line," she said, lightly touching a small crease about the length of a dime. "It runs parallel to your life-line here."

"What does it mean?" Julie asked.

"Let me see your other hand." Star glanced back and forth between the two without saying a word. After a minute, she lowered Julie's hands. "Have you recently found something? Something that's been hidden for a long time?"

Amazed, Julie exclaimed, "Yes, I found some old papers and a little book!"

Star shook her head. "No, something else."

Julie rummaged through her purse and pulled out the vial for Star to see.

"May I?" Star asked.

At Julie's nod, she took the vial, opened it, and smelled the contents. She replaced the lid and handed it back to Julie, who placed it back in her purse.

"You have a very unique opportunity given to only a few. The small line I showed you, the rare one, is another life. Another life, before you were born. A person's dominant hand shows me this lifetime; the nondominant, shows traces of their other lives." She grabbed Julie's hands and raised them for her to see. "Most people have the same handprints with some slight variations. You have two entirely different prints. One from this life." Star tapped Julie's right hand. "And one from this one." She tapped her left hand. "I have seen this before where one past life has a great influence on a current one, but the small mark by your life-line tells me that you have been given a chance to do something that most of us cannot."

"Chance? What kind of chance?" Cold sweat formed between Julie's shoulder blades.

"You have the opportunity to see who you were," Star answered.

"You mean like watching a movie or in a dream?"

"The gift means something different for each person. I cannot say how you will experience it. What I can tell you is your window is closing soon. You must act by tonight or you will forfeit your chance without a second invitation."

"Act by tonight? How? What do I have to do?"

"Light two candles, purple and silver, and burn a stick of sweet grass incense. Marie Laveau's Voodoo shop should have what you need, and the candles will have already been consecrated. You must then reconstitute the contents of the vial with oil, either almond or olive, and rub it on your feet, your hands, the center of your chest, and your third eye." Star lightly touched the center of Julie's forehead.

Julie listened with growing unease. "And if I perform this...this ritual, then what?"

"Then you will see whatever you were meant to."

♀

Julie held the door open with her foot so she could get into her house while juggling bags from Marie Laveau's shop and the corner Rouse's grocery. She set the bags down, locking the door behind her. "This is crazy," she muttered as she emptied the bags, lining the items up on her kitchen counter.

As she did, a low noise sounded in the background. It was her cell phone vibrating, alerting her to two missed calls. She hadn't realized she had left it at home. She dialed her voicemail. The automated voice spoke, "You have two messages: First message, October thirty-first, three pm."

"Juliana, this is Heath. I just checked my messages. Didn't I tell you that you might find something? It's very possible I'll be able to translate it for you. Hang on until I get there. I'm hoping to see you around five." His voice was cut off.

"Next message," said the automated voice. "October thirty-first, five pm."

"Juliana, it's Heath, again. I'm caught in evening traffic—Hey! I have the right of way here!—Sorry about that. Anyway, looks like I might not make it to your house until around six or so. Hope that's okay. See you soon."

"End of messages. You have no saved messages, you..." Julie snapped her phone shut. The small LCD screen on the outside of her phone flashed 5:15 pm. The day had flown by. She threw her clothes off and jumped in the shower.

While getting ready, she decided to prepare "the ritual" before Heath got there so she wouldn't feel like a fool setting up some crazy Voodoo production. She poured the olive oil into the vial and shook it well. She put the candles on top of her stove and lit them. She brought a plate into the bathroom and lit the stick of sweet grass incense. Finding the scent a little strong, she opened the window a crack.

Julie went back to the kitchen counter and took some oil from the vial and rubbed it on the tops of her feet. She didn't want to make oil footprints on the floor. She glanced at the clock. 5:55 pm. Heath would arrive at any moment.

She rubbed the oil lightly on the center of her chest and then thoroughly on her hands. She would save her forehead for later, when Heath was there *and* if she decided to do the ritual all the way. She still didn't feel totally committed to this experiment. She jumped when her phone rang. She picked up the phone, scrambling not to drop it out of her oily hands.

"Hello."

"Julie?"

"Yes?" She didn't recognize the man's voice.

"This is Vic."

"Wow, Vic, I didn't expect you to call so soon."

"Yeah, well, miracles do happen," he replied dryly. "I brought your stuff to my friend. He only translated a few sentences for you. He said it sounded like Hoodoo Voodoo crap and refused to do anymore than that. I told you he was a paranoid son-of-a-bitch."

"I understand. Whatever you have is great. Besides, I have a friend who might be able to read the rest." Julie cleared her throat. "What was he able to tell you?"

"He only translated three sentences, but here goes. '*Neu naiz denboratik harantz zungana heldu daitekeena.*' That one says, '*I am the one who can reach you beyond time.*' '*Entzun nire ahotsa.*' is '*Hear my voice.*'"

Julie heard a knock at the door. It must be Heath. "Just a minute!" she hollered.

"Don't be forever!" James hollered back.

Julie rolled her eyes. "Go on, Vic. I'm sorry for the interruption."

"Okay, the last bit, '*Zure arimari nigana etor dadin agintzen diot, ene aingeru ederra.*' It says, 'I command your soul to come to me, my beautiful angel.'"

"Wow," Julie rubbed her forehead thoughtfully. "That's sort of beautiful. I wonder if it's poetry or..." her words trailed off. The heavy scent of the sweet grass swirled around her. Fear gripped her as she realized that she had just unconsciously rubbed the oil from her hands onto her forehead and completed the ritual. She lost her grip on the phone and it fell with a loud thud, sending the battery skidding across the floor. She could hear banging on the door.

"Dawlin', are you okay?" James yelled in concern. She tried to call out to him for help, but her body refused to obey her mind's orders. The last thing she saw was the floor rushing up to meet her as she was enveloped by darkness.

It was true what they say; hearing is the last to go. Acutely aware of every sound, she could not move at all. She heard James frantically bang on the door when she didn't answer him. She heard Heath approaching and ask James what was wrong. She heard Heath move the rock that hid her key. She heard the dirt as it was displaced. The key in the lock grated her senses.

The sound of the men thundering into the house hurt her ears. Heath gasped when he bent over her. She longed to tell him she was glad he was there, that he made her feel safe. She felt Heath's hand on her wrist. Her pulse beat strongly against his fingers.

What is this?" Heath said. He lifted her hand and smelled it. "Juliana, what have you done?" His voice sounded choked. "Call 911!" he ordered. "Now!"

James fumbled noisily with her phone, trying to put it back together. Their voices faded into the background. Julie felt herself being drawn deeply into her own inner silence.

Is this what it's like to die?

CHAPTER SEVENTEEN

A crackling noise surrounded her. It came from everywhere and nowhere, penetrating deep into the bodiless darkness that had overcome her. She listened to the sharp rustling, aware but without fear. *What is that?*

As the sound continued to echo around her, clarity came to her thoughts. *I know what that is. Simon left the alarm on a static radio station again.* She tried to wake up so she could turn off the annoying alarm. The more she struggled to wake, the more aware she became. The crackling became more focused, coming from the front and left of her.

Wait, she thought. *That's wrong. Simon and I are divorced. It must be my own alarm.* Her frustration subsiding, she fought to wake herself further. As she did, the noise persisted with an occasional popping.

No. That's not my alarm. I remember. I was getting ready to meet Heath. She could now sense her body breathing, but felt wholly unconnected to it. She lay on something soft and comfortable instead of the hard floorboards where she had fallen. She tried, but was unable to send messages to her body to make it move. While rising to a higher state of wakefulness, she realized what the sound really was. Even though she couldn't feel the heat, the noise was a roaring fire in a grate.

Did Heath light a fire?

Then with rising dread, she remembered the ritual, the phone call, the darkness, and Heath worried by her side. He wasn't by her side now. The only sound she heard was the wood-burning fire.

Though her mind panicked, her body continued its slow, even breathing undisturbed by her emotions. *This is not a hospital. Where am I?* The more anxious Julie became, the more she felt the heaviness of her body. Her muscles were like lead and still refused to obey her commands when she tried to stir.

She heard a door slide open and footsteps. She inwardly held her breath although her body kept on breathing steadily. *This is crazy*! She willed herself even harder to wake up. *Fight it*! *Fight*!

She silenced her inner voice when footsteps strode toward her. A presence bent over her and smoothed the hair off her forehead.

"Wake up," a deep voice coaxed.

Heath? I'm trying!

"Christine, wake up," commanded the unfamiliar voice.

Not Heath.

Her heart skipped a beat. Adrenaline surged in her body. She desperately wanted to tell the stranger he was mistaken. She managed to raise the fingers of her left hand.

"Good," the man said with approval.

He saw her move! She focused on her heavy-laden eyelids. *Open. Open.* They moved slowly. Her vision was out of focus, but she could tell that near her stood the blurry figure of a man. She was unable to keep her eyes open long and they closed of their own accord.

"The effects of the potion will take some time to wear off. You will be completely fine when it does."

How did he know about that? Where was Heath? Where was James?

"Christine, I have missed you." The man's voice sounded pained.

Julie opened her mouth to speak. Nothing came out. Her tongue felt thick and clumsy. She kept trying. She was determined to set the record straight.

"Not Christine." Her voice was a dry, rasping whisper.

The man leaned closer to her, and his breath warmed her ear. "What did you say?"

"Not Christine. Julie. Juliana François."

The man inhaled sharply. "Repeat that."

With relief, she repeated, "Juliana François."

The air stirred as he pulled away from her. His retreating footsteps crossed the room, and he left with a slam of wood against wood. She couldn't fight the urge to succumb to sleep any longer. Letting go was easier to do now, knowing that the stranger had understood her.

♀

The secret pocket door slammed into place by the force of Erik's rage. *Impossible!* What trickery was this? The woman wouldn't have the ability to lie to him in her altered state, so he knew she spoke the truth. He paced the hall outside the chamber in fury. He wanted to charge into the room and shake the answers out of her, answers that wouldn't come because she was in no condition to respond to an interrogation.

A sudden rush of understanding gripped him like a vise. Now, not only did he *not* have Christine, but he had lost Naomi also. What had he done? What nightmare did he send her to? He imagined Naomi's confusion as she woke up in an unfamiliar house surrounded by strangers. Guilt pulled at his gut; everything he had promised her was a lie.

"Marie," he snarled, pounding his fist against the wall. This was *her* doing. The only variable that had been beyond his control was his reliance on her portion of the potion. He was going to kill her.

He pictured pulling the noose tightly round her proud neck and the satisfaction of hearing her gasp for breath. He wanted to look into her eyes as she died. Would she find herself so superior then? Taking a deep breath, he quelled his anger. He wouldn't kill her yet, he reasoned with himself, at least, not until she fixed this mistake.

With steely control, he pressed the latch to open the hidden chamber and walked in again to look at his wife. Naomi's body was sound asleep along with the woman inside it, Juliana. He stared down at her and for once in his life, a quick answer failed to come to him.

This was a complication he had never once considered. He knew that one way or another, this mistake would be remedied. Whoever this Juliana was, she would sleep several more hours. He would deal with Marie and return without Juliana even knowing he had gone. He would make this right.

♀

Erik stood back within the wooded area on the north side of Congo Square. He had just spent an hour gazing through Christine's windows, watching her with her son and her husband. He had to be sure she *was* Christine and *not* Naomi. And she was, in every way, confirming for him that Naomi must be wherever the stranger had come from.

Oblivious to the cold air, his only focus was to confront Marie. He scanned the crowd of worshipers while they swayed and danced to pounding drums under the moonlight. A large pyre in the center of the square burned brilliantly as revelers threw animal innards into a cauldron on a smaller fire nearby. The smell of wood smoke and incense permeated the air.

A pause in the beating drums happened simultaneously with the appearance of a short, squat, dark-skinned man. The revelers ceased their frenzied dance, giving the newcomer their attention. Erik kept his eyes on him as well, for the moment.

The man shouted something unintelligible to Erik's normally acute hearing to which the crowd replied as one. "Sanctified by blood!"

Erik's eyebrows involuntarily rose as a tall figure shrouded in white shuffled forward before the now silent, motionless crowd. The short man held up a chicken by its legs for all to see. It writhed in his hands desperate to free itself. "The sacrifice is made to sanctify us all!" In his other hand, he raised a sword. The sharp steel blade gleamed in the firelight, and spectators in the crowd bowed down as he passed it before them to see.

"Let it be done!" He decapitated the chicken in one fell swoop with blood spraying the stranger's white shroud. The crowd roared with approval and drumbeats began again along with the sensual gyrations from the ecstatic participants.

The shrouded individual was assisted to the ground where, lying still, the remaining blood from the lifeless bird was shaken upon the linen along with oil from a clay pot. The chicken's head was tossed into the large fire then the squat man dropped the body, feathers and all, into the cauldron and joined the enraptured dancers.

Erik scanned the crowd once again. Faces of all colors shone in the blazing light although, the majority were the darker-skinned citizens of New Orleans. The crowd's shouts and chants escalated again amid the scent of fresh blood and sweat mingling in the air. As he moved to the outer edge of the crowd, he saw what sparked their enthusiasm.

Marie, barely covered by a gleaming white dress, slowly, sensually moved around from the other side of the bonfire, her curves embraced by a large, dark snake that undulated in unison with her. A few members of the congregation fell prostrate before her. Marie continued the exotic dance while the snake sinuously writhed around her body.

The rapturous crowd gyrated in tandem with the rhythmic drumbeat, but once Erik locked his eyes on Marie, everyone and everything in his periphery became insignificant. He took one slow, deliberate step after another toward her, the worshipers moving out of his way, parting like the Red Sea.

He didn't bother to look at their faces. He wasn't David de la Croix tonight. He had taken the risk of revealing his own face, so that when Christine had woken, she would have seen it was him. Silence and stillness spread among them as he passed. The dancers stopped dancing and the chanting faded into muted tones from the few who had not seen him yet.

As he reached the inner edge of the circle, the drumming stopped, and the only sounds remaining were whispered murmurs and the crackling of the blazing bonfire. Marie stopped dancing and opened her eyes. Erik stood before her, making no attempt to conceal his contempt, which he was knew made his face look more gruesome.

The slightest flicker of surprise crossed her face, followed by the usual insincere smile.

With expertise, the Voodoo queen unraveled the reluctant snake that tried its best to stay anchored to her body and handed it over to a waiting follower. "See to it Zombie is put in his cage," she commanded. The crowd watched in utter silence as the man hurried away.

"Behold!" Marie called out while opening her arms to the crowd. "Even the son of the Devil seeks my counsel." A rise of whispers shot through the spectators. Encouraged by their reactions, she grabbed Erik's hand and raised it high into the air with her own. "I alone, Queen of Voodoo, can bring solace to the Prince of Darkness." Erik snatched his hand back with a scorching look, while Marie kept hers up to the level of her eyes.

Erik narrowed his eyes and hissed loud enough only for her ears. "My noose would find its mark around your neck, witch, if that was what I desired."

Unfazed, Marie continued to address her captivated audience. "Denizens, you do yourself honor to continue celebrating St. Remigius' Feast Day." She motioned and a brightly dressed woman came forward from the edge of the crowd. "Priestess Kyah will preside over the service until I return to sanctify our offerings."

With a thin finger, she pointed to the men by the drums. "Play."

A soft beat emanated from the drums, steadily growing louder as Marie walked away from the crowd with Erik close behind her. She glided with little effort into the forested area while Erik glared at the back of her head. Farther in, hidden from any prying eyes, he grabbed her arm and pulled her around.

She looked sideways at her arm then back up to Erik's face. "You dare touch me?"

He let go. "You should be grateful my hand is all I placed on you."

"I don't fear you," she sneered. "You have sought *me* out, not I you."

He let his face harden. "Only to make you fix your sabotage."

Marie's eyes smoldered, but curiosity also glimmered in their depths. "What sabotage?"

"Do not act the innocent one, witch." He ground the words out through clenched teeth. "The potion you gave me was altered."

Her face lit up with bitter triumph. "*Not* by my hand."

"Liar!" Erik pushed her against a tree. "Nothing happened as it should! My angel remains at her home, *not* with me. My wife is gone and another resides within her. This is your doing." His eyes raked her face. "And you *will* fix it." Her laughter caught him off guard. He let go of her, incredulous, while her mirth rang out into the stillness.

"Foolish, foolish man," she managed to utter, shaking her head. Her eyes sparkled in the sliver of moonlight that cut through the trees. "Oh, man that you are. Can't you see? Don't you know? You cannot pull a soul into a body where it does not belong." The pleasure faded from her face. "*I* cannot fix this. Only *you* can." She walked past him, casting a look over her shoulder. "And you must figure out how to do so on your own. You'll not get any help from me. I don't provide aid to my enemies." She disappeared among the trees.

He let her go.

He didn't trust a word she said, but he might need her later. He half-heartedly slipped in and out of the shadows until he made it home. He stared at the outline of the magnificent house that he was supposed to share with Christine. Without her, it was no more resplendent to him than a thatched hut. Tonight was a monumental failure, and he didn't like to fail. He grew weary of the mockery that was destined to be his life.

Once he had returned to the secret chamber, he turned one of the mahogany chairs facing Naomi's body and sat down heavily. *Only I can fix this. Can't put a soul in a body it doesn't belong to.* He rested his weary head in his hands and realized how old he felt and how alone he was. He should have taken a chance on a life with Naomi rather than be alone.

Only I can fix this. He sat upright. *Not fix it. Reverse it.* Yes. He rubbed his chin. He would send the stranger back as soon as he figured out how to do so. It seemed much clearer to him how to call a soul than to send one on its way. He owed it to Naomi to get her back. He would remove any unpleasant memories and then spoil her as his life-long companion. Once he achieved that, he would spend his time determining whose body Christine belonged to and try again. If there was anything to be learned from this, it was that it could be done.

♀

Julie woke up from strange dreams of hot summers, bare feet on dirt roads, and playing with a coonhound. She could smell the pine-scented air, feel the warm breeze, and taste cool water pumped from behind an old wooden house. She yawned and turned onto her side, reveling in being able to move her body on command and breathe at will.

She slowly opened her eyes. Blue walls. She blinked. French doors with floor-to-ceiling curtains on either side. She turned over and sat up. *Blink*. Large mahogany bed. *Blink*. Burning embers in an ornate, white fireplace. *Blink*. Man in chair facing bed.

Julie sucked in her breath. Her heart began beating erratically. This was not her house. She did not know the sleeping man in front of her. Her heart pounded so hard now she was sure he could hear it bouncing against her chest. Fear coursed through her veins.

Where was she?

CHAPTER EIGHTEEN

Julie covered her mouth, smothering her instinct to scream. She stared warily at her kidnapper sleeping in the chair across from her. The man's skin seemed pale white in contrast to his dark hair. The profile of his Romanesque nose sloped down to firm, sensual lips framed by a well-defined jaw line. His body was long and lean. He wore a dark shirt with the first few buttons undone. His black slacks clung to muscular legs.

Her grogginess subsiding, Julie surveyed the room, looking for an exit. She could see a patio outside of the open French doors. There was a gas-lit lamppost next to a fountain in the center, illuminating a very high brick wall that would be hard to scale, but maybe not impossible, if she had to.

Ahead, slightly to the left of her bed, was an open door to a small room where she could see a tiled floor and a sink. Past the sleeping man was another room accessed by an opened archway with a small dining table and a piano. To her right were a bookshelf and a chaise lounge. *No exit doors*. Something was wrong with this picture. Her heart began to pound in her ears, again.

Gong.

Julie jumped out of her skin at the unexpected sound. The clock on the mantle had its hour hand on three. The man turned his head, eyes still closed. Julie smothered another gasp with her hand. The other side of his face was not right.

Gong.

His skin looked unnatural. It was raised with alternating reddish-pink and white areas. The damage extended down his neck as well. She could not see how far down. From this angle, his once-handsome features now appeared sinister.

Gong.

She watched, wide-eyed, as his eyes flicked open, midnight blue, and returned a piercing look. Dropping her hand from her mouth, she could not look away. She could see past the deformity to the arresting intelligent eyes that threatened to hold her gaze captive.

"Juliana, is it?" She recognized the rich timbre of his voice. He was the man who had spoken to her earlier.

She nodded, keeping her expression flat. Inwardly she trembled, but she resolved not to give him the satisfaction of seeing it.

He leaned forward in his chair. "I want you to tell me where you live."

If he abducted her, he should know where she lived. "Why do you need to know that?"

"I would like to return you."

"Oh, you don't have to do that. Show me to the door and I'll find my own way home."

He shook his head. "I'm afraid it is not as simple as that."

As she stood from the bed, her legs shook with a combination of weakness and fear. And when she spoke, against her will, her voice trembled. "Why? I don't need your help. I'm perfectly capable..."

The light material of her clothes brushed against her body and her words trailed away as she looked down. She felt the blood drain from her face as she realized she was dressed in a sheer nightgown with a thin robe.

How did I get into these clothes? Jesus, Mary, and Joseph! She looked up immediately crossing her arms over her body, closing up the robe.

As if he could read her thoughts, he spoke. "I have no intention of harming you. I want to send you home as quickly as possible, but I need your cooperation to make that happen."

If he doesn't want to harm me, he must want a ransom.

"Please, whoever you are, I have friends who can pay you whatever you want, if you let me go." She would work the rest of her life trying to pay Heath and James back if they would front the money to this man.

"Money cannot fix this." His voice sounded almost sad.

"Look, this is a big mistake. You have the wrong person."

He sat back in the chair and studied her thoughtfully. "Quite right, you *are* the wrong person."

"Then why? Why did you take me?" Before giving him a chance to respond, she continued. "Did you abduct me from the ambulance or the hospital room?" She paced, hoping she could reason with him. "My friends will be so worried. Please," she extended her clasped hands. "I beg of you, let me go."

Julie froze as she noticed that her hands were the deep, rich color of cinnamon. She unclasped them, holding them up at eye level, and turned them over. She slowly ran her gaze up the length of her matching cinnamon-colored arms. A chill ran down her spine. *Who was she?*

She looked beseechingly at the stranger to answer the question she couldn't seem to ask. His expression was guarded. Out of the corner of her eye, she could see him stand up as she made a mad dash for the bathroom, searching for a mirror. Bare walls! *Who doesn't keep a mirror in the bathroom?* She spun around, bumped into the man, and stared up at his very solemn face.

"A mirror," she gasped.

He led her to a small chest of drawers with a four-piece silver set—hair brush, clothes brush, comb, and mirror—on top of it. She grabbed the small hand mirror and held it to her face. Golden eyes looked back at her and ringlets of honey-colored curls framed the cinnamon-colored face in the mirror. The full lips opened at the same time Julie's cry pierced the air. She let her arm fall limply at her side, mirror still clenched in her hand.

"This is just a dream. It isn't true." She spoke out loud, trying to convince herself.

"It is true." The tall stranger contradicted her.

She needed a better look at herself to comprehend what was happening to her. "Why don't you have a real mirror I can look in?"

He measured his words carefully. "I thought that an adjustment period might be necessary until the idea of your circumstance became palatable." He paused. "I can bring one for you later, if you wish it."

She looked into the hand mirror again. The woman's saucer-eyes stared back, causing Julie's stomach to twist in knots. "I think I'm going to be sick." She barely made it to the toilet before her clenching gut made her vomit. She sank to the floor, exhausted—physically, emotionally, and mentally. This *had* to be a mistake. She thought back to the events just before she woke up. She was supposed to be viewing a past life, not experiencing this nightmare.

She glanced at the man observing her from the doorway. She ignored his watchful eyes and picked the mirror up from the floor, willing herself not to scream. She must approach this logically. She searched her brain for a rational explanation.

She studied the reflection. It wasn't a woman at all but a girl, maybe eighteen years old, if that. Julie touched her face and watched the girl's hand do the same. *None of this can be real. Maybe it is an elaborate hoax? She wouldn't put it past James to do something like this.*

But Julie knew she grasped at straws. A hoax like this would have taken a lot of work and expense to pull off. It was not a plausible explanation, but the alternative just could not be possible. She leaned over the sink to rinse out her mouth.

"Listen to me." The man crossed his arms, looking very intimidating. "We can do this the hard way or we can work together. One way or the other, I am going to correct this unfortunate error."

"So what happened? What am I doing here?"

He spoke slowly. "Shall we say simply that an experiment went awry?"

She raised her eyebrows as she shuffled past him and dropped into the nearest chair, worn to the bone.

"The end result is that you are in my wife's body and I would like to get her back."

His wife? Cradle-robber.

"Wait a minute!" She eyed him with suspicion. "If she's your wife, why do you keep her locked up in a room with no doors?"

His smile twisted his mouth. "My wife could come and go as she pleased. It is *you* who needs to be kept under lock and key." She started to speak, but he waved her next question away with his hand. "The circumstances are complicated and I do not have to explain myself to you. These are the facts as I wish you to know them. Now, do you want to go home?"

"Yes." Julie straightened. A gnawing feeling of guilt edged its way into her mind. She thought about her own little "experiment" that had gone awry. She was pretty sure that her own actions contributed to this bizarre chain of events. Her voice wavered. "Can you get me home? What I mean to say is...can you put me back into my own body?"

"I am going to do everything in my power to make that happen," he said with an air of authority. What other choice did she have but to trust him?

"It might help if I knew your name," she said.

"Erik."

"Just Erik?" she asked.

"Yes." He pushed off the wall and sat in the chair across from her.

Julie leaned back into her own chair, her strength waning. She felt as if she wore this body like a heavy suit. "What do you need me to do?"

"To start, I need you to answer a few questions for me."

"Okay."

"Where do you live?"

"New Orleans," she said, rubbing her head. She felt a sudden headache. "If you mean the address," she mumbled, "it's on the 900 block of St. Peter." Julie didn't feel comfortable just yet giving him the exact address.

"Where?"

"St. Peter, St. Peter!" She winced as she repeated the street. When she spoke, it felt as if a dagger had jabbed her head. "Why?" She closed her eyes and continued to rub her throbbing temple.

"This may be more complicated than I thought." He spoke softly. "I think you need more time to adjust." He assisted her to her feet. She didn't argue with him, allowing him to walk her to the bed. Her head pounded so badly now that the pain blinded her. She didn't have the energy to fight him even if she wanted to.

"I will bring you something to eat in a little while." He covered her with the blanket. "If you should wake before I return, for your own safety, do not attempt to leave this room." He paused. "There could be dangerous consequences if you do."

She heard his warning through the aching pain. "Okay, wait for you." Her tongue felt thick again. "Dangerous," she slurred. She only intended to rest her eyes. At least, until this headache subsided. As she drifted on the edge of sleep, images seeped into her mind.

Again, she found herself walking barefoot on a dirt road. She veered off the path to soak her feet in a manmade pond. She had only been there for a moment when a cow bell rang. She jumped up and headed back to the old country house. She had an ominous feeling. She was late for something.

As she walked, the scenery changed. Then she was inside a room that was bare but for a few pieces of furniture. She held an ornate brooch in her hands. It was a beautiful gift, and she felt happy because someone she cared about had given it to her. With tears in her eyes, she looked up to thank her benefactor.

It was Erik.

She fell back from the moment, observing through the eyes of the woman as the scene played itself out. She didn't hear the conversation between them and she couldn't tear her eyes from Erik's face.

It was completely normal.

♀

Erik fastened the floor-length mirror to the bathroom wall. He felt more alive than he had in quite some time. A few hours of sleep had done wonders for him. He realized he had not been thinking clearly before. Where were his accolades? Who would congratulate him on his extraordinary feat? There was no one but himself to marvel at his genius.

He had done it!

He had conjured a living soul.

He looked into the bedroom at the sleeping woman. So, it didn't go according to plan. He could live with that for now. He'd root this out and send Juliana back to the body and family she had come from.

An old familiar wickedness began to take hold of him. By the time he sorted this whole tangle through, he'd have Naomi *and* Christine. This whole debacle made him realize Naomi belonged with him, too. He would be her guardian and her protector. While Christine, his most cherished possession, would complete his broken life with her love.

He stood back, making sure the mirror was level and lowered his gaze to his reflection. He stared without blinking at the blue eyes given to him by his mother and the features, the perfect parts, at least, given to him by his father. He raised his hand to touch the rough, marred side of his face.

He had forgotten that his face had been exposed the entire time. Even though Juliana saw his atrocity, she had been unfazed by his appearance. Her level of concern was appropriate given her situation, but never once had he seen fear in her eyes. That fear he saw in all others, even from Christine when she had first seen his face.

He walked to Juliana's bedside and watched her. As irksome and inconvenient as this whole matter was, he was fascinated by her. Naomi's expressions had changed, the inflection of her voice sounded different, and her mannerisms were altered. Who was this person inside Naomi's body?

It was obvious that Juliana was still confused. Some lingering memories of Naomi must be affecting her. Why else would she give the same street as Naomi's address? After her rest, ready or not, she would tell him everything. It was imperative that he go to Juliana's home soon. For wherever she came from, Naomi would now be in her body and she would need comfort. He would soothe Naomi's fears and reassure her that he'd have her back home as soon as possible. And, depending on the circumstances, he might remove Naomi from that household and keep the two women together while he sorted this through.

Yes, that was most definitely a viable option.

He would take Naomi back.

She belonged to him.

And he always took what was his...

CHAPTER NINETEEN

Julie ran a finger over her lips. They tingled from the pressure of Heath's mouth on hers...her last dream before waking. She wanted to go home. She missed her life, flawed as it was. She missed James and their wonderful dysfunctional friendship and she desperately wanted the opportunity to explore where her budding relationship with Heath would take her. Yearning pulled at her heart, then indignation took its place.

Who did that Erik person think he was? She didn't need him to solve this situation. She had her own people who loved her, friends who were invested in her welfare and not their own agenda. They would help her. She would explain everything to them and they would go with her to find Star.

Star would know exactly what to do. If only she could find a way out of here, Julie would try to convince everyone of her true identity. They were all open-minded people and by now, it should be obvious to them that something was different about her, if she had indeed switched places with Erik's wife.

Julie tiptoed around the set of rooms looking for any sign of Erik. Relief flooded her as she realized she was alone. She ran to the French doors, checking once more over her shoulder before she opened them and stepped into the bricked garden.

Once she entered the courtyard, she realized it was enclosed inside the house. There would be no escape this way. As she considered other options, a dazzling illusion of the sun edged its way across the domed ceiling along with images of clouds blowing by. The false sun felt as warm as if it were producing the heat of real sunlight.

A cool breeze blew ringlets of hair across her face. She tried tracing the source of the air and noticed small openings between the edge of the back wall and the ceiling. She went to the back and held her hand out in front of one of the slits and felt the constant flow of air. Whoever had designed this courtyard had taken the trouble to attend to the littlest details. But for all the details, it gave her no clue as to where she was. For all she knew, she could be in Argentina.

In the center of the courtyard, next to the lamppost, a fountain bubbled merrily and she heard the faint sound of birds chirping, although there were none in the room. Large green potted plants ranged along the walls and around the fountain. Clinging to one side of the brick wall, ivy climbed its way toward the ceiling.

In one of the corners, a stone bench sat diagonally, and in the opposite corner stood a circular wall of brick only as high as her hips. It was filled with a myriad of colorful flowers, and in the center of this raised garden, a statue of two lovers lay in the earth. Julie gazed at the finely chiseled features of the man and woman.

Jesus, Mary, and Joseph! It was the statue from Lafitte's Blacksmith Shop Bar. What had Smooth said? The statue had disappeared and was returned one night many years later. And she was staring at it right now, no longer at the bar where it belonged.

She shook the thoughts from her head. Dwelling on the statue would not help her discover an exit. From her quick assessment, it didn't seem that any exit route would be from the garden. She stepped back inside the bedroom. It had no obvious door. She would have to think outside the box.

Outside the box...good one, Julie...seeing as I'm pretty much trapped inside a box. Her eyes raked the set of rooms that formed a very large square space. There had to be a door here; Erik came and went by some means.

Old mystery movies often had hidden doorways and passages. If there was a secret entrance, and there had to be one, it was cleverly disguised.

The fireplace.

Surely there was an item to move on the mantle or by the floor that would cause the fireplace to swing back and reveal a secret passageway. She lifted the clock. Nothing. She moved a jewelry box. Nothing. She shifted both candlesticks. Nothing. She ran her fingertips slowly along the edge of the top and sides of the mantelpiece. Nothing.

Her heart sank and frustration welled in her. She kicked the fireplace poker stand, knocking it over. She screamed, sat down, and cradled her throbbing toe in her hand, inspecting it for damage as a purplish bruise blossomed before her eyes.

What had she been thinking? What if she had seriously hurt herself? She needed to center herself and think logically. Losing her cool would only jeopardize her efforts. And it didn't help that the unnerving click of the swaying pendulum of the mantelpiece clock sounded as if Erik were turning a key into the lock of the door she couldn't find.

Yes, Erik was very clever, but she would show him. She *would* find a way out. Her eyes slowly scanned the entire room, stopping as they rested on a bookshelf. She ran to the shelves, pulling books off in hopes that one would slide the bookcase open. She wiped her clammy hands on her gown after casting aside the last book. Nothing.

What else? Maybe the walls?

She tapped the walls, listening for a hollow echo. With each disappointment, she felt more determined and yet, more shaken. She rubbed her hands up and down each groove of the walls, feeling for some imperfection, any indication that the wall might be false.

Her arms and knees ached from the effort of bending low and then reaching up along the walls as high as she could. She didn't find anything. It seemed as if Erik were challenging her, seeing whether she could rise to the occasion.

Maybe she would have better luck in the bathroom? The warm tile felt glorious to her bare feet. She had not paid attention to the details last night, so she took her time to look at the bathroom with fresh eyes. She let her hand linger along the edge of the large claw-foot tub as she observed the unusual toilet.

The porcelain was covered by a complicated pattern etched in blue, and the seat rim was much smaller than she was accustomed to. There was no lid on the seat and high on the wall behind it was a water tank with a pull string attached. Possibly it was some kind of European model or a restored antique.

She inspected the rest of the bathroom and caught sight of herself in a mirror. Erik must have hung it while she slept. Mesmerized, she walked closer. There was the girl she had seen last night; this time she could see her from head to toe.

So this was Mimi.

Among her many dreams last night, in one the girl was berated by a wiry woman, with very cold eyes. Before the snippet ended, the woman hollered with a raised hand, "Mimi, you'll mind me if it is the last thing you do!"

Viewing the girl at different angles, Julie shook her head and watched the honey-colored curls swing. Mimi was beautiful.

♀

Usually one to make sure each step was well-planned, Erik was instead fueled this evening by recklessness and wild abandon. Without much thought or reason, he stormed through the de Marigny's front doors, stalked through the dark foyer, and ran up the staircase. His senses heightened as he listened for any sound of activity, but he heard nothing. The household was asleep.

He should have had Christine. He felt bitter disappointment, but he would not be the only one feeling intense emotions this evening. He had decided to make his presence known. He would leave this family in little doubt that he yet lived.

He centered his weight so each step he took toward the boy's room was soundless. He did not wish to wake the occupants of the house just yet. The little beau stood up, wide awake, contentedly gumming the rail of his crib.

"Hello, little namesake." Erik projected his whisper to the baby's ear. The boy bounced up and down on the mattress, laughed, then held his arms up to Erik. Erik's keen hearing picked up a gentle stirring from the bedroom down the hall.

"I have not much time to spend with you, son." Erik crossed the room. "I wanted to take the opportunity to introduce myself. I am your godfather." Erik bowed low before the boy, who laughed at the marvelous game. He reached his arms out to Erik again. Of course the child did not fear him; his imperfections were hidden under wax and white powder.

"I wonder," Erik mused out loud as he picked up the child. "If you saw the real me, would you be so eager for me to hold you?" The baby immediately reached for his nose. Erik stopped his hand. "No, little one, I am not here to play, not this time. I promise to come again. I am going to teach you everything I know." The baby's steel-grey eyes watched Erik's mouth as he spoke. "I will protect you. I will guard over you. You have been given to me by name, and I always protect what is mine."

The baby smiled up at Erik, oblivious to his meaning, but Erik knew his subconscious absorbed every word. The child turned his attention to Erik's shirt and he clumsily picked at the shiny, silver buttons. Erik cradled his petite godson and sat in the rocking chair, pushing the chair back and forth with his heels. He sang to the boy an age-old lullaby from the Pyrenees of France, his childhood home.

He controlled the range and volume of his voice to remain within the walls of the nursery. The child struggled to keep his eyes open while Erik rocked.

Ellendora had sung this very lullaby to her children, his half-siblings, sitting around her, as he watched through the window. The song told the story of a wise boy who faced the Laminak with bravery, never asking for what he wanted as a foolish child did, since fairies in the song did the opposite of what one asked.

"Ask for what you do not want, and your true wish will be given," Erik ended, looking down at the sleeping child.

Erik felt a surge of love accompanied by a deep misery. He placed the child in the crib and stood board-straight, throwing his head back with his mouth opened in a silent cry. The child should be his. This family should be his. Despair gripped his soul as he grabbed the rail of the crib to prevent himself from sinking to the floor.

He was not a shadow. He would not be ignored.

Until he could have Christine's love, he would settle for her fear. He reached under his coat and pulled out the gold engagement ring he had given to Christine, the same one she had slipped onto his dead finger, and placed it on the blanket next to the sleeping child.

Erik made his way down the hall, pausing outside the door where he could hear the slow, even breathing of two people. He tried not to picture Christine lying next to Raoul as he listened to the faint rustling of the sleepers' movements. Without a sound, he cracked the door open, looked for her feminine figure, and spoke.

"Christine." He projected the whisper to her ear. "Check on the child." Instantly, her slim silhouette sat up in the bed. Erik moved away from the door.

"Raoul." He heard her lean over to her husband. "Get up. I think something is wrong with Philippe." Erik heard the bed creak under her shifting weight, the quick flutter of material as she put on her robe, and footsteps as she crossed the room.

"Come back to bed," Raoul replied, half-awake. "There is nothing wrong with Philippe. He is sleeping."

Erik's gut burned at the sound of Raoul's voice.

"No." She continued to shuffle toward the door. "I have to check on the baby."

Erik stepped farther back into the shadow of the hallway and watched longingly as Christine hurried to the nursery. He fought the urge to go behind her and run his fingers through the long, soft tresses swaying across her back. Oh, how he missed her!

But, he waited instead...

Christine's loud scream tore through the house. The pitch was high, beautiful, and flawless.

He sighed.

The momentary connection he felt with Christine broke as Raoul's half-dressed figure dashed down the hall. Her screams now mingled with the frightened cries of the child.

"Christine! What is wrong?" Fear laced Raoul's voice.

When Raoul disappeared into the room, Erik descended the stairs, hopped the banister, and landed without a sound on the floor below. The whole house came to life. He didn't have much time, but he wanted to hear, he needed to hear...

"He's alive, Raoul." Christine's voice shook.

"Who's alive?"

"Erik."

"No..."

"Yes, look..."

Erik wished he could have seen Raoul's face when Christine showed him the ring, but he had already made his way down the street. In moments, he'd be blocks away.

What a successful night! What a brilliant morning! The dawning sun shone upon him and he continued on with a spring in his step. Yes, indeed, he *was* alive, very much so.

When he made it as far as Canal Street, he hailed a cabbie. "To the French Market, my good man." As soon as he returned home with the fresh produce, he would make breakfast fit for a king. *Or a prince*, he grinned. And when he was done cooking, Juliana would also enjoy the spoils of his celebration.

♀

Intent on finding a way of escape, Julie had shoved the obvious to the back of her mind. *I am inside someone else's body.* Now, confronted by the reflection in the mirror, she could no longer avoid it. She ran her hands along the shapely curves of the body, firm breasts, narrow waist, flat stomach, fine hips, and shapely thighs. Mimi had a natural, sensual beauty. Julie turned sideways and noticed her voluptuous rear. So completely unlike her own body.

She began to feel as if she had taken up residence. This body felt as comfortable on her as her own had. And that fact disturbed her more than the stranger in the mirror.

She tore her eyes away from her reflection to continue examining the bathroom. She held on to the waning hope of finding a way out and back to her home and to her life.

She opened the closet door. The shelves held a stack of clean towels and a jar filled with soaps, homemade by the look of them. She opened the lid and took a few out to smell. The small lilac, lavender, and rose-scented bars fell from her trembling fingers to the floor as she tried to put them back. One soap ricocheted off the floor and hit the closet wall. It sounded odd.

Cautious about raising her hopes, Julie rapped on the back of the wall closet half-heartedly with one knuckle and heard a slight, but definite echo. The lower down on the wall she knocked, the echo got louder. Under the last shelf, which was about three feet from the floor, she tapped again. The space behind the wall was definitely hollow!

Now, she had to figure out how to open it. She pressed against the stubborn wall, but it didn't budge. She looked around for a button or lever, anything that looked like a triggering device. She assessed the sides of the wall, then the floor, where she noticed something out of place.

A small piece of shoe molding jutted out slightly farther than its firmly anchored fellows. She held her breath as she pushed it back and heard a soft click. The wall under the bottom shelf swung open, and she fought back tears of relief.

She leaned forward, peering into the dark passageway. It was narrow. She'd have to crawl through. She imagined every creepy, crawly thing waiting for her in the darkness. She consoled herself by the shadow of light at the other end and the fact that Erik must have travelled through many times before, so hopefully, nothing, such as a huge roach, clung to the wall. Taking a deep breath, Julie put one hand in front of the other and crawled into the darkness.

CHAPTER TWENTY

Julie crawled out the end of the tunnel and jumped to her feet. The well-lit hallway she now stood in was lined with doors, three to her right, three to her left, and a larger, deeply etched door at the end of the hallway. One of these doors had to be an exit.

She alternated sides, trying the doors closest to her. The first two were locked; the third opened to a brick wall. Her stomach tightened as she questioned the wisdom of continuing on, but she had not come this far for nothing. Again, the next two doors were locked and the third opened to a brick wall. That left the impressive door at the end of the narrow hall.

Her hand trembled as she held the handle. Open it? Don't open it? How many horror movies had she seen in which at a moment exactly like this, she yelled at the stupid girl *not* to open the door? She knew it could lead to some unknown horror, but if there was a chance it could lead a way to freedom, she *had* to open it.

Her heart hammered against her ribs as she turned the knob. It moved easily. She pulled the heavy door open, feeling the resistance of weighted hinges. She placed herself between the door and the jamb to prevent it from closing. Darkness mocked her from the adjacent room. She slid her hand along the smooth, cold glasslike wall, feeling for a light switch.

A current of air issuing from the room smelled like cut grass and fresh rain, giving her hope. This had to be the way out, if only she could see. She'd have to navigate slowly, feeling her way. She took a brave step into the room and as if sensing her presence, the ceiling illuminated, blinding her with bright light. She let go of the door to shade her eyes, realizing her mistake too late as the door slammed shut behind her.

She swung around. The door was no longer visible, only mirrored walls, six of them with beveled strips that mimicked the outline of where there could be a door. Then the walls began to move. The light from the ceiling reflected back at her from every angle of the mirrored walls, highlighting a large, iron tree anchored from floor to ceiling.

Before Julie had time to consider what purpose the tree might serve, the mirrored floor vibrated under her feet and a faint whirring sound drifted up as the lights flickered. The brightness dimmed and she spun around to see a three-hundred sixty-degree view of a tropical forest inside the mirrors. The jungle floor was under her feet.

The images had such depth that she could almost believe she was really in the middle of a jungle. Was that a leopard crossing in the distance? She backed away until she bumped against the metal tree.

Something buzzed near her left ear, and she swiped at it. A large fly-like insect sailed past the other side of the mirror. An oppressive heat radiated into the room, feeling like a typical New Orleans summer day at one hundred percent humidity. As perspiration formed on her skin, Julie slipped out of the thin robe she wore, but it only provided a momentary relief.

A loud roar reverberated inside the room. Julie turned around to find herself face to face with a male lion shaking his massive mane and roaring again. He bared his teeth, staring at her through the glass. Panic shot through her, even though she knew none of what she saw was real. The lion turned its aggression toward a lioness which ran away in fear, dropping a lifeless gazelle from her mouth. The lion ripped the gazelle into pieces and gnawed on it contentedly.

"Ewww…" Julie uttered, more determined to get out.

She started on the opposite side from the lion, pulling on the beveled strips along the mirror attempting to find the door, without any luck. Surprisingly, in spite of the increasing and unyielding warmth of the room, the mirrored walls remained cool to the touch.

Sweat dripped down her back, and more beads slid down her face, narrowly missing her eyes. She grabbed the robe from the floor and wiped her face and neck. Within seconds, her skin was wet again. She tore the lace off the edge of the thin robe and used the strip to tie her curls up into a pony tail.

God, it is hot. She wiped her face again. *To hell with this.* She was not beyond asking for help. She pounded on the mirror. "Erik! Let me out!"

As she moved around the room, pounding and yelling, her damp nightgown clung to her legs, impeding her movement. She gathered the material. If only she had a pair of scissors. Then she noticed the tree branches. There was a sharp-ended branch sticking off one of the lower limbs. When she touched the iron tree, just like the mirrors, it did not absorb the heat generated by the room.

Julie climbed the tree. She used the sharp branch to rip through the fabric of the gown, then tore the skirt apart until what was left hung just above her knees. She wiped her face again, letting the material fall to the floor. She climbed higher and banged on the impenetrable mirrored ceiling in frustration and on the verge of tears, very thirsty, and drenched in sweat.

A familiar sound pinged inside the room. As it grew louder, she recognized the patter of rain. She climbed down the tree and watched enviously as the drops fell all around her behind the mirrors and pooled under the glass beneath her feet. Her thirst grew so severe, it tempted her to lick the mirror to quench it.

The sun made a rapid descent into darkness without tribute to twilight. She swallowed, hoping the sudden night would provide some relief from the heat, but she quickly found the darkness just as suffocating under the muted rays of the moon. Worse still, every manner of unknown insect serenaded her while the forest floor rustled with their movement.

Julie crumpled to the floor in defeat. She had been slow cooking for hours. She did not know how much longer she could endure it. She gazed up through the metal branches to the stars and moon above her, staring for a while until she heard a click. Something swung in the darkness, breaking her from her spellbound gaze.

The thing continued to sway from one of the larger branches higher up the tree. She pushed herself up on one elbow to get a better view and realized it was a thick rope. No. Not just a rope, but a noose. It swayed as though pushed by a gentle breeze, beckoning any who was weary to claim its embrace. It hung from underneath the branch as though it had always been a part of the metal structure.

Drained of all energy, without the strength to hold herself up any longer, Julie crumpled back to the floor with her lips and throat dry, her tongue parched, and her skin soaked. All she could think about was having a drink of cool water. If only there was a way out of this room. But there was...

Julie imagined someone climbing the tree, slipping the noose around their neck, and jumping. One could certainly get out that way. *Jesus, Mary, and Joseph.* She shook the horrible thought from her head just as the constant whirring noise got louder and the walls moved once more.

A bright speck of amber-gold light hovered in the horizon, and like the oncoming night, the morning appeared without ceremony. This time the sun's merciless rays brought with them the torturous sound of lively, bubbling water. And on the distant edge of the desert that filled her three-hundred sixty-degree view, she saw an inviting waterfall cascading into a pool surrounded by large palm trees.

Her hopes crashed again as she remembered that none of these images were real. Julie succumbed to the mounting heat, remaining limp on the floor, looking at the desert through apathetic eyes. She welcomed the oncoming flashes of her delirium, looking down at her own feet as she walked down a dirt road.

"Bijou!" she heard herself call out. She veered off the dirt path toward the edge of a wooded area and the protection the trees provided from the baking sun.

"Bijou!" Why wasn't she coming? She was usually an obedient dog. Julie listened for a moment for a response. What she heard did not belong to an animal. Heavy breathing filled the space behind her. A shiver ran down her spine, and she froze. She forced herself to turn around to confront the presence at her back.

The man stood larger than life, his expression clouded by frustration. He stared down at her with small dark eyes, his grimace deepening the lines on his face and jutting his prominent chin even more forward. She did not know what she had done, but he seemed upset with her. She did not want to be alone with him and tried to pull herself out of this moment. But she was held captive by this memory, forced to experience something that did not belong to her.

Every moment that Mimi allowed Julie to see something, the memory became a part of her, allowing Julie to know things. Little bits of knowledge would settle over her. She knew all the people in the dreams she'd been having even though she had never seen them before.

For instance, Julie knew the man standing before her was named Joe B and that Mimi didn't fear him. In fact, Mimi felt very comfortable and safe; it was Julie who felt threatened by his stance and the desire in his eyes. She wanted to make an excuse and dart around the man back to the open road. All Mimi wanted to do was find Bijou.

"I keep hollering for Bijou and she doesn't come." Julie was forced to put her hands on her hips and stamp her foot. "Are you sure she's here?"

"Deeper in." He pointed with his large, beefy hand.

Julie felt danger to the deepest depths of her soul while Mimi naively walked farther into the wood, isolating them from any chance of help.

"Bijou, Bijou!" she called out.

This is not a good idea. Turn around, Mimi. Get the hell out of here. But Julie was forced to walk onward as Mimi wished.

Julie's heart plummeted as she was slammed to the ground, the wind knocked out of her. *Jesus, Mary, and Joseph!* She'd physically *felt* that hit. While Julie struggled with the fear coursing through her veins, Mimi assumed a large branch had fallen off a tree, knocking her down. Shaken, but not concerned, Mimi got to her feet.

Large hands forced her back down, turning her over. Joe B's heavy frame straddled her, pinning her to the brambled floor. For the first time, Julie and Mimi agreed: they were in trouble and needed to get away. Julie felt the raw ache on her wrists from his unyielding hands and the small pricks of pain along her backside where sharp sticks and rocks dug into her skin.

Julie felt everything. She was bombarded by sensations. And she could do nothing. Julie wanted to lift her knee right into his groin, but Mimi was paralyzed by shock and dawning awareness.

Joe B leaned closer to her. "I didn' want it to be this way, you know." He glared at her as if this were all her fault. "I tried to do this the right way," he said, trying to convince himself. His voice softened while he caressed her face with a calloused hand. "I don' want to hurt you."

Mimi turned her head, her voice quivering. "Don't hurts me, Joe B, I'm a good girl."

Julie wanted to scream. She knew it to be true. Mimi had never been touched by a man before. More memories flooded through her. Joe B had asked Mimi to marry him many times, and Mimi had dismissed each offer. Mimi never saw it, but Joe B had wanted her since he first laid eyes on her.

Julie felt Mimi's brief moment of happiness turn to dread when Joe B let go of one of her wrists, but didn't set her free. Instead, he loomed over her while Mimi turned her head to the side, trying to avoid the smell of sweat, alcohol, and body odor emanating from him. He put his nose to her hair and inhaled, nuzzling her neck as he murmured words she could not make out. Mimi struggled against him and Julie was relieved that something finally drove Mimi to action.

She put her free hand flat on his chest and tried pushing him off her.

Find your voice Mimi, Julie encouraged her.

"No!" she screamed. "Joe B, no!"

His stunned face turned dark, and Julie knew Mimi had just made a huge mistake. Unaware of the storm brewing inside of him, Mimi still pounded on his chest and shouted. Julie felt the agonizing sting across her face from the large hand as it struck her cheekbone so hard that her head twisted from the force and spit flew from her mouth.

He ripped her clothes from collar to hem. Mimi tried to kick him off her, which resulted in another fierce blow that sent pain searing through her skull. Julie had never felt pain like that before. Her face pounded with residual aching waves while her vision blurred in her left eye from the immediate swelling and she tasted blood in her mouth.

"Help!" Mimi cried out.

Julie could hear Joe B struggle with his belt buckle as Mimi tried to twist herself around. He dug his hand deeply into her small shoulder. Julie saw stars and found herself flat on her back again. Joe B's eyes were wild and animalistic, his breath quick and ragged as he pulled off her underclothing. Mimi fought him the whole way, resulting in another fierce strike to the face that made Julie dazed and confused.

"You're gonna belong to me now." That was all he said before Julie felt a tearing burn between her legs and heard Mimi's screams echo in the wood in unison with her own inward cries of pain.

They both drifted in and out of consciousness during his relentless assault. Mimi cried, screamed, and begged, but Joe B ignored her pleas. With his eyes closed, he placed one of his large hands over her mouth to muffle anything else she might say, pleasure etching his face.

Over his rhythmic motion, Julie heard a faint rustling in the woods that grew louder. *Someone had heard her*! *Someone was coming*! A blur of brown and black soared over her onto Joe B.

Bijou.

Growling and with her teeth bared, Bijou bit into Joe B's flesh. He let Mimi go to fight the angry coonhound. To Julie's relief, Mimi wasted no time in scrambling free. Dizziness washed over her as she stumbled in the direction of the road.

Keep going. Keep going. Julie couldn't wait to see the sandy dirt road again.

She limped onward, her heart lightened by the hope of freedom until she heard the howl of an injured dog. Mimi stopped, debating between running back to help Bijou or continuing on to safety. Julie trembled. She felt Mimi's concern for the dog, but Julie wanted to get away. The thundering weight of Joe B broke the silence as he pushed through the trees after her.

"No!" Mimi cried as she ran again, her own freedom superseding her concern for Bijou. Large arms wrapped around her legs, causing her to fall to the ground, flailing. Joe B stood up, holding on to her legs, dragging her back into the secluded wood.

Julie sobbed unheard.

Not again.

CHAPTER TWENTY-ONE

Erik, still happy from his successful exploit, hummed as he unloaded the fresh produce onto the kitchen counter. A flood of rapid notes pulsed through his mind and he realized some time had passed since he had felt like composing. The swell of trumpets, joined by haunting violins and crashing cymbals, converged in his mind. His fingers played imaginary piano keys.

He raised a hand to silence the other instruments in his head in order to concentrate on the piano bridge-passage. He attempted the transition phase again without success. Something interrupted his concentration. Willing his fingers still, he froze, listening for the anomaly disrupting his genius. A very low whirring encroached upon his senses.

He recognized the low disturbance. It was a sound that he had heard many times in Persia and once in France. It was the sound of his torture chamber. His lips twisted into a satisfied smile as he strode toward the hidden chamber. Raoul, the fool, entrapped once again!

Erik's smile faded as it dawned on him that even if Raoul had seen him leaving this morning, he had gone straight to the French Market, not home. It could not be Raoul. No one else would have reason to break in, yet. Erik picked up his pace. No one would want to break in, but one person would want to break out.

He rushed through the maze of trap doors and hidden corridors toward the metal enclosure. The only people who had ever survived its relentless design were Raoul and the Daroga, and only because he had set them free. All the others had taken their lives within four to five hours of the chamber's warm embrace.

He reached the exterior room, sparing a glance at the time clock that had started counting the moment the machine turned on. It had been triggered a little over three hours before. He yanked open the metal door and peered through the two-way mirror. His heart sank as he saw Juliana on the floor.

Foolish, foolish woman.

He shook his head. He had warned her not to try to escape. Yet, there she was, on the floor crying out and wrestling with an unseen opponent, the unrelenting heat apparently affecting her mind.

He pulled the large lever that turned the machine off, and pressed his foot on the small spring nail near the chamber door until it sank, releasing the lock. He rushed inside, swamped by the stifling heat, and knelt by her side.

Juliana cried out in hoarse agony. The sound struck a chord in his heart. He had never heard anything like it before. He tried to wrap his arms around her so he could remove her from the room, but she fought him off with every attempt.

Even though the heat escaped from the room and the temperature dropped, Erik knew he had to get her out of there. Her full lips were dry and cracked, her skin hot and drawn, and her eyes sunken. He touched her again, and a fist slammed into his mouth. He staggered back from the pain and surprise, tasting blood.

Juliana continued to flay and scream. "No! Get off me!" She raised her head, looking at the empty space behind him. "Why are you doing this to me?" she cried out while her body arched in what appeared to be pain. She sobbed. "Joe B, I'm a good girl. Why?"

Erik's blood turned cold. He felt as if he had been hit again, not by a fist, but by the sudden understanding of what played out before his eyes.

This wasn't Juliana.

This was Naomi, reliving the very memory he had tried so hard to access. And he didn't have to guess what took place. He felt her agony mingle with his own despair and anger. He vowed to never forget who caused her dishonor. Joseph Alphonse Batiste would pay the ultimate price for what he had done to Naomi. But for now, he would give Naomi peace.

As she struggled against the memory, he knelt by her head, battling to control his own emotions and his voice. "Naomi, you are safe. Be still now, wife. I will not allow anyone to hurt you again." He embraced her. "It is my hands holding you now. You cannot be harmed."

She stopped moving, relaxing in his arms. Her wild eyes closed, and the lines of pain faded from her face. Erik breathed a sigh and gathered her closer to him, but she began to scream again. He could not contain her violent movements and at a loss, he released her.

"You son-of-a-bitch!" Naomi fought the air again. "You filthy, stinking animal!" She gasped for air. "Help!" she yelled, twisting her head to the side to look beyond Erik. "Somebody help us!" Then she muttered urgently, "Mimi, fight him. Fight him!" She turned her head forward, fury on her face. "You won't get away with this Joe B!"

Staring in disbelief, Erik wiped the sweat from his brow. This entire display went beyond his imagination. Naomi had never uttered a foul word. This was Juliana fighting the same memory. It was beyond reason.

"Somebody get me out of this nightmare!" she screamed.

Her request jolted Erik into action. "Juliana, wake up," he commanded. Her wild movements slowed, but she still breathed rapidly from the exertion. Erik smoothed the damp curls from her face. "Wake up. You are safe with me." She relaxed just as Naomi had done before her. Her cheeks were reddened from the heat and her dry lips quivered. She opened her golden eyes, gazing directly into his.

"We were raped," she uttered.

♀

Julie's hands clawed at the forest floor while Joe B pulled her farther back into its depths. Her clothing was ripped and torn by sharp sticks and prickly brambles along the way as was the soft, sensitive skin of her stomach. With her mind in overdrive, she barely felt the superficial wounds. She knew if she were free to do so, she could defend herself and get away from this man whom Naomi once called friend.

She yearned to grab a large, bat-sized branch she saw on her right and whack the living daylights out of that asshole until he let her go. But Naomi, in fear, continued to grasp at roots and other useless forest debris as she was pulled farther into the undergrowth.

They passed the clearing from where she had just escaped. Naomi cried out. Julie saw Bijou lying motionless on her side, her chest rising and falling unevenly.

Naomi started kicking her captive legs, slowing Joe B. "What did you do to Bijou?"

Joe B halted, flipping her over to her backside while he turned his large, muscled arm for her to see. His shirt sleeve had ripped, and the edges were stained with blood. "That bitch bit me so I kicked her." He shook his head. "I don' want to hurt nobody, Mimi. But it's gonna be all right. You *have* to be with me now."

"I don't want you!" Naomi spat, to Julie's surprise.

A strange expression crossed his face. "No man will have you." He tightened his grip on her ankles and his brows furrowed over his darkening eyes. "Pastor Edwards said you was to be my wife. The Lord told him so. He tells me over and over to be patient. But you keep telling me no and I can be patient no more." His eyes moved down from her face. Naomi hurriedly pulled the edges of her ripped blouse over her exposed breasts. "I'd rather go to hell than not have you." He leaned towards her.

"You can't make me love you!" Naomi glared defiantly at him, tears of anger and shame running down her face. She jerked back when he attempted to wipe them away.

"I hope you will one day, until then...." Again, he launched himself upon her. Naomi fought valiantly, screaming and kicking. Julie at last felt as if she weren't forced to be a helpless victim. Until, without forewarning, her entire body went limp.

No, Julie moaned inwardly. Naomi's body remained still. *To hell with this! I'll be damned if I'm just gonna lie here.* She summoned all her will power to fight on her own against the relentless assault.

"You son-of-a-bitch!" To her amazement, she spoke the words out loud and commanded Naomi's body, resulting in a swift punch to his chest. Joe B hesitated a moment, surprise etched on his face by her vulgar words. She took the opportunity to hit him again and again. "You filthy, stinking animal!" She spat more insults at him. His dark eyes clouded over with anger, and his large hands grabbed her neck.

"Help! Somebody help us!" Julie struggled to breathe, clawing at his hands. "Mimi," she muttered. "Fight him!" But she didn't feel Mimi's thoughts with her anymore and knew she now faced him alone. She looked him dead in the eyes and heard her voice rasp out, "You won't get away with this, Joe B."

A gunshot echoed in the air, and Joe B relinquished his hold on her neck long enough for her to scream. Julie saw a bright-skinned woman with gray hair poke Joe B in the back with a rifle.

"Get off her, Joe B." She jabbed the tip of the rifle into his back again. Relief flooded through Julie. It was old Hortense Berry, Mimi's neighbor.

Joe B stood up with hands raised and turned around. "You're gonna want to be minding your own business, Hortense," he said through tight lips.

"That's Mrs. Berry to you, and I'm making it my business." Her thin arms jerked the gun to the right. "Now, move away from Mimi."

Joe B rushed at the frail, wiry woman. He fought her for the rifle and Hortense struggled to maintain her grip on the barrel. Julie's heart sank. She could guess how this fight would end. He would kill Hortense, then brutalize Naomi again and maybe kill her as well.

"Somebody get me out of this nightmare!" Julie screamed.

Out of the madness, a soothing voice called her name. "Juliana, wake up."

The pain ceased, and she became a silent observer once more. Joe B wrenched the rifle from Hortense and turned it on her just as two men stepped out from the trees, brandishing guns of their own. Without having ever met them, Julie knew they were Hortense's farm hands, Elijah and Ben. Joe B looked back and forth between the middle-aged, healthy men and the guns in their hands, then dropped his rifle and ran away.

Tender hands smoothed the hair away from Julie's face, and a reassuring voice reached her through the memory. "Wake up. You are safe with me." When she opened her eyes, she saw Erik's face. She never thought she'd be so happy to see him again. Her lips were dry and she found it difficult to form the words, but she had to let him know what happened.

"We were raped," she muttered. It was a relief to speak the words, to tell someone, even if that someone was Erik.

He looked away while scooping her up into his arms. "No one can hurt you now."

Did he not understand what she was saying? She struggled to raise her head and look him in the face.

"I know who did it. I can describe him. We have to go to the police." Her voice became more urgent with each word. "He has to be arrested before he can do this to someone else," Julie moaned under her breath.

Erik kept his eyes averted. "There is no need for that."

What! What can he mean there is no need? Mimi was brutally raped. Julie had felt every pain, every humiliation of the horrific ordeal for herself. Joe B had to be caught and punished.

"He must pay for what he has done," she bit out in righteous anger. And even as she spoke to Erik, she could still see snippets of what transpired in the forest.

Helpful hands lifted Naomi up and assisted her to Hortense's house where she was cleaned and given fresh clothes.

"Oh, he will," Erik said, carrying her away from the mirrored room. She vaguely noticed walls opening and closing as they moved farther away.

Hortense took Naomi home in a horse-drawn wagon because she was too sore and weak to walk.

"How?" Julie insisted. "How can he be held accountable if you don't alert the authorities?"

Finally, he looked down into her questioning face. "Because I am going to kill him."

He said it as easily as if he were asking someone to pass the salt, but the look on his face held an unspoken, steely anger that made Julie shudder. He lifted his gaze from her face and continued to carry her with little effort.

When Hortense's wagon arrived at Naomi's house, Cora and Eugene ran out to meet her, both appearing concerned.

Julie relaxed in Erik's arms. She didn't know whether to be comforted or alarmed by his words. One thing she knew to be true: he was on her side. Ordinarily, she didn't believe in the death penalty, but in Joe B's case, she would make an exception. Her conscience smote her. She knew by Naomi's memories that Joe B had suffered horribly and faced his own trials in life, but it didn't give him the right to hurt and humiliate others.

As soon as the sound of the wagon's wheels receded into the distance, Cora cracked a heavy belt across Naomi's back, forcing her to the floor. Eugene taunted her, calling her a whore. They beat her senseless, but before they did, they let her know once she was in a suitable condition, she would be taken to New Orleans and sold to a Madam.

After all Naomi had been through, this was what they did for her? Julie tired of reliving Naomi's memories. She wasn't interested in doing this anymore. Not another minute. She was exhausted from the heat, from the memories, from everything…

"I want to go home, Erik." A sob caught in her throat.

"And so you shall." He placed her down on the bed in the chamber from which she had escaped.

"I am going to let you go."

CHAPTER TWENTY-TWO

"Yes, let you go. That would be best," Erik said, more to himself than to Juliana, as he walked away from the bed toward the bathroom. Once released from his custody, Juliana would return to her family and he would simply follow. No need to interrogate the girl. She had been through enough trauma already. Besides, his hands were tied; Naomi would be the one suffering by his methods, or at least her body would, if he forced the answers from Juliana, so he had to release her. Out Juliana would go and he, directly behind her.

Erik turned on the tub's faucet and saturated a small towel with the cool water issuing from it, left it running, and returned to Juliana. "Put this on your forehead. We need to cool you down."

She accepted the towel and pressed it to her face, neck, and chest, giving him a curious glance as he opened the French doors, allowing the circulating air to come in from the garden room. "Your face." Her eyes continued to catalogue each feature. "It looks normal."

He delayed his response until he could control the contempt he felt. "Like it better this way, do you? I'm able to cover my imperfections when I choose," he said coldly, pointing at the wax and white paste.

"No." Juliana repositioned herself in bed. "Well, yes *and* no." She continued to press the wet towel to her skin, appearing more revived. She tilted her head. "You look handsome either way."

Her words seared his heart, causing an irregular beat. Fiery hope and icy disbelief flowed in union through his veins. No one in his life, certainly no one of the fairer sex, had ever described him as handsome. He could not have heard correctly, even though the words swirled repetitively inside his head. *You look handsome either way...*

He thought of Christine, who recoiled at the sight of his face. And yet, across the room from him, staring with Naomi's golden eyes, Juliana's expression was sincere. This woman found him attractive. Could it really be true? The only people in his travels to welcome him without abhorrence were the Tonkin pirates. Erik's face was a merit to that band of men, making them more feared.

Not capable of responding to Juliana's compliment, he chose to avoid the subject. "I have drawn a bath for you to freshen up before you leave. I will have something to eat and drink waiting for you when you get out of the washroom, and I will get you a dressing robe from the closet to wear. After you have eaten, I will bring you some of Naomi's clothing."

"Okay."

He pulled the robe off the top shelf of the closet and noticed the trap door ajar. He closed it and broke the shoe molding lever to prevent access to it again.

"Erik?" Juliana called.

He turned off the faucet and returned to her, placing the robe on her bed. "Yes?"

Her eyes searched his face, trying to read him as one would a book. "Were you speaking metaphorically, or are you really going to kill Joe B?"

That name sent a wave of fury through him, and although he tried to keep his reaction from frightening her, he felt his facial muscles tighten. "He forfeited his life the second he placed his hands on you." With a slight shake of his head, he corrected himself. "When he touched Naomi, he became my enemy."

Juliana sat up in bed, her golden eyes opened wide, placing her hand to her chest. "No, you were right the first time. It happened to me, too. I don't understand it, but I experienced blow by blow what happened. I can describe to you the pain he put your wife through because I felt it all. How can that be possible?"

Erik ran his hands through his disheveled hair, sinking into the nearest chair. He looked down at his hands, willing them to stop trembling as he concentrated on the silver band on his left finger. He did not want to know blow by blow what happened. Had he been successful in getting Naomi to tell him that memory in its entirety, he would have stopped it, erased it from her mind, and then he would have hunted Joe B down and exterminated his worthless life. He still intended to do just that, but he had more pressing matters at the moment, Juliana and Naomi.

"No," he finally voiced. "I am at a loss. I cannot explain what happened."

"Did you know," she persisted, "that her family blamed her for what Joe B did?"

Erik's insides clenched like a fist at this revelation.

"They beat her mercilessly. They were going to sell her to a Madam in New Orleans…" Her voice faltered.

"No more!" Erik commanded with hands raised. If he were to control his emotions, he could not listen to another word. He feared he would not be able to restrain himself if he allowed his anger free rein.

She acquiesced, sinking back into the pillows. Her brows creased, but it did not seem to be from concern over his outburst; her gaze was distant as if she were absorbed in thought. He took the opportunity during her silence to dim the gas lights in the room and light several candles. The blazing glare reflected in the mirrors of his torture chamber could have caused temporary damage to her eyes. He wanted her completely recovered before sending her from the house.

Erik cleared his throat. "Juliana, I trust you will not need my assistance to prepare yourself." She shook her head. He felt her eyes on him as he walked over to the sconce closest to the bookshelf and turned the small knob underneath it. The door in the wall slid open. "I also trust that I can rely on you not to leave this room again until I show you the way."

She gave him a faint smile. "Oh, you can count on that."

♀

Erik stared hard at the knife in his hand while he cut slices of the baguette he had baked the day before. A few hours ago, everything had made complete sense. He was going to exorcise Juliana, summon back Naomi, claim Christine—by whatever means possible, in spirit or body—and cherish the two women for the remainder of his life. He had believed himself in complete control of his circumstances. Now it appeared that he was just another pawn in life's chess game.

And his "death list," as he called it, grew by the day. He dunked the sliced bread into the mixture of eggs, milk, and cinnamon he had prepared. With each slice, he counted the names: the scoundrel he had helped Marie exonerate; Joe B; and now Eugene and Cora Heming, Naomi's cousins, the very people who should have protected her.

There was little in life that Erik regretted. He prided himself on his ability to uphold the code of gentlemanly behavior, and holding to that code, he had never killed a woman before. Cora would be his first, but for her offenses toward Naomi, he could overlook her sex.

Erik could change the game at any time. He had an arsenal of herbs in his greenhouse. It would only be a matter of calculating the exact formulary to send Juliana away. For a few minutes in that mirrored room of horrors, he had seen Naomi's personality break through. Risking her safety in any way was not acceptable. Until he could understand how she and Juliana could exist in the body simultaneously, all things would stay as they were. He had to be sure of exactly what he was dealing with.

His stomach growled as the scent of warm bread and spices wafted around him. He was tempted to eat, but fasting would keep his mind sharp. He willed his hunger away and garnished her plate with fruit and cheese slices as he continued to think.

In an hour or so, Juliana would be free to roam the city at her leisure. Of course, he'd follow in the shadows, as always. Every step she took, his footsteps would echo. She would unknowingly lead him to all the answers he needed.

He covered the crispy bread with warm, buttery cinnamon-sugared banana slices then added a cup of freshly squeezed juice and a pitcher of water to the serving tray. When he reached the chamber, he knocked softly on the wall before he opened it. Juliana didn't answer, a bad sign. His shoulders tensed as he imagined finding an empty room. He stepped into her quarters and placed the tray on the dining table. He heard a soft splash of water from the bathroom.

She was still taking a bath.

"Juliana," he called to her. "Your meal is served." She did not respond. He approached the bathroom to repeat himself, halting just before rapping his knuckle on the slightly ajar door. Through the gap, he saw her glistening cinnamon skin, rivulets of water dripping down her curves...

Erik averted his gaze to the ceiling, leaning against the wall to hold the weight of his trembling body. Inhaling deeply, he could smell the soapy lilac bubbles.

"Juliana." His first attempt to speak was so low he barely heard his own voice. He cleared his throat and looked down at his feet, anywhere but at the slightly open door. "Juliana." The sudden splash of water told him he had startled her.

"Yes?" Her reply was quick.

His mind went blank except for the last breathtaking image of her. What had he wanted to tell her?

"Yes?" she repeated again, a little louder. Water swished as she moved inside the tub, caressing her skin, her wet, beautiful skin.

"Erik?"

Hearing his name broke him from the spell. "Your meal...it is on the table, when you are ready."

"Oh...thank you. I'll be out in a few minutes."

He lingered against his own will. He wanted to retreat from the room, but he also wanted to engage her in conversation, so he would have reason to be near her a little longer.

"I am going to leave...I'll return soon...to bring the clothes I promised."

"Great. Thanks."

Erik hesitated then turned on his heel and left the room without looking back. He needed to get his head cleared of this foolishness. He had too much at risk to make mistakes. He strode down the hall, determined to push everything from his mind except the formation of a well-constructed plan. However, at the back of his thoughts, not completely suppressed by the urgency of his task, the smell of lilac water pervaded his senses.

♀

After she heard the wall slide shut, Julie let out her breath, leaning back into the tub. She didn't know why she hadn't put two and two together before. Perhaps the oil she had applied to her skin, even though she was no longer in that skin, had ingredients that had left her disoriented and confused. Her thoughts had been muddled by the unsettling circumstances and by her fixation on trying to escape. She had not noticed anything strange because everything in Naomi's life seemed normal to Naomi.

But the wheels in Julie's mind finally clicked...

The Red Light District had faded into obscurity decades ago. New Orleans no longer had "Madams." And, the more she thought about Naomi's memories, she realized that Hortense's furniture and household items had all been antiques, as were Eugene and Cora's. They all wore outdated clothing. Erik's clothing was less datable, black slacks and shirt.

What had Star said to her?

The gift of seeing a past life was different for everyone.

Naomi was *her* past. She was in the body she had occupied during this period of her soul's existence. Her heart plummeted, and she drew her knees to her chest and squeezed her arms around them, rocking. What had she gotten herself into?

Fear settled deeply into her soul. *Think. Think.* Star said there was only a small window of opportunity open to see her past life, and then the moment would pass forever. She never said anything about being able to return to her life: Juliana François, divorcée, SSI recipient...

When she thought of it that way, her life kind of sucked. But, it was *her* life, damn it! And if there was a way to get back to it, she would. She had to. There was so much she hadn't done yet. She thought about Heath and what could have been or still could be.

A part of her knew it was pointless to leave Erik's house for the streets of New Orleans. Who would be there for her to find?

But still, she couldn't just wait, hiding complacently within these walls. She needed to do something. Leaving this house would make her feel more proactive and give her the sense that she had some control.

The smell of Erik's food crept into the bathroom through the small gap in the door, and Julie's stomach rumbled. She hadn't realized how hungry she was, and a savage thirst overcame her. Knowing that Erik could return at any time, she rushed to get the bathrobe he had laid out for her on the bed. After tying the robe's belt, she let the towel drop to the floor as a gust of wind blew the French doors wide open.

Her damp hair swirled across her face. Another gust caused the candles to flicker and blow out. The smell of smoke filled the bedroom that was now lit only by the dimmed overhead lights. She jumped as a third surge of air gracefully lifted the drapes on either side of the doors, and Erik's lean outline appeared inside the faux garden.

"Don't be afraid." His voice carried softly.

She wasn't scared. She never really was where Erik was concerned. She knew that now. A part of her, from a life she was just starting to remember, knew that she could trust him.

"There are many doors to this chamber–" he added as he placed a trunk at the foot of the bed. Glancing over his shoulder at the table then back to her, he frowned. "You have not eaten."

"I was just about to." Julie sat at the table, and poured herself a glass of water. The cool liquid relieved her parched throat. "Ah..." she gulped. She turned around to see Erik pulling garments out of the trunk and laying them on the bed.

"One would have sufficed–" she attempted a lighthearted dialogue.

"I have always been under the impression it was a woman's prerogative to choose," he said.

Breaking eye contact, he walked around the room, adjusting each light so that by the time Julie took her third bite of the savory French toast, the room was much brighter, illuminating previously unexplored portions of the dining area. To her left was a raised platform that looked like a stage with a backdrop of stained-glass windows. A row of lights lined the edge of the stage and the entire construction was framed by thick, red curtains.

Julie narrowed her eyes.

Who would imprison a woman in solitary quarters and take the time to build a stage inside? Never mind that, who would build a torture room to bake people to death? Julie gave Erik's back a troubled look. What had he said earlier?

His wife can come and go as she pleases, but the room was designed to keep me in here. Only problem with that explanation is that he had never expected me in the first place.

Besides the obvious, something was terribly wrong here. Now that she thought of it, this man never seemed surprised that someone different was in Naomi's body...he was only surprised that it was her. Who *was* supposed to be in this room and inside this body? Even though her soul feelings as Naomi told her Erik was to be trusted, her own instincts sent up red flags of suspicion. The sooner she got out of here, the better. She needed to trust her own judgment. She feared that the longer she stayed in Erik's presence, the greater the chance that Naomi might win out.

"Was it to your liking?" Erik's inquiry interrupted her thoughts.

She looked down at her empty plate. She had been so absorbed in her thoughts that she hadn't realized she had consumed the entire meal. Plastering a Cheshire cat smile on her face, she stood up and praised him. "Delicious." She walked away from him to the bed. She would never let him see how vulnerable she felt. "Now, let's see what I'm going to wear." Julie looked at the garments displayed across the bed, a deep purple monstrosity, a lacy pink number, and a cream-colored ensemble, all old-fashioned, long-sleeved, front button-up modest tops and ankle-length skirts.

"That one." She pointed to the off-white outfit.

Erik scooped up the remaining clothes and nodded toward the chest. "You will find undergarments in there. I will return in twenty minutes to see you on your way." Then he disappeared through the courtyard the same way he had come.

Eighteen minutes later, dressed in Naomi's clothing, she finished lacing up and tying a bow on the old-fashioned heeled shoes then began to brush her hair. What was she about to face outside of this house? Where would she go?

She knew the first place she'd visit was her own house or what once was her house or would be her house. She sighed at the complexities of turning back the hands of time. Maybe she was here for a reason...to make a difference in her past life, to change something. Maybe once she did that, she could go home and live both lives happily ever after.

On schedule, Erik reappeared with a length of light blue material in his hands. He held it out to her. "Here, put this on."

She took the cloth and went to the bathroom mirror. She tried to tie it around her waist, but it was too wide and thick for a belt. Maybe, it was a wrap? She draped her shoulders with it and hung it over the crook of each arm, turning sideways to get a better look at her reflection. Erik stood in the doorway, staring keenly at her, his expression unreadable.

"Let me help you with that." He gently pulled the material from around her shoulders. His fingers expertly swept her curls up and wrapped the material around her head, tying the ends into a knot close to the nape of her neck.

"Is this necessary?" she stammered, touching the wrap. He nodded, still keeping his face impassive, but she thought she saw a flicker of something in his eyes.

An unwanted tenderness pressed on her heart. Julie hadn't considered what this situation might be like for him. As much as she wanted to be out of his presence, she realized that it must be hard for him to let her leave, considering she'd be walking out the door in his wife's body. Even though it blew her mind to realize that technically, *she* was his wife.

What would he do if he knew that little fact? She considered her thought for exactly one second. *Hell no!* She couldn't risk the chance of Erik changing his mind. Right now, she had to do this on her own, and besides, he probably wouldn't believe she was from the future. The words sounded ridiculous in her own head.

She turned back to the mirror, drinking in the finished product. Oh…man. Add some hoop earrings and an apron, and she could be a member of an acting troupe doing a historical reenactment. She stared a little longer, but there was no point in putting off the inevitable. "Well, I guess this is it. I'm ready."

"This way." Erik made a sweeping gesture with his arm.

Julie followed him through the door in the wall, taking quick steps to match his long strides as he walked down the dark, narrow corridors. At the end of the hall, he placed his hand on a side panel. She heard a click, and another door opened, flooding the corridor with light. She could see shadowy movement through the white floor-to-ceiling curtains on the windows on the other side of the sparsely furnished room. And, more importantly, she spied the front door. Her heart began to beat faster. In mere moments, she'd be out that door and free.

As she walked on, the wood floors echoed under the heels of her shoes. At the door, Erik unbolted the multiple locks while she took two steps down, crossed the room and stepped up four more steps to enter the foyer. She peered around the foyer wall to the rooms on the other side. They also had more steps alternating up and down. Not one room was on the same level with the others.

She stiffened. Was it a coincidence that last night James told her a story about a house just like this one? Could this be the Devil's mansion? She shuddered and dismissed the thought. She could only handle one disaster at a time.

The front door creaked open to the clop clop of horse's feet and rumble of carriage wheels. On the street, Julie could see the horses and buggies, men with hats and canes, and women dressed as oddly as she. She hesitated, feeling rooted to the spot. Erik stepped back to the end of the foyer where she stood, his piercing blue eyes watching her.

"Have you changed your mind?"

She mutely shook her head, casting her eyes down. She could not return his gaze. She knew he'd be able to see the doubt running through her head. Of course she was uncertain now, faced with the reality of the world she was about to enter from the safety of Erik's sanctuary. But what was the alternative? Waste away in this protective cocoon? That was *not* an option. Yet why weren't her feet moving forward? Her gaze wandered to a newspaper lying on the top of a side table in the foyer. She could see the headline from where she stood.

PEACE COMMISSIONERS TO MEET!

Above the headline was the paper's name: *Daily Picayune.* She rushed forward, snatching the paper up to read the article.

"Representatives from the United States and Spain to meet on September 29th to discuss terms of treaty to be signed officially ending the Spanish American War. President McKinley to delegate..."

Hardly able to comprehend the words, she looked at the upper right-hand corner for the date: September 26, 1898. She was unable to prevent her voice from shaking.

"Erik, is this today's paper?"

"No."

His lack of disclosure frustrated her, but she refused to show it and instead spoke sweetly. "I feel I have lost a few days." *That was an understatement.* "Could you tell me what day I woke up?"

His eyebrows rose. "October 1st."

Thirty days earlier...I did the ritual on October 31st. Trying to be nonchalant, she pursued it further. "And the year...is it correct?"

"What other year would it be?" His eyes narrowed slightly.

Julie let out a false laugh to cover her rising hysteria. "Of course it's 1898...what *was* I thinking?" She put the paper back on the table.

A million thoughts ran through her head. She hadn't paid much attention in any of her history classes. Knowledge of this time period seemed to be missing from her mental data banks. She'd have to rely on any past life memories Naomi chose to reveal.

Julie silently asked God to forgive her for being discontent with her current life and for violating any spiritual laws by listening to Star, and she bargained with Him—*I'll say 10 Hail Marys, 12 Our Fathers, 7 Apostles' Creeds, and as many Glory Bes every day for a year if you send me back the moment I step through the door*, she promised.

She gingerly approached the door and stopped just at the threshold, trying to keep her composure. She closed her eyes, emptying her mind of all thoughts but one. *Let me go home. Please, let me go home.* She took a deep breath with her eyes still closed, and crossed one foot over the doorsill.

CHAPTER TWENTY-THREE

The shrill whistle of a passing steamboat startled Julie. She opened her eyes and saw her feet firmly planted on Erik's front porch. She looked up to see the top portion of the boat's smoke stack releasing a trail of white smoke in the air as it slowly moved south down the Mississippi River. Disappointed, but not surprised, she exhaled as she resigned herself to her fate. Apparently living in her past would continue to happen no matter how many prayers she offered to God. There wouldn't be any "take-backs" for her. She had wanted to see her past and for better or for worse, see it she would.

Under the shadow of the porch roof, she and Erik stood in silence as she surveyed the neighborhood's activity, trying to determine exactly where she was. She smelled air free of fog and exhaust from the RTA. Instead, it held the unmistakable odor of horse manure.

As a horse and carriage passed, the occupant's laughter carried to the porch. An elegantly dressed white woman, wearing a wide-brimmed hat, animatedly moved her gloved hands as she spoke to her companion. Juliana looked down at her bare hands and plain clothes. She touched the material wrapped around her head.

In this lifetime, she realized, she was born into a class much lower than she had been accustomed; made more apparent to her when two more well-dressed women sauntered down the sidewalk with an ebony-skinned woman following a few feet behind, eyes cast down, wearing a white turban, and shuffling under the weight of several heavy packages.

Asking Erik to help her seemed less distasteful now. She realized being in her past would be more challenging on her own. And, Erik didn't seem in any rush to make her leave. He remained at her side, letting her move at her own pace. Only, Julie couldn't find the words to voice her desire for his help, so there was no reason to prolong the inevitable.

Turning to tell him farewell, she stumbled, grabbing the railing post just in time to prevent herself from falling; something was caught under her shoe. She raised her skirt to her ankle and bent over to get a look at it.

"Stop!" Erik commanded, the tone of his voice making her freeze.

He pulled out a handkerchief and bent down on one knee before her. In fascinated curiosity, she watched his hand slide between her ankles with the handkerchief and felt him tug the offending item from under her heel. He stood up with a small red bag held inside the hanky. He stared at the bag, a muscle twitching in his jaw. If looks could destroy, his glare would have incinerated it. With a grimace, he wrapped it securely in the handkerchief and deposited it into his pocket.

"What is that?" Julie asked. If she didn't know better, it looked like a gris-gris bag.

"A calling card," he answered, a dark look crossing his face. "Nothing to concern yourself with."

His face blank and unreadable again, Erik took her hand and placed a few coins into her palm. "In case you're in need of a cabbie, lodgings, food…"

She looked at her palm. The gold coins did not have Lincoln or Washington looking up at her. Lady Liberty stood proudly on the fronts and an eagle with an O stamped underneath its feet on the backs, and written in raised lettering were the denominations of five and ten dollars. These were relics, not to be used, but collected and treasured. In her day that is, she had to remind herself, not this day.

"I want you to send word to me when you have settled, wherever it is you intend to go. You are to let me know you have arrived safely. And if I can be of any assistance, I expect you to call upon me."

She nodded. Part of her still wanted to spill her guts and tell Erik everything she had guessed. Tell him about her life and who she was…where she was from. She could use any help and guidance he could give her. She didn't want to navigate the city alone, and he deserved to know the truth. But this truth was a lot to swallow. In fact, it was downright giving her indigestion.

"Thank you, I will," Julie managed to finally answer. "Umm…before I go, could you tell me what street this is?"

His eyes glinted with curiosity at her question. "St. Charles."

"Okay." At least now she had some bearings as to her location because from where she stood, the landscape was almost foreign. Squaring her shoulders, Julie stepped down the front porch, crossed the stone steps in the yard, and opened the wrought iron gate. She turned to give Erik a final wave of goodbye, but an empty porch and closed front door met her eyes instead. This was it. She was officially alone, feeling terrified and exhilarated.

She knew this wasn't the birth of New Orleans, but it certainly seemed to be in its infancy. Instead of the shaded canopies of majestic oak trees with Spanish moss hanging from their hundred year old limbs, sunlight poured down on St. Charles Ave., leaving nothing untouched, including the young oak saplings swaying in the slight cool breeze. Another steamboat's smoke stack slowly inched its way down the river, and Julie followed in the same direction. She stayed on the brick-paved sidewalk, avoiding the dusty dirt road with unsightly piles of horse dung scattered upon it.

A bell clanged, and she swiveled around to see a streetcar lumbering up the road towards her, not on its customary route, the neutral ground, but on the street *and* being pulled by mule. Staring in disbelief, she stood still. As it passed by her, she saw the passengers looking out the windows and read the sign plastered to its side.

PROGRESS AT ITS BEST!
Electric lines under construction
to serve the Crescent City by 1899.

She looked back at the neutral ground and sure enough, the lines were in the process of being laid down. Like the power lines, she realized every little change around her would be the foundation for her life later on. All the things she took for granted were the careful forethought of generations before her.

"Hey, girl!" A scruffy red-haired man called to her from the side window of the streetcar. "Best be moving on to where you belong." The look of contempt on his face made Julie shudder. She couldn't walk fast enough.

In her hurry, she almost bumped into another light-skinned woman wearing a light pink-colored turban. The woman nodded to Julie and whispered as she walked past her. "You should know better than to look them in the eyes." Julie nodded back, taking note of her advice.

As she continued, Julie passed the area where the future interstate overpass to the Greater New Orleans Bridge would be. At the barren place where the bridge connected the east and west banks of the city, she could see the expanse of clear sky on the afternoon horizon. This New Orleans would take some getting used to.

By the time she reached Lee Circle, her feet were tender and throbbing. These old-fangled shoes offered no arch support at all. She sat on the first bench she came to, looking up at the statue of General E. Lee standing on top of his columned pillar, stoically facing toward Lake Pontchartrain. What had she learned in her short stint at college? He faced due north because one never turns one's back to the enemy.

It felt good to see his familiar face, a timeless friend in this out of time experience. She had passed his statue many times in her future life. Her eyes welled with tears. What was happening to her, Juliana François, right now? If she was here, her lip trembled, was it possible she was dead in the future? She thought about her cherished friendship with James and Heath's charming smile, but a ruckus distracted her.

A bunch of excited children ran around the circle shouting, "A horseless carriage! Make way for the horseless carriage!" Behind them, an awful honking noise made them scatter from the middle of the street as the buggy rolled its way closer. Sure enough, the vehicle looked like a carriage, an open front seat and four spindled wheels, without a horse.

The handsome gentleman on the plush seat turned a small wheel, directing the path of the antiquated car. He followed the circle, lifting his hat to the awed onlookers. Another gentleman lifted his cane in the air to hail the driver, who stopped the carriage by pulling a long stick backwards, keeping the buggy idled in place alongside the sidewalk.

"Isidore," the man on the sidewalk shook the driver's hand while his eyes admired the vehicle. "I didn't think your automobile would be here for a few months!"

"A series of fortunate events made it my lucky day," answered the jovial owner. "Care for a ride?"

"Don't mind if I do!" The man climbed up next to his friend. "So how fast does it go?"

Isidore patted the side of the buggy. "A fair speed, Charles. It's a 4 horse-powered engine, you know." He released the brake and steered the buggy forward.

"Leave it to you, Isidore Newman, to own the first one in the city." The man named Charles laughed. "Now, what's this I hear about you wanting to open a school?"

Their conversation faded away along with the voices of the hollering children skipping and hopping behind the retreating car. Julie watched the car in stark amazement until she couldn't see it any longer, realizing she had just glimpsed the founder of one of the most prestigious schools in New Orleans *before* he had founded it.

A loud bang coincided with the sharp vibration of her bench. Julie jumped up, turning toward the noise. A police officer stood frowning at her, his baton in his hand. "Better be moving along, missy." The officer's apparent dislike unnerved her, but his thick French accent made her cringe. His voice bitterly reminded her of her ex-husband, Simon.

Her heart in her mouth, Julie did not dare to speak. She nodded with her eyes cast down and walked away. She had never been treated this way simply because of the color of her skin. It unnerved her to say the least. She didn't have the emotional strength at the moment to dwell on such blatant discrimination. She just wanted to go home. The urge to get to her house became overwhelming. If she could just get inside, she felt everything would be okay. So, street after street she walked, determined to make it home. That is until she reached Lafayette Square.

Her heart panged with recollection of the building right across from the park. The marble three-story building with two rows of columns, Gallier Hall, would be the place where she and Simon would hold their wedding reception. And now, the sign in front read, *CITY HALL*. This landmark also reminded her there were only six more blocks to Canal Street from here, then another six more to her house. Almost home.

Her feet throbbed. She wished she could take the streetcar or grab a cab—or carriage, rather, certainly not what she thought of as a cab, but she was worried she would do or say something wrong. She didn't want to chance it. It would have to be onward on foot, one painful step at a time.

Throngs of people walked up and down Canal Street, in and out of different stores. Julie halted when a group of giggling girls blocked her path, oblivious to her presence. The eldest looking stepped to the front of the pack.

With an air of importance, she spoke. "I have to stop in Godchaux's to buy some perfume." The other girls looked impressed. "Go on ahead, and I'll meet you under the clock." She pointed down the street. Julie's eyes followed the direction of the girl's finger to a clock affixed under a department store, D.H. Holmes written above it on the façade of the building.

The D.H. Holmes' department store had closed its doors just around the time Julie was the same age as the very girls skipping off to rendezvous there. The older one, who remained behind, crossed her arms and threw Julie an ugly stare. "And, what are *you* looking at?"

Stunned by the child's behavior, Julie cringed, but dutifully dropped her eyes to the ground like the other women of color, while a surge of anger and resentment began to build up inside her. She had never comprehended how life in New Orleans had been so unfair. To know about it was one thing, to live it was another.

Once she crossed the busy thoroughfare, Julie breathed a sigh of relief, shaking with anticipation as she stepped onto Royal Street and closer to home. She noticed more changes along the way. Some of the buildings she recognized as houses were businesses, some businesses were houses, but the feel and energy of the streets, the architecture— iron lattice work, huge locks and hinges on the doors, balconies, inner courtyards—and the colors and smells—*oh, yes, they were exactly the same*.

She glanced down the passages between the buildings to courtyards with their fountains and parterres, some with statues half hidden in roses and vines. She picked up her pace, feeling the call of home, and no longer registering the pain in her feet from the poorly made shoes.

As quickly as she walked, it seemed the people headed toward her walked just as fast. Others crossed over to the other side of the street. Puzzled, Julie slowed her stride to watch them. Some faced stiffly ahead, while others looked back nervously as they scurried away.

When the sidewalk cleared, she saw a very tall, light-brown-skinned woman wearing a turban like her own, only it had seven knots and it was a golden-yellow. Large hoops swung heavily from her earlobes with each step.

A young girl, shabbily dressed, stepped from a doorway, carrying a basket of goods in her arms. Too late, the girl realized she had stepped in front of the woman. She bowed deeply and walked backward into the store and out of the way. The woman gave her an approving nod in return and continued on toward Julie.

Julie could see this woman garnered respect and even fear from the people around her, but she had no clue to why or how she should behave. Should she move from the woman's path? Bow? Stop? The woman continued to saunter forward, a slow smile pulling at her lips. She came to a standstill about three feet from Julie and assessed her with a sweeping glance.

"Ah...Miss Heming...or is it Mrs. de la Croix now?"

Julie turned to look behind her, knowing the woman could not possibly be speaking to her. The street was empty, save for a few faces peeking from behind glass store fronts. Julie could feel her eyebrows shoot up in surprise. "Are you speaking to me?"

The woman gave a hearty laugh that didn't rise to meet her eyes. "So, he's done it already, has he? I've been expecting you."

Julie shifted on her feet. This woman did not make any sense. All Julie could muster was a "Sorry-I-don't-know-what-you're-talking-about" look.

"Monsieur David de la Croix—" The woman paused.

Julie shrugged her shoulders. She watched the smile leave the woman's face.

"Perhaps you know him as Erik."

Julie stiffened. *That* was a name she *did* know.

"You aren't Naomi anymore." The woman didn't pose this as a question. She stepped closer to Julie. "I can help you. I can send you back." At her words, a shiver traveled down Julie's spine, as if someone had just walked over her grave. The woman leaned closer, whispering to her. "Come with me and I can undo what he has done to you."

How did this woman know?

"You...you can send me back?"

"Oh, yes." The woman gave a nod of her head, another smile shadowing her face. "But it will come at a price."

"A price? All I have is fifty dollars."

A genuine laugh erupted from her lips. "Not that kind of price. You will have to do something in exchange for me. You possess something I want."

What could I have that this woman would want?

"I don't know your name," she continued to speak, giving Julie a piercing look. "But I *know* who you are."

"What?" Julie stammered.

"You are one of Naomi's incarnations and I can send you back to the life you should be in *if* you do one little thing for me."

Thoughts of home flashed in her mind—her own bed, James mooching her food, nights walking in the Quarter...Heath...

"What do you want me to do?" Julie blurted. Her insides churned with doubt as a greedy look flickered on the woman's face.

"Annul Naomi's marriage to Erik. Make me her guardian so that I may take care of her."

That's it? That was all the woman wanted? Could it be as simple as that?

"You want to take care of her?" Julie repeated.

"Yes." The woman answered, practically hissing as if a snake about to bite. "Erik means well, but he does not know our customs, our ways. Naomi should be with her own people, yes?"

There was truth to that. Erik, wealthy and with the right skin color, could never understand the discrimination Julie had to endure today. How could he possibly shelter Naomi from that? Presented with a quick fix opportunity for both herself and the welfare of her past self tempted her. Only thing is, this woman gave off mixed signals and Julie had a bad gut feeling about accepting the offer. Before Julie could make her decision and answer, a figure dressed in black inserted himself between them. The man had his back to her.

"Marie," Erik said, his voice low and angry.

Julie peered around his back.

"Erik," Marie replied with equal enmity.

Julie could sense the palpable energy of mutual dislike pass between them just as one would feel a negative charge in the atmosphere right before a thunderstorm. The two stared at the other, until Erik turned his back on Marie to look at Julie.

"Juliana," he said softly. "Are you well?"

She nodded.

"Juliana, is it?" Marie raised her eyebrows.

Erik rounded on her. "Do not speak to her, do not look at her, do not even *breathe* in her direction."

"Why?" Marie challenged him, amused. "What are you going to do about it?"

Ignoring her, Erik threw the red bag at Marie's feet. "And don't come to my house." Several of the business doors slammed shut, hands turned *Open* signs to *Closed* in the nearby windows.

Julie recalled pictures that she had seen of another strong and powerful woman that reminded her of this one. Another woman that used gris-gris bags. She wondered…*Marie…could this woman be Marie Laveau, the infamous Voodoo Queen*?

Dead for a century, her legacy still lived on strongly in Julie's time. In high school, Monika's mother scared them one night after they had gotten in much later than curfew. She told them that Marie Laveau would come visit them while they slept and pull their toes for misbehaving. They stayed awake all night.

Did Erik know he was playing with fire?

Marie looked at the gris-gris bag at her feet, flicked her eyes to Erik's face. She turned to Julie, but directed her comment to Erik. "Juliana can decide for herself who she will and will not speak to."

Erik moved closer to Marie, briefly blocking her eye contact with Julie. "I am warning you to stay away from my wife." The dangerous edge and possessiveness to his voice sent a thrill deep inside of her. For a second, she wondered what it would be like to be his.

It seemed Erik could hold his own against the Voodoo Queen. Mesmerized by the standoff, Julie glanced back and forth between their faces. Marie disclosed no discernible emotion to his strong reaction.

"Juliana is not your wife. Even she knows that." Marie tossed Erik a coy look, baiting him. Erik's eyes darkened and his lips twisted in anger. Julie saw him slip his hand into his pocket, clenching and unclenching his fist. Marie noticed also, her eyes staring warily at his movement. "I'll be on my way." She brushed past them and then turned. "E-r-i-k," she slowly enunciated his name. "Consider your actions as a personal debt to me. In the end, you are going to lose tenfold." Next, she cast her eyes on Julie. "If you should need to find me, I have a house at the Lakefront. Anyone can tell you where it is." With her back straight and head held high, Marie sauntered off with her jingling bracelets the only sound on the empty street.

Erik grabbed Julie by the elbow, turning her toward him. "You *will not* consider going to that woman's house."

She jerked her arm away. "Don't tell me what to do." She spun on her heel, walking away from him. She could see St. Peter Street in tile on the corner sidewalk. Nothing else would delay her. She was going home.

He followed beside her. "That woman means Naomi ill will, Juliana. You cannot go."

She marched forward. "Erik, things are very complicated and there's no time to explain it to you right now. But the truth is, she might be the only person who can help me. I haven't ruled out that possibility."

"*I* can help you. Juliana, trust me."

She felt as if an invisible hand had blocked her path, so she paused. A nagging voice in her soul said, without words, *yes, trust him.*

No. No. She rejected the message. *I need to figure out what is happening first.*

"You realize I will not allow you to go," he said with finality.

"Won't allow me..." Julie stood with her mouth open about to argue, but decided not to entertain him and walked again, Erik keeping up alongside her. She turned left on St. Peter.

"Do you not have somewhere else to be?" she asked Erik as she crossed Bourbon Street. She walked past what would one day be The Cat's Meow. Vague images of the night she sang and met Heath flicked across her mind. It was now someone's personal residence.

Only one more block. She practically skipped.

"No. I am not going anywhere until I see you safely..."

Julie stopped and put a hand up to silence him.

There was her house! She had made it. A sense of security flooded her. If she could just get through the front door. She didn't know how she'd manage it. Maybe she could ask for work? As she pondered, a different familiarity washed over her. The quality of light and shadow, the horse and carriage coming down the street, another turbaned woman crossing the road...she had seen this once before...the night she had put the bracelet on her wrist...

The world felt as if it had been put on slow motion. She turned her head toward the street window of her house and saw her own face looking out between the curtains. The face she had looked at in the mirror for the last thirty-three years. She glanced at Erik, who stared intently in the same direction. He had seen her too! Erik rushed toward the house, and Julie followed at his heels.

CHAPTER TWENTY-FOUR

Juliana's lips were parted, her features etched in shock. Following the direction of her stare, Erik found himself looking at his own home, the one he had purchased for Naomi. And there, looking out the window was a woman with shoulder-length brown hair. He could tell her complexion was fair, but her features were not as easily discernible. She looked down the street in the opposite direction. As he rushed across the road, the woman stepped back from the window, disappearing from view.

The hair stood up on the back of his neck. No one should be in that house. He had sent the Krause sisters home days ago after the wedding, instructing them their services would not be needed, for an indefinite amount of time.

He heard Juliana catch up to him as he opened the door. "Stay here." His voice came out in a low growl. He didn't mean to speak so harshly, but for all he knew, the Voodoo witch could be behind this, and he'd prefer to take the brunt of anything Marie may have planned.

Adrenalin coursing through his veins, he burst into the house and charged straight to the living room. The heady scent of perfume lingered in the air, a mixture of jasmine, ylang ylang, sandalwood, and vanilla—easily identifiable, but a combination he had never encountered before. Otherwise, the room was empty. She couldn't have gone far and there weren't many places she could hide. He heard a soft rustling and spun around ready to confront the unwelcome guest.

"She's not here," Juliana said, walking into the room. He had asked her to wait outside. He had never met such a disobedient, headstrong woman.

"Have you no regard for your safety? I directed you to stay outside the house for a reason," he snarled.

She gave him an indifferent look and walked toward the window where the woman had been. She wrapped her arms around herself, trembling. The unoccupied house was chilly. The fall days had been warm, but the nights had been cold. Feeling a little remorseful for being so harsh, he took off his jacket and held it out to her.

She considered his offering for a moment, then took the jacket and put it on, looking back out the window. "Stay here while I check the rest of the house. Please?" He spoke with as reasonable a voice he could manage.

"I won't move from this spot," she murmured.

Satisfied, he wasted no time searching the remainder of the house. Nothing was disturbed. Everything was in complete order and more importantly, it did not smell unusual. The woman's perfume was only in the one location. He smirked, feeling superior. At least the scent was permanently registered in his olfactory memory. He'd remember the aromatic combination and with it, he'd be able to identify its owner if he were to ever come across the smell again.

It was a small consolation to him. How did the woman simply disappear from the house without a trace? *He* was the master of illusion. Marie could not be capable of a trick such as this on her own. She must be working with someone else.

If the witch didn't stop her antics, he would force her to stop. Erik slammed his hand against the wall in disgust. His tolerance wore thin. He had killed many others for far less. The only element that held him back was the slight chance he might need Marie to send Juliana back. Once he knew for sure that he had no further use of her services, Marie wouldn't cause him any more problems. Permanently.

He strode back into the living room and true to her word, Juliana was still there. She had remained staring out the window, her tignon now on the floor at her feet and her honey-colored curls cascading down the back of his jacket. He felt the blood rushing through his body along with a sudden weakness. The image of her wearing an article of his clothing, took his breath away.

"We can leave now," he said casually. "But I insist you let me walk you the remainder of the way to your house or better yet, tell me the address and I will escort you there by cab."

Without turning around, she commented, "Oh, I'm not going anywhere."

Obstinate woman! First, she had disobeyed him at every turn and now, when he asked her to stay put, she decides to cooperate and take him literally. He spoke patiently to her.

"You cannot stay here. As I said, it is not safe. You may go back home with me or I will take you where you want to go."

She spun around with such a look of fierce determination, it took him off guard. "Let *me* tell *you* how it's going to be. You can go back to your home or you can stay here with me, but I'm not leaving this house."

Taken aback by her strong words, Erik shifted his weight to his heels while he considered her response. With the exception of Marie and the Sultana, no woman had ever stood up to him in such a manner. Naomi certainly would not, neither would Christine.

He found Juliana maddening and intriguing all at once. Her response was such a stark contrast to Naomi's gentle nature. It piqued his curiosity. Who were her family, where she was from, and how did she grow to be such an independent thinker?

He rubbed his chin as these thoughts pressed on his mind. What could her motivation to stay here be? Why not go home now? Could she sense more memories from Naomi? So be it. He would not fight her on this. Instead, he would let events unfold and see what came of it. Patience after all, was his greatest virtue.

"Well, then," he answered. "If we are to stay, I shall have to see about warming this house up and getting the stove started." Juliana exhaled, relaxing her shoulders. Apparently, she had been preparing to put up a fight if he had not consented. "As the first order of business," he continued. "I am going to lock the door. In the meantime, make yourself at home."

She placed her hand on his arm just as he had turned to go. Through his shirt sleeve, he could tell her hand was cold, but to him, where it rested, it felt as if a wave of lava coursed under his skin. With a great effort, he lifted his eyes from her hand and attempted to appear unaffected by her touch.

"Erik, thank you." He saw a trace of turmoil cross her face. "I need to be here. I can't explain it to you any better than that right now." He inclined his head in a way he hoped conveyed acceptance of her gratitude and her explanation, then backed away from her feeling relieved as her hand slid off his arm.

After securing the front door and lighting a fire in the sitting room fireplace, he left Juliana quietly warming in front of it to scour the kitchen for any food that might have been left behind by the Krause sisters. He found a tin of biscuits and a small chunk of left-over cheese. Neither looked very appetizing, but they would have to suffice for tonight.

When he reentered the sitting room, he placed the tray of biscuits and cheese near Juliana should she want to eat. He didn't speak. Instead, he walked directly to the piano and began to play. The music was his voice. With his head bent and eyes closed, he caressed the keys with the familiarity of a lover, coaxing the minor chords to fill the room with all he could not say. He played for his mother, for Christine, for Naomi, and for his loneliness...

♀

The radiant fire did nothing to prevent the occasional chill that shot down Julie's spine. She couldn't stop thinking, analyzing. She had felt instinctively she needed to come to this house, but she never expected to see herself in the window or to feel the hope that surged through her when she had. Did she really think she would be able to enter the house and talk to herself—warn herself—when she knew full well when she had seen the past days ago, she had only been there for a few moments and she hadn't met anyone?

It was the same room she had seen that night—busy wall-paper and old-fashioned furniture, and eerily, it held the scent of Chanel No. 5, the perfume she had worn for the picnic dinner at James' house, the dinner with Heath. She was amazed to realize she had actually been physically in the room only moments before. Except this time, she couldn't get back home by removing an antique bracelet.

And what were the odds that the very house she would own in the future was one of Erik's properties in this time? The tie that bound her here seemed to be Erik. It had to be. He was the connecting factor, the reason for her, Julie, to engage in this lifetime. Hadn't Heath told her that a soul could reincarnate to help another soul learn a lesson? Maybe as Naomi, she could not help Erik, but as Juliana, she could make the difference. Discovering what he needed, solving that problem might be the very point that would allow her to go home.

She didn't realize she had been swaying as she sat in the fireside chair. The soft flow of music had ushered around her for quite some time, steadily growing louder, filling the room and swelling with an intensity she could no longer ignore. The melody was haunting, it was beautiful, and it was so very sad.

Julie rose, finding herself drawn to the piano. Erik played the mahogany grand masterfully.

Engrossed in the melancholy of the music, he bent his head over the keys, making the dark hair that hung over his face look black in contrast to the blue wall and the amber light of the fire.

She made it half-way across the room and froze. She felt her insides clench as wave after wave of icy currents cascaded down her back. Her peripheral vision closed in on her making it seem as though she were looking through the wrong end of a telescope, while her thoughts relived the memory of a different piano and a different player.

Heath. Playing for her. The Blacksmith Bar. The vision of another man playing. This was the moment. Erik was the man. This real-time experience would be a remembrance in the future. Was it even possible for a person to have déjà vu of their déjà vu?

Did she gasp? Did she cry out? Something she did caused Erik to look up and stop playing. His somber gaze searched her face as the memory of Health's shining brown eyes faded from her line of sight.

She could only imagine how she looked to Erik, standing in the middle of the room with her eyes practically bulging out of her head. She heard the piano bench scrape against the floor as he stood up.

"Juliana?" He asked, concern written over his face, one of the rare times it had ever revealed his thoughts to her. He turned to look at the empty space behind him, then back to her. "What is it? What do you see?"

"Nothing..." she lied.

The room felt uncomfortably warm now. And she needed a drink. Badly. She saw him walk around the piano toward her, but she maneuvered the other way, taking off his jacket and tossing it onto the chair by the fire.

Alcohol.

Her eyes scanned the room. Surely, Erik had some in the house. Didn't people in the olden days keep alcohol for medicinal purposes or something?

If she had to tear the kitchen apart, piece by piece, even if it meant she had to drink cherry cordial or some strange equivalent...her nerves begged for relief and it didn't matter where it came from.

"Juliana, what...?" She heard Erik's questioning voice behind her. But Julie had found what she had been looking for and gulped the dark, numbing liquor right from the decanter sitting on the dining room table.

After the first swallow, she recognized by the black licorice taste, it was absinthe. What was it with men and absinthe? She remembered Health's preference for it; James liked it, and now, Erik as well. She didn't see what the big deal was. Frankly, she'd be happier with an ice-cold beer. Julie took another long swig and felt the familiar warmth spread through her body, strength garnered from the alcohol elixir.

She turned around to Erik's astonished face. He pried the half-empty decanter from her unyielding hands as she attempted to get the bottle back to her mouth. She intended to drink it all. She wasn't going to let him have it just like that.

"It is not meant..." He looked from the decanter firmly in his own hand back to Julie. "A lady should not..." He frowned. Julie began to laugh. Erik suddenly looked very funny. The man, with such a rigid personality and controlling ways, stood before her looking as if he were constipated.

She continued to laugh as she stumbled away from him to the fireside chair and plopped down onto the cushioned seat. The several gulps of absinthe were effective enough for now. She bent over to remove the blasted foot deformers people of this time called shoes. *Why hadn't she thought to do this earlier?* She rubbed the sore arches of her feet. *God, what a relief!*

"Juliana, I am gravely concerned by your behavior." Erik's tall shadow stood over her. She looked up at his face. Yep, he was telling the truth. He watched her warily.

"You don't have to be *gravely concerned*," she mocked him. "Everything is fine now." She continued to rub her feet, sighing as the pain in her arches began to ease.

"You are mistaken, I fear. Everything is not fine. Absinthe, if taken in large quantities, can be poisonous. You might have not have concern for your own welfare, but it seems I need to remind you to honor Naomi's body. She is not a woman familiar with spirits. Granted, on very rare occasions, she might partake in them sparingly, but they are not something she would indulge in, tumblers full."

Julie threw her head back in a smile. *Oh, the irony!* She leveled her gaze directly into his eyes. "Oh." Her voice came out strangled. "I beg to differ, Erik, because I can assure you, Naomi truly appreciates 'spirits.' She just doesn't know that she does yet." Then she added under her breath, "It might take her about a century to figure it out."

His eyes narrowed. "What do you mean?"

"It means we have to talk. I've figured a few things out today." She looked down from his searching gaze, feeling uncomfortable. How in the hell could she tell him *she* was Naomi? "I just need a minute." She continued to knead the tender sole of her foot as she thought.

Before she realized what he was doing, he knelt before her and gently massaged her feet. "Let me do this for you."

She sank back into the chair, letting her hands drop as he stroked the soles of her feet, sending undulating currents of welcome respite throughout her body. Her taut legs relaxed, her tense shoulders dropped, and the overall stress on her body from the past day's events, including her long walk, seemed to ebb away under his warm hands. The pleasure of it was almost torture.

"I want to ask you something." Erik's soothing voice resonated in her head.

"Hmmm…" she assented, feeling as though she could deny him nothing.

"Where were you going?"

"To my house." She closed her eyes as his hands continued their rhythmic movements.

"There are only two more blocks on this street. Which one is your house?"

"*This* is my house."

"I think you are confused. This is Naomi's house. Where is your house?" he persisted.

She felt her forehead crease as she thought about his question. "I'm not confused. It is your house now," she acknowledged. "But it will be *my* house…later."

"I see." The tone of his voice sounded patronizing. She was pretty sure he didn't 'see' at all.

"And what of your family?"

The peaceful, foggy feeling in her brain started to evaporate. She rubbed her forehead. "I don't like to talk about them, okay?"

"Will they not be missing you?"

She inhaled.

Visions of blood smears on the floor, her parents' bludgeoned bodies, and the grief of their deaths washed over her. Maybe it was the absinthe, maybe it was the stress, but the memory was as fresh to her as the day it had happened along with the pain and the guilt. Had she had been home that night…maybe…

She choked on the uncontrollable sob that wrenched from her chest, unable to stop the hot tears streaming down her face. Her eyes flew open. She wasn't feeling tipsy anymore. Erik stood up with the decency to look uncomfortably disconcerted.

"They're dead. Please, don't ask me anything else—" she finally managed to blurt out.

Erik knelt down beside her again, looking ill at ease, misery lining his face. Again, he spoke softly, yet with authority. "Do not cry, Juliana."

The moment her name left his lips, a feeling of peace washed over her. Her tears subsided into a few left over sniffles. She raised her arm to wipe her wet face on the sleeve of her shirt. Erik placed a warm, comforting hand on her arm. With his other hand, he reached into his vest pocket and pulled out a handkerchief. Something shiny came out with it and fell with a tinkle to the floor. She blew her nose and watched Erik pick it up. Her mouth fell open as she saw the bracelet dangling from Erik's hand. She saw silver balls with a silver charm attached.

"Let me see that—" she said hoarsely, her heartbeat quickening.

He tried to put it back in his vest pocket. "This is a gift for..."

She waved away his explanation and grabbed the jewelry from his hand, turning the face of the charm upward. On the front was a complicated braided pattern—interwoven blonde hair with an inscription on the back, a single word: *Nightingale*. Although in her day the bracelet contained a pattern of brown hair, it was unmistakable.

"Oh my God." This was unbelievable. She raised her eyes from her hand.

"What is it?" Erik asked.

She held her hand palm up, the piece of jewelry resting there for him to see. "This is my bracelet."

CHAPTER TWENTY-FIVE

"Your bracelet?" Erik could not suppress his disbelief.

Juliana nodded her head vigorously. "Yes, it's mine."

"That's not possible." It had been many months earlier in Paris when he had unfastened the latch from the owner's wrist as her hand had brushed against the theater curtain he had hidden behind. "This bracelet came to New Orleans with me from France."

"Oh...so *you're* the one who brought it here." She arched an eyebrow. "How did you come to own it, by the way?"

Erik suppressed his annoyance as he stood up again. "What are you implying?"

"This is a one-of-a-kind creation...Jenny Lind's daughter wants it back, but it will never happen though, will it?" Juliana sighed while looking at the bracelet in her hand.

A jolt of shock enveloped him. How could she possibly know? Erik relaxed the tension in his jaw, but his voice still came out gruff. "Explain yourself."

"I want to, really, but you're making me nervous." She looked up at him with troubled eyes. "If you sat down..."

Erik deposited himself into the other fireside chair, crossing his leg over his knee.

Leaning forward, Juliana spoke to him entreatingly. "I need you to keep an open mind."

He remained silent, inclined his head forward, and waved his hand indicating she should get on with it. *Keep an open mind.* He was one of the most forward-thinking men in his generation. What he found difficult to keep was possession of his patience even though it was his greatest virtue.

She took a deep breath, exhaled, and searched his face. "I know you might find this difficult to believe, but whatever problems you are dealing with, I'm certain I have come to help you resolve them. I believe this is the reason I am here."

He opened his mouth to reply, but she was too quick for him.

"No, don't say anything," she interrupted. "Let me get everything out before I lose my nerve, and then you can ask me whatever you want." She stood up and began to pace back and forth in front of him.

Erik leaned farther back into the chair. He would hear what she had to say, but working on the potion to send her back was about to become his top priority. Juliana's mind seemed to be coming unhinged by his conjuring and he imagined it could be affecting Naomi as well.

"I'm not sure where to begin. I guess it all started with the bracelet. No." She frowned, talking to herself. "That won't do. He won't understand how I got it." She looked at him again. "I'll have to start with the hard stuff."

From where he sat, it *was* possible she was on the verge of a mental collapse—first, the emotional outburst, the bracelet, the house and now, talking to herself. Or maybe she was having ill effects from the absinthe? She had consumed quite a large quantity.

"There is no way to sugarcoat this, everything I have told you is true. I am the owner of that bracelet, I live in this house, and my name is Juliana François. There is only one little detail I've left out." Her brow furrowed and her expression became pensive. "My birthday is August thirteenth," she paused. "*Nineteen seventy-six.*" Her words hung in the air.

Erik's mouth felt dry.

"And before I woke up here in Naomi's life, I was supposed to meet up with a friend." She paused again, reflecting. "God, he hasn't even been born yet." She let out another deep sigh. "And just minutes before I was to meet him, I ended up here. The year was 2009 when I left."

Her story was completely ludicrous, of course, but he wouldn't tell her that. Masking his feelings, he rubbed his chin thoughtfully, starting a mental list. *Sweet grass, juniper, clove, and yarrow would be the first combination to try. If that doesn't work, maybe nettle and buckthorn would.*

She let out a shaky laugh. "You can't imagine how relieved I am that you are taking this so well. I mean, I've had a hard enough time trying to accept the truth myself." She sank back into the chair across from him and smiled. "You know, it feels so good to get this off my chest. I didn't realize what a weight I carried. I mean, if I were in your position, I'm not so sure I would be so gracious—"

He wasn't sure what to make of her. During the few years of his childhood spent with Ellendora, he'd experienced one whose mind was truly unstable, enduring her irrational behavior, disconnected thinking, and exaggerated body language. Yet, here Juliana was, albeit nervous, but very sincere. She certainly believed what she was saying. Could she be telling the truth?

Sitting straighter, Erik's heart quickened at the thought. Perhaps, not only did he possess the power to conjure a soul, but also the ability to force the applications of time to bend to his will. His spirit lightened. Why not? If it could be done, *he* would be the one to accomplish it. It was certainly unconscious on his part, he had acted on pure instinct. He warmed with a deep self-satisfaction. Imagine what he could achieve if he actually put his mind to it. He needed to know the truth, the absolute truth from her. Erik suppressed the urge to smile. The absinthe, he had a way to infiltrate her mind, and he was going to put it to good use.

"And that's when I knew!" Juliana's voice jarred him.

"What?" He had been tuning out everything she had been saying.

"That's what I'm trying to tell you. About a hundred years from now, I will put on this bracelet." She held it up to the firelight. "My house will change. My living room will look just as yours does now, and I will walk to the window to look out. The bracelet will start to burn my skin and I'll take it off." She stared at her wrist with a distant look in her eyes. "Next thing I know, my house will return to the way it was, and the last time I'll see that bracelet is right before I hide it in the back of my closet. The next day, I will end up here with you."

Erik found her comments perplexing. *What could the bracelet possibly have to do with this?*

"Don't you understand what this means?" she asked fervently. "The reason why I knew no one was in the house is because *I* was the woman in the window. I know because it had already happened and also, well...because the perfume I wore that night was still in the room."

"You were the woman in the window?" He could not keep the incredulous tone out of his voice. Erik recalled the brief glimpse he had gotten of the woman—slender and petite, shoulder-length brown hair, and fair skin. That was Juliana? The intoxicating scent belonged to her? A surge of keen alertness crept through him. He felt very much alive at the moment. He leaned toward her. "Tell me what happened directly before you woke up here."

"Follow me." She jumped up and led Erik to the second bedroom. She put her hands flat against the wall that separated the second and third room. "I knocked down this wall to make my room bigger and discovered a loose floorboard, this one." She pointed downward toward a piece of flooring peeking out from under the wall. "When I lifted it up, I found a box that had a vial of some kind of powder, a roll of parchment paper, and a journal." She spoke without taking a breath. "I was told to reconstitute the powder with oil and rub it on my skin. Then James' friend called me and translated the words on the parchment. Next thing I knew, I couldn't move. I fell to the floor. Then I woke up in your house."

She rubbed oil on her skin?

He could not get the thought out of his mind. Who put the powder there? Who told her what to do? He got the sinking feeling he had conjured her in complicity with someone else. His ego deflated. And he felt a twinge of something else, who was James?

"Slow down, Juliana," he said with a calm he did not feel. "You said that the parchment had to be translated. What language was it written in?"

"That's the thing...so unusual." Her curls shook as she tilted her head in thought. "I should be able to remember what it's called, but it was the first time I'd ever heard of it before." Apprehension stirred in the pit of his stomach while she searched her mind for the answer. "I don't know." Her face was lined with frustration. "All I can tell you is that hardly anyone speaks it anymore."

He remembered the first words he had uttered when he thought he was calling Christine. *Entzun nire ahosta.* "Was it Basque?"

Her eyes lit up. "That's it!"

Before she could ask him how he knew, he pressed forward. "Who told you to reconstitute the powder?" Again he surged his question into her mind, demanding she answer.

"I..." she hesitated. "Star, a Voodoo practitioner told me what to do."

"Why did you listen? Why did you do it?" If the practitioner was anything like Marie, Juliana's best interest was not at the heart of this advice.

"She read my palm," Juliana said defensively. "She told me that I had the chance to see my past life. I didn't want to pass up the opportunity."

"And where did it get you?" Erik felt cross. Star's meddling had prevented Christine and Naomi from making the transition. Now, Naomi was possibly slipping in and out of the future, no doubt frantic and disoriented, perhaps beheld as a ranting madwoman.

"Look, I didn't have much time to think it through. The 'window of opportunity' was going to close by the end of that day. It was a now-or-never choice." She crossed her arms. "In hindsight, it was probably not the best decision I've ever made in my life."

Her life? It dawned on him he knew nothing of her life. Was she married? Did she have children? But his momentary curiosity was overshadowed by his concern for Naomi.

"Not the best decision?" he sneered. "And what of Naomi? Have you given any thought as to what has happened to her?"

"Obviously not!" She glared at him. "I didn't give any thought about what would happen to me at all." She stomped past him, heading out of the room.

"You?" He grabbed her elbow. "I did not say you."

Her arm trembled in his grasp and he could sense her trying to control her anger. She spoke to him slowly, as if to a small child. "Haven't you been listening to anything I said?" An ironic smile pulled at her lips. "I *am* Naomi and *she* is *me*. She is my past and I am her future."

♀

Juliana rubbed her arm as soon as Erik let go of it. His face, even in the shadow of the dimly lit hallway, looked stunned. He leaned against the wall, rubbing his hands over his face and through his hair. She knew exactly how he felt, having experienced something akin to that when she had figured out the situation for herself. If she smoked, now would be a great time to light one up.

He blinked a few times, all the while keeping his eyes on her, his lips twisted slightly in a grimace. Whatever he used to make his appearance look normal had partially worn off. The right side of his face looked scarred again.

"If this is true," he questioned her. "Where is Naomi?"

Juliana licked her dry lips. "I'm not sure, but if we are the same soul...well, I suppose she is with me, here, now."

"And what of your body?" He studied her, revealing none of his thoughts. Did he even believe her?

"Erik, I'm scared to even guess." She shuddered. It was true. She felt Naomi was with her, especially in the mirrored room when she was reliving Naomi's rape. Now, not so acutely, but she knew about people and feelings from Naomi's life that she could not possibly know about on her own. If what she suspected was true, where did that leave her in the future? Could her body exist without a soul? Had her actions caused her own death?

He pulled a small leather book from the other vest pocket, opened it, and held it out to her. "Tell me. Did the writing look like this?"

Her heart skipped a beat as she flipped through it. The pages were filled with writing in what she recognized to be the unique Basque language, scribbled in red ink. Some pages held diagrams and lists.

The leather-bound book was in pristine condition, not well-worn like the one from the chest, but there was no doubt in her mind that it was the same one.

Her voice came out breathless as she clutched the book in her hand. "This is the exact book I will find under the floorboards. How did you get hold of it?"

He walked back to living room fireplace and stoked the logs with a poker, keeping his back to her. "It is mine." He turned around, his expression inscrutable. "It seems that our destinies *are* intertwined, Juliana."

Her heart did a quick leap. She felt vindicated by his acknowledgement. But where did they go from here? She would need to understand Erik's role in their circumstances in order for them to move forward. In order for her to help him, she told herself.

"Why then–," she hesitated. He raised his eyebrows in polite encouragement for her to continue, so she struggled to gather her thoughts. "I am wondering, what exactly you and I—I mean, you and Naomi—what were you trying to do the night I arrived?"

His blue eyes stared hard at her for a few moments before he finally answered. "You may not like what you are about to hear."

She gave a small smile. "Could it be any worse than what I've found out about her life already?" He stiffened and Julie remembered the cold fury on Erik's face when she had told him about the rape. She felt so distant from that experience now, as if it had happened eons ago. The real fact was that for her, it had.

"Perhaps not," he consented as he sat back into the chair. "None-the-less, you may find it distasteful."

"Just say it." Julie much preferred for the Band-Aid to be pulled off in one quick yank rather than slow and torturous.

"We were in the middle of... an exchange, if you will. Naomi has affections for another and so do I. Most happily, for our sakes, the people in question are married to each other." He cleared his throat. "On the night you arrived, I expected another woman, Christine, to be in Naomi's body and Naomi..."

"Would have been in Christine's," Juliana finished. "I don't know. It doesn't feel right to me." She felt a flush rise to her cheeks. "I feel the love Naomi has for you, Erik. And these are words I would never use, but she holds you in such high regard. She trusts you implicitly. Why would she give that all away? I don't sense any affection for another man."

A twisted smile tugged at his lips. "No doubt when you meet Monsieur de Marigny it will all come flooding back to you. Raoul's charms appear to be irresistible to any woman he bestows them upon, including Naomi."

She had difficulty grasping his explanation. "Even if we, I mean, you and she, 'loved' Raoul and Christine, they apparently love each other. Why would we come up with this crazy scheme to swap places?"

"Because, Juliana, things were not as they appeared to be. Naomi became a confidant of Christine when she assisted with the baby."

"They have a baby!" Julie interrupted, becoming more uneasy by the minute. Being adopted, this struck a chord in Julie. She would never tear a family apart. Why would Naomi?

"A baby," he smoothly continued. "Named after me."

Julie felt her jaw drop open.

"What you don't understand is that Christine and I were engaged before..." He paused a moment. His eyes looked glassy in the firelight. "She believes me to be dead and has gone on with her life, but her heart still harbors love for me. I am sure of it, and so was Naomi, or she would have never agreed to exchange her life for Christine's."

His argument compelled and settled over her, daring her to reject it, but she still had questions. "Well, there is one person left in this complicated puzzle who gets the short end of the stick. What about Raoul? He loves Christine. Why would he want me, I mean, Naomi?"

Again the twisted smile accentuated Erik's misshapen face. "Raoul's affections for Christine are questionable at best. He is seldom home, they quarrel in front of Naomi, and when all was said and done, he would be none the wiser. His wife would still be with him, her soul would be with me. Naomi had feelings enough for the both of them."

She reflected on his words. For every question she had, he had a ready, plausible answer to give in return. Disturbing as the answers were, the words from his mouth were oddly reassuring, and she felt inclined to accept them. She concentrated hard to fight the fogginess in her mind.

"Okay, if this went down the way you say it did, why were you going to keep Christine locked up in that house like a prisoner?"

Again, Erik was at the ready, keeping his voice slow and even. "Imagine the shock she would experience seeing me since believing me dead." He leaned toward her. "And you, yourself, can attest to the shock of waking up in another's body, another's life. It was for her benefit that I wanted her there, only until she could become accustomed to her new reality and embrace it with calm and resolve."

The fire crackled in the silence that followed. Juliana sighed. This was the crazy stuff of soap operas. Her first instinct was to disbelieve it, but again, Erik's voice reverberated in her mind soothingly, convincing her it was true, or was it her memories as Naomi reminding her that it was?

"What are we supposed to do now?"

"What if?" Erik began, stopping abruptly.

" 'What if—'what?" her heart quickened.

He raised his eyebrows, his expression hopeful. "What if you have come to make this happen, physically?"

She threw him a quizzical look until the answer dawned on her. "You mean somehow get Raoul and Christine to break up?"

He nodded.

"Why don't you just go see her, let her see for herself that you're alive?"

"This must be handled very delicately. I could not appear on her doorstep so suddenly, without warning. She would likely think me a ghost."

She considered his logic. This whole situation was unorthodox, insane even, but if it was the truth, what choice did she have? "If this is really the problem, maybe I'll get to go home once we make it happen."

"My thoughts are in unison with yours. Why else would you be here?" Erik's demeanor was relaxed and convincing.

"So what is the plan? How do we go about doing this?" Julie would have to rely on his expertise. She didn't know any of the social etiquette in this time period, let alone how to get around the racial discrimination.

"I wonder…" Erik looked at her. "You mentioned that a palmist told you that you were able to see your past, correct?"

"Yes," she nodded.

"Normally, I am a very private person. I keep my life compartmentalized. You would only know what you see of me and nothing further, but it seems for an occasion such as this, I will have to make an exception."

"You can't mean literally that no one knows you. Surely Christine *knows* you, your life."

A shadow crossed his face. "Christine knows only of her life with me, but not of my life."

She could understand the fleeting expression on his face. It was sad not to be known by anyone. But at the same time, she felt honored and had a mounting anticipation at the thought that he would reveal a part of himself to her. She saw a glint of mischief in his eyes when he spoke.

"I spent several years living among gypsies."

"Real, live gypsies?" she asked, surprised.

"Is there any other kind?" His genuine smile, followed by a warm chuckle, gave her a glimpse of a much younger Erik, perhaps how he looked in his nomadic life with gypsies. "It was then I became acquainted with the art of palm reading. I am quite knowledgeable, in fact."

"Really?" Juliana found herself returning his grin.

"Yes, really." Erik quickly became the most unusual man she had ever met, next to Heath.

He continued. "If your lines told the story of coming here, perhaps they will reveal to me the next path you should take." He reached out for her hand. "Shall I give it a try then?"

Feeling light-hearted, relieved of the weight that had been bearing down on her, and with a sense of purpose and direction, she held out her hand to him. "You shall."

He kept his eyes on her face while turning her palm away from her line of sight toward the light of the fire. He looked down, frowning at her upturned hand.

"Impossible!" he stood in disbelief, letting her hand drop.

"What is it?" Panic rose in her gut as he paced the room. "Tell me what you saw."

He stopped dead still, facing her. The look on his face held a mix of disbelief and sympathy. He did not answer her. She stood up and walked closer to the fire to let the light shine on her palm then looked down at her hand to see for herself why he would react in such a way.

She looked up into the sad blue eyes staring back at her, the eyes that already knew her distress. She looked down again at both hands for good measure…two blank palms reflected back at her in the light.

Smooth…with no lines at all.

CHAPTER TWENTY-SIX

This could not bode well.

It was uncommon enough to see a Simian line—a solitary mark across the palm—but, among thousands of truth-seekers, he had never seen a palm without lines at all.

Erik racked his memory to no avail, trying to remember Naomi's hands before Juliana inhabited her body. How could it be that he wouldn't have noticed something such as this before now?

Juliana's wrenching cry of "Oh God!" filled the room, causing a pause in his heartbeat. Her golden eyes searched his face, begging for reassurance. For a moment, the briefest moment, he had none to give her. He could only infer, as she apparently had, it must mean she had no future.

Unless…

"Pardon my behavior." Erik bowed his head penitently. "I was taken aback for a moment and in doing so, misinterpreted the meaning of your palms," he said, the lies flowing easily.

Perhaps not a lie, he reminded himself. Juliana relaxed her stance, letting her hands hang limply at her side, hope and curiosity lighting her eyes

"Under the circumstances, I think it would be fair to deduce that your story, here and now, has yet to be written. You have a blank slate, if you will." She blinked a few times and looked down at her palms again, considering his words.

"That certainly makes sense," she acknowledged, her voice much lighter. She blew a quick breath of air, placing a hand over her chest. "For a moment there I thought—"

"So," he refused to let her finish her sentence. "I think we should move forward with the plan we discussed a few minutes ago. It will need some fine tuning to be successful." He saw a flicker of doubt cross her face. "It must be done. It is for the best, Juliana." He intoned the words, so that his suggestion penetrated her mind, and watched the uncertainty erase from her face.

"Yes, yes…of course, you're right. What do you need me to do?" Juliana sat down, looking up at him.

That was a good question. He thought on it for less than a moment.

"I shall write a note on Naomi's behalf to Christine explaining your absence, requesting a visit in a few days' time." He was confident it would be enough time to teach Juliana the floor plan of the house, who lived there, and how to behave becoming to a woman of her station. She was a gentleman's wife to be sure, but one of color, and there were no exceptions to that.

"And what excuse do I have for not visiting sooner?" She arched a brow.

"You have been recuperating from an unfortunate fall or misstep, one in which you hit your head—not seriously, but enough to require a few days rest."

Yes, that would do nicely. Christine would automatically attribute any misspeaking or odd responses by Juliana to the injury and excuse her behavior.

"I want you to get back into her house, back into her confidence. I want you to find out everything you can, see for yourself that Christine was meant to be with me. Convince her to give in to her feelings for me."

Juliana's jaw dropped open. "Are you crazy?" Her voice cracked. "Christine thinks you are dead! That is *not* a good plan."

"I want her to remember me, to think of me, to long for me. If you can get her to that place, I will do the rest."

He pictured himself whispering in Christine's ear as she slept, coaxing her from the bed, urging her to leave with him, his godchild in tow. The boy was part and parcel, a package deal, and he welcomed it. His own family at last!

Erik had taken extraordinary measures to honor his promise to Christine and Raoul, the promise to set them free. But, it seemed that the very Universe told him Christine belonged to him body *and* soul. It was time to give up the notion of owning her soul alone. It was all or nothing and he was not accustomed to walking away with nothing.

MOTHER AND BABY MISSING—the headlines would be sensational. The community would rally to search, but after months passed for some, or years passed for others, people would no longer seek them, accepting that neither would return. He would have to work hard at it, but in the end, Christine would believe it had all been her idea and they'd leave New Orleans, perhaps for the Pyrenees, and make a home together.

Juliana rubbed her face, fatigue lining her eyes. "I don't know. Why don't we make a more definitive plan after I've gotten in there and checked out the situation for myself? Look, it's late and I'm tired. Can't we start this again in the morning?"

"Most certainly." It would be good to have Juliana out of his way for a time. He had much to do in the next few hours.

♀

Erik paced his stride to match the rhythmic music of a local brass band even as the tune faded behind him. The music of New Orleans resonated in the veins of the people here. He found it easy to embrace this town as his own.

The wind had changed from southeasterly to northern, bringing an unwanted sting of cold to his face and hands. As he continued on his errand, he thought about the constant shifting of events. Although these shifts were troubling to him at first, once again hope burned in his heart, so much so that the cold did little to bother him. He could endure all things if in the end his reward would be a life with Christine.

The hope surging in him turned into the deep familiar longing that usually inhabited his heart. He knew time would best be served traveling by carriage, but he had a restless energy that could only be put to rest by constant movement, which he did, placing one foot in front of the other. After delivering the notice for reinstatement to the Krause sisters, all he had left to do was deliver "Naomi's" letter to Christine.

A light was on in the nursery window when he arrived at the de Marigny's home. Christine must be up with the petit garcon. Smiling, Erik dropped the letter into the mail slot, slipped around to the side alley of the house, and climbed the drainpipe. He couldn't wait to see her face, even if a pane of glass separated them. Not for long though; he could almost taste the sweet victory of having Christine as his very own.

Instantly, the moon became dark in his eyes, and his smile twisted into a grimace of rage. Slumped in the nursery rocking chair with a pistol in his lap, Raoul slept soundly. The fool! Did that man think gun powder and metal would prevent Erik from taking what he wanted? Did Raoul have the gall to believe that guarding the child could stop him from taking what was rightfully his?

He would rush upon Raoul as if a lion to its prey…instead of sharp claws, a rope…instead of a lion's roar, a man's rage. Erik swung his hand back, preparing to break the glass, but a sudden thought stilled his hand in mid-strike.

What would Juliana think?

He didn't know where the unbidden thought had come from, but the prospect of her thinking ill of him quelled the rage. He lowered his hand, glanced once more at Raoul with contempt, then quickly descended the drainpipe. He had to refocus. Juliana agreed to help him. She believed she had come to assist him and he needed her to do just that.

She intrigued him greatly. He could learn much from her...new technologies, philosophies...the knowledge of what the future held. She could answer so many questions that haunted his mind. But there was more to it than that, he knew.

This woman looked at him with Naomi's face, but the golden eyes now embodied depth, character, and an infuriating mule-headedness he'd never had to battle with. He shook his head while tenderness stole over him. Her eyes were the only ones that saw his face and never flinched, hers and hers alone.

She chose to gamble on him and he intended to give her the grand payout. He walked up the steps to the porch of his grand St. Charles Avenue home. Inside he would start to compound an herbal mixture in preparation for sending her back. She depended on his help in return and he would not let her down.

He would forever be in Juliana's debt for her part in delivering Christine to him. Once she returned to her own time, her own life, he would lavish such luxury and care on Naomi that it would take her breath away. Naomi would not have to lift a finger or want for anything. True, Naomi might never understand why he would abandon her to be with Christine, but that could not be helped. She didn't know it, but she would be his savior, and he would honor her accordingly.

♀

Footsteps echoing on the hardwood floor and the clanging of pots and pans stirred Julie from her slumber. It had been a sound sleep without any dreams at all, at least none that she could recall. She remembered everything from last night though. Today, she and Erik would make some decisions about how to move forward.

She pushed the blankets away, but gripped them tighter when she realized she heard female voices in the house. Erik hadn't told her anything about visitors. What now? She was about to get up when two robust women bustled into her room.

"Guten morgen," the first woman said as she hurried across the room with a bright smile and opened the curtains, letting the sunlight stream in.

"Now, sister," said the second woman, carrying a tray of food, reproached the first. "Speak English. You know our Mimi doesn't understand the language of the mother country. Sit back now, Mimi."

Julie did as she was told and kept quiet. The woman placed the tray across her lap and unfolded the napkin while the other laid out clothes from the wardrobe. Both strangers were rotund, big-boned, well-endowed women with mousey-brown hair.

"Bea," said the one arranging clothes. "What did you do with the blue skirt?"

Bea sighed. "I brought it with us, Agnes. I just ironed it. Go look in the living room."

Agnes winked at Juliana as she left the room.

"Honestly." Bea squeezed lemon into the cup of dark liquid on the tray. "She'd forget her head was on her shoulders if I weren't here to remind her."

Julie gave her a small smile, but still kept quiet. Obviously Naomi knew these women well. Why didn't Erik give her a head's up so she could fake her way through this a little better?

"So," Bea gave her a knowing look, then began to cut up the links of sausage on her plate. "How's the lady of the house this morning?"

"Fine." Julie thought short, simple answers would be best for now. "Really, Bea, that's not necessary. I can…" She was going to say, cut up my own meat, when a spoonful of food was thrust into her open mouth.

"Now, now," Bea patted her hand. "Monsieur de la Croix explained everything about your fall. How dreadful! We don't want you to worry about anything today. Agnes and I will attend your every need." Bea put another spoonful of food in Julie's mouth.

Julie swallowed the warm buttery grits in one gulp. She was going to kill Erik.

"Where *is* my husband?" She tried to ask nonchalantly once she had swallowed.

"Don't know, dear. He wasn't here when we let ourselves in. Don't worry your pretty head about it. I'm sure he will be home soon."

♀

There was no denying the sisters cared about Naomi, but Julie had had quite enough of their attentions for one morning. After being spoon-fed breakfast, bathed, and dressed without privacy, she was ready to be rid of them. And while trying to act grateful, it was difficult to quell her annoyance of their smothering, and the irksome fact that Erik wasn't there as a buffer. Where was he? They were in this together, yet she felt as if he had left her to drown by herself.

Once Julie had promised to sit quietly and work on her needlepoint did the Krause sisters leave her alone. Only Julie didn't know how to needlepoint. However, she could go for a good book right now to take her mind away from the here and now, although she was pretty sure Naomi probably couldn't read.

This sucked. The sisters would more than likely have twin coronaries if they walked in and discovered she miraculously learned to read over night, but she couldn't sit for hours pretending she knew to how to work a needle and thread either. Unless...

Julie gave frequent looks over her shoulder as she quickly browsed the small assortment of hard-bound books inside a cabinet with jester's faces carved into it. Finally finding one of interest, she pulled it off the shelf...*Great Expectations*...at least she had heard of this one. She plopped into the chair closest to the window so she could peek out on occasion. She kept the needlepoint hoop on her lap to cover the book if one of the sisters came in. And if they were too quick for her, she'd say she only flipped through the book to look at the pretty pictures. That's the best solution she could come up with.

An hour later, engrossed in Pip's story, a rap on the door startled her. Her heart leapt. Perhaps Erik was finally home? But why would Erik knock on his own front door? She pulled the sheer curtain away from the window and saw the back of a tall man as he stood on the sidewalk, walking stick raised to tap on the door again.

She got up and looked down the hallway. Neither Agnes nor Bea must have heard the knocking. Julie struggled with two deadbolts and several other locks in order to open the door. She rolled her eyes at Erik's excessiveness. She couldn't decide if he was being overprotective or just being paranoid. She swung the door open just as the man had raised his walking stick to rap on the door again.

Several things about the man struck her at once. He was extremely tall, possibly seven feet, at least. His glossy hair, pitch-black, revealed itself from under the old-fashioned, yet stylish hat he wore. His facial structure had perfect symmetry with a Romanesque nose very similar to Erik's.

"My card," he spoke in a sonorous tone, while quicker than thought, he was on the top step of the stoop, brandishing something small toward her. She noted his body was well-proportioned as he stood with graceful ease, patiently just inside the doorframe. He was the closest thing she'd seen to Herculean. He was larger-than-life, and handsome, but that wouldn't quite describe him. Julie found him to be beautiful, really beautiful.

She forced herself to wrench her eyes away from him and take the card. It was hand-painted with a picture of the walking stick he held in his hand to the left of the border—shaft overlaid with etched silver topped by a large, round quartz crystal as the handle. Stylized rays of light spread out from the crystal across the card and in the center was the man's name.

Izak Ulloa

"Might I prevail upon you to fetch Monsieur de la Croix or whatever he may be calling himself these days? In fact," he gave her a wicked, attractive grin that took her breath away. "Why fool ourselves by this merry game? If you would kindly let Erik know I am here." He tipped his hat at her.

Julie felt oddly calm, unsurprised by the arrival of this extraordinary man or how he happened to know Erik's real identity. She found herself filled with an overwhelming urge to please this Izak. So, in her most apologetic voice, she tried to explain Erik's absence.

"He isn't here. I don't know where he is or when he'll be back." Izak gave her another dazzling smile, almost as if he knew already that Erik was away. "May I help you with something?" she added.

"Yes, you may." He leaned in toward her, not crossing the threshold, his green eyes boring into hers. Their iridescent quality captivating her. All she could see was shade after shade of green in layers like peacock feathers at the center of his eyes and an outer iris rimmed in black. "You can invite me inside."

He's right. She thought. *I should let him into the house.* She spread her arm back to gesture him inside as she was about to vocalize the invitation. At the same time, the back screen door slammed as Bea rushed into the hallway, interrupting the discourse.

"We'll be having none of that, Madame de la Croix. You know perfectly well no one is allowed inside while the master of the house is away." She moved Julie away from the door and started to close it. "I'm sorry, sir. You will have to come back another time."

"Most understandable," Izak acquiesced, stopping the door with the palm of his hand. "Before I depart, let me leave this along with my card." He withdrew an envelope from his vest pocket and motioned for Julie to take it. She hesitated for a moment, but stepped in front of Bea and accepted it, rewarding Izak with a shy smile. He smiled down at her and winked, speaking in a conspiratorial whisper for her alone to hear. "Tell him to consider this as a gift from me. Tell him the de Marignys will be in attendance. Tell him all the players will be in play." He tipped his hat again, leaving faster than her eyes could register.

"Lord that tall fellow sure can move," Bea commented as she locked the door again.

What could his message mean? She looked at the thick envelope in her hands. She turned it over to open it and felt a small slap on her hand.

"What has come over you, Naomi? Monsieur de la Croix opens his own mail." Bea took the envelope and placed it on the silver card receiver on the small entry table next to the door. "Heaven knows what would have happened if I hadn't come in just when I did." She shook her head. "A stranger in the house, think of that. You must have hit your head harder than was thought." She led Julie back to the chair she had been reading in. "Sit here and I'll bring you a nice cup of hot tea."

The remainder of the day passed by without further incident since Julie did nothing more than sit in the living room, staring out the window. She couldn't concentrate on the book that hung loosely from her hand. She vaguely recalled eating supper served to her on a tray in the same chair and could not seem to recall when daylight turned to twilight then to dusk.

The only constant thoughts running through her mind were about Izak—how he looked, his smile, his voice. She should have let him in. Why hadn't she let him in? Someone stopped her from doing so.

She could hear the sisters' hushed whispers of concern. Should they leave her alone in such an odd state or stay until Monsieur de la Croix returned? As they bickered over their dilemma, Erik walked in the front door.

Good. She had a message to give him. Now what was it?

♀

Erik was bone-tired. He had been pushing himself too hard for too long and it took a toll on his body. He disliked weakness in people but not more so than in himself; he should be above all that. It frustrated him that he actually required the basics, food, water, and sleep, like the regular masses.

He had just spent the last several hours meticulously hand-penciling the layout of Christine's house to review with Juliana this evening. He had tonight and tomorrow to ready her for the delicate undertaking. But first, he might try for a bit of quiet, to rest his eyes and revive his senses.

He opened the front door and placed the rolled blueprints on the entry table, hung his coat on the hall cabinet's hook, and caught a glimpse of himself in the mirror, his powder and paste were smeared, darkened shadows haunted his eyes, and his hair was disheveled, no doubt from the countless times he had run his hands through it in frustration. He was fortunate the darkness had long set in and the hallway was poorly lit.

"Oh, thank goodness, sir," Agnes greeted him by the door with Bea directly behind her sister in the hallway, glancing from the living room then back to him.

He looked at the wall clock. "It is half-past the hour. Did I not instruct you to leave at six, no exceptions?"

"Yes, sir, you did." This time Bea spoke. "But, Mimi has not been quite herself this afternoon and…"

What did Juliana do? He could only imagine.

"I thought I clearly explained to you about that. She is not herself right now as a result of a nasty bump to the head."

"Yes, sir, you did," she repeated. "She was a little less like herself this morning, too true, but what I speak of is how she has been since the gentleman caller left."

Erik stiffened. *Did Joe B find her?*

"What caller?" His voice rang out, startling the sisters.

"I've not seen him before, sir." Bea scuttled past him, retrieving the card and envelope from the small table. "He left these for you," she said, handing them to him. "We'll be on our way now, but we thought you should know." Agnes nodded in agreement.

"You did the right thing," he acknowledged, as they walked past him out of the door. "Take tomorrow off. I will stay with Naomi the entirety of the day myself."

The sisters exchanged worried looks at each other. "Yes, sir," they both said. He closed the door behind them, bolting it shut.

Erik looked at the card, dismissing it since he was not familiar with the name. He tapped the envelope against the palm of his hand as he walked into the living room. Juliana sat in the chair closest to the window, a dazed look on her face. She jumped up when her eyes lit upon the envelope.

"I've remembered!"

"What have you remembered?" Had she gained some new insight into Naomi's life?

"The message Izak asked me to give you."

"You spoke to him." It was not a question, but disbelief. He controlled the tone of his voice, barely keeping it level. He was irritable before, now a flood of additional unwanted emotions threatened to explode. Juliana could have single-handedly jeopardized her safety and Naomi's. What if it had been Alphonse at the door? What if it had been Marie or if this man was in league with Marie? Foolish woman! Was there no end to her outlandish independence?

"What was the message?"

Juliana's eyes became more unfocused, her voice monotone. "'Tell him to consider this as a gift from me. Tell him the de Marignys will be in attendance. Tell him all the players will be in play.'"

Erik recognized immediately that Juliana was in a hypnotic state. He should have noticed it earlier by the dazed expression on her face, but he had overlooked it. He was livid at himself for his inattentiveness and seethed with fury toward the newest complication, Izak. Who was this man?

He grabbed her face more roughly than he had intended and forced her to look into his eyes. Garnering all the strength he could muster by drawing from his anger, he commanded in a voice no man on earth could refuse, "*Awake.*"

CHAPTER TWENTY-SEVEN

"Awake? Don't be crazy. I'm not sleeping. And get your hand off my face." Juliana pried away his fingers. She pointed to the envelope. "Are you going to open that or can I? I'm dying to know what's inside." She averted her eyes back to Erik. "Those two women you sent to watch me, nice as they are, wouldn't let me near it. And speaking of being watched, thanks a lot for letting me know they'd be here today. I really appreciate it." Her voice held an edge of sarcasm.

It appeared Juliana was unaware Izak had infiltrated her mind. Erik didn't want to alarm her, so for now, he thought it best to keep that knowledge to himself.

"I put a note in your room telling you in detail about Bea and Agnes before I left this morning. You didn't see it?"

"Obviously not." She crossed her arms. "Next time, tell me in person. I've got enough to deal with without being blindsided by something like that."

"As you wish," he said with a nod.

"So, my curiosity is killing me. Aren't you going to open the envelope?" she asked, her annoyance seemingly dissipated.

He slumped into the nearest chair, closing his eyes as he spoke. "Not before you tell me about the man who left it."

"Didn't you see the card? It's from your friend, Izak. Izak Ulloa."

Erik sighed. "That, my dear, is the issue. I do not know an Izak Ulloa." He opened his eyes to see the curious look on Juliana's face.

"That's odd because he certainly seemed to know you."

"How do you mean?" He sat a little straighter as an uncomfortable sensation gripped his stomach.

"Well, he called you Erik." Julie waved her hands as if trying to draw an explanation. "He gave me the impression that you knew him, too. He acted as if he knew what—you—we were planning."

Erik searched his numb mind without finding any recollection of an Izak. Maybe Izak masqueraded under a false name just as he did. In any case, there was no one other than Juliana who was privy to Erik's intentions. Even Marie had only a vague inkling of his true goal now.

Marie.

He gripped the arm rest with his free hand until his knuckles turned white. This had to be something to do with her. No one else in New Orleans knew him as Erik.

"Did this Izak mention Marie?"

"No." She shook her head. "Why? Do you think she has something to do with his coming here?"

"Perhaps," he said, looking down at the thick envelope. "I do not see putting off the inevitable any longer, for you will not rest until I open this, and neither shall I." He teared at the seal then thought better of it. "Juliana, stand back." He directed her toward the hallway. "I do not want you near this in case…"

He didn't have to finish his sentence. Juliana moved back without argument. He ripped the envelope open with one yank. The card he pulled out was an invitation with elaborately scrolled lettering announcing a Masquerade Hallowe'en Ball at the Commercial Hotel for 8 o'clock on the 31st of October. Along with the invitation were two tickets for admission, paid-in-full.

What had been Izak's message?

The de Marignys will be there. All the players will be in play.

Hmmm….it did seem Izak knew too much. The calling card he left did not bear Izak's address on it, only his name, another complication for Erik to deal with. Once Juliana spent her days with Christine, he would spend his looking for this Izak, to confront him without constraint.

"What does it say?" Juliana asked, entering the room.

He flipped the invitation over for her to see. "It appears that we are invited to a ball."

"What?" She grabbed the paper, her eyes quickly perusing the words. "You're kidding! I've never been to a masquerade with full costumes and masks."

"My friend, *Izak*," he bit out the name." Must be very well-connected. Admission to this ball was sold out months ago." Erik felt wary about the invitation. It was most likely a trap. By attending, he could be leaving himself and Juliana vulnerable to any mischief Marie and Izak might be planning.

Juliana's face lit up. "This is really kind of thrilling. I mean to see how people do things now and to be there, be a part of something I've only read about. It's not as if we don't have balls, we just do it differently."

Her eyes sparkled, those golden eyes.

"So, are we going?" She bestowed on him a beautiful smile so deep that a dimple appeared on her right cheek. "It will give me something to look forward to."

Erik felt tempted by the desire to please her. "I do not know…"

The fact that the ball was for "whites only" was the least of his worries. The real question was should he give into Juliana and walk into a trap or stay home and wait for them to set up another one? If they did go, at least he would already be guard rather than to have them surprise him by some other means later on. He had so many misgivings, but he knew he could turn the tide in his favor. He had time to figure out Marie's plan and be prepared.

He'd never let anything happen to Juliana—never—even if it came at great cost to himself. He would not deny her such a small pleasure. A costume with gloves and long sleeves along with heavy make-up, powdered wig, and a mask would conceal her race. Perhaps, Marie Antoinette? He could get her into the ball. It was the least he could do.

♀

Erik looked up at her; his eyes held a sheen of purpose. "Yes."

"Really?" Her disbelief must be written all over her face. She had been certain that she would have to argue her case in order to convince him; yet, he had given in so easily.

"Yes." He gave her an indulgent smile.

Squealing with delight and without thinking, Julie enveloped him in a hug. It was an instantaneous, natural response. It didn't even register until Erik stood up and returned her embrace. Overcome with the unexpected realization that it felt wonderful to be in his arms, she pulled away from him. She looked into his ragged face and saw something flicker in the depths of his eyes. Had he felt something too?

"However," he stressed as he pulled further back. "You will have to go incognito."

She laughed. "Isn't that the whole purpose of a Masquerade?"

"For most it might be that simple, but you will have to change the identity under your mask if you wish to attend." He turned her around to the ornate mirror hanging above the jester's cabinet, and rubbed a hand down her cinnamon-colored arm. "Your skin, as beautiful as it may be, will deny you admittance."

The anger she would have felt at this discovery was abated by the warmth of his hand on her skin. She turned around to face him again and her voice came out breathy. "Then you are the perfect person to disguise me." She touched the side of his face. "You have it down to an art."

Erik cleared his throat and changed the subject. "Do people still dance in the twenty-first century?"

Images of Patrick Swayze in *Dirty Dancing* crossed her mind. She stifled a laugh. "Oh, we do, but I'm pretty sure our style of dancing would not be appropriate for a masquerade."

"Then we will need to add dance to the list of things you must learn while here. I am quite an accomplished dancer. Before long, I can assure you that you will be also."

Suppressing the smile that threatened the corners of her mouth, she managed to utter, "I look forward to it." And she spoke the truth, especially if that meant she had an excuse to be held in his arms again. Technically, he was her husband, after all.

"Come." He beckoned to her as he walked out the room. "There is something I want you to see." Julie followed as he grabbed a roll of papers from the hallway, took them to the dining table, and laid them out for her to look at. As he smoothed the curling edges down, she saw a detailed sketch similar to a blueprint, but in color.

"Is this Christine's house?" she took a no-brainer guess.

"Yes," he answered as he placed crystal tumblers on the ends of the paper that refused to remain flat. Satisfied, he stood back. "It is important that you can navigate confidently within her home. I want you to look through all of these and familiarize yourself with the layout."

That sounded reasonable. There would be only so much that Julie could blame on a "bump on the head." It wasn't as if she had been comatose and woke up with amnesia or something.

"Sure, sounds like a great idea." She leaned over the table and looked closely at the detailed outline of the exterior of the house while Erik crossed the room to settle into one of the fireside chairs. "Where did you say you got these?" She turned her attention back to Erik, who silently gazed into the flames.

"I drew them myself." He answered with a lazy tilt of his head, blinking heavy-lidded eyes. "That is why I have been gone all day." He leaned back against the chair. "I presume you can manage to figure things out on your own. I would like to rest a few moments if you are agreeable."

Why hadn't she noticed the fatigue in his voice or the shadows beneath his eyes before? And she realized the only time she had seen him sleep was when she had woken up at his St. Charles house.

"When was the last time you had any sleep?"

He raised a brow with curiosity at her concern. "About 50 hours ago, give or take a few," he replied.

"What? No wonder you look so worn-out." She had never considered what Erik had been doing. She had been preoccupied only with her own worries and concerns. "You are going to sleep right now, Mister." She went to the sitting room and grabbed the small lap blanket Bea had covered her with earlier "on account of the drafty windows."

Erik pushed up from the chair when she re-entered the room.

"Stop right there," she commanded, pointing her finger at him. "Sit down." His eyes widened slightly at the order, but he complied with her demand. She covered him with the blanket then grabbed a small cushioned stool from the corner.

"I don't know what you were thinking. Lack of sleep lowers the body's resistance to infection," Julie fussed as she lifted his feet and gently deposited them on the stool. It had never occurred to her that either one of them could get sick. "Have antibiotics even been discovered yet?" she mused out loud to herself. Erik protested as she knelt to remove his shoes, but she silenced him with a stern look. "Would you like a pillow or are you comfortable as you are?"

"I am quite comfortable," he said thickly, a strange expression on his face.

She gave a nod of satisfaction. "Good. Now while you sleep, I'll start to memorize the blue prints."

She returned to the table and passed another cursory glance over the exterior of the house. She didn't really need to spend much time on that. What could she learn from it really? She would not be expected to memorize the landscaping or the stones used to pave the walkway. She moved one of the tumblers, allowed the top sheet to roll up, and placed the tumbler back on top of the remaining sheets.

"Oh—" She involuntarily uttered when she saw the diagram of the first floor. She flipped through the pages underneath in growing amazement. Each page was an exact replica of the house, down to the wood grain in the flooring, plaster work on the ceiling, and wallpaper on the walls. She could make out the pattern on the dishes in the dining room, detect the melted wax on the candles of the candelabra, and clearly see a complete replica of a large oil painting of a beautiful woman with long, chestnut hair holding an infant in her arms on the living room wall. The hallways, the bedrooms, kitchen, every room of the house was sketched down to the finest detail. It almost felt as if she were invading their privacy.

Erik's ability to draw...to capture so completely...was unbelievable. His talent was so evident in all the pages. It must have taken him hours to do. She felt her forehead crease with her concern.

How could he possibly know in this kind of detail what Christine's house looked like, unless he was some kind of Peeping Tom, or worse, had somehow gotten inside the house? She shuddered as a chill ran down her back. There was something more involved going on here.

Julie glanced back at Erik sleeping in the chair. His body was relaxed, and there was a peaceful countenance to his scarred face. She watched his chest slowly rise and fall. The man who portrayed such self-assurance and confidence when awake now presented an innocent vulnerability. What was going on inside of that mind of his? Julie wondered if what they were about to do was actually emerging from a darker side of Erik.

She shrugged her misgivings away. They had a united goal and once it was reached, she would go home. It was that simple. Julie sighed and looked at the blue prints once again.

♀

Erik jumped to his feet with his hands at the ready. It took a moment before he realized he had woken up to an empty room save for muted shadows lingering in the corners. He relaxed his stance, releasing the breath he had been holding in. He was safe and so was Juliana.

His heart plummeted as he scanned the room again. *Where was Juliana?*

In his socked feet, he slid nearly the length of the floor in his haste to get to her room. Relief flooded over him as he looked at her sleeping form sprawled across the bed. A spark of irritation flickered in his soul. He had let Marie and her henchman, Izak, get to him.

His dreams had been disrupted by a faceless man dragging Juliana toward an entryway through the midst of a crowded room of vibrantly costumed revelers. When Erik tried to go after him, the floor turned into quicksand and pulled him downward, rendering him helpless. A laughing Marie held the door open for the scoundrel as he continued to shove the panicked Juliana outside. The harder Erik attempted to free himself, the further down he sank into the floor. He was completely powerless. Even now, awake, the echo of Marie's laughter still rang in his ears.

He had had enough! Marie would die—sooner, rather than later. There wasn't room for the two of them in New Orleans. He would not allow her to ruin anything for him or anyone else whom he cared about.

He continued to stare at the sleeping Juliana. He found himself attached to her, although he knew he had no right to. He felt...he didn't know what he felt. She astounded him. No one had ever considered him. He had never been given common courtesy by humanity, let alone have someone worry about his welfare. No person, no woman had ever shown him kindness of any measure as she did. She had attended to his needs with sincerity and concern. What she had done for him last night might seem trivial to most others, but to him…he was indebted forever.

He had never felt he owed anything to anyone before. The obligation felt unusual. Now in the bathroom, he attempted to wash away his contempt for Marie and the strange new stirrings he felt for Juliana as he splashed his face with water. He looked in the mirror above the sink at the scarred flesh of his face, raw and taut. He was a freak. Most people thought so when gazing upon his face. And who could love a freak?

No one.

That was why he had to resort to trickery, smoke and mirrors, deception and suggestion. He didn't want to be alone and he loved Christine. It shouldn't matter how she ended up with him. What he wanted was all that mattered.

Juliana would have to look at him as he was. He had washed off what little there was left of his paste and wax, and there was none to be had at this house. She would have to bear his appearance for a while. After dark, he would go to the St. Charles house and reapply the mixture to once again walk among society. Until then, they would remain in the house.

Tomorrow, Juliana would visit Christine.

Today, he would be the teacher and she the student.

Let the game begin.

CHAPTER TWENTY-EIGHT

Julie tied the last knot on the end of her tignon and examined the effect in her vanity mirror. She had practiced several times yesterday until she had gotten it right. Erik had really put her through her paces, guiding her through with repetition and memorization of all possible things she might need to know to the point that she would feel confident, capable even, of blending in. She'd know soon enough, wouldn't she?

Her newfound confidence did not prevent the tangle of nerves inside her from stealing her appetite. She didn't have much experience with performing, but she could remember the flutter of nervousness in the pit of her stomach just before her dance review as a child. The feeling was like that only magnified by a hundred.

Julie saw a hint of disappointment cross Erik's face when she had politely refused the breakfast he had fixed for her, but she couldn't worry about that now. She appreciated the effort, but he would just have to understand. She wouldn't have held it down.

Erik had been most attentive the entirety of the previous day. He wasn't distracted by anything else, she was his sole focus. And he had been very patient with her as she learned, never demanding, but gentle and kind. They talked for hours. He answered all of her questions about her position in life and what she could expect while at Christine's house.

However, the most memorable part for her was later on that evening when Erik played waltz music on the old-time record player, or phonograph as he called it, and began her dancing lessons. Julie messed up terribly in the beginning; stepping on his feet because she had been too busy trying to explain to him about iPods, and doing an awful job at that since she didn't really know how they worked. But, toward the end of the lesson, they danced in comfortable silence. She had learned to anticipate his movements and follow accordingly. She glided in his arms.

She had closed her eyes, soaking in the rhythm of his breathing and the light pressure of his hand as it lingered on her back. He pressed her body a little closer to him, and she had wondered if he might feel something for her. However, she had dismissed the thought as quickly as it had popped into her head. Erik had made it quite clear from the beginning that he loved Christine.

When Julie excused herself for bed later that evening, all she could hear was Eliza Doolittle from *My Fair Lady* singing in her head "I could have danced all night." And she wondered if the more she got to know Erik, would he manage to take her life and turn it upside down like Henry Higgins did for Eliza, and would she love him for it or regret the day she met him?

She squared her shoulders and walked out of the bathroom.

"How do I look?" She struck a few Vogue poses for Erik.

She had caught him off-guard with her silliness and the room filled with his genuine laugh. The broad smile on his face reached his eyes, softening the lines in his face from the manikin-look caused by the wax and paste. She preferred him without it. Erik was a very attractive man, more so when he wasn't being so serious. Julie laughed in return and it eased some of her tension. She longed to play the fool for him if it meant the reward of such a warm response.

"Quite impressive," he applauded congenially as he crossed the room. He clasped both of her hands in his own, preventing her from doing any more posing and his face settled back into its usual sensible expression. "Juliana, it is time to refocus your mind and ready yourself for the day ahead. You will have to rely on yourself to…"

"I know…I know," she interrupted, the pleasure of the moment already faded. "You won't be there to help me." She sighed. "I'm as ready as I'll ever be. Let's just get this over with."

He released his gentle grip on her hands. "The carriage already awaits you. I shall send it to collect you at precisely four o'clock this evening," he said as he escorted her to the door and opened it for her.

She stepped outside into the cool October morning, holding her wrap a little tighter around her shoulders. The horse shifted, nickering impatiently. Julie turned around, her nerves getting the best of her. "Erik…"

He opened the carriage door, his expression remaining even. "You will be fine, Juliana," his voice calmed her. "I promise you that." He took her hand and assisted her inside, shutting the door.

She leaned over to look out of the carriage window. Erik conversed with the driver, dropping coins into his palm. With a small ache of longing, she watched Erik return inside the house as the carriage lurched forward.

♀

Once Juliana's coach had departed, Erik headed straight to his desk and wrote inquiries to the upper echelon of New Orleans as to the residence of one Izak Ulloa. With Juliana on her way, he could now invest his energy in locating this man.

While writing, his mind wandered to Juliana. He had actually enjoyed himself yesterday. She was an intelligent woman, easy to converse with, and charming in her own way. It was not common for women to speak their minds as she did, but he found it an attractive quality. Shocking at times, but always entertaining, he never knew what would come out of her mouth next. He shook his head and smiled.

And what of her countenance?

She seemed to accept him as he was, scarred and mangled. She was at ease around him although his face was bare, uncovered the entirety of the day. It didn't seem to matter to her.

But, he wouldn't accomplish much if he kept thinking about Juliana. There was too much to be done. He redirected his attention to writing. He had just sealed the last of the correspondence when someone knocked on the door. From the living room window, he could see a young boy, around the age of eight. He looked further down the street, both ways, but saw nothing unusual. He opened the door.

"Monsieur de la Croix?" the guttersnipe chirped.

Erik nodded.

"For you." The child held out a letter. Erik glanced down from the outstretched hand to the too-small muddied clothes and worn shoes. Did the child have a home or did he live on the streets as Erik had? The boy shook the letter. "For you, sir…from Monsieur Ulloa."

Izak.

A chilled anticipation shot through Erik, and without considering the boy further, Erik tossed him a five-dollar gold coin, took the letter, and closed the door. Elegantly slanted, firmly printed, no smudges—Izak's handwriting was perfection, but irritation rose in Erik at the familiarity with which he was addressed by this man.

Erik,

It surprises me that you have yet to seek me out. I would have expected more from you. I think you will find that we have much to learn from each other, and there are mutual interests for us to discuss. I can imagine what you are thinking, but on my honor, as a gentleman, I assure you that I extend a white flag of peace. Luncheon with me. Today. One o'clock. I can be found at the transcribed address below. Looking forward to the pleasure of your company,

Izak

The gall of this man! To assume Erik would drop everything he might have planned to attend a last-minute invitation...no, practically a *command* for his presence at Izak's house for lunch. Erik did not bow to the will of any man.

However...

He didn't want to postpone this meeting any more than Izak did. It would most likely consist of a droll proposition by Izak on behalf of Marie, the puppet-master. He was confident that one of two things would be the result of this encounter: He would reprogram Izak's mind from under the influence of Marie, or if that was not possible, dispose of him. Either way, it would be a day well-spent.

His thoughts churned with possibilities. It would be a pleasure to flex his mind against an equal and prevail. A tête-à-tête, if you will, of the most dangerous kind. He savored the possibility of a challenge, and he hoped that Izak would not disappoint.

One o'clock.

That would give him time to stop by his residence and retrieve a few items, just in case. Preparation had always been the key to his success. And since he would be in the vicinity of the de Marigny's home, he would discreetly lay his eyes on Juliana and Christine, making sure all was well before traveling farther uptown for lunch with Izak. This was going to be a good day. He was certain of it.

♀

From the window of the carriage, Julie could see the façade of the home from Erik's blueprints. In spite of the rapid rate of her pulse, she descended from the carriage and walked around the side of the house to the kitchen door where she raised her shaking hand and knocked. Heaven forbid she should enter through the front door like regular folk. Even though she was a welcome guest, here to assist the family, she could only gain entry by the kitchen. A small flame of resentment flared in her, one more degrading example of how people of color had to bear the indignity of discrimination.

She wasn't employed by the family. She received no recompense for visiting. Naomi was sent months ago by Erik, known to them as Monsieur David de la Croix, as a favor to assist Christine with the baby. Naomi and Christine became close friends in the process. However, because of her skin color, she was still forced to obey the "rules" of society. Her blood boiled thinking about it. This society stinks.

The door opened, revealing an elderly woman, stooped and frail with her café-au-lait skin pulled tautly over her skeletal frame. If not for the faint rosy glow on each cheek, it would be reasonable to assume she had one foot in the grave. From Erik's description this would be Orelia, one of the few live-in staff.

Her gaunt face broke into a genuine smile. "Is good to see you, Mimi." Julie smiled, nodding in return. "Mme. Christine waits in the sitting room. She been dere nigh on an hour now." She shuffled back and let Julie inside.

"I'll just see myself in then." Julie walked past Orelia into the kitchen, unwrapping her tignon as she went. No sense taxing the old woman when it was quite possible Orelia could die from the exertion. As she walked, she recognized everything from Erik's painstakingly accurate drawings. Thank God for small favors. She peered into the sitting room. Christine sat in a chair near the window concentrating on her needlework.

So this was the person Erik was madly in love with.

Julie fought against the tiny jolt of jealousy that struck her as she gazed at Christine. She was a very pretty girl in her early twenties, with porcelain skin and long chestnut-colored hair, the exact likeness to the portrait Erik had captured on the blueprints.

Julie cleared her throat.

Christine squealed with delight and smothered Julie in an embrace followed by a kiss on each cheek. "I'm so happy, Mimi. I've missed having your visits." She sang out merrily with a heavy French accent. "Come....come sit down. Are you well? I must insist you do not do too much. Today we visit only, yes?" Without giving Julie a chance to reply, Christine continued. "Philippe, he has missed you, too, I think. He should wake soon enough."

Philippe...that would be the baby.

"And, Raoul? Is he home too?" Julie asked tentatively, looking over her shoulder.

"Sadly, no," Christine replied as her countenance fell. "He will not be home until long after the sun sets. He works very long hours most days. But," she brightened a little. "He looks forward to seeing you. Perhaps you will dine with us on Friday?"

Julie gave her most appreciative smile. "I would be honored to have supper with you on Friday." She was glad to know that Raoul would not be present for today's visit. It would take some of the stress off of her as she worked on getting Christine to forsake her marriage.

Julie shuddered at the thought. She wouldn't have dreamed in a million years she would try to destroy someone's relationship. But here she was, doing just that.

A soft cry floated down from upstairs. Christine tilted her head. "Ah." She smiled. "That would be Philippe now. Wait here." She hurried out the room and Julie could hear her footsteps fading up the staircase.

So far, so good. She let out a breath.

She didn't realize how young Christine was. If Christine lived in the twenty-first century, Julie would be quick to say that the de Marignys were playing house, but young people during this day and age shouldered a lot of responsibility and took it seriously.

Another thing that surprised her was how delighted Christine seemed to see her as if Mimi was her only friend in the world. Julie felt sorry for her. She got the sense that besides the house staff, Christine had very limited contact with people. Did she live a lonely and isolated life? Julie had to figure out if it was by Christine's choice or if Raoul controlled the situation. No wonder Erik wanted to rescue Christine. And Julie knew Erik would devote his time and attention on Christine. Once he put his mind to something, it was his sole focus.

"Look, bebe." Christine swept into the room, speaking to her son. "Look who has come to visit us." The little fellow's eyes lit up when he saw Julie and he stretched out his arms to her. Julie took Philippe to her hip. He wrapped one hand around her arm and the other went immediately to her hair, gently pulling at her curls in fascination. "See, Mimi, I told you he missed you."

"It seems he has." Julie looked into the clear, grey eyes of the child for the first time. He certainly was a happy baby. She could see why Naomi liked to spend time with Christine and Philippe. In spite of her lowly circumstances, they made her feel accepted.

Between the two of them, they entertained the delighted child with peek-a-boo and silly faces until he rubbed his tired eyes. And before Julie knew it, just like the snap of her fingers, the morning had passed. Julie held Philippe while Christine picked up his playthings from the floor. She paced the room with the tired child, but stilled as a shadow caught her eye.

She looked over her shoulder at Christine, who folded the blanket they had spread on the floor. Since Christine was occupied, Julie stepped back to the sitting room window to gaze through the sheer curtains. It was nothing, only a pair of birds flying in and out of the gardenia bush close to the house.

Or was it? Julie leaned closer, clasped her free hand to her mouth to suppress her gasp as the shadow popped up in the shape of a man, a man who looked as startled as she to be seen. Erik's familiar face quickly erased of all surprise followed by a semi-smile, and a finger held to his closed lips, indicating she should be silent.

She stared at him in amazement. What in the hell was he doing outside the window? Spying? She quickly checked on Christine, who placed the folded blanket on the sofa, oblivious to the immediate drama. When Julie turned back, he was gone. She rubbed the crease on her forehead, fighting the thrill of happiness at unexpectedly seeing Erik with the creepiness of the whole situation.

♀

A mixture of simultaneous emotions flooded Erik. With his agility, stealth, and cunning, no one had ever seen him when did not want to be seen. Yet, fate would have it that Juliana, his golden-eyed beauty, would be the one to lay eyes on him. And in some strange twist that he couldn't quite explain, it comforted him. They shared a secret. They were partners in this endeavor. He was glad for this silent exchange.

Erik watched the emotions that crossed her face range from surprise to shock to happiness. He hushed her with a finger lest she speak. His heart sank seconds later when a flicker of something akin to disgust replaced her joy. When she turned her head, he took the opportunity to make his escape.

What she must think of him? Peering from the outside in had been such a natural part of his life, he hadn't considered what anyone else would think if he were ever caught doing so. He had lived outside the rules of society. All that existed in his world were *his* rules.

And lately, he felt as if his world had been turned upside down. He wanted to help it right itself, but every move he made in that direction only got him mired in more complications. But he vowed that at least one of those complications would be resolved as of today.

He stopped across the street from Izak's house, rubbing his hands together to warm them as he stood in the shadow of a massive oak tree, surveying the Prytania mansion. He couldn't help admire the massive wrap-around veranda and Corinthian columns that flanked it. He approached the house's gate and noticed a plaque fastened to it that had "Maginnis house" written in gold lettering. Erik's eyes narrowed as he searched his mind. He couldn't place where, but he had heard that name before. It would come to him eventually. His immediate concern was that the sign didn't read Ulloa.

Trust nothing.

He knocked on the door.

A very attractive, middle-aged woman answered. Her hair swept up into a loose bun and her clothes were well-made and expensive.

Erik's senses were on alert. It was uncommon for the lady of the house to answer her own door.

Lifting his hat, he offered her a polite bow. "Good day, I am David de la Croix."

The woman gave him a vacant stare without acknowledging his greeting. From deep in the house, a man's voice boomed. "Lizzie, don't be rude. Invite our guest inside."

"Won't you come in?" Lizzie said without hesitation, stepping aside to allow him entry.

The entry hall was grand and tastefully decorated with a rich red color on the walls and ceilings, the trim work in white, and high-back mahogany-carved chairs lining the walls. Red carpet ran the length of the floor with about a two inch gap on the ends revealing beautiful Cypress wood underneath.

"Take his hat." The man's voice ordered.

"May I take your hat?" she parroted, grabbing it from his hand. Erik could see Lizzie was under some type of hypnotic state.

"Bring him to the parlor and offer him a drink." The man's voice sounded bored. The woman gestured for Erik to follow her.

Erik eyed her with caution as she led him into a room filled with plush sofas and chairs, large gold-framed mirrors on the walls, and beautifully crafted trim work on the ceiling and around the windows.

"May I fix you a drink?" Lizzie motioned to a decanter on the liquor cabinet; an amber fluid nearly reached the stopper.

Trust nothing.

"I thank you, but no." Erik dismissed the offer.

"Surely you will not deny yourself the pleasure of a drink?" came a man's deep voice from behind him.

Erik spun around. In the doorway stood a well-bred aristocratic man, statuesque with a handsome, unblemished face.

"Let me introduce myself." The man held out his hand. "I am Izak."

CHAPTER TWENTY-NINE

Erik appraised Izak as they shook hands. More than a foot taller, around the same age, in fit health, and a firm grip. None-the-less, Erik felt he could overcome Izak if the situation came to that.

Izak barely gave Erik a cursory glance before he turned to Lizzie. "You may go now. Make sure the entire family is at the table for our luncheon." Lizzie's gaze went unfocused for a moment then she backed out of the room as commanded. Izak walked to the side table with the decanter on it and poured two drinks. "Have a drink with me, Erik," he said, turning back to face him. "I insist."

Erik accepted the drink. Turning his back to Izak, Erik perused the décor as he casually walked the length of the sitting room. "You have a magnificent home."

"Yes, I have particular tastes." Izak answered.

Erik spun around, startled to find Izak standing less than an arm's length away from him. He had heard no footsteps, no rustling, no indication at all that there had been movement behind him. He would never have turned his back otherwise.

Who was this man?

"That is why," Izak continued, with a tilt of the head. "I chose this house." A brilliant smile emerged on his face. "Well, it was *one* of the reasons." Erik took the opportunity to search Izak's face. Curiously, he saw nothing special behind the common green eyes.

Izak swept a hand toward the door and arched an eyebrow. "Shall we join the family for lunch?"

Erik gave a stiff nod and followed his host, dumping the contents of the glass into a potted plant as he left the room. There was no anticipating Izak's motives at this point, but Erik would vigilantly assess the situation to see if a connection between Izak and Marie would reveal itself.

The dining room was adorned with multiple elegant chandeliers over a mahogany table that sat sixteen. The center chairs were occupied. On one side sat the woman, Lizzie. Next to her were two other women, one grandmotherly and the other, a fresh-face debutante. Across from the women sat an older man, and a young couple. No one in the family acknowledged their entrance. Instead, they stared ahead at each other, expressionless.

Erik's eyes scanned the far end of the room where there was a large fireplace with two wingback chairs facing it. On the armrest of the chair to the left of the fire, Erik noticed a man's motionless arm and the slight silhouette of his shadowy profile on the wood floor. So by his count, there were eight potential adversaries should this meeting take a turn for the worse.

Izak motioned for Erik to sit in the chair at the head of the table closest to the door through which they had entered. Meanwhile, Izak settled at the other end nearest the fireplace, his tall frame overshadowing the table. Strategically, Erik had a good position. He had means of escape by the door that led to the hallway or the one that most likely led to the kitchen, and his back was to the windows of the dining room that faced the street. If need be, he would not be opposed to jumping through one. It bothered Erik though. Surely Izak could see this advantage, why would he allow Erik to have it?

The door to his left swung open as several house staff in starched uniforms entered with heavily-laden trays of food, placed them on the table, then turned back through the door to retrieve more. Izak watched with approving eyes as every bare spot on the table was covered with food: ham, roasted turkey, lamb chops, casseroles, butter beans, rice, bread, pork, sausages, sweet potatoes, puddings, pies, cakes, and all available seasonal fruits.

"Ephraim," Izak commanded as he unfolded his napkin and placed it on his lap. "Serve the soup." Ephraim ladled soup into their bowls then exited the room, leaving them alone.

With a sweeping glance around the table, Izak announced, "You may eat." He lifted his spoon and tasted the soup. "Delicious."

The rest of the party lowered their eyes, mechanically depositing their spoons into the soup, raising them to their lips, and swallowing as one. Erik's hands remained on the table.

Izak laughed. "You refuse my food just as you disposed of my drink?"

"I am afraid I did not bring an appetite with me," Erik answered coolly.

Izak reached across the table, cleanly wrenched a leg off the turkey, took a savage bite, and swallowed the chunk of meat whole. Erik found his blatant disregard of table manners disgusting and turned his head away. Lizzie and the rest of the family continued to eat their soup unconcerned with Izak's behavior.

Izak's voice broke the silence. "Do you think it makes you strong to abstain?"

Izak's common green eyes had now acquired a layered iridescence. Erik slipped a hand into his pocket and gripped the rope inside tightly, reminding himself that he still held an advantage.

Izak cleaned his hands thoroughly with his napkin. "Strength doesn't come from denying yourself, Erik. It comes from indulging in all that you want. For instance," he leaned over, gently lifting Lizzie's arm off the table to kiss the inside of her wrist. "Later, I will indulge in a dessert that you cannot partake in." He kept his gaze fixed on Erik, a self-satisfied smile spreading on his face. "We all have desires and we both know you want something, or should I say…*someone*, very, very much."

"Stay out of my affairs," Erik said, grateful his voice remained soft and deadly, not betraying his inner trembling. "I do not know what Marie has been telling you…"

Izak gave a dismissive laugh. "I do not associate with that woman. If it were up to me, I would rid the world of her, but all the players in the game have a right to play. Now," he placed his hands flat on the table. "Ask me what you really wish to know."

Erik returned his gaze, feeling his face twisting as he suppressed a sneer. "Who are you?"

Izak stood, intertwined his fingers, and paced by his end of the table. "What to do? What to do?" he murmured more to himself than to Erik. "I had anticipated you might ask that question first. Shall we say that I am an interested bystander, or observer, if you will?"

"Not good enough." Erik slammed his hands on the table as he stood. The dishes rattled from the force of his hands, yet the family continued their mechanical eating, undisturbed. "Who *are* you?"

"Who am I?" Izak repeated, amused. Erik felt his core burning. The tickle of fear that had tried to take root was overcome by his anger and irritation.

"That's a complicated question." Izak stepped away from the table.

Erik followed suit, moving away from his end of the table so that they faced each other at dueling distance. "I am very capable of handling complicated."

Erik blinked.

He knew instantly it was a mistake. As his lids closed, he saw Izak move faster than most eyes could register. By the time his lids had opened again, Izak had grabbed him by the neck, and he found himself dangling a foot in the air.

Erik clawed at the hand closed around his neck for a minute, then regaining his senses, he stopped. It was a futile effort, he knew well just how futile. Hadn't he watched many a man do the same as he choked the life from their bodies? Instead, he defiantly gazed down into the hypnotic green of Izak's eyes.

"Can you handle this?" Izak tilted his head, silently appraising Erik, his eyes seeming to penetrate through the wax and paste. "Pity about your face... most unfortunate." Izak's voice had a much deeper quality to it than before. He set Erik back on his feet, letting go of his neck. "I stopped her, you know, but not before she ruined you."

"What?" Erik managed to gasp, rubbing his neck, the words not quite sinking in.

"Your mother...Ellendora."

Dazed, Erik stumbled back into the nearest chair. Izak's words were not making any sense to him. "What do you know of my mother?"

How could he possibly know her?

"I had been gone for months, you see. I was not aware of your mother's...condition." Izak leaned against the wall. "You had been born hours earlier and the smell of blood was still in the house. Your mother had no midwife to assist with the delivery. She slept, no doubt exhausted, when I arrived."

"What are you saying?" Erik interrupted, his head reeling.

Izak continued. "It is not in my nature to let an offspring survive, but I was forced to make an exception in your case." He smiled wryly. "It was not long before your mother woke and saw me...as myself. And all hell broke loose, or should I say she thought I had broken loose from hell? She tore at her gown, spat at my feet, and attempted to kill you. You were, after-all, half-mine."

Erik felt glued to his chair. He couldn't be hearing correctly.

"You would think that I would have seen it coming. Usually, they try to kill themselves and leave the child to me, but," he said, shrugging his shoulders. "You were your mother's priority. Sulfuric acid did that," he gestured to Erik's face.

A leaden sensation settled in the pit of Erik's stomach. "Are you telling me that *you* are my father? Impossible! You cannot be much older than I." In spite of his disbelief, Erik found himself scrutinizing Izak more closely. Now he noticed the similar jaw line, nose, and lips that he himself had.

"I am not telling you anything other than the truth, if you are willing to hear it." Izak paused.

"Go on." Erik's voice sounded oddly constrained in the silent room. The other guests had finished their soup and sat at the table motionless, staring ahead as they had before.

"I pushed your mother out of the way, but the acid had already left her hands. It splashed against the edge of your crib and landed partially on your face, neck, and chest. I tended to you as quickly as I could, but the damage was already done." Izak idly examined his fingernails. "I attended to your mother next. I admit, I had been a little overzealous, suppressing her memories to the point where her brain disengaged, but I was angry." He eyed Erik. "I find it very hard to constrain myself when I am angry, not so unlike you, I think?"

Erik had once broken through his mother's memories. He knew she had done this to him, but he never really knew why. He had always thought she had been distraught over the death of the father he resembled so closely, not that it was out of revulsion of his very existence. That was why he had been forced to cover his whole face with a sack.

"Why now?" Erik's throat constricted. "Why seek me out now, after all these years?"

Izak laughed richly, pointing a finger at him. "Your conceit is refreshing. It really is." He sobered up, cocking his head to the side. "I have been with you the entirety of your life."

"No—" Erik shook his head in disbelief. "I have never seen you before."

"Do you honestly have the audacity to believe that you would see me if it were my desire for you not to? You, who hide in the shadows, disappearing like vapor in the night." Izak's voice grew deeper again. "Your stealth and agility, your ability to coerce, to confound…you have inherited a watered-down version of my own abilities. Unlike you, I can walk abroad in daylight and still pass unseen. Unlike you, I do not require spirits to loosen the mind in order to control it. So I say again, I have been the silent observer of your life as I saw fit to watch it."

"Let me rephrase the question," Erik bit out. "Why have you chosen to reveal yourself to me now?"

The warmth of Izak's smile echoed in his voice. "Now *that* is a good question. Let's just say that things have gotten interesting, too interesting for me to simply watch on the sidelines. I want to offer my services."

"You are here to assist me because my life circumstance *amuses* you?" Erik's voice cracked. "Where were you when I was hungry? When I had to steal to feed my belly? When I was at the mercy of gypsies? When I was beaten and mistreated?" He stood up again, enraged at the injustices he had suffered while this man who called himself father sat back and watched it happen. "You could have given me opportunities. You could have given me a life without misery. Why did you leave me to suffer such cruelty?"

Izak's face grew hard. "This has always been your choice. I did not embrace this life sojourn you embarked on. I never agreed with it. But there are laws that even I am forced to abide by." Izak walked to the window. His voice softened. "But that is all in the past now, Erik. We can move forward from this moment on, if you so choose it. I can be a very valuable ally."

"Why now?" Erik persisted.

Izak turned back, his face aglow. "There is something powerful at work at this very moment. I sensed it the night Juliana arrived. It is an ancient power outside of either one of us. It has been a long time since I have felt its energy. I want to be a part of it."

"And if I say no? If I take Juliana and leave this place?"

"Then, flesh of my flesh, blood of my blood, I will seek you out." Izak smirked. "There is no place you can hide from me." He inhaled deeply. "I can *smell* you from miles away."

This revelation did not surprise Erik for he knew at once Izak spoke the truth as he also had a very keen sense of smell.

"I am not completely at fault in this—" Izak elaborated. "I am bound from interfering in your life without your consent. I regret that I have not offered before now. I would like for us to move past this."

Erik rubbed his hands through his hair. He didn't want to think about that just now. He turned toward the table. "Who are these people? Are they my family?"

Izak's contemptuous laugh bounced off the walls. "No, Erik, they are not family. I am afraid you and I are the last of a very ancient line. But where are my manners? You have met Lizzie Maginnis. Next to her is Corrine, her daughter, then Grandma Meryl. On the other side we have Grandpa Melvin, Josephine Maginnis, and her husband, Richard."

"Yes," Erik said, annoyed, "but *who* are they exactly?"

"They are the family unfortunate enough to have invited me into their house."

A foreboding feeling stole upon Erik. "Are you going to kill them all?"

"I do not have to kill to be satisfied, Erik. So...no, when I leave here, they will not remember my stay at all. This," he swept a hand toward the table. "It is what I do. I have been the guest of many of these fine New Orleans' families since following you here. All have survived, more or less." His face lit up again. "Ah...but I have forgotten the guest of honor, the very reason for choosing this house, this family to reintroduce myself." He walked to the back of the room, placed his hands on the wingback chair, and effortlessly turned it around.

"May I introduce, Mathew Maginnis?"

When the chair stopped in place, Erik saw a young man sitting in the chair. He had blonde hair and a boyish face, a face that Erik had seen somewhere before. A photo from the *Daily Picayune* flashed in his mind of the very same man on the court steps with the headline *MATHEW MAGINNIS EXONORATED*.

Erik gritted his teeth. He had helped this man go free in exchange for Marie's potion even though Mathew had been guilty of taking advantage of a young woman. Mathew's head lolled to one side and Erik noticed a bluish tinge to his fingernails and mouth. Mathew was dead. Izak lifted the man's head upright for Erik to see more clearly.

"This is my peace offering. I killed him earlier today, for you..."

CHAPTER THIRTY

It had been a long time since Julie had spent a day in the company of a woman. After her falling out with Monika, her back-stabbing best friend, she had pretty much hung out with James and his buddies. James was the closest thing she had to a good friend. She didn't know whether she could ever trust a girlfriend again.

Julie felt very comfortable with Christine at first. Christine seemed so familiar; the way she tossed her hair, how she expressed herself with her hands, and the way she moved. Julie supposed it could have been due to the unconscious recognition of past times Naomi had spent in Christine's company. But as the day lingered on, even though Christine had been kind and hospitable, Julie felt an unexplainable mistrust stirring in her gut.

After little Philippe had been fed and put down for another nap, Christine played the piano and sang. Even though Julie didn't understand a word since the song was in Italian, it was the most beautiful one she could ever remember hearing. Christine's voice was angelic.

As she watched Christine sing, a twinge of jealousy pulled at her heart. Julie could see why Erik was so enamored. And she knew she had no hope of competing against the lovely and talented young woman.

She stiffened.

Where had that thought come from? There was no competition. When this was over, Julie was going home.

"Now," Christine turned the pages of her music book, "shall we sing together, as we used to?"

"No," Julie politely refused, thinking about her performance at the Cat's Meow. The second she opened her mouth to sing, Christine would know she was a fraud. "But, I've been here all this time and forgot to give you Philippe's christening gift." She crossed the room to retrieve her sachet purse. "I really wish I could have been there."

She smiled when she reached in her purse to pull out the handkerchief. Just thinking of Erik diligently completing the cross-stitch work that Naomi had started. It was sort-of comical seeing a grown man concentrating so hard with needle and thread, not to mention doing it so well. She withdrew the handkerchief with the baby's name stitched in blue, Philippe Erik de Chagny-Marigny. She held it out to Christine.

"I know he is a bit young for a handkerchief, but you can hold on to it for him until later."

"Why it is just lovely! Look at the stitch work." Christine held the handkerchief up to her eyes to examine it more closely. "It's flawless and I thought you were just learning." She smiled at Julie. "You are quite talented."

Julie felt her face flush at the undeserved praise. Erik's stitch work. Erik's talent. "Tell me again, Philippe is named after Raoul's brother?"

Christine nodded. "Sadly, he is no longer with us, but I think it is a beautiful way to honor his memory, yes?"

"Yes." Julie agreed. Here was her chance to introduce the subject she had come for. "And is the Erik he's named after a family member as well?"

Other than a slight blanche, Christine's expression did not alter at the mention of Erik. She busied herself with clearing the piano of the sheet music. "Erik is the reason Raoul and I are together. He made our union possible." She shrugged without looking up. "I felt honoring Erik honored my marriage to Raoul." She closed the lid of the piano and sat down on the mauve velvet settee near the window, unable to look Julie in the eyes.

Julie joined her. "I am so curious," she began tentatively. "Might I ask about Erik? What was he like?"

Christine's eyes made a nervous dart to the door. "Erik is unlike anyone you will ever meet in your life. He had the ability to do anything, change anyone." Christine placed her hand on her throat in deep thought. She lowered her hand and shook her head. "Some things, Mimi, are better left buried."

"Buried? Has he passed on, too?" Julie prodded.

"Yes," she answered. "At least I thought so, until recently." She clasped and unclasped her hands. "Mimi, do you believe in ghosts?"

Before Julie could respond, a loud commotion at the door drew their attention. She looked back at Christine, whose face had lit up with delight.

"Raoul is home early!" Christine rushed out the room.

Julie cautiously approached the hallway. She saw Christine embraced in the arms of a relatively tall, blonde-haired man, his hand entwined in his wife's hair. She heard him speak in a thick French accent, "Your hair is as soft as silk."

Julie, rooted to the spot, felt as though the wind had been knocked out of her by his words. He was a complete stranger to her, but his words were ingrained in her head, spoken to her when she was once a wife herself.

He cupped Christine's face in his hands. "Did I ever tell you that you have the most mesmerizing eyes?" As his deep voice rang out, Julie's legs felt weak.

Christine replied, blushing, "Every time I see you."

At that moment, involuntary tears blurred Julie's vision. She knew why Christine had been so familiar to her. It had nothing to do with Naomi. Everything seemed so clear to her now. She had not come back here for Erik at all. Shaken and unable to move, Julie was stunned by her own epiphany.

She was here for herself.

She was in this past life to set things right for herself.

She knew without a shadow of a doubt who these two people were to her.

Christine would, one day in the future, return to the world as her best friend, Monika, the betrayer. And Raoul, who would eventually repeat those very words to Julie, would be her no-good cheating ex-husband, Simon.

Julie's heart pounded furiously in her chest.

Given this opportunity to re-live her past life meant she had the choice to change it. What had Heath said? It all seemed so long ago. Sometimes people spent different lifetimes together.

Searing anger burned inside of her. She would most certainly put her time in this life to good use. Every tear, every agony she experienced, she would return to them one hundred-fold. Nothing would stop her from breaking that marriage up.

This had just become personal.

♀

Erik's heartbeat became erratic as he tried to comprehend the scene before him. He was no stranger to death, but the ghoulish way in which Izak stood behind the body of Mathew Maginnis was eerily inhuman and distasteful.

"Am I supposed to be grateful?" Erik asked. Killing Maginnis was to be *his* revenge. *He* should have been the one to exact justice on this scoundrel, and then to play a requiem for Maginnis' soul in tribute to a life extinguished.

Izak's eyes turned dark green, his face contorted with rage. "Yes!" He pushed the chair with such force that it soared forward and skidded across the room, ejecting the dead man to the floor. Lizzie Maginnis turned her head at the disturbance. Izak's searing gaze rested on her face. He uttered one word. "Forget." Lizzie closed her eyes and turned back around.

Erik stood his ground, his own anger serving as an anchor. Izak had no right to interfere. He was perfectly capable of handling his own life his own way without "assistance." "I do not want your gifts," he bit out. This time, he didn't blink.

"I thought this would please you, Erik." Izak spoke calmly, his face relaxed again. "After all, Mathew took advantage of a vulnerable woman. You wanted him dead."

"What makes you think you know what would please me?" Erik crossed his arms.

The all too familiar brilliant smile crossed Izak's face. "You told me." He pointed to his temple. "I can read your thoughts when your emotions are strong, as I can with all who share in my bloodline."

The bravado Erik had sheathed himself in crumbled, at least the outer layer; he didn't like the idea of someone getting inside of his head. "Who are you?" he whispered.

Izak opened his arms as one would when beckoning an embrace. He answered just as quietly. "I invite you to see me."

With cold disdain, Erik looked at the man from his head down to his feet. "I see nothing."

In a matter of milliseconds, Izak moved from Erik's line of sight, retrieved something from the other side of the room, and returned to the exact same spot. As he stood there, Erik could see the iridescent quality return to Izak's eyes.

"See me," Izak repeated, his deep voice echoed unnaturally off the walls, growing louder. He struck the end of the walking stick he now held onto the floor. Its crystal handle absorbed the light in the room until it began to glow. "*See me*," he commanded once more.

Erik squinted. Was it a trick of the light? Izak remained stationary, but something extraordinary happened in very quick succession. Izak's appearance changed constantly, morphing from moment to moment. His hair retreating backwards until it was short, then grew to shoulder-length, then even longer, and back to short again. His clothing changed with each physical alteration, from to kilt, to doublet and tights, to archaic chain mail, to flowing majestic robes. His face never altered, neither younger nor older, except the expressions: one minute solemn; then cruel; next strong, a trace of despair; and rounded off by a look of such fierceness and pride that Erik sucked in his breath. He had never been a very empathetic person before, but Izak projected his emotions, centuries and centuries old, onto Erik, who steeled himself against the rawness of it all.

With a massive effort, Erik pulled his teary gaze away from this unnatural vision and managed to utter, "*What* are you?"

"I am an Earth Walker."

"What is an Earth Walker? Is that what I am?"

"You?" Izak answered, deeply amused. "No, you are human...for the time-being."

Erik, still reeling from the enormity of the experience, sank into the nearest chair, trying to make sense of it all. Whatever Izak was, Erik did not feel he meant any harm.

Izak spoke as if he could read Erik's very thoughts at will. "If I had meant to harm you, you would already be dead." He sat back at the head of the table with his faux-family, leisurely sipping from the drink he had fixed earlier. After silence stretched between them for a few minutes, Izak spoke once more. "I have already told you I am bound from interfering with you or your plans without your express permission and," he drawled. "Even if you gave it, would be dependent on my desire to do so. At the moment, I'm feeling generous, so say the word, and allow me to wreak havoc."

Erik wanted no part of this proposed havoc. He wanted peace, peace of mind and heart. Above all, he wanted to love and be loved, wholly without condemnation. Izak was powerful, with abilities Erik could only dream of. But Izak seemed more dangerous than helpful. Erik could make his plan work on his own. He had to trust in himself.

He did trust himself.

Erik stood. "I will have to regretfully decline."

"No matter, it is your choice." Izak waved him off, seemingly unconcerned.

Erik made his way to the door.

A word of caution before you go... the deep, resonate voice pervaded his mind.

Erik stopped, but didn't turn around.

This plan of yours...your life here...was put into motion centuries ago. Rules have been bent on your behalf, Erik. Be sure the choices you act on do not make it all in vain. Erik tried to block Izak from his head, but the words penetrated just the same. *If you should change your mind...if you should have need of me, call to me. I will hear you.*

Without responding, Erik exited the house, slamming the door behind him with a force that he wished he could use to shut Izak out of his life. Making his way back to the main thoroughfare, he swore he could still hear Izak's distant laughter.

Regaining his composure, he looked around, and hailed a cabbie. It was late. He pulled out his pocket watch. Juliana should be home by now. It would be a relief to get back to her and concentrate on their plans.

♀

Inside the small Creole house, Julie paced the floor with purpose. She had never experienced a manic high before, but she was pretty sure she was on one. A million scenarios flashed through her mind on how to seduce Raoul.

She could brush against him, put a little more sashay into her walk, flirt with her eyes, and flatter him with her words. After Raoul had become accustomed and receptive to her behavior, she would try to find him alone and...

All Julie had to do was to entice Raoul away, by any means necessary, regardless of Christine's feelings. After all, in the future, Christine-reincarnated-as-Monika, wouldn't have any boundaries when it came to Simon. So why should Julie? Then Erik could miraculously appear, back from the dead, and sweep Christine off her feet. Everyone would have exactly what they wanted in the end.

A rattling at the door jarred her thoughts.

Good. Erik's home.

Julie was fit to burst. She couldn't wait to tell Erik everything. He entered the living room and before he could even acknowledge her presence, she cornered him.

"You will not believe the day I had." She couldn't control her nervous energy, hovering around him as he sank into a chair. He seemed a little paler to her than usual, but she dismissed it. Something extraordinary had happened. She didn't have to speculate anymore as to why she was given this opportunity for a "do-over."

He motioned for her to sit. "Tell me."

"Erik, you are just a pawn," she blurted out, taking the seat across from him. His mouth tightened, but other than that he gave no sign her words affected him.

He arched an eyebrow. "How did you come to that conclusion?"

"Because the reason for my being here is bigger than you can imagine, it's about Karmic debt. A debt owed to me."

"Can you elaborate?" his brow furrowed.

"Oh yeah, I can elaborate," her voice rose an octave. It made her angry every time she thought about Monika and Simon. "It means

Christine, that no-good hussy you are so infatuated with, is going to get what she deserves."

Erik rose, anger flashing in his eyes. "I am going to tell you once, and only once," he enunciated his words. "Do not speak of her in that way."

Julie balled her fists at her side and stood up as well, too angry to feel any concern over his misplaced sense of gentlemanly protectiveness. "Oh, she's all politeness and sweetness now, but you just wait. She is not what she appears to be."

Erik sighed. "You are not making sense, Juliana."

"It makes perfect sense to me!" She said in a strangled voice, trying to force back the tears.

Erik's anger dissipated and an uncomfortable look passed his face when a few of her frustrated tears managed to escape down her face. "Calm down." He gave her arm a clumsy pat. "I will listen. Promise me you will calm down."

"How can I?" she choked. "How can I, when I know she's going to stab me in the back and twist the knife while she's at it?"

Erik's astonishment turned to disbelief. "Utter nonsense! Christine would never be capable of such violence." He handed her a handkerchief. "Here, wipe those tears."

"I'm speaking figuratively!" Julie shrieked in frustration, grabbing the handkerchief. "She's going to betray me!"

"Betray you?" Erik gave her a skeptical glance. "How could she betray you? That is not possible."

"I assure you it is." She sniffed.

"Christine is not going to betray you." He attempted to reassure her.

"I've got news for you, Erik. For me, she already did." Julie crossed her arms. "In the future, she is going to steal my husband."

Erik's lips parted. "You were married?"

"Well, I'm not anymore, thanks to Christine," she said sarcastically. "I've been divorced for a few years now."

"Who were you married to?" he asked her, the creases around his eyes deepening.

"Simon François," she paused. "But you know him as Raoul." She turned on her heel and left the room, satisfied by the stunned look on Erik's face.

CHAPTER THIRTY-ONE

Shoulders hunched against the sting of Juliana's words, Erik swore under his breath as he watched her walk away. Could what she had said been true? If it was, he was being humbled to the utmost degree.

To prevent his knees from buckling, he reached deep within his core for strength. Not even an hour had passed since he had met with Izak. There had been no time to come to terms with all *that* entailed, and Juliana's sudden announcement was more than his brain could currently absorb. The agony in his heart jolted through him. It didn't seem that he would ever factor into the equation. Now or later, Raoul would always be the one to end up with the women he cared about.

He felt so set apart from the world. When Izak had bestowed on Erik a glimpse of his undying existence, the biggest impression Erik gleaned was an overwhelming loneliness. Is that all there was to look forward to, a solitary lifetime of loneliness? Was Erik to be sentenced to always look from the outside-in, excluded from the world's beauty?

No.

He stood tall, centering himself with deep, even breaths; a method to controlling one's emotions he once learned while in the Middle East. There was nothing he could do about the future, but he'd be damned if he would allow anything to affect his carefully-laid plans. Things would continue as intended.

He was not Izak.

He was a man unto himself.

He deserved happiness.

He deserved to get what he wanted. And what he wanted was...

He closed his eyes and saw two conflicting images: one, a slender woman with doe-eyed innocence who had an angelic voice, and the other, a shapely golden-eyed charmer who saw past his mask.

It had always been Christine for him.

He wavered for a moment. Was it still?

He had to clear up these outrageous accusations. The fragility of a woman's mind could easily create issues where none were to be had. Erik strode after Juliana, grabbed her by the elbow, turning her to face him. "What basis do you have to make these assertions?"

Instead of pulling away from him, she stood her ground, holding his gaze with an equal resolve. "I can tell you anything you want to know. And while we talk, we're going to need to discuss your plan—" she extricated her arm from him—" because as of today, I'm changing it."

Erik set his jaw. *Was it to be a battle of wills, then?*

Because he was a fair-minded gentleman, he would hear her argument, but he doubted she could sway his decision. It would be his way without contest though at this point, even he started questioning which way was right. For over an hour, Erik sat listening to Juliana's story word for word.

To have both her best friend and her husband deceive her in such a manner, his heart seared with the pain and humiliation she expressed to him. He knew how it felt to be rejected, to have his love abused, disregarded, to have the object of one's affection choose someone else. He knew how it felt to not be enough.

In her voice, he heard her anguish. He felt the betrayal. It took everything he possessed to stay seated and dismiss the urge he had to take her in his arms to try and erase the pain she harbored in her heart. He wanted to show Juliana he could cherish her as she deserved to be cherished. He wanted to be the one to eradicate the damage Simon and Monika had done, or were going to do.

However, along with his desire to console her, a niggling dread at the back of his mind prevented him from acting on those thoughts. He couldn't face the possibility that she might react unfavorably to his attempt to comfort her. If he gave up his control, his power, and she rejected him…

"I thought I had let it go—" Juliana's shoulders sagged as she plopped into the nearest chair, raising her tear-stained face to Erik's. "I thought I had forgiven them." She sniffed. "I had bought a house—" she looked around her. "I moved on with my life. I had even met someone new." She sat still in thought. "But tonight, somehow, everything came flooding back to me as if it had just happened." She looked up to heaven. "God, thinking about this could drive a person mad!" Then in a reflective voice she whispered, "All of this is messing with my head because in my heart, I know that really…it hasn't even happened yet."

She covered her face with her hands for a moment, removed them to rub her temples, and to look at him, pleading with her eyes for him to understand. "They look nothing alike, but…I swear to you, Raoul is Simon…he *has* to be. I heard Raoul speak to Christine the same words as Simon did to me, the same—" she shuddered— "body language. It's him. I know it." Juliana pressed her hands to her heart. "I *know* it."

"Perhaps you are seeing what you want to see." Erik wanted her to hear reason, admit that her perception could be mistaken.

She continued on as if he hadn't spoken a word. "And I couldn't put my finger on it, but all day," Juliana cleared her throat. "*All day*, Christine reminded me of someone, and when I saw them together, I just knew. There must be traits or behaviors that carry over with us from lifetime to lifetime. I am sure this is no coincidence. Besides, I've been told that people often spend several lifetimes reincarnating together."

Again, Erik held back the torrents of emotion ebbing and flowing inside him. He wanted to shake some sense into Juliana, to convince her that this belief was all imagined on her part. Because if it wasn't, he would be very tempted to throttle Raoul, leaving scars for every invisible one that would be left on Juliana.

But what was he thinking? The man was innocent of the charges Juliana laid at his feet. It hadn't happened yet. He couldn't dole retribution out on the innocent. And even if he wanted to, Erik could never lay a hand on Christine. No matter how infuriated he was at her for hurting Juliana, and for choosing Raoul again in another life to come. But surprisingly, out of everything Juliana had just confided in him, his mind focused on one thought.

"You said you met someone new, did you mean a suitor?" He kept his irritation from his voice. The idea of someone else being with Juliana disconcerted him.

"Do you believe in fate?" she asked, neglecting to answer his question.

He rubbed his chin. *Was this a diversionary tactic?*

Had she asked him that question days earlier, he would have told her that he believed one made one's own fate. But now, what had Izak said? This had been put into play centuries ago. "That there might be something greater than us affecting the outcome of our lives?"

"Exactly." Her eyes lit up. "That's what I'm thinking. I mean, it's the only thing that makes sense." She sat back further into her chair. "The *suitor* you asked about...his name is Heath. We only saw each other twice, so I don't think he'd qualify as a boyfriend really. But, he made me think starting over with someone else was possible just when I had decided to give up on love."

Erik shifted in his chair thinking about what he would like to do to Heath if they ever met in a dark alley. It irked him that someone moved Juliana in this way and it wasn't him.

"I couldn't see it then, but the more I think of it, Heath did not come into my life for that reason. He must have been sent by fate, or God, or some higher force, or whatever you want to call it, as a messenger. If it wasn't for him, I wouldn't have considered the possibility of past lives or reincarnation. If it wasn't for him, I wouldn't have known about this opportunity to come back to a part of my past existence and change it. This is *my* chance to teach *them* a lesson." Her voice rang with a tone of finality.

Erik paid close attention as Juliana related her talk with Heath regarding reincarnation, her understanding of why it occurred, and the karma attached to it. He was not unfamiliar with the idea of reincarnation. His travels among many peoples and countries had exposed him to this belief, but he never subscribed to it. It was never something that affected his life before.

And just as Erik would grasp a partial understanding of reincarnation, it would slip away like water through his hands. It was so hard to swallow the idea of Christine as anyone else, as this Monika without loyalty or kindness, without honor or morality. He would have to take a tremendous leap of faith to accept everything Juliana said. But if seeing was believing, Juliana was a walking testament to the fact that reincarnation was true.

He tried to recall Juliana's face in the window, the body of the woman who was once Naomi and now reliving Naomi's life. He had had such a brief glimpse of her. Had he only known who it was he saw, he would have tried to get her attention, make her look his way.

"How exactly do you plan on teaching them a lesson?" Erik already suspected, but he wanted Juliana to speak her intentions out loud. He pressed his lips together at the wild look that crossed her face.

"An eye for an eye!" she jumped up. "I'm going to seduce Raoul and steal him away from Christine. I'm going to—"

"I do not think that's necessary—" Erik cut her off.

Juliana's eyes bore into him. "Are you naïve? Did you think you'd just waltz off into the sunset with Christine on your arm and that would be the end to your happily ever after? What exactly do you think will happen to Naomi once you are out of the picture? Or have you even thought hard on that? If this is an exchange of wives, then Raoul and Naomi will know each other as man and wife. Comprende?"

Erik uncrossed his legs. That thought hadn't mattered much to him before.

"The difference now is that I'm going to make sure that I give Christine a glimpse of her husband with me *before* your little exchange. I want Christine to find out how it feels and I want her to hurt as much as she hurt me."

Although aghast by Juliana's plan, Erik kept himself composed, when speaking to her. "Think about what you are saying. This is not who you are. Naomi would never hurt anyone in this manner." He remembered Naomi's timid nature, her attractive shyness. "What I have proposed is an equal exchange where all parties have what they want." Who was he fooling? He wasn't even convincing himself with that argument.

"If you haven't noticed," she retorted. "I'm not Naomi anymore and you are no expert on what I am and am not capable of."

"Absolutely not." It was time to put an end to this nonsense. "This is not acceptable." He shook his head, rejecting the very idea. "I forbid it."

Juliana stood up, hands on her hips, her voice rising to an uncomfortable octave. "You forbid it? I wasn't asking your permission."

He rose from his own chair, looking down at her flushed face, no longer from tears, but from anger. He admired her feisty spirit, but he would not encourage it. "I cannot allow you to do so."

Her eyes flashed. "How dare you! How dare you presume to tell me what I can do! This is my life and I will live it as I please!" Erik gritted his teeth as she wagged a finger in his face. "I am going to break that marriage up my way and that's final."

"Do not force my hand, Juliana," he said darkly.

She broke her gaze, pacing the floor. "Oh my God, oh my God!" She threw her hands up in the air. "What do you care anyway? You, who are so willing to dump your wife on another man. You, who obsesses over another man's wife. And, by the way, just so you know," she tossed him a look he was unable to decipher. "I didn't get the feeling that Christine's 'memory of you' was such a good thing."

Juliana was right. Everything she had just said was the truth, although he wouldn't admit it to her. He couldn't defend himself against it, so he allowed her to rant on. "And, *pray tell*," she mocked him. "What is to prevent me from doing as I please once I'm inside their house, Erik?"

"I will," he answered firmly.

♀

The audacity of that man! Julie stomped her foot on the floor in tandem with a loud clap of thunder. Bad weather had moved in. It seemed the universe felt her anger. "How are you going to do that when you are nothing but a ghost to those people? You can't step foot inside that house without ruining your 'carefully crafted plan'."

"I can be anywhere and everywhere." He didn't elaborate further.

What kind of freakishly impossible answer was that? She wanted to slap that man, at least once. His vague answers made her feel even more frustrated. Her face was so tight with stress; she thought she might have to get knitting needles to free her eyebrows.

Julie had told her story many times to different people, but very rarely did she reveal her feelings to them. All that hurt and anguish had tumbled out of her so easily when she spoke them to Erik. In his eyes, she saw sympathy. His face had softened, making him seem compassionate. During those moments, she had felt they shared a connection.

And now, he annoyed her. Talking about his plan and what she couldn't do. Didn't he see that there was something greater orchestrating this whole remarkable event? Granted, he had played a huge role in bringing circumstances about, but he had deluded himself with his purpose, blinded by his own wants. Contrary to his beliefs, the world didn't revolve around him. And though she had never thought so before, incredulous as it might sound, apparently, the world revolved around her. She cringed at the conceited thought.

Julie wanted to have her way or at the very least get her point across. Why didn't he understand what she had to do? It was so obvious to her. It would be nice if he had her back, but she was perfectly capable of doing what was needed without him.

She had wanted to dissect the comment of Erik being "everywhere" as he put it. Because all that meant to her was that he peeked through windows, convincing himself he was actually a part of the view. She wanted to call him out on all of his selfish ideals. Now that she saw things more clearly, she realized nothing out of his mouth served a purpose to anyone but him. He always appeared so calm and collected. But why wouldn't he? It was her world that was turned upside down, not his.

Julie didn't know where all this bottled-up hostility came from. It bothered her that she wanted to lash all her frustration out on Erik. She wasn't normally so mean-hearted. This past-life experience did not seem to be changing her for the better.

Or maybe it was a little bit of Naomi coming out in her? For once taking the opportunity to dictate how her life should be and not feel oppressed by rules and racial laws of the current day. How was Julie expected to fix two of her lives at once? It was a tall order, and it felt as if there was a lot riding on her decisions. One bad choice could change both of her lives forever.

The disgruntled silence between them seemed to last for hours as she mulled over her thoughts. Julie knew Erik would not back down. She didn't intend to either, but it was late, the day had been a long one, and a truce seemed like a good idea.

"Maybe I am jumping the gun on this," she conceded. "I think I'll sleep on it and we can talk about it tomorrow."

Erik's eyed her with skepticism. "That is an excellent idea, Juliana. In the meantime, why don't you freshen up and I will see to supper?"

She nodded, giving him a brazen stare. "And for tonight, maybe we should skip my dance lessons."

He hesitated a moment before answering. "As you wish."

Once in her room, Julie leaned against her closed door. It was official, she was a nut case. And her reasoning on that assumption had nothing to do with Christine or Raoul. It was directed at her somewhat bruised feelings.

Why didn't Erik insist on making her have her lessons? If she were Christine, he'd be all over her like white on rice. She had suggested skipping tonight out of anger, simply to hurt his feelings, but instead, here she was consoling herself. She had grown accustomed to her daily lessons with Erik. She enjoyed their time together. He had been a considerate partner and a patient teacher.

She hugged herself, trying to shake off the growing desire of belonging in Erik's arms. Was this Naomi again or were they her own feelings?

♀

Did Juliana honestly think that he was fooled by this sudden cooperation? She had given up far too easily. She was most likely in her room devising some plan he would just as soon deal with in the morning. Erik felt weighted by his own problems that needed to be processed tonight.

Supper.

They both needed to eat. A Creole woman sold meat pies every evening a few corners down. That would have to suffice. He grabbed his coat and walked out into chilly night. He pulled his collar up to break the cold bite of the wind. Another clap of thunder beckoned the coming rain. With a storm on the way, the streets were considerably less crowded, so he could see the peddler woman clearly from the front door.

A customer had just walked off with a wrapped pie when Erik reached the stand. The woman shivered each time the wind blew.

"How many sir?" she inquired with her leathered face tilted up. He noticed her wrinkled hands tremble as she waited for his response, her thin coat and hole-worn shoes provided little warmth.

"I will buy them all."

Her face lit up as she wrapped the meat pies in paper then handed them to him. He gave her a five dollar gold piece and walked away. "Sir, your change," she called after him.

"Keep it." He wasn't sure what made him do it. He felt pity for her. A woman her age should be in the warmth of her house surrounded by grandchildren, not on the streets trying to make a meager living.

"Thank you. God bless you." Her voice carried to him. At the same time, another conversation caught his attention.

"I believe Monsieur Lapierre is expecting me." The man's familiar deep voice made Erik halt.

"Yes, sir, Monsieur Lapierre received your card earlier." Turning, Erik caught sight of a manservant stepping back from the door of the house across the street. "Won't you come in?"

The tall gentleman at the door turned toward Erik and flashed him a knowing grin. Izak then turned and addressed the man. "Well, if you are inviting me in…"

"Yes, sir," the butler answered as Izak stepped inside the home. "May I take your hat?" That was the last Erik heard before the door shut.

Erik closed his eyes and cleared his mind. *What are you doing, Izak?*

Izak's laugh echoed. *Whatever can you mean?*

Startled by the response, Erik's eyes fluttered open. He had hoped for a reply, but hadn't really expected one. He steadied himself and concentrated his thoughts again.

Why are you here?

To be closer to you should you have need of me.

Erik swore. *Go away. I do not need you. Not now. Not ever.*

That remains to be seen, Izak replied. *Now leave me alone. I am busy working.*

Erik's attention was drawn to the house. In one sudden movement, all the windows went dark. He felt sorry for the misfortunate occupants of the Lapierre house, but not strongly enough to interfere. Erik walked the short distance to his own house while pondering this new development.

There was no escaping the inevitable. As much as he had preferred to keep knowledge of the Earth Walker to himself, he would have to tell Juliana all he knew about Izak. Maybe that was what Izak wanted.

Was Izak trying to force Erik to involve Juliana or coerce Erik into action? He stopped inside the hallway of the small Creole home and hung up his coat. He heard Juliana calling from her room.

"Erik, is that you?"

"It is," he answered. "I have supper."

Keeping Juliana blissfully unaware about Izak, who he was, and what he was capable of had been a comfort to him for the brief few hours he had held his tongue. But now, even if it was by Izak's design, Erik would have to tell her, for her own safety. This situation could not be ignored. Izak would not fade into the background. In fact, he had just become part of the scenery, much too close to home.

CHAPTER THIRTY-TWO

Erik listened to the soft patter of rain against the window throughout his restless night. He hadn't told Juliana about Izak. In fact, nothing had been resolved as they had eaten supper in silence; he engrossed with his thoughts and Juliana with her own. Today would be different. By evening time, everything would be settled to his satisfaction.

Control was to be relished.

Compartmentalizing his life and manipulating the outcomes in each area had always worked for him; spectacularly so, until each compartment had slowly merged with the other, integrating into one life experience. Was nothing sacred anymore?

The dappled light of early morning made a feeble attempt to penetrate through the rain and into the room. He sat on the edge of the sofa, staring absently at the muted light and thinking about what he wanted to say to Juliana. All the words he had left unspoken last night.

Magnificent, a deep voice breathed into his mind.

Startled by the intrusive thought, Erik sprinted to the window, muscles at the ready. A quick glance showed him an empty rain-soaked street. Just as he began to relax…

No… the voice reprimanded. *Look up.*

Erik raised his eyes to see Izak walking barefoot gracefully from slate roof to slate roof until reaching the house across from the window. Izak knelt down on the slick surface with a rapturous look upon his face. His wet hair and clothing were whipped by brief gusts of wind as black clouds hung low in the sky behind him.

Again, you deny yourself the pleasure.

"The pleasure—" Erik began, then remembered that he need not speak out loud. *The pleasure of what? Sitting on a roof drenched in freezing rain?*

Izak flicked his astonished gaze down to Erik. *Curious. You cannot see, can you?* He gestured his hand at the downpour. Erik heard Izak's continued mumbled thoughts. *His affinity for music, I assumed…*

You will come here. Izak indicated the roof.

A slow smile pulled at Erik's mouth. Control was to be relished. *I will not.*

Izak's eyes looked past Erik further into the room. *Perhaps Juliana might appreciate what I have to offer.*

Erik stiffened. He hadn't even checked on her this morning. He made haste to her room disregarding gentlemanly propriety as he swung open the door without knocking. Juliana lay asleep, tangled in her spread. Her sleep seemed restless also. A brief tenderness stole over him before fury rose in his chest at the thought of Izak's interference.

Leave her out of this, Erik growled.

Then come to me, came the unperturbed reply.

Erik stormed out of the house onto the wet street, giving Izak a defiant stare. "I am not in the habit of granting concessions to madmen." He blinked up through the cold, stinging rain. "What could possibly merit such attention?"

"Sit next to me and I shall show you," Izak spoke idly as he continued to gaze into the rain.

Every fiber of Erik's being rejected any further involvement with Izak, but until Erik found a way to rid himself of this Earth Walker, it would serve better to placate Izak than to antagonize him. A carriage trundled up the street and Erik stepped back to the shadow of his stoop.

"You need not hide," Izak voice carried over the noise. "I will conceal you from their sight."

Acting on a faith he didn't feel, Erik boldly crossed the street, climbed the drain pipe, and crouched low next to Izak on the slate-top roof. Erik's gaze swept the darkened skyline and saw nothing extraordinary except for the rain. Rain bouncing off rooftops, hitting windows, shutters, metal pipes, and the brick walk below. He steeled himself against the cold sting that penetrated through his clothes.

"What is this about?" Erik bit out in irritation. Was Izak trying to distract him for some other purpose? Maybe to lure him from the house, leaving Juliana unprotected? Another carriage fought its way through the muddy street and stopped in front of the Creole cottage he had just vacated. Two rotund women emerged and let themselves into the house.

Erik smirked as the carriage pulled away. He had sent the Krause sisters a request yesterday evening. He didn't want Juliana to have a moment alone with her thoughts until he had the opportunity to engage her in a sane, calm discussion about her intentions. And now, they served a dual purpose. Juliana would not be alone while he entertained Izak's folly.

Izak's attention rested briefly on the women. He gave Erik a sideways glance. "You needn't have gone through the trouble. Had I wanted to harm either of you, your lives would have been forfeit long before now." Izak shifted his position and looked forward again. "I want you to still yourself and listen."

As much as Erik wanted to resist this man, he felt equally compelled to obey him. So, he closed his eyes to listen. Once he tuned out all thoughts, Erik noticed the slight differences in the sound and rhythm of the rain—dull echoes from the roof, tings from the windows, clanks from anything metal, and the splats against brick.

Do not be startled, Izak's thought was softer than the noise. Erik felt the light pressure of Izak's hand against the back of his head. *Now...open your eyes*, Izak's voice held an air of expectance.

Erik opened his eyes to a blaze of colors. He gasped in surprise.

Resplendent! Magnificent!

It was beauty beyond imagination.

The stunning vision dancing before his eyes was awesome to behold—for every sound created by a surface as the rain made contact with it, a stream of color shot outward intertwining with other hues in a spiraled dance. Rain on the roof produced shades of silver. The higher sound created from the window's glass was a mixture of yellow and orange. Metals emanated darker hues of greens and blues. And shafts of bronze bounced off the brick. All colors sprinted outward from the sound, dissipating only to be replaced by the next color behind it, except for the ground, whose colors spread outward like ripples on a pond's surface.

Izak removed his hand from Erik's head and the colors disappeared back to clear drops of water and the mundane music of the rain.

"Extraordinary," Erik breathed out. He turned toward Izak. "This is how you see all of the time?"

"Yes." Izak's green eyes glinted, his expression serene. "Every sound has a color. But the rain always remains surprising. I never know what I might see. And it never fails to provide—" he sighed deeply "—a rare moment of contentment, even peace." His voice took on a harder edge. "I block it out as I choose. It can make for ineffective combat as you may well imagine. Colors are distracting at the wrong time."

"Why share this with me?" Erik couldn't keep the question at bay.

Izak kept his unwavering gaze on Erik. "I assumed that by the natural course of genetics, I had passed on the ability to you."

Erik leaned back on the roof. The cold rain had tapered off and specks of sunlight broke through the clouds. "What gave you that impression?"

Izak followed suit, leaning back on the roof, and turning toward Erik. "You are a composer of intricate music. You took up residence in an opera house. You groomed a young woman's voice to express shades of color I have rarely had the pleasure of seeing. I thought that was what drew you to music. If you found the beauty of nature stunning, imagine what you would see from an orchestra or from the human voice?"

Erik imagined Christine singing, picturing indigos and violets intermingled with silver and gold flowing along the notes that passed from her lips. His mind began to create a song of such terrible beauty, composing it solely by the colors he imagined it would produce. An all-consuming renewal of his desire for Christine flowed over him.

He wanted her for himself.

Raoul was not in love with Christine. He was deceived by her. Her voice, a result of Erik's own creation, was a Siren's, a lure to ensnare an unsuspecting man. Erik was the true source and cultivator of Christine's talent and therefore, the rightful possessor of the woman herself. Oh yes, he would move forward with his idea as originally planned.

"Give me this ability," Erik demanded feverishly.

Izak nodded in appreciation. "I wish that I could, but—," he sat up straighter. "You are either able to use it or you are not." He skimmed his eyes over Erik. "You are soaked." Until Izak drew attention to it, Erik hadn't realized he shivered.

"Come with me. We do not want your body to succumb to some unpleasant illness. Unlike mine, it is not immortal." Izak stood up and walked the rooftops toward the Lapierre home on the corner.

Erik hesitated.

Was he being guided by Izak's influence or by his own free will? He did not feel out of control so, should he follow Izak, it would be of his own volition. As curiosity got the better of him, he also lithely walked the rooftop in Izak's shadow. It was the right decision: To learn more of Izak meant Erik would discover more about himself.

♀

The slam of the front door, combined with the thuds of heavy footfalls and the familiar bickering voices of two women, roused Julie from her sleep.

Oh crap! It's Agnes and Bea.

Julie shot up in bed, disentangling herself from her covers. "If I don't get up and start getting myself ready, they're liable to try and bathe me again," she mumbled to herself. She poured water from the pitcher into the basin and washed her face. The cold sting shocked her into instant alertness. She grabbed her clothing and attempted to dress as fast as humanly possible. She heard a soft knock on the bedroom door just as she found a discarded stocking and rolled it up her bare leg.

"Mimi."

Julie didn't answer. She hoped Agnes would go away and by the time she returned, Julie would be fully dressed. More persistent knocks followed.

The door swung open. "Mimi, it's time to wake up." Agnes bustled into the room, a surprised look on her face. "Why you're half-dressed already!"

"Yes." She thought up a lie quickly. "I will be walking to the de Marigny home today. Doctor's orders: exercise, fresh air, and—" Julie tossed a glance to the window. The outside pane was still wet from last night's rain, but unmistakable signs of a clear morning were evident. "—sunlight."

Agnes frowned, doubt crossing her face. "Surely the doctor would object to you being out in this cold weather?"

"Not if I bundle up. And I should definitely remain warm from the exercise." Julie laced up her shoe, pretending she didn't see Agnes' concerned expression. "Really," she said as she stood up and smoothed out her dress, smiling at the disgruntled woman. "I've walked it before. It's not that bad."

Agnes shook her head. "Monsieur de la Croix did not mention this in his note."

"That's because we decided last night, *after* the note was sent," Julie improvised. "And," she raised her hand to prevent Agnes retorting. "Dependent on whether it was still raining or not. As you can see," Julie tossed a look to the window. "It's not raining anymore."

"I don't know." Agnes put her hands inside her apron pockets. "I think I should talk to Bea," she mumbled on her way out the room.

"If you must," Julie called after her as she finished tying the knots in her tignon. She felt slightly bad ducking out on Bea and Agnes. Their love for Naomi was genuine. They were getting paid to be there, but Julie knew they would be there regardless.

A trickle of annoyance swept over her. Why did Erik put her in this position? Again, he hadn't mentioned anything about them coming over and again, he was nowhere to be found. Where had he disappeared to?

She snorted.

He was probably looking in windows. In fact, she could guess whose window his face was plastered to, Christine's. What was it about Christine that both Raoul and Erik wanted so badly? Christine was pretty, but Juliana had seen much prettier women. The world contained many beautiful, exotic women, one only had to open a *Sports Illustrated* magazine to see a sample.

What did Christine have that Juliana didn't? She looked at herself in the mirror. She was beautiful too. Women in the 21st century would kill for her skin color. They laid their bodies out in the sun, spent hours in tanning booths, or even had their skin spray-painted in the hopes of achieving the sun-kissed likeness of Naomi's skin. And she had so much more to offer…

But not in this life.

She sighed.

In this time, her darker skin was a detriment, looked down upon. She had her answer: Christine was a white woman in the nineteenth century. Christine had it all.

Wait! She willed herself to stare at the mirror again. *What am I thinking? I am Julie. Julie François. This is Naomi's life, not mine. Why am I even worried about this*? Juliana held her head high and swept out of the room. As she strode down the hallway, she paused to listen to Bea and Agnes' hushed voices carrying from the kitchen.

"Something is different with our Mimi," Agnes whispered. A scraping of metal and the creak of the oven door followed before there was a response.

"She hasn't been the same since she hit her head," Bea conceded. "But there are stranger things happening with Monsieur de la Croix, one minute telling us *not* to come over then the next minute sending notes for us *to* come. This arrangement has gone topsy-turvy, but I daren't say anything. And you shouldn't either."

"We can't just let her walk the streets by herself, Bea."

"I don't like it either, but it isn't for us to stop her."

Julie released a small breath of relief knowing she would not have to fight Bea and Agnes to get out the door.

"Mimi," Agnes addressed her as she entered the kitchen, ignoring Bea's warning look. "Why must you walk? Stay home and we shall call a carriage for you later."

"My sister is just concerned about such a long journey by foot." Bea tried to smooth over Agnes' persistence on the matter.

Julie hugged the women with sincere gratitude. She appreciated their maternal caring. It had been such a long time since someone had displayed that kind of concern. It made her ache for her own mother. However, it seemed her uncharacteristic display of emotion bothered them even more. She had to do something to relieve their anxiety.

"Can you keep a secret?" she asked while trying to think one up as quickly as possible.

"Of course we can," they said in unison.

Images of baby Philippe flashed in her mind. Julie began to girlishly twist a button on her dress in feigned bashfulness.

"You know I've mentioned how much I adore Christine's baby. Spending so much time with him has brought out certain feelings in me." She placed her hand lightly on her belly and gave the women a knowing look.

Their eyes lit up. "You mean to say that you and Monsieur de la Croix…" Agnes gasped.

"Yes," Julie bobbed her head in confirmation. "We are hoping for little ones of our own as soon as possible."

"All the more reason to let the carriage take you later on," Agnes asserted.

"No," Julie countered. "The walk will strengthen my constitution. The doctor said so. And once I am with child, I will be confined to the house and unable to enjoy long walks outdoors." She didn't know where she was coming up with this stuff, but it sounded good to her.

Bea looked at Agnes. "A little one to take care of…imagine that!"

Julie knew she had won. There would be no more talk of carriage rides. She grabbed her purse and coat. She wasn't going to give the sisters a chance to change their minds. Time was of the essence. Erik could come home at any time, and then her plans would be squashed.

The walk would give her time alone to think.

As Julie walked away from the house, Bea and Agnes stood in the doorway waving, smiles on their faces, probably with visions of children dancing in their heads. She suppressed a laugh. It was so wrong of her to play on their hopes.

A sudden pang hit her. She turned away and continued to walk, the smile gone from her face. For a second, she had recalled the memory of James dancing a jig as she had walked off down the same street, in the same direction in the hopes of meeting up with Heath, before she had chosen to confront her past. Her future seemed hazy to her now, making it easy to push the memories from her head. No need to focus on that. Besides, she needed to figure out what her next move would be.

She knew Raoul would be home Friday for dinner. Christine had invited Naomi as their special guest. In the meantime, she would try to discover any weaknesses in the marriage and use it to her advantage…when the time came. If she ran into Raoul before then, it would be a bonus.

A wave of guilt swept over her. Erik was right about her, although she wouldn't admit it to him. Planning to seduce Raoul was not like her in the least. She would never have dreamed of splitting up a husband and wife. Could it be that this shift back into Naomi's reality warped her own sense of morality?

But everyone crossed the line sometime, she reasoned.

She wanted the option.

And nothing had been done yet. Julie knew that just by devising a plan, she had entered a grey area. She didn't want to do something she would regret now and possibly in the future. And it didn't help that her conscience urged her to tread carefully. She didn't have to make her mind up until the last moment, but if she chose to go for it, circumstances would be set in place to make it possible.

Julie's breath was stolen from her chest as an arm like a band of steel wrapped around her waist hard enough to force a gasp out of her, jolting her backwards into a side alley. A rough hand covered her mouth as she was pressed up against someone and pulled further back away from the main street.

"I don't mean to harm you none," the stranger's rich Irish brogue whispered in her ear as she struggled to free herself from him. "Just hold still now and this will be over quick enough." With his free hand he pulled her tignon from her head and threw it to the ground. His fingers entwined among her curls. "Such pretty hair—," he breathed in deeply, "—smells good too."

Oh hell no!

She lifted her knee up and aimed her foot backwards where his groin should be. A swift kick to the nuts would bring this creep down. Anticipating this move, the man swerved to the side and her foot swung in empty air. She made her body rigid when his hand left her mouth and she felt the hard coldness of a blade against her neck.

"Now why would you want to go upsetting me like that?" His voice shook as he dragged her toward the back wall of the alley. If she screamed, he was liable to slice her with the knife. Maybe she'd have better success reasoning with him? He seemed uncertain of himself.

"I have money in my purse. Take it all," she calmly informed him. He swung her around, staying behind her and continued forward.

"Your money won't do me any good. It won't cover what I owe. Now just hold still." He pushed her body flat against the wall. The left side of her face was pressed against the cold brick. He pulled her head back by her hair.

"I'll try to make this quick."

♀

"Two whiskeys," Izak commanded.

Erik waved his hand in silent refusal.

"One whiskey for me and dry clothes for us both," Izak amended. The butler blinked his glazed eyes in response and left the room. Izak turned his attention to Erik. "You do not have to repeatedly shun my hospitality. I cannot compromise you without your express permission."

"Excuse me if I do not trust your word blindly," Erik answered.

"I would expect nothing less from you." The corners of Izak's mouth twitched. "Even if it is becoming tiresome," he muttered as he sat, casually stretching his long legs.

The butler returned with clothes and a crystal tumbler of golden liquid. *Poor sap*, Erik thought, *his every move, every thought under captivity courtesy of Izak.* A deep unease settled in his stomach as Erik remembered exercising that same dominance, although not to the exact degree, on Christine and countless others. His appetite for control was innate, it seemed.

With all of his wet clothes on the floor like a pile of autumn leaves, Izak stood immodestly in the middle of the room. Erik couldn't help notice Izak's broad muscular shoulders sloped down to a toned abdomen and powerful thighs, his towering frame of perfection very much akin to a demigod. In some ways, Erik recognized that on a slightly smaller scale, he was a duplicate of Izak, except with puckered and scarred skin marring the perfection.

The butler assisted Izak into dry clothes as Erik stepped behind a chair to change on his own. He would always wear his skin with shame. He could not reconcile himself with being disfigured.

"Tell me," Erik broke the silence while pulling up his trousers, "Where are the others?" He tucked in his shirt and waited for the soft click of the door catching after the butler left the room. "The owner and his family?"

"There will be no ears to overhear us. No eyes to pry. They all slumber in their beds." Izak swallowed his whiskey in one gulp.

"Eternal slumber?" Erik countered, disliking Izak's methods.

"Not yet..." A dangerous glint entered Izak's eyes. "For now, I am sure their dreams are sweeter than nectar." Over the course of Erik's life, it hadn't been normal for him to care about such things and the family meant nothing to him, but somehow caring about those people made him feel human.

"What you did up there," Erik indicated the roof. "What was that?"

"Anyone in my family line is able to experience it, but using it independently is another issue." He placed the tumbler on a side table, clasping his fingers thoughtfully. "I have a theory about that...to be discussed at another time. There are more important matters to discourse at the moment."

"Such as..." Erik prompted, curious to hear what Izak might reveal.

"My bloodline goes back for centuries." Izak leaned forward. "Have you read the Bible, Erik?" Erik had a sudden flashback to his childhood. Standing stoically in a corner, his head covered with a cloth, and his hands covering his ears as Ellendora hollered scripture verses at him.

He grimaced. "I am familiar with it."

"Let us fit my story within its parameters shall we? Your mortal mind will not be able to comprehend what I am about to tell you otherwise."

Erik cast Izak a cold stare.

"Let us start at the beginning." Izak ignored Erik's look. "God created the Earth. On the sixth day, He created man: Adam. And for this man, He created woman: Eve. He gave them reign of the Garden of Eden, until they fell from grace and were cast out." Izak paused, waiting for Erik to speak.

"Those are the basic facts as I know them," Erik shifted in his seat, a discomfort settling upon him. Where was Izak going with this analogy?

"The days neither number six nor seven as man counts a day. And what most humans do not know is that there was another woman in the 'Garden of Eden.' Another woman *before* Eve was created. That woman's name is Lilith," Izak spoke in a whisper. "A woman so old that she has forgotten the sound of spoken words."

Erik sat in stunned silence. It sounded as if Izak implied Lilith still lived.

"Oh yes, she still lives. She will never know death." Izak answered Erik's thought, leaning more intimately toward Erik. "For you see, she left the garden *before* the fall of man. Her lips never touched the symbolic apple, so death does not touch her."

"What?" Erik kept his dazed emotions from his face.

Izak relaxed back into his chair. "This is all a figurative analogy. Again, you could not truly embrace the truth. I tell you this to help you understand."

"Why are you telling me this?"

"The woman in the garden…," Izak paused, "…had several children."

" And Lilith," he enunciated, "is my mother."

CHAPTER THIRTY-THREE

"So that would make your father—," Erik interrupted.

"Adam," Izak answered. "But my father has many names." Izak paused, inhaling deeply. "Do you smell that?"

Erik took in the odors around them: the fresh clothing on their bodies, a hint of whisky, and burning wood in the fireplace. Erik didn't smell anything unusual. "No."

Eyes closed, Izak pointed to the window facing Royal Street. "Juliana is on the move."

Erik leapt from his seat and pulled the curtain back. Looking down, he caught a glimpse of Juliana as she turned the corner. Erik heard Izak inhale again.

"She is being followed. He is an inexperienced hunter."

Izak was right. Erik saw a man stop at the corner, nervously look around, and turn on Royal Street, keeping his distance from Juliana. Erik had never seen the man before. He was neither beggar nor rich, his clothes were plain, and so was his face.

"This meeting is at an end." Erik meant to exit the room, but Izak held him back.

"You will never reach her in time."

Erik stiffened. He was Juliana's protector. He was strong, capable, and fast, faster than most men. "I will manage." He jerked his arm away from Izak and swung the door open.

"He has her already…second alley to the right. I smell their fear. You cannot help her, but *I* can. I can reach her before he blinks thrice, but you must give me permission to intercede."

Dare he trust Izak? For all he knew, Izak set up this charade to trick Erik into granting his consent. He didn't have time to debate Izak's sincerity because there wasn't time to waste.

With a hard swallow, Erik nodded.

"You must speak the words." Izak opened the second-story window, placing one foot on the ledge.

"Save Juliana." Before Erik could blink, Izak was gone.

♀

"Wait!" Julie begged. "Please, don't kill me." The man's trembling hand hesitated; Julie could see the knife out of the corner of her eye. It

PRINCE OF CONJURERS · 239

shook in mid-air for a few seconds then slashed downwards. Barely missing her neck, the knife brushed past her in a flash of shadow and wind.

She was suddenly freed from the man's grip and heard him crash into the side of the house to the left of her. She skirted away from the wall and saw her attacker crumpled on the ground, gripping his stomach. A large man towered over him.

Her savior's deep, smooth voice echoed in the alleyway. "You will not leave this alley alive." He lifted the assailant up by the scruff of his neck with very little effort. "Before you die, you will apologize to the lady for trying to kill her."

"No sssir—," the captive man stuttered, his brogue barely audible. "I wasn't to harm the lady. Honest to God, sir. I only came for this." He raised his hand up. Clutched within his fingers was a large chunk of curly, honey-colored hair.

Julie gasped and felt her hair, a large section was missing. The tall man also turned to look at her. She recognized him in an instant, those unmistakable green eyes. Izak Ulloa, the man who had introduced himself to her as Erik's friend.

"Indeed." Izak set the man down. "This is interesting."

"Juliana!" Erik careened full-speed into the alley. His gaze swept from Izak, to the stranger still clasping Julie's hair, then to Julie herself to whom he quickly approached, pulling her into a tight embrace. As he held her in his arms, the wall they had built between them last night fell away like sand, and Julie breathed in the comfort of his presence. He gave her hand a squeeze before he let her go, piercing the attacker with his eyes, a dangerous glare now replaced the look of concern.

Izak extended a placating hand in Erik's direction. Turning back to the man, Izak questioned him. "What is your name?"

"Niall Doherty." He tossed an apprehensive look back and forth from Izak and Erik. "Don't kill me please. I have a wife and three small children."

"Your lies won't save you." Erik moved toward the cowering man.

"Wait," Izak commanded. "He's telling the truth." Julie noticed Izak's eyes swim with an iridescent quality, his voice grew deeper. "What brought you to this alleyway today?"

"Please, my youngest son was very ill. I feared for his life." Niall did not raise his eyes from the ground as he spoke. "I've not been long in this country and heard rumors of a woman who could cure my child. The woman gave me a powder to put in his drink and it cured him. The only payment she would accept—," he finally raised his eyes, pointing to Julie, "—is a lock of *her* hair." Niall's face flushed. "If I don't bring this hair to Mamzelle by tonight, she will remove the healing magic from my son. I can't lose my son."

"She *cannot* have any part of my wife!" Erik fumed. A small stirring awoke in Julie at his words, *my wife*.

"Peace." Izak calmed Erik. "Marie plays with fire. She is bound to the same constraints as I am though she must not know it." Izak rounded behind Niall so fast that Julie wasn't sure her mind comprehended the movement. He tilted Niall's head at an awkward angle.

"Jesus, Mary, and Joseph…" Julie whispered, staring, immobilized in horrified fascination as Izak plunged his teeth into Niall's exposed neck. Erik shielded her behind him, backing them both slowly away from the two men. Curiosity burning in her chest, Julie craned to peek over Erik's shoulder.

Izak released his hold on Niall. The man seemed dazed and confused as to what had just taken place. His hand went immediately to his neck. "Don't worry, Niall," Izak crooned. "It's just a flesh wound. No harm done." With a flourish, Izak pulled out a handkerchief and casually dabbed at his mouth.

Panicked, Niall turned to flee. Only moments before, Izak had been behind Niall but now, he blocked the mouth of the alley preventing Niall's escape. All she could do was watch this play out as her feet remained rooted to the spot. Erik did not move to help the man either.

Julie felt a surge of sorrow for her attacker. He seemed to be a good man who was being used by Marie, a woman who proved to be ruthless and conniving. If there was a question in Julie's mind before, there certainly wasn't one now. Julie would *never* accept help from Marie Laveau.

"Niall, Niall, Niall…" Izak shook his head with disapproval. "I have not finished with you yet." Izak stood within inches of the trembling man. "Be still," he commanded. Niall stopped shaking. "I want you to take a message to your Mamzelle. Show her the souvenir I have given you," he said while tracing a finger over Niall's neck. "Tell her if she continues to interfere, she will no longer be afforded protection from me. Tell her—" Izak smoothly pulled Julie's hair from Niall's clenched hand— "I am saving her from herself."

Izak moved aside. "You may go." Niall stiffly ambled forward.

"Halt," Izak commanded. "I have one additional condition for Madam Laveau. She would be prudent to assure nothing ill befalls you or your family. For as of this moment, you are under my protection. Now be gone." Izak waved the man away.

Julie continued to stand behind Erik, soaking in the strength he emanated.

"Vampire." Erik's voice softly echoed her sentiments.

"I think not," Izak dismissed the utterance, disgust clouding his face. "Vampires are monstrosities of nature. I have found very few worthy to remain alive. You would be wise to remember that before you liken me to them."

Erik stepped forward, keeping as much distance between Izak and Juliana as possible. "What you did just now…I assumed…"

"A vampire is only a pale imitation of its creator." Izak continued, bridging the gap between himself and Erik. "You would have better comprehension of what you just witnessed had we not been interrupted, if you better understood my origins."

♀

Erik leaned forward, whispering to prevent Juliana from hearing. "I am nothing like you in that way."

"You wouldn't be." Izak acknowledged to Erik's great relief. "A matter for another time," he said in a louder voice, turning to Juliana. "It would seem Marie Laveau has a very keen interest in you." He held out her hair. "I suggest you destroy this."

Erik snatched it out of Izak's hands, securing it in his pocket. "I'll handle that."

"Of course you will," Izak said, his expression bemused.

"Thank you for saving me." Both men turned at the sound of Juliana's voice.

Izak bowed low. "A pleasure."

"There are stories…but…I didn't know there were people …like …you." Juliana stared at Izak with saucer-wide eyes. "But you say you aren't a vampire. I'm confused. What are you exactly?" Although she acted brave in her speech, she stayed close to Erik.

Izak glanced at Erik briefly before he answered. "I have walked the Earth a very long time. It is from my immortal bite with a human that a vampire breathes life."

"I see." Juliana stepped alongside Erik. "You create vampires, but you are not one. Are there more people like you?" Erik had not had a chance to voice the question himself, so he turned a curious eye to Izak.

"There are some, but most have accepted the end of their existences." A sad countenance briefly brushed Izak's face. "I have accepted the inevitability of one day choosing the same path, but until then, I remain to attend to some unfinished business."

Juliana appraised Izak then turned to scrutinize Erik, and then back to Izak, an awareness dawning. "The two of you look like you could be brothers." She let out a deep breath. "Erik, is there something you haven't told me?"

He shifted under her gaze. "I had planned to tell you yesterday, but our conversation regrettably took a turn in a different direction." He stressed the last part. "We will discuss this when we have privacy."

"Let me unveil the mystery." Izak interjected. Erik shot him a scorching look, daring him to continue.

Izak ignored him. "Considering our resemblance, the fact is undeniably clear that we are related. However—" he said loudly over her attempt to react—" have no fear, sweet Juliana. Erik is very much the mortal, or as you would be more inclined to say, a human version of my lineage."

Juliana tore her eyes away from Izak to Erik, then to the street where passersby ambled past the alleyway. "You're right. This is no place to carry on a conversation." She put her arm through his. "I think it would be best if you were to take me home now." He felt her hand tremble though she gave no other sign of being disquieted.

Erik walked with her to the fallen tignon. She picked it up and regarded the material with a momentary frown. She shook it free of dirt and began to wrap it around her head. It occurred to him that the tignon was as distasteful to her as his mask was to him. He gently reached up and took the ends out of her hands and tied the knots for her. Juliana held back as he directed her forward toward the street.

"Izak." She looked behind her. "When you bit Niall...did you make him a vampire?"

Erik didn't like the way Izak's eyes never wavered from Juliana's face as he approached her. "No, of that you can be assured. It is much more complicated than a simple bite." He flashed her that brilliant smile Erik was starting to dislike. "But it does give me certain advantages."

"Oh—" she turned around. "I *don't* want to know what *that* means."

I want to know, Erik thought.

Izak continued to smile at Juliana's back as he answered Erik. *I can penetrate Niall's mind from great distances to read his thoughts or direct his actions.*

Erik frowned at his answer. Placing his hand on the small of Juliana's back, he started toward the street, and yet again, she resisted him. "Izak, aren't you coming with us?"

Erik nearly bit his tongue in surprise.

Izak's harmonious laugh echoed in the confined space. "Not today. My work here is done for the time being."

"It seems as if we are all on the same side. We should stick together, don't you think?" Juliana persisted.

"Oh, you are sadly mistaken," Izak seemed to enjoy her surprise. "The only side I am on is my own." He nodded at her. "Good day." And with that, he sauntered onto the thoroughfare, leaving Erik as stunned as Juliana looked.

The ride home was quick and uneventful. Erik was glad Juliana held her tongue since it gave him a few minutes to collect his thoughts. If he could figure out Izak's motivation, he would feel more at ease about his father's new role in his life. But, he could not wrestle his thoughts into submission. His mind and body were in a state of war with each other. Looking down at his side, a thrill of sensations shot through him: pleasure, fear, longing, and happiness from Juliana holding his hand the entire way home.

♀

Bea and Agnes rushed into the hallway, concerned looks clouding their faces as Erik and Julie came through the front door.

"Monsieur de la Croix, what—," Bea's sentence hung in mid-air. Julie knew they were surprised to see her and Erik home again together so soon, but there was a flicker of horror in her eyes. Past her, Agnes also had a look of restrained fright. Did they fear a reprisal from Erik?

"Is there a problem?" Erik's stony voice carried throughout the silent house. Something was wrong. Julie whipped around to see Erik's cold stare and marred face. She hadn't registered until now that his face had been exposed this whole time. Seeing him that way was second nature to her now.

Bea swallowed, looking everywhere but at Erik. "No sir."

With averted eyes, Agnes asked to take his coat. His face softened in surprise as he handed it to her.

"I think a hot toddy is in order, Monsieur de la Croix." Bea patted Julie's hand. "And hot tea for you." Bea and Agnes made such an effort to correct their earlier reactions. Julie felt as though her heart would burst with gratitude. She could well imagine if she was treated so contemptuously because of the color of her skin, Erik had probably faced equal or greater discrimination because of the disfigurement of his.

Julie grabbed Erik's hand again and led him to the small settee in the sitting room. Each sat giving the other small glances as they waited for the drinks. There was no point in diving into conversation since they would be shortly interrupted. But, feeling uncomfortable by the silence, Julie struggled to make small talk.

"This is not my favorite room in the house." She played with a doily on the table.

Erik gave her an odd look. "Nor mine."

Encouraged by his reply, she elaborated. "The furniture doesn't match and the wall-paper is so busy, it makes me nervous to look at it. Who decorated your house?"

His lips pulled back in a smile so natural and genuine, it made her return it. "You did, I'm afraid. Well," he conceded. "Naomi did."

Julie laughed at the irony. "Why did you let her? It's plain awful."

"Yes it is." He appraised the room. "But it made her happy. I could not deny her that." Julie nodded.

"Well, you might be interested to know that I don't share Naomi's idea of what is aesthetically pleasing." Julie was discovering that she and Naomi were different in many ways. "Did you know I can't sing?"

Erik raised his eyebrows in interest. "Is that so?"

"Christine wanted to sing with me the other day and I refused. Thank God she assumed I had problems because I 'hit my head.' But the truth is...I am tone deaf."

"Curious—" he mused. "I would like to hear you sing one day."

"No you wouldn't," she countered. "Have you ever heard a dying animal cry?"

"Of course."

"Then you've heard me sing. I sound just like that."

"I am sure you grossly exaggerate." He relaxed into the chair.

Julie thought back to the time she sang at the Cat's Meow. "No, I'm not." She felt her cheeks flush with embarrassment at the thought. "But one day, if I'm feeling generous, I might give you a small preview." She shrugged. "Maybe."

"I look forward to it."

Bea entered the room carrying a silver tray with two cups. She placed one in front of Erik and the other in front of Julie. "Agnes and I will be leaving early...to...tend to...um...our neighbor who is recuperating from a cold." Bea added to her clumsy excuse. "Doctor's orders." She gave Julie a meaningful look. "And everyone should *always* follow doctor's orders."

Erik gave Julie a questioning glance.

"That will be fine." Julie managed to answer, her cheeks feeling a familiar flush. Bea hurried to join her sister in the hallway, where within seconds, Julie heard the front door shut.

"I assume you know what that was about." Erik lifted his cup.

Without preamble, Julie gave him the truth. "The sisters are under the impression that you and I would like our privacy—" she looked away, speaking as fast as humanly possible. "In order to start making a baby."

He choked on his drink. "I beg your pardon?"

CHAPTER THIRTY-FOUR

"Don't make me repeat myself." Julie cringed under his gaze.

"How *exactly* did they get that impression?"

"I think you know it came from me," she admitted. Julie wished she could guess the thoughts that swam behind Erik's eyes, eyes that seemed to bore holes into her with silent expectations, searching for something.

"If we were to have children," he finally spoke. "They would be quite handsome." He rubbed the scarred side of his face. "I was not born this way.

"My mother—" he stood up and walked to the window, turning his face from her. "My most beloved mother, gave me life then tried to take it from me the same day." When he turned toward her again, his eyes were moist. Julie pretended not to notice, although she ached for him. Erik gave her a cursory stare. "You need not pity me. I do not remember it at all. Besides, it is the remainder of my life that has given me more pain because of her choice that day."

Julie couldn't resist the wave of compassion that washed over her. Her empathetic heart couldn't comprehend how anyone do that to an infant, to a helpless child...

"Oh, Erik—" Tears welled in her eyes. "I'm so sorry to hear that." She wanted to embrace him, to comfort him, but she didn't dare do so for fear that he would withdraw from the conversation. As it was, he stood stoically before her, without revealing any reaction to her emotional reply.

"There is more to my story." He sat down again. "In fact, some of the pieces were just filled in for me."

"You don't have to tell me if it's too painful," Julie interrupted, thinking about how difficult it was to discuss her parent's murders although; a huge part of her hoped he wouldn't take her up on that half-hearted offer. She wanted to know.

Erik held up his hand. "I simply want you to listen for now. There are things you need to know about me."

"Okay..." she readied herself.

"I never knew why my mother did not finish...shall we say...her task? And it seems I owe my father for intervening and sparing my life. He saved me and then abandoned me to an indifferent parent and a life of—" his sentence lingered for a moment before he caught himself. "A story for another time, perhaps...

"Juliana, what I am trying to tell you is that I have never known my father. Never knew what his name was or what he looked like, until now."

"You've found your father after all these years?" she breathed out in an excited whisper.

Julie had always said she wasn't interested in finding her own birth parents, but deep down in the smallest recesses of her soul, she did wonder about them. As she considered this, she remembered the resemblance between Erik and Izak and the declaration that there was some kind of family tie. Had Izak, the ancient Earth Walker, come to reunite Erik with his father? Was that what he meant when he had told her he had unfinished business?

"A more accurate account in this situation would be that *he* found *me*. In fact," Erik stared at her again. "He left his card with you a couple of days ago."

"Izak," she mumbled as dread started at her toes and made its way to her fluttering heart. What did this mean? Was Erik some kind of inhuman creation?

Erik kept eye contact. He seemed to steel himself for rejection or condemnation from her, but she would have to disappoint him as she recalled Izak's words from earlier.

Have no fear, sweet Juliana. Erik is very much the mortal, or as you would be inclined to say, a human version of my lineage.

At this point, she didn't know why she bothered to let anything shock her. It seemed this was all part and parcel of this life review. For all she knew, when the full moon arrived, she might transform into a wolf or banshee or something. She would completely accept this soul experience, without question. No matter how strange things got.

"How do you feel about this?"

Erik's brow shot up in disbelief. "What?"

"How do feel about finally meeting your father? Or finding out he saved your life? Or that your father is whatever in hell an Earth Walker is?"

"I understand your question, Juliana. I am in amazement that you posed it." He touched his chin, studying her again. "Quite honestly, I expected a different reaction from you."

"Well, you should know by now not to expect the ordinary from me."

"Duly noted." He graced her with a small smile. It was nice to see the change in his demeanor.

"How do I feel about this, you ask?" He stared at the wall. "I cannot lie," his eyes flashed as an odd expression crossed his face, one Julie had seen before, but had not yet learned to read. "I feel validated. Izak defies all things that we thought we knew about the world and in doing so he gives credence to my differences. And I am intrigued...intrigued to learn what I am because of him. Meeting him explains so much about myself. I feel exhilarated, liberated by the knowledge that I now have some idea of my true origin.

"And I hate him," Erik spat out in such an unexpected change of emotion. Julie jolted back into her seat, surprised. Anger smoldered in his eyes. "He deserted me to a life you *cannot* imagine. He should have let me die."

"Oh no!" Her choked reply surprised them both as Julie realized she couldn't imagine life without him in it.

His face softened. "You are being kind."

"Did he explain his absence to you? Can you forgive him that and move on? He is here for you now." She hoped to divert their conversation from her outburst.

"Maybe if you would lead by example, I could follow."

She tilted her head, unsure what he meant.

"Can you forgive Christine and Raoul? Can you let go of their future transgression?"

"Oh." Julie said, unable to give him the answer she knew he wanted to hear.

"I thought not."

Julie did not want to dive into that subject again. There was only so long you could beat a dead horse. "So, where do things go from here?"

"I am not definite on that." Shaking his head, Erik pursed his lips. "I do not trust him completely. As you heard from his own account, he is a willing ally when it suits his purpose, a purpose he has yet to disclose." Erik closed a hand over hers. "Whatever he is, Izak is powerful. He may have many more abilities we don't know about. If you should ever encounter him without me present, use the utmost caution."

"I promise."

He accepted her answer with a nod. "Now," his tone became more businesslike. "We have someone of more immediate concern to discuss."

"Marie," she guessed.

"Her actions today were a blatant attempt to create some way to bewitch you."

"With my hair? Do you *really* believe she could do that?"

"Do not scoff at her abilities, Juliana. If it were not for her, I would not have been able to bring you here. She is very talented at potion-making. I regret to admit that I needed her assistance."

"So that's why Marie told me she could send me home," Julie realized out loud.

"Is that what she said to you before I intervened?" He gave the empty room a scowl, exhaling a long breath before speaking again. "It is true. Marie could likely send you back to your life, but it would cost Naomi dearly. Do not," he clasped her hands again. "I implore you, do not accept Marie's assistance. I *can* get you back. I promise."

Her heart brimmed with emotion. "I believe you, Erik. I can wait until you can make it possible. I would *never* accept Marie's help, never." It seemed to her that for once, she and Erik had come to the same understanding: Izak was the lesser of two evils, for now.

"Very well," Erik said, pulling his hands away. "Let me tend to you."

"Tend to me?"

He gave a gentle tug on her tignon. "Your hair is a bit of a mess. I will be back in a moment."

Julie slowly unraveled the material then ran her fingers through her uneven tangled curls. Niall certainly had made a mess of it. She turned when she heard Erik entering the room, hands raised, showing her a pair of scissors in one and a hairbrush in the other.

She sighed occasionally during the minutes Erik brushed the knots out, the soft strokes relieving all the tension in her head. It felt like heaven. Placing the brush on the table, he gathered her hair with his hands, and pulled the remaining length behind her back. She heard the clip of the scissors and saw snippets of hair falling to the floor. He worked in concentrated silence while she enjoyed the calming sensation of his hands in her hair.

"This will have to do," he said, walking around her. "Take a look." Erik extended a hand, assisted her out of the chair, and led her to the hallway mirror.

Framing her face was a shoulder-length mop of curly hair. Julie tossed her head, watching the strands sway since they were now free from the burden of the heavy weight they once carried.

Behind her in a gentle manner, Erik pulled the ends together checking the accuracy of the cut. "I know a woman's hair is her luxury. I apologize for the shortness of length. Niall did not leave me much choice in the matter."

"No." Julie gave the Erik in the mirror a small smile. "I like the style. It's more...me." She turned around to face him. "Since we don't really know how much time I will remain here...you know...helping with this wife-swap thing—"

Erik's brow furrowed. "I really wish you would not reference it in that way."

"Alright," Julie sighed in exasperation. "Helping you reunite with your 'fiancée.'" She removed a loose curl from her face. "Do you think, in the spirit of change, that you and I could wipe the slate clean and start fresh?"

"*You* want something from me." Erik crossed his arms, a knowing look on his face.

"And *you* do beat all, Erik, so suspicious of everyone and everything. Maybe," she conceded. "You might be justified. I can't imagine what kind of life you have had. But, in saying that, we don't know how long we might have to live with each other. Wouldn't it be nice if we just used this time to get along?"

"We have had our moments, Juliana, but on the whole, I have not felt in discord with you, *except* when you do not get your way."

"Or you yours—" she teased.

The light of his smile reached his eyes. "Touché."

"So—"

"Ah-ha! Here it comes." His lips twitched.

"*So*," she said more seriously. "Seeing as I haven't much to look forward to personally—"

"Do not say that, Juliana. I can afford you any comfort. I can give you any want you might have."

"I am banking on that," she smiled up at him. "Look, we both know that my time here is limited, could be days, could be months. I know you will see to Naomi's welfare. I am not worried about my past self. But I would like to enjoy myself here, now, in the present. And," she looked up to the ceiling. "God knows there isn't much to keep a soul occupied in this time period." She didn't know how people functioned without television or computers to help fill the day. She found the days long and most often, boring. "And at this point, I am facing possible threats from Marie and Izak."

Erik stood in grim silence. She knew he could not refute that.

"I want to continue my dance lessons. I want to attend the Masquerade ball. That's all I ask for."

Erik let his arms fall at his side. "Not only will you be there," he promised. "But I will see to it that you are the most alluring guest in attendance. Beautiful attire, graceful presence, and sublime dancing—" he took her hand and gave her a playful spin— "will have the gossipmongers whispering of disguised royalty in their midst."

She flung her arms around him in a grateful hug, one he spontaneously returned. It was nice to know there would be a spot of happiness amongst all the unpleasantness. She knew when she returned to the twenty-first century, her life would be changed forever by the little things in this one.

"Thank you," she whispered in his ear, after planting a kiss on his cheek. She breathed in as she pulled away. He smelled like soap, wind, cedar wood, and fresh rain. Time seemed to slow. She raised her eyes to his face which displayed a multitude of emotions, one in particular catching her attention: temptation. And without thought, she leaned in and kissed his lips, soft and lingering.

She pulled back again. One look in Erik's eyes told her she had opened Pandora's box and she yearned to partake in its contents. He claimed her mouth with a raw passion that sent mind-numbing, toe-curling electric tingles shooting through her. She leaned closer into him and slipped her hand into his hair, responding to his touch, and savoring the experience. Each passing moment increased his fervor, as she strained on her tip-toes to close the gap between them.

There was no more Christine, no Raoul, no Simon, and no future for her with Heath. There was no time, no plans, and no endings. Erik was the only person in her new world...Erik and his ongoing, passionate kiss.

"Enough!" Erik staggered back from her, his ragged breathing matching her own. Stunned, Julie stood there, silent. Was that regret she saw in his eyes?

He turned his face away, speaking to the wall. "I suggest you change clothes and ready yourself for your day at the de Marigny's. We do not want to disappoint Christine with the absence of your presence." He turned his back to her in an unspoken dismissal.

Well, hell! What was she supposed to do with that? The fire in her veins cooled, but her cheeks burned hot. Flying down the hall to her room, her hands trembled as she changed into new clothes and tied a clean tignon around her head. His reaction was so humiliating. It wasn't as if she had taken advantage of him. Her senses weren't that dulled. What had just taken place was most certainly mutual.

Julie tried to keep her emotions in check as she popped her head into the sitting room and announced to Erik she was ready. He rose from his chair and walked her to the front door. When the door opened, she could see a carriage waited to transport her for a "fun-filled" day with Christine. Erik hadn't wasted any time and neither would she. She stepped toward the threshold, but a light hand on her wrist held her back.

"I want to assure you," Erik said in a strained voice. "I will never again lose control with you."

"Really?" she felt affronted. "Well, that's real good to know. But answer me this, what do you intend to do if I am the one out-of-control?" He let go of her wrist. The desperate look in his eyes tried to tell her something, but she was too worked up to decipher the message. Instead, she descended the two steps, crossed the walk, jumped into the carriage without help, and slammed the door. This time as it trundled off, she didn't look back.

CHAPTER THIRTY-FIVE

"Damn it all to hell!" Erik slammed the door, his heart pounded with fire. His illusion of contentment had just been shattered. Pacing the length of the hallway, he could do nothing to prevent images of Juliana from flooding his mind. The very thought of kissing her left every inch of him longing.

All this time he had clung to the memory of the first kiss ever allowed to him. But the light brush of his lips on Christine's forehead was a vacant promise to him now. His desire to take Christine as his own dwindled with each second he had held Juliana in his arms. He no longer wanted the controlled passivity a union with Christine would bring. Juliana's actions changed that for him today.

It seemed so long ago he had believed Christine's response to him was love. That he had believed she saw past his deformity and saw a man. Everything he thought he knew no longer made sense. What did he know of love?

Nothing...

And this morning, in an instant, his defenses had been stripped away by Juliana, leaving him feeling naked and a stranger to himself, unable to recognize his own feelings.

He might not know what love was, but he certainly understood passion: his penchant for music, the pleasure of a woman's voice, the wind on his face, the world at his fingertips...and Juliana in his arms.

Passion might not be love, but it was a beginning...

It was not Christine, but Juliana who saw into him, past the exterior. And that was what he feared and hoped for the most. What if she gazed too deeply and was repulsed by who he was or unimaginable still, could endure the sight of him in spite of his many shortcomings? Maybe one day her passion could turn into love?

He knew one thing with certainty; his life had been irreparably changed. Just as the moon reflects the sun, Erik swore a silent oath that he would strive to be a better reflection of the light regardless of his relation to Izak or his own unsavory past. He wanted to be good enough to deserve Juliana. For however long he might have her in this lifetime.

Erik leaned against the hallway wall, his legs suddenly weak. What did he know of goodness?

Having spent his life walking in the shadows of this world, he had just come to the most shocking realization: He was human. And not the best part of humanity at that.

If you are finished emasculating yourself, there is something you may want to see. The familiar voice dripped with condescension into his head.

Is your mission in life simply to torment me? Erik retorted, tired of the intrusion. Izak's rich laughter grated his insides.

I think you are doing just fine tormenting yourself without any help from me.

Erik pushed himself away from the wall, anger welling deep within. *Get out of my head and out of my life!*

*Hmmm...*Izak purred into his thoughts. *And how will you make me leave you, Erik? Ah...I see it in your mind. You picture the catgut rope in your pocket around my neck. You mean to choke the life from me. Tear me to pieces if necessary. To kill me as you have done to so many others.*

Erik realized there would never be the element of surprise. Izak would always be prepared against any assault from him.

You think you are one of them? Izak taunted. *Think again. You are more like me than you could possibly imagine. They will always see you as a monster. They will never accept you, but I...I see your true nature, Erik. Your anger, your fury makes you beautiful. You are more powerful than these people you surround yourself with could imagine.*

Izak's words flooded in rapid succession one after the other into Erik's mind threatening to drown out his resolve.

If you want something, take it. There is nothing in this world that does not belong to you. Forget these petty dreams of yours. Abandon this life and join me. There is the whole world for the taking!

That appeal to his ego might have been tempting a few months ago. In fact, a very small part of him even now bristled in keen interest at the thought. But what if what he wanted was love? Love that was not coerced, not orchestrated, or taken, but freely given? Year after year, he discovered there was little satisfaction in getting what you want without being able to fully enjoy it. It took a lot of energy to make someone do as you wish.

I shall have to respectfully decline.

Erik heard Izak's resigned sigh. *No matter. I am almost to your door. Let me in.*

I think not. Erik shook his head in emphasis. *You are not welcome in this house.*

Izak didn't respond, but within seconds, Erik heard a sharp rap on the front door.

"Go away!" Erik slammed his palm against the door.

"Now don't be that way. As I said, there is something you will want to see."

"You know," Erik gazed at the ceiling. "I don't think I'm interested in seeing anything you want to show me."

"Even if it might affect Juliana?" The deep voice carried easily through the door though he whispered the words.

Erik removed his hand from the door, curling it into a fist. Izak knew his weakness. He knew Erik couldn't take a chance when it came to her. With reluctance, he opened the door.

Izak stood in the doorway, crystal-topped cane in hand and a smug, all-knowing smile on his face. "Are you not going to invite me in?"

Erik shook his head. "Just show me from right where you are."

"That is not possible. We are going to need some privacy." He rested the crystal to the side of his temple. "What I have to show you is in here and you are wasting time. Our thief may be up to mischief. Do you not want to know what happens?"

Yes he did. He definitely did, but he didn't want any unwanted visits to his home later, especially when he wasn't around.

"You may enter under a few conditions." Erik agreed with reluctance. "Your stay is only welcome for the duration of this visit and terminates once you leave."

"Of course, as you speak, so it shall be done."

Not trusting Izak's flippant reply, Erik did not yet offer the invitation.

"I swear." Izak raised a compliant hand.

Believing that Izak would be bound by the verbal guidelines he set forth, Erik swung the door open wide and Izak sidled past him into the house. Locking the door behind him, Erik followed Izak into the small living room and watched as Izak's hands lightly touched the piano in the corner, an odd expression crossed his face.

Uncomfortable with the strange intimacy, Erik broke the silence. "So, when do we do this?"

"No time like the present." In a fraction of a heartbeat, Izak had his hand behind Erik's head. Erik blinked several times to focus, his vision flickering. He realized that although he could see his living room, he also saw another room through the eyes of someone else, both views coexisting at the same time.

The bits and pieces of the decor he was able to see were lavish. The owner had very good taste, but Erik didn't get a satisfactory look at his surroundings as the person's eyes darted around. He felt the man stand, then sit, his chest rising and falling with anxiety. Erik could feel fear building inside him...the man's concern for his child and his fear compromised Izak's power.

No fear, Niall. No fear, Izak crooned.

Niall's muscles relaxed and he breathed easier. He was calm by the time the door opened and a tall, striking woman entered. Erik would have recognized her without her swinging hoop earrings or her tignon, knotted seven times. Marie Laveau was unforgettable even when one wanted to forget her.

"I trust you would not be here unless you have come with payment for your son's healing," Marie said with saccharine sweetness as she placed a cold hand on Niall's arm. Erik jolted his own arm back in surprise. He had felt her touch.

Izak looked at Erik with mild interest.

Niall stood. "No, Mamzelle."

"What?" The false welcome erased from her face. "Then what is the meaning of your presence here?" Her voice sounded strained, but controlled.

Do not look away from her, Izak guided Niall.

"I've been sent with a message," Niall said, looking straight toward Marie. Erik could see anger flash in her dark eyes.

"A message?" her voice rose an octave. "A message important enough to sacrifice the life of your child?"

Erik saw Marie through watery eyes as conflicting emotions tore through Niall: regret, loss, defeat, and anguish. He was unable to speak, but nodded in response.

"Well?" Her question hung in the air.

Niall clumsily fumbled with the collar of his shirt. His fingers brushed against the two swollen puncture marks on his neck as he pulled the material to the side and exposed his skin. "I was instructed to show you this. I've been marked."

Marie swept up to him for a closer look, her lips thinned. She stepped back, crossing her arms. "It does not negate your debt to me."

"You aren't to interfere," Niall mumbled.

You must speak with authority, Izak urged. The crystal on Izak's cane glimmered and Erik felt a surge of energy flow through Niall.

Niall spoke louder. "None of this has anything to do with me or what you say I owe you. He does not want you to interfere with the girl."

Clicking her tongue, Marie considered his words. "I can see that you have become a pawn of Monsieur de la Croix, no doubt. He is a master of disguises." Her eyes flicked over to his neck. "And a proficient in trickery."

Izak raised an eyebrow. "I do believe she just paid you a compliment."

After a few moments of consideration, Marie continued with her thoughts. "He would go through elaborate lengths to dissuade me from pursuing Mimi. This will not work and it does not release you from your obligation. Mimi is too valuable to me, valuable to my business. Get me a lock of her hair or your son will succumb to his unfortunate illness when it returns and mark my words, if I don't have Mimi's hair in my possession by nightfall, your son's illness *will* return."

Niall's mind fluttered through the message Izak had commanded him to repeat. He wanted to finish, but Erik could feel Marie's response unsettle Niall.

Izak smirked. "She thinks to break your hold on him, Erik. Little does she know whom she is truly dealing with." A wicked gleam crossed his face in the light of the crystal. "Let us show her, shall we?" Without giving Erik a chance to respond, Izak closed his eyes and spoke in Basque to Niall. "Sleep."

Erik's vision from Niall's perspective went dark and he felt Niall's head fall forward. But before it touched his chest, Niall blinked, gazing at Marie through narrowed eyes. He felt Niall's lips spread into an ugly smile. The same smile mirrored on Izak's face.

"Woman," Izak and Niall spoke in a unified voice richer and fuller than any human could manage. Izak moved Niall face to face with Marie. "You would do well to heed my warning for it shall be spoken but once." Erik could only imagine Niall's unholy appearance with Izak at the helm.

Erik felt a tinge of jealousy at the obvious horror on Marie's face. He had never inspired such a reaction from her, but he reveled in it, satisfied to see her visibly quake. And almost as if fueled by Erik's unspoken approval, Izak slowly backed her against the wall, leaned in close, and breathed in her scent. Erik smelled fear, hatred, incense, and vanilla along with something very faint, under the surface that he could not discern, although Izak seemed to.

"Tread carefully, Voodoo Queen," Izak warned. "You are protected by the bond of the ancients, but once you breach that protection, I can do with you as I will." He ran a finger down the front of her bodice, but she angrily swatted it away.

Amused, Izak grabbed her chin and forced her to look him in the eyes. "You are fond of informing people that there is a spiritual cost to everything they do. I am here to remind you that *your* soul-debt is mounting. Just give me an excuse to collect."

Marie tore herself from his grasp and maneuvered far away from him, fleeing to the other side of the room. "I don't answer to you, whoever you might be." She raised her head. "I commune with the Loa. They and they alone are my judge."

"Your first, among many misconceptions." Erik heard the familiar condescension in Izak's voice. "You only think that you do."

"Who are you?" She glared at him, incensed.

He swirled his hand and leaned forward in a mocking bow. "Izak Ulloa."

"I've never heard of you."

"You would not have." Erik could feel Izak tiring of this tête-à-tête. "Let me be clear with you, Marie. Do not interfere with Juliana and Erik." A devious look crossed her face and as if reading her thoughts, Izak amended his previous statement. "That includes Naomi Hemming. Juliana and Naomi are to be considered as one. As you do to one, you do to the other."

"I have been wronged." She challenged him.

"Wronged? I think not. Has your ego been stepped on? Perhaps. Let this go before you cause yourself irreparable harm." Erik was surprised by a sliver of compassion coming from Izak. "Under any other circumstances, I would be the first to extend my encouragement."

Izak casually ran Niall's hand through his hair. "Since we understand each other, I will take my leave of you then." Marie remained silent as Izak-as-Niall approached the door.

What about Niall? Erik interjected, concerned for the man's safety.

Izak spun Niall back around. "One more thing you need to know. Should harm come to Niall or any member of his family, I will pay you a visit, in my own form. A visit you will severely regret." He then carried Niall as arrogantly as possible out of the Maison Blanche. Erik felt a speechless Marie's eyes boring into his back. Once the building was far enough behind him, Izak whispered, "Awake." Erik felt Niall's consciousness once more.

Run home and never seek out Marie Laveau again, Izak told Niall while pulling back his and Erik's energies. Izak removed his hand from the back of Erik's head and Niall's vision abruptly disappeared from Erik's sight along with the light from the crystal on Izak's cane.

"I do believe some refreshments are in order," Izak said as he sat down on Erik's love seat.

The short-lived camaraderie Erik had felt evaporated. "Don't get too comfortable. One drink and then you leave."

"Is this the gratitude I get for neutralizing your nemesis, making the way clear for you to continue your plans?" Izak asked in feigned offense.

"Thank you for that," Erik said, handing Izak a full tumbler of whiskey.

Izak nodded and downed the drink in one swallow, slamming the tumbler onto the small side table much to Erik's annoyance.

"I will see you out now," Erik motioned toward the hall.

"Not so fast," Izak crossed a leg over his knee. "We need to talk."

CHAPTER THIRTY-SIX

"Your hair!" Christine gasped as Julie unrolled her tignon. "Whatever possessed you to cut it?"

Telling Christine the truth was not an option. Julie sighed, hoping that by the end of this past-life experience she would be able to recognize the truth from lies; she ran her hand through her short curls. "My hair becomes tangled and knotted since I have to wear it wrapped so often. I find it easier to care for this way."

Of course *that* woman wouldn't have considered what Julie had to endure. Christine was born with many liberties denied to Naomi. Being forced to wear that blasted material on her head on a daily basis was just another thing on the list of perturbing mandates of this life.

Understanding lighted on Christine's face in the form of a guilty blush. "Now that I look at it closer, I think it's just lovely."

Julie managed to give her a small smile.

"I thought we might go to Canal Street today for a little shopping. Before we do," Christine rattled on. "How about some refreshments? Tea? Coffee?"

"Coffee, please."

She leaned into to the hallway. "Orelia!" After waiting a few moments, she called again. "Orelia!" Giving Julie an apologetic smile, Christine started walking off. "She's a little hard of hearing."

Julie couldn't say she was sorry to see the back of her. Had she known they were going shopping, she wouldn't have taken the damn tignon off in the first place. Leaning back into her chair, she gazed out of the window, half-hoping that she would see Erik's face peering back at her again. Her stomach tightened as she pictured his eyes flicking to her lips and the kiss that followed. Her anger at him had fizzled out on the ride over as she forced herself into a nineteenth-century state of mind.

It had occurred to her that his response could be due to some genteel morality of the time period. He might have believed that he had sullied her honor. Was Erik only trying to be a gentleman?

Or perhaps his reaction stemmed from feelings of betrayal. Erik was convinced his heart belonged to Christine and Julie had violated those feelings. Sure he had responded to her ardently less than an hour ago. What hot-blooded man wouldn't? But, on the downside, he had quickly made sure she knew it wouldn't happen again.

Or perhaps he felt something for her and was not ready to admit it to himself yet?

If only she could be certain. If only he had elaborated on what he meant, not that she had given him a chance to do so. He was so difficult to read, Julie couldn't be absolutely sure of the reason. Anyway, no sense speculating. She had a mission to accomplish and she couldn't do that with her mind wandering.

Putting on her best game face, she turned toward the hallway at the sound of approaching steps. She rose to her feet in surprise as Raoul entered the room instead of Christine.

"Oh," he uttered, startled at finding her there as well. "I was looking for Christine."

Julie's mouth went dry and her words came out a bit breathy. "She's in the kitchen with Orelia."

This was her opportunity. She had Raoul alone.

"Ah." He nodded, smiling. "You know, I believe Orelia is nearly one hundred years old. I have tried countless times to bring in more help," he said, shrugging his shoulders in amused resignation. "But she chases them all out of the kitchen."

Julie stared at his mouth as he spoke, bewitched by the sensuous curves his lips made as they wove around the heavily accented words.

"She has been with my family before the war or so they tell me. I believe she fears being replaced, but she will always have a home with us."

Julie thought of how easily Simon had replaced her with Monika and her throat tightened. "I think everyone fears being replaced."

His eyes studied her face as he considered her opinion. "You might be right." He shifted his weight, staring a bit more obviously now. "There is something different about you."

Julie's breath caught. Was it a possibility he could sense that she was not Naomi any longer? Was he drawn to her as herself?

"Yes, definitely something different." He rested a finger on his lip. "Is that a new dress?"

"No," she replied while looking down at the frock. At least she didn't think so.

"As sure as you stand here, I can plainly see that there is a change, yet it escapes me."

Maybe, Julie wasn't going to have to do anything to compromise Christine and Raoul's relationship. It might be part of her history already. Raoul seemed to be interested in her of his own accord. It didn't help that his intense stare elicited memories of her past and a heated flush crept up to her cheeks as she remembered Simon's stamina.

She tucked a lock of her hair behind her ear when a light bulb went off in her mind. Raoul was observing the obvious. "Oh!" She breathed out in realization. "It's my hair. That's the difference. I cut it."

Raoul crossed his arms, staring in appreciation. "So you have and it becomes you."

His compliment weakened her resolve. She was supposed to be the one in control of the situation and instead, Raoul made her feel rattled. She couldn't let his disarming and sensual aura disarm her. He was still the enemy or would be...

But with those eyes staring at her, again, she felt her resolve waver and suddenly, switching spouses didn't seem so distasteful. Yes, maybe Erik's original plan wasn't so bad after all.

Raoul took a seat and shuffled through a stack of magazines. "I'll wait for Christine to return."

Erik.

Her heart raced. She felt sick with uneasiness.

What had she been thinking?

She hadn't.

She stared hard at the oblivious Raoul, who now completely disregarded her presence. It seemed she was the only one who had been affected by their little exchange.

She could try and plant the seed right now in Raoul's head for an indiscretion with her.

Then she recalled the smells of cedar wood, soap, wind, and fresh rain that were imbedded in Erik's clothes and that emanated from his warm skin.

She could make Christine pay for the pain she would inflict on Julie later as her friend, Monika.

She could almost feel Erik's tight embrace...

"*You could destroy her life like she destroyed yours,*" an inner voice whispered.

She relived the thrill from the pressure of Erik's lips, the kiss that rocked her world...

She found now, the problem was, she didn't feel much like hurting Raoul and Christine anymore. Her heart pounded with joy at the clarity that streamed through her. She finally put the pieces of the puzzle into place.

She wanted to be with Erik. What that meant, she did not know. What she did know was it would be in her best interest and Naomi's in this lifetime to be with him. Now she had to convince that stubborn man it was true.

At the same moment, another certainty flooded her mind. She understood the probability was high that Monika and Simon's betrayal of her was only as a direct result of what she intended to do today. The minute Julie changed her mind, she felt lighter. The burden of such a decision now removed from her conscience.

With new resolve, she squared her shoulders and replied to Raoul, "I will go tell Christine you are waiting for her."

"I'd be much obliged, Mimi." He gave her a brief nod then in a dismissive gesture, chose a periodical, and read unaware of what had just transpired or rather, what hadn't.

Julie couldn't help smiling. She had just battled the worst part of herself and won. She strode with a keen purpose toward the kitchen. Her new mission: get to know Christine and find out her connection to Erik. She needed ammunition if she was going to convince Erik to let Christine go.

Orelia's shaking hands poured steaming coffee into delicate china cups while Christine hovered behind her, watching with anxious eyes. Julie cleared her throat to announce her presence.

Orelia started and coffee splashed onto the fine silver tea tray.

Julie winced in sympathy.

Christine lifted three fingers, and mouthed, "Third time."

Not wanting to make a big deal out of it, Julie pretended to study the grain patterns in the floor. "There is a certain gentleman in the sitting room who would like to talk to his wife." Julie paused for a moment. "I was surprised to see your husband at home," she added.

"Yes." Christine became flustered as she hastened to remove her apron; her cheeks suddenly stained a pretty pink. "Please don't mention that to Monsieur de la Croix. We so seldom see each other with the constant deadlines Raoul has to oversee. We wanted a little …time …together."

By the soft emphasis Christine placed on "time," Julie knew exactly what she meant.

"Your secret is safe with me." Julie had no intention of telling Erik that Raoul was home. It would only add fuel to the fire. "Why don't you join him and I will help Orelia." She turned her attention to Orelia, trying to be considerate of the elderly woman's feelings. "If you don't mind my help?"

Orelia nodded. While they cleaned up the mess together, Julie's mind raced. Christine did not seem to be a woman harboring feelings for another man. The shy blush and the light in her eyes at the mention of Raoul told another story. That woman loved her husband. Erik was wrong.

"Is not right," Orelia's raspy voice interrupted Julie's thoughts.

Julie wiped up the last of the spill. "What's not right?"

"You," Orelia said, pointing a bony finger at her.

Julie furrowed her brow, at a loss as to what the old woman could mean.

"Walkin' round da place like you lives here...callin' da Master and Mistress by dere given names. You should be ashamed. You should knows your place. Is not right," she mumbled as she shuffled to the sink.

Flabbergasted, Julie couldn't think of how to respond. It was true. She considered herself as the couple's equals when clearly no one else saw her as one. Maybe because Raoul and Christine emigrated here from France, they didn't adhere to the strict code of segregation embraced by the Deep South. They were friendly to her and accepted her, but in reality, she had the wrong skin color.

A cascade of memories overtook Julie, and she sank into the nearest chair while Orelia cleaned the dishes, muttering her disproval. Naomi recalled other dinner invitations with the de Marignys spiraling from happiness to disappointment at the unexpected arrival of white guests. Naomi asked to eat alone in the kitchen. Dark looks from the work staff at her preferential treatment. Other shopping trips not with Christine, but for Christine, walking a few feet behind her, receiving dirty glances from department clerks if her attention lingered too long on an item. Always having to enter through the back door.

Naomi and Christine weren't true friends, rather they were only friends of convenience. Why hadn't she realized it before?

Orelia turned around again. "You needs be careful, Mimi. How many times I tells you not to trust so much? Never ends well, child."

Orelia shuddered, looking around at the empty kitchen. "Dere's somethin' wrong with dis place. Mistress and Master don't know it, but I sees," she pointed to herself, whispering. "I sees."

Julie found herself whispering back, transfixed by Orelia's wide eyes. "What do you see?"

"Da One Who Watches."

Julie swallowed as she pictured Erik gazing through the window the last time she was there.

Orelia mumbled on. "Sad eyes in da shadows...always watching...watching. Eyes follow da Mistress. Da Mistress, she be finding things in da house left by Da One Who Watches."

"What kind of things?"

"I know not. But da Mistress be screamin' and screamin' and da Master, he get angry and stay up wit a pistol, guarding against The One Who Watches." Orelia sat down with a tired sigh. "Dat one comes and goes and dey never sees, but I sees."

Julie's heartbeat became irregular. The One Who Watches had a name. And that name was Erik. "Does he know you can see him?" Trying not to give away her concern, she poured the coffee and prepared the tray.

"I never says it was a man." Orelia gave her a sharp look. "I only sees the sad eyes." She thought a moment then shook her head. "Da eyes never looks at me."

"Have you tried telling Chris...I mean...the Mistress what you have seen?"

Orelia's eyes narrowed. "I is old. Dey think I can't do my job. I's not wantin' for dem to think I's crazy too."

Good point, Julie thought.

"I prays for Da One Who Watches. I prays for peace for dat soul."

"From your mouth to God's ears, Orelia."

Leaving the wizened woman sitting at the kitchen table, Julie grabbed the tray, hoping her hands wouldn't shake, and walked toward the sitting room to bring Monsieur and Madame de Marigny their coffee.

Staying here, going along with Erik's charade, was not a good idea and she would not be coming back. If Erik still wanted *his* Christine, he would have to find another means of getting her. Julie would not be a maidservant for anyone. As soon as she served this coffee, she would give her excuses and leave. Christine would have to be disappointed about her shopping excursion because Julie was going home.

She was going home to Erik.

CHAPTER THIRTY-SEVEN

"This is not the time." Erik felt drained from connecting with Niall and Izak in such an intimate way. "We'll talk later." He motioned toward the door. "Take your leave now."

Izak stared at him coolly, pulling out a cigar from his vest pocket. "Have you ever considered why Marie is so determined to get her hands on Naomi?"

"Consider?" Erik repeated in annoyance. "I don't have to 'consider' that. Marie has told me more than once. And you heard just now for yourself."

"Erik," Izak sighed as he lit the cigar. "There are so many other women with pretty faces at Marie's disposal. Why Naomi?" He leaned forward. "Think carefully. Why Naomi specifically?"

"There can be no reason." Erik racked his brain. "She is a person of no consequence. She's only been in the city for a few months, not long enough to make any poor alliances."

Izak nodded and sent a ring of smoke toward the ceiling. "Then there is only one reason that makes sense."

"Which is?" Erik prompted.

"You."

Doubtful, Erik sat down.

"Think about it," Izak reasoned. "Marie is fixated on Naomi only because she can see you want her so obviously."

"Why would that be? Marie and I have had no connection, no interaction except..."

Izak sat back, casually crossing his leg.

"...when dealing with Naomi." Erik stood up. "Oh, so her issue is with me is it?" He grabbed his coat on his way to the door.

"Where are you going?"

"To confront Marie of course. This ends now. Today." He reached toward the door handle when he felt a hand on his back.

"Peace," Izak whispered. The urgency of resolving the issue diminished. As it did, a keen irritation toward Izak took its place.

"Do not use your will on me," Erik seethed.

"Listen to reason then. If you still want to confront Marie after, then by all means, do so. I will not get in your way."

Erik kept a suspicious eye on Izak as he sat down again. He'd listen, but this would end today.

"You may find this hard to believe, but I do not think Marie knows why she wants Naomi."

"What kind of game is this?" It did not make sense that Marie would not know her own mind.

"No game. I did not sense anything from her except for a very fierce desire where Naomi is concerned. Maybe even a hint of jealousy. Have you given her a reason to feel jealous, Erik?"

"Absolutely not!"

Izak smiled at his quick denial.

"Another interesting note I should mention: Marie cares naught for Juliana. She will send her back, but that is only because she does not know the truth."

"What is the truth?"

"I think Marie believes you conjured another soul into Naomi's body. What she might not realize yet is that the soul awake in Naomi is Naomi—her future self. You will have the advantage if she does not believe this to be the case."

"How so?"

"Juliana owns the right to her past. She has the choice to change it in any way...such as to give Marie permission to do as she wishes with Naomi."

"Even if that is true, you seem to think that *I* am the key to all of this?"

"It does feel that this runs deeper than what the surface reveals," Izak said with a thoughtful pause. "There is an easy way to answer your questions. If you are willing—"

"What now?" Erik interrupted.

"Let me see Naomi's past."

As Izak spoke the words every muscle tensed in Erik's body. "What does that entail?"

"I would only need a taste of her blood."

Erik jumped to his feet, repulsed. "Never. You will *never* touch her." He trembled with fury at the thought. "If you need to see the past, you take my blood, you see my past."

Izak shook his head. "I already know your past. What we need to figure out is Naomi's part in your past, if any, and what that has to do with Marie."

"Then take Marie's blood, drain her dry if you must. See her past."

"Gladly, but I cannot interfere where I am not asked and I do not think we want to alert Marie to our concerns."

"Damn it all to hell then! We shall have to move forward without knowing."

"I assure you, it is painless."

Erik pictured Izak's mouth on Juliana's neck, pictured his teeth sinking into her skin, and his heart twisted. "No, you cannot have her."

"Cannot have her?" Izak raised an eyebrow. "I was merely interested in assisting you. I am not invested in this adventure, you are. If you should change your mind, call out to me."

Erik was relieved at how easily Izak let the subject drop. He was even more pleased as Izak put out his cigar and stood to leave. That is until he noticed the subtle flare of Izak's nostrils, the shift of his gaze to the door, and the hint of a smile on his lips at the same moment a knock echoed. Wary of Izak's reaction, Erik didn't move.

"Are you going to let the lady wait all day?"

Erik wasn't expecting anyone. "Whoever they are, they will go away."

"I think not." Izak opened the door before the words were out of his mouth. "Juliana, what a surprise to see you home so soon," Izak said, tossing Erik a look that said anything but.

Erik started forward wanting to put as much room between Izak and Juliana as possible. But as he did, an odd resistance slowed him down and he felt as if he pushed through water, his movements unbearably slow. Again, Erik saw the subtle flare of Izak's nostrils before he spoke.

"Juliana, you are bleeding."

Horrified, Erik watched her lift an ungloved hand to look at the small drop of blood on her index finger. "It's nothing. I just scratched my finger on the door."

"Let me assist you with that," Izak offered. Before she could refuse, before Erik could utter no, Izak wrapped his lips around her finger and drew back slowly. "Mmm..." Izak murmured with his eyes closed, stepping back, his eyelids fluttering.

Erik, finding himself free to move, made it to the bewildered Juliana's side. "Did he hurt you?" Erik examined her finger which now showed no evidence of having a wound.

Juliana shook, looking at her finger. "No, I'm not hurt. What's happening? What did he do to me?"

"No!" Izak's cry was inhuman.

Erik shoved Juliana behind him and backed them down the hallway deeper into the house. Izak's eyes, stark green, were open and staring directly at Juliana. He lifted his head up and howled another unholy cry. Erik noticed the crystal on the walking stick next to Izak's chair began to glow.

At the same time, the howl of despair changed to rage. Erik could sense the power in the room building and Izak seemed to tower over them. Not tower, Erik realized. Levitate. Izak's feet were no longer on the ground.

"Jesus, Mary, and Joseph—" Juliana muttered in fear.

"Viper!" Izak roared, flying forward.

Erik braced himself for the impact, keeping himself between Juliana and Izak. A wall of force surged into him and cast him aside. He leapt back to his feet in an instant, but knew he wouldn't make it to Juliana in time. Izak drew his hand back, but was held in mid-strike as if by an invisible force.

Juliana sobbed on the floor, cringing away from the blow that didn't come.

Izak's drew his fury back as he sank to earth. "If I was not bound from hurting you, you would be dead. You are poisonous. You destroy a tree from the roots up. You rip families to pieces."

"No," she cried, tears on her face. "I swear. I have done no such thing." Her golden eyes begged Erik to look at her. "That's why I came home. I couldn't go through with it, Erik. I couldn't break up their marriage. You were right. I'm not that kind of person."

A warm feeling settled over Erik, Juliana was still his. *Still his...*

"Give her to Marie," Izak demanded. "Let fate decide what she deserves."

Erik turned cold eyes to Izak. "I don't believe in fate. I make my own way."

Izak held his ground. "I do not speak of Christine and Raoul, Erik. Her destruction goes far deeper than the trivial human pursuit you have set your mind on." Erik could feel another surge of power beginning to swell between them. "I will not allow you to have him." Izak's mouth twisted with the words, eyes on Juliana again.

The fear Izak caused Juliana fueled a power to build in Erik as well, anger. His heart ached to see her wide eyes and trembling lips as he heard her barely whisper in response. "What happened when you tasted my blood? I have a right to know."

"And help your cause? I think not."

"Honestly, I have no cause. I...I just want to go home." Juliana looked back and forth between Izak and Erik.

"I have a better idea," Izak told Erik. "I should wake Marie's sleeping mind and see how it all plays out."

"No!" Erik snapped, stretching his arms out toward Izak. He felt anger surge through his body into a concentrated point of energy that burst from his hands. Izak flew across the room, slammed into the wall, and sank to the floor, laughing. Astounded, Erik looked at his hands. *What in hell?* From the corner of his eye, he saw the crystal glowing.

"Well, well, well, this is an interesting turn of events." Izak's eyes held hope as he stood up. "Maybe you will solve this problem without my help." He looked at Erik and then gestured at the cane. "I think I will leave it in your safe-keeping...for now." He smoothed his rumpled suit.

Erik shook, his body feeling weak and ill-used by the experience. Juliana came to stand at his side, aiding him to stay upright.

"Don't worry, you will feel like yourself in a few minutes." Izak's reassurance was no comfort to Erik. "I think I will take my leave."

"Don't go to Marie." Erik managed to get out.

"I am bound from action. I will not be allowed to if it is against the design."

"If you find that you can, don't." Erik felt his strength returning and clenched his hands. "Swear to me."

Izak tilted his head in consideration. "Yes. I swear." He flicked his gaze to Juliana. "I will leave you to ruin yourself."

Erik felt Juliana shiver against him as she struggled to form the words. "I don't know what I have done to deserve your hate."

"Hate?" Izak's eyes remained clear and unperturbed as he sniffed in disdain. "I would not honor you by using the word hate. What I feel for you has no name."

"Get out," Erik commanded. The crystal started to issue a soft glow and before Erik could utter the words again, Izak was gone.

CHAPTER THIRTY-EIGHT

Izak's accusations after he had tasted her blood sent chills of dread down Julie's spine. Her soul obviously had layers of lives-lived and in one of them she had left a distasteful mark on Izak. By his account, she was the scourge of the earth and it made her feel suffocated by the thought.

It was just an hour ago that she had felt as if she walked on air. Letting go of her vendetta against Simon and Monika was the best decision she had made in a very long time. Didn't walking away from that count for something? Sinking into the nearest chair, Julie gripped her stomach until the knots began to unravel.

"Erik," she murmured, the irregular beat of her heart stealing her strength. What if he had lost faith in her? Losing his support would leave her empty. She needed Erik to believe in her.

"Erik, I—"

He held up his hand, silencing her. "I don't believe one word out of Izak's mouth."

Relief crashed over her. But then she recalled the fierceness in Izak's eyes.

"He believes it."

Erik set his jaw. "He's wrong."

"But—"

"I would know, Juliana," he said with conviction, leaning against the wall across from her. He slid down to the floor, exhausted. "I am certain of it. I would know." He pressed a hand to his heart.

I hope so, she thought, still unconvinced. Apparently that Earth Walker felt she had wronged him in a very grievous way. Only she had no memory of it. Rubbing the oil on her skin took her farther than she had ever wanted to go.

Erik stared up at the ceiling as though he counted the small cracks in the plaster. Julie found herself studying him, mapping the lines on his face. She much preferred him without the wax and paste that covered his scars. She had the urge to wipe it away to reveal the real Erik. But she resisted that urge as she noticed the fatigue around his eyes when his gaze moved from the ceiling to the cane and from the cane to his hands, palm-up, contemplating them with a mixture of wonder and awe.

"I have never done anything like that before," he mumbled.

She had been just as surprised to see Izak fly across the room from the invisible force that had surged from Erik's hands.

"I feel so drained," he said, rubbing his face.

Julie eased herself out of the chair and sat next to him. She took his hand into her own, but he quickly pulled it back, appalled.

"Whatever just happened, I don't know how to control it. I might hurt you with the very hand you hold."

"You won't."

His eyes searched her face. "How can you be so sure?"

"Because I just know," she said, pressing a hand over her heart. "You would never hurt me." She took his hand in hers again and this time, he allowed it. "We'll figure this out together, Erik."

We have to, she prayed.

Julie's attention moved to the crystal-topped cane that lay on the floor in front of them. What if anyone could touch it and make it work? What could she do with power like that?

Erik squeezed her hand, distracting her from her thoughts. "So serious," he said, releasing his grip and gently brushing a wisp of hair off her forehead.

"Yeah, well, some serious stuff just happened. I'm just sorting it all out."

"Indeed," he agreed.

Again they sat in silence. She didn't know what was going through Erik's mind, but she couldn't seem to shake the idea of using the cane. All she had to do was reach out and take it. Just as she worked up the nerve, Erik grabbed it first and scrambled to his feet, almost as if he had anticipated her thoughts. He turned it over in his hands, thoroughly inspecting the now quiescent object. He stopped, piercing her with an intense gaze.

"This cane in my hands is like a forgotten word or a scent I cannot place. I feel a sense of recognition that I cannot explain." He turned his attention to it again, peering at from it several different angles with an intent frown. "I'll be damned," he swore without fire in his tone, only speculation.

"What?" Goosebumps broke out on Julie's arms.

"There is a very thin coating of copper under the silver overlay. See?" He dangled the tantalizing cane in front of her face and pointed out the reddish-orange sheen.

"Is that significant?"

Erik gave a quick nod. "Copper is a conductor."

She followed him into the sitting room and watched him as he clenched the cane between his knees, his fingers exploring the crystal top. She wondered if maybe he thought there was a notch or button that could be pressed to activate it.

As she watched him, she remembered Izak levitating and Erik flinging Izak across the room. Neither man had been close to the cane. How could she ever hope to get it to work?

Erik stood again. "It will have to wait until I can take this device to my home to analyze it further." He strode to the coat closet and hid the cane inside. "We don't want to arouse the Krause sisters' curiosity, do we?"

"No." She shook her head, pretending she had no curiosity about the cane herself. She would have to figure out a way to get her hands on that thing before Erik left later in the evening.

"I seem to recall." Erik approached her. "Hearing you say you have changed your mind. Is that so?"

"I have." She blushed. "I have changed my mind about many things."

He nodded with a pleased look. "Why don't you tell me about it while I make the house more presentable?" His eyes darted to the hallway where the scuffle took place.

Julie followed as Erik straightened out the floor rug, adjusted crooked pictures, and put jostled furniture back into place. She cleared her throat.

"You were right, Erik. I couldn't bring myself to..." She shrugged. "I just couldn't do it."

With his back to her, she could not see his face, but he seemed to stand taller. "That said," she ventured on, "I have also decided I am not going back to their house either. I will not be a party to this scheme of yours, Erik." She hurried to justify herself as he turned to face her. "I don't know how you got the impression otherwise, but Raoul and Christine, in my opinion, love each other."

His eyes gave nothing away, but Julie noticed Erik's mouth tighten. "That is no longer material as I have also changed my mind on a few matters as well."

"You have?" His response surprised her.

"Juliana, I think you will agree there are too many complications that take precedence over what I might or might not want at the moment." Refusing to look at her, he wiped a mote of dust off the wall. "My only goal at present is to arrange it so that you make it to the ball you are so longing to attend and then–" Erik moved past her into the living room, still speaking, "–secure a way to send you back to your former life."

"Oh." Julie tried to hide her disappointment. She had expected a fiery exchange. She thought she'd have to defend her position, make him see reason, and convince him to give up this fixation with Christine. Instead, he was being evasive about his sudden change of plans. It was anticlimactic and confusing.

An uneasiness churned inside her. Since she woke up in this mixed-up mess, her biggest desire had been to go home. But Erik's announcement didn't make her feel as happy as she should be. It made her anxious.

She wasn't sure she was ready to leave just yet.

♀

The room was cozy, warmed by the fire flickering in the hearth nearby. As Julie lounged on the sofa, staring at the mingling flames, she mulled over the dancing lesson she had with Erik after dinner. Being so close to him, soaking in his nearness, had reminded her of their kiss that morning and she repeatedly found her eyes focusing on his lips. And although Bea and Agnes clapped and called out encouragement regarding her progress, it was inevitable that each time she was distracted by her thoughts, she stumbled.

Erik made up for her lack of grace each time by pulling her a little closer to prevent an all-out tumble and keeping them from even missing a beat. Each time he pressed her closer to his chest, it only caused her thoughts to turn back to the kiss and the whole pattern would repeat itself over again.

They twirled about in tandem to the outdated music and Julie soaked in every minute of it. His smell, his heartbeat, his warmth, and his hand on her back while the other gently held onto hers as he effortlessly directed their every step. She felt drawn again to his face, tempted to repeat her impulsive behavior from that morning only this time, Erik would kiss her without reservation and sans wax and paste.

He noticed her staring and whispered into her ear. "I wish I could always have the face I have on now."

A pang of guilt hit Julie as she realized he had totally misread her scrutiny. She didn't want him as the image of perfection. She found him attractive just as he was, flawed. It was a part of who he was and he was all the more beautiful for it. And as soon as she had the opportunity, she would clear up this misunderstanding. But she could understand his desire to fit in. He would not have to hide who he was ever again if he had the face he had been born with.

And just like that, clarity penetrated her mind as light does through stained-glass, and she knew what she would do for Erik if she had the power to do so, power a certain crystal-topped cane could produce.

She would heal him.

She would heal his face.

She was grateful Erik had insisted on keeping to their normal routine for the Krause sisters' benefit. And she'd insisted that he not leave her alone tonight, to which he consented. She didn't feel safe being alone with Izak so furious at her. And it would be her only chance to get to the cane before Erik removed it from the house.

With a smile on her lips, she slid her hand under the sofa and felt the smooth, cold crystal. She had grabbed the cane from the closet and tucked it under the sofa while Erik saw the Krause sisters to the door. Now all she had to do was to wait for Erik to fall asleep.

She touched the cane while Erik was in the back of the house and wished with all her heart he would just make an early night of it and go to sleep. No sooner had the thought crossed her mind than the crystal warmed under her touch and she heard a heavy thud and the sound of breaking glass.

Heart racing, Julie froze when she reached the back bedroom and found Erik unconscious on the floor next to a shattered water pitcher.

"Erik!" She shook him.

No response.

She pressed his wrist for a pulse and relaxed when she felt the slow and steady pressure. Then she heard a light snore. Astounded, Julie realized that the cane had responded to her wish.

She tried dragging Erik into the bed. And although she struggled, panted, and jostled him, he didn't stir. His body was limp and heavy. Not wanting to waste any more time, she placed a pillow under his head and covered him with a blanket then kicked the broken glass to the side as she rushed to the living room, retrieving the cane. Returning to his side, she took a deep breath.

With one hand on the crystal and the other on Erik's scarred face, Julie closed her eyes. "Okay, Erik," she whispered. "Let the healing begin."

CHAPTER THIRTY-NINE

Show me how to heal Erik, Julie wished. Without opening her eyes, she felt the crystal warm under her palm—her other hand, against Erik's skin, tingled. A low hum of energy surrounded her. Luck was on her side. His healing *was* going to happen. When he woke up in the morning, Erik would no longer have to hide himself behind powder or paste. His skin would be flawless because of her.

With eyes askance, she gave in to the desire to peek at his transformation, gasping as she did. Instead of the bedroom, she saw ancient buildings of smooth white stone. Beneath her hands, she still felt the cane and Erik's face while her vision became enveloped by a different place and another time, picture perfect except for hazy clarity around the edges of her view. Her heart, heavy with uncertainty, beat furiously. Instead of healing Erik like she had asked, the cane was doing something different and she had no control over what that might be.

"You should not wander around by yourself this time of day."

Julie peered up at the source of the quiet reprimand, a handsome man. And by the expression on the face of the one he spoke to, his words were a welcome interruption. And why wouldn't they be? He was tall, muscular, and sensual, even to the eyes of a little girl. The child lifted her face toward the man with a faint smile on her lips.

Doe-like eyes peeked through the wisps of red hair blown across the girl's face by the salty wind, and Julie could plainly see the admiration in their warm amber depths, even if the man could not. Not more than ten years old, the girl stood still, waiting to see whether the man would say anything else.

Julie felt a sudden surge of energy from the crystal feeding her information. She knew she wasn't living this experience as she did when facing Naomi's memories. She was a part of it, around it, inside of it, and viewing it all at once. She felt a connection to the child and could sense her emotions and thoughts while remaining a separate entity.

So, Julie knew that although he left broken hearts of lovers in his wake, to the child, he was kind, always. Placing a flower in her hair as he passed, giving her a fresh-picked fruit to fill her belly or handing her a shiny coin to buy herself a sweet treat. And like the women who eagerly called his name when he walked the city streets, she also longed for his attention. For in her young heart she knew that little girls eventually grow up.

"Go back to the temple, Akasha." The handsome man tousled her hair. Julie looked back in the direction of his gaze.

The temple stood stories high with jewels embedded in the walls themselves. The stones reflected an iridescent radiance in the rays of the setting sun, lighting the square with its multi-colored resplendence. Above the carved entrance she could translate "Temple Beautiful" even though she didn't recognize the language, the same language spoken by the man, who was gracefully striding off toward the outskirts of the city.

Akasha's little feet made no noise as she disobeyed the man and followed suit. Along the way, as she hid behind columns and bushes, Julie sifted through the curious little girl's thoughts, discovering she was born a Daughter of the Law of One and raised in the Temple Beautiful to be a priestess since birth. The man was not a Son of the Law of One nor was he a Son of Belial. He walked among the citizens, but was not held to their beliefs or their ways.

Again the crystal grew hot under her palm and a flash of images assaulted her: Akasha in the temple. Studying. Learning. Curious. Whenever Akasha would question High Priest Mai-Ra about the man, he would give her only a tight-lipped frown in response. Then he would redirect her to her studies of metallurgy or astrology. And she tried very hard to put her mind toward her work, but without answers, her thoughts would wander back to the handsome man, whose appearance was never quite the same, but always similar. The girl's thoughts were transparent and easy for Julie to absorb. So, this evening, she knew Akasha sought to find the answers for herself.

The girl's thin frame shuddered even though the evening was warm and humid. This man lived within the Sekhat-Aztlan and no one walked through the Field of Reeds, except for the man and his kin. There were cities beyond and more beyond that, but everyone traveled to their destinations on boats, avoiding the Field of Reeds. Her curiosity won out over her fear, but the latter was a close second.

Hiding behind the man-sized vase that adorned the front of the apothecary's building, Akasha leaned closer to the cool stone, shielding herself from the view of a woman rushing past. Akasha recognized her as one of the many love-struck females that chased after her friend.

Akasha bristled as she watched the curvy temptress grab the man's arm, pulling him to a halt. The woman was the wife of a wealthy copper trader *and* a practicing Daughter of Belial, all reasons for Akasha to dislike her. But, she shook off her dislike for the adulteress and interceded with prayer for her sins as was her duty. Sacrifice, prayer, love, and acceptance were the actions of a good priestess and ones she found herself embracing daily on behalf of the man.

"Arak," the woman called his name, a pretty pout on her lips. "You mean to leave without kissing me farewell?"

"Sybelle," Arak pained an unnatural smile as he extricated his arm. "How many times must I tell you not to touch me unbidden?"

"You did not mind my touch earlier," Sybelle swayed closer, leaving nothing but a hair's-breadth between them.

"That was then," he said, uninterested. "This is now." He stepped away from her. "Go home to your husband and leave me be, woman."

Her delicate features creased into ugly lines at his contempt. Akasha jumped at the sound of Sybelle's hand making contact with Arak's face and then flinched as the long nails scraped skin away, drawing blood. Unfazed by her reaction, Arak calmly dabbed the bloody wound with a piece of his tunic, staring down his nose at her.

"Are you finished?" his expression was one of boredom.

Infuriated further by his indifference, Sybelle raised her arm for another strike that Arak intercepted faster than a blink of an eye.

"Stop," he said. His soft voice, imbued with power, carried on the wind to Akasha and Julie. "You will go home, Sybelle. You will forget me." He paused for a moment, staring at her hard. "No," he reconsidered. "Not forget me." He let go of her arm and tilted her face up to his, forcing her to look into his eyes though she struggled. "You will always yearn for me. Knowing for the rest of your life with every beat of that wicked heart of yours that I will forget you the moment I walk away. You are nothing to me." He let go of her face and she stumbled back. "Now go home to the husband whom you do not deserve."

Arak turned on his heel and walked away without a backward glance. Precious moments passed while Sybelle, hands clenched at her side, shook as she stood in a silent fight against his order. Finally, with a stiff back, she turned and shuffled back in the direction she had come from. Akasha scurried from her hiding place, trying to get Arak in her sights once again. Though she had never been where he was going, she at least she knew the way.

Julie was neither corporeal nor spirit, but her mind remained present and it continued after Akasha, curious to figure out what all of this had to do with Erik, if anything. As the girl hurried, Julie hoped Akasha wasn't endangering herself going so far from the sanctuary of the temple. The sun, on its descent to the horizon, lit the sky with diffused colors as it sent tendrils of light into the atmosphere. Julie wasn't sure how much time was left before darkness would blanket the area.

Akasha hesitated as she approached the vast reed bed. She looked at the retreating sun and Julie knew that they both shared the same concern. If Akasha turned around now, she might make it back to the temple before dark. But she had come too far to turn back. Besides, she would already have been missed for supper and a very disapproving Mai-Ra would have sent someone to look for her or he might have taken the task on himself. Knowing her so well, it wouldn't be difficult for him to figure out her intentions, and even less time before someone reached her. If she wanted answers, she must move forward.

The reeds swayed in the wind giving no indication of which way Arak had gone. Akasha plunged forward blindly through the marshy landscape, hoping she chose the right direction. A family of birds hidden in the tall grass flew skyward in a rush of squawks as she crashed past. She kept a fast pace, afraid of any other creatures that might be hidden in the reeds. Akasha slowed as she began to hear voices, crouching lower in the thinning reeds to peer into a clearing just ahead of her. Julie knelt by the girl and watched.

"You are a bloody mess, brother," a dark-haired man, with his back to the reeds, said to Arak. "Who was it this time?"

"Sybelle." Arak shrugged, looking down at the stains on his tunic. "What is the damage to my face?" He touched the deep scratches.

The man sighed. "Let us have a better look in the light."

The man waved a long-fingered hand, lighting up a large crystal by the front door. And in tandem, other crystals placed around the yard also glowed as the last glimmer of twilight was extinguished.

"Hmmm…" Arak's brother grabbed his face and looked closely at the scratches. "If I did not know better, I would think the woman had talons." He let go of his brother. "You will live, but it will leave scars."

"I should get changed, then." Arak began to disrobe. Julie wanted to place her hand over Akasha's eyes, but the little girl was far less undone by the man's nudity than Julie, who couldn't take her eyes away from Arak's firm, muscular buttocks as he walked toward the furthest building from the reeds, giving a shrill whistle as he got closer to it. "Atezaina, send them out!"

Single file, one after the other, men, teenagers, and young boys exited the home in descending order. They varied little in their appearance. Julie only noticed subtle differences as to how full the lips, wide the eyes, or defined the jaw. Each had black hair, green eyes, and the same resemblance as Arak. It was disconcerting to see them fill the yard, expressionless and obedient.

"The Empty Ones," Akasha breathed in disbelief.

A catalogue of thoughts from Akasha blindsided Julie. Akasha had heard stories of those born soulless, the *Arimarik Gabe*. She had even overheard Mai-Ra discuss a baby born a few years ago without one. The enlightened priests from the Law of One had united in prayer for the pitiful creature. They communed with the souls awaiting their time for physical manifestation and petitioned for one to step forward into the child, yet none did. It was decided that Mai-Ra was to take the child, a boy, to live in the Temple Beautiful until such time as a soul could be found for it, but Akasha never saw the baby and never found out why or what happened. Did he now stand before her as one of these unfortunates?

"God, is that even possible?" Julie whispered, stunned as she watched Arak pacing in front of the replicas of himself. Knowing that she could not be seen by others in this vision, Julie left Akasha in the reeds to get closer to the men.

"The pickings are slim." Arak tossed a look back to his brother as he considered the four men closest to his age.

"You need to be more careful, Arak. You are going through them like water," his brother answered. "If you do not watch it," he chuckled. "You will have to use a juvenile for a while."

Arak scowled in response and turned back, motioning to the elderly man to the rear of the line. "Atezaina, I will take that one." He pointed to the male directly in front of him. As the old man corralled the others back into the house, Arak hollered into the wind. "And be sure to feed them well. They are looking a bit scrawny for my taste." The old man nodded.

Julie crept as close as comfortable and squatted behind a barrel. Although certain they couldn't see her, she still felt too vulnerable to stand out on the open. Only feet away, the brother stood with his back to her still.

"Hurry up, while the night is young," he said, his voice holding the distinct resonance of impatience.

"Yes, yes..." Arak waived him off then reached a hand out toward the closest crystal.

A burst of light streamed to his open palm. Arak's eyes rolled back and his body collapsed to the ground, leaving a transparent image of someone who looked very much like Arak standing over it. The image moved into the man that was just chosen and disappeared.

"Ah..." the replica's face became animated, a brazen smile on his lips. "I do love a new body," it said as it stretched and flexed its muscles.

"Glad you like it, brother. Now, take care of the other one so we can be off." He motioned to the discarded body now standing, its face blank.

"With pleasure." The new Arak grinned, wrapping his arms around its neck, and twisting its head. Julie felt bile rise in her throat at the sickening crack that reverberated as the bones snapped.

"I meant send it to the house," Arak's brother said with scorn. "Do you not think that was a bit wasteful? You could have worn it around the yard if one of the others needed mending or got sick."

"I will be more careful with this one." Arak patted his brother on the shoulder as he walked past.

"Be sure you are," his brother said, while turning to follow.

Another surge from the crystal under her hand reminded her she was only an observer to these events. But it didn't stop her from having actual physical reactions in response to what she witnessed as her body sat next to Erik's in her small Vieux Carre cottage. At present, a cold sweat chilled her as she stared in disbelief at the brother as he passed the barrel she was slumped against. She almost lost her lunch when he stopped and peered in her direction, staring hard.

Could he see her?

Iridescent green eyes in a familiar, beautiful face turned away from her while his undeniable, signature smile was generously bestowed upon his brother as the Earth Walker threw an arm around Arak's shoulder.

Izak Ulloa...

...Erik's father.

...Arak's brother.

...and her enemy.

CHAPTER FORTY

Shaken by Izak's presence, Julie forced herself to stand. The men headed toward the main house. The whole keep your friends close; keep your enemies closer seemed like a good mantra right about now, so she started after them. Before taking a step, she turned, certain she'd heard a muffled sob.

With streaks of tears on her face, Akasha crept toward the fallen body that once housed Arak's soul. She gently straightened his head, crossed his arms, and closed his eyes while mouthing silent prayers. As Akasha continued her quiet ritual, Julie noticed soft wisps of light siphoned from the crystals in the yard to settle around the pair in a gentle luminescence.

Julie stiffened as the crystal nearest the main house door released swooshes of light that flew past Izak and Arak to hover over the prostrate Akasha. At the same moment, Arak grunted and stumbled backward pulled by the light.

"Brother," Arak groaned, reaching out his hand. Izak grabbed his arm and held firm, his muscles bulging.

"Hold on," Izak growled with the effort, his eyes tracking the light to the source of the trouble, Akasha. "I can fix this," Izak said, looking into Arak's eyes. "I will have to let you go."

"Do it!" Arak grunted through gritted teeth.

Izak released him and Arak flailed to the ground, dragged backward by an unseen force toward Akasha, who was oblivious to the havoc her prayers caused. True to form, Izak moved faster than Arak, faster than the surging light, and before Julie could blink, he seized Akasha, lifting her into the air by her neck.

"Let her go!" Julie shouted, running forward. No one heard Julie's cry.

"Put her down," Arak ordered, as he staggered to his feet. A flood of relief overcame Julie knowing she would not be forced to watch Akasha choke to death.

"What?" Izak turned an incredulous look at his brother, his eyes swirling shades of green.

"You heard me." Arak held his gaze, walking toward them. Akasha's red face turned an ugly shade of blue as her little fingers weakly pulled at Izak's hand. He dropped her without ceremony and she crumpled to the ground, coughing in desperate gasps.

"What does it matter to you?" Izak marveled as Arak bent next to the girl and held her to his chest, soothing her. "Have you taken leave of your senses? Do you mean to keep her as a pet?"

Arak glared up at his brother. "Of course not." Akasha buried her face in his tunic and wrapped an arm around his neck. Arak's face softened as he looked at her. "I like her."

"You like her," Izak repeated, biting out each word as he crossed his arms. "Are we to build her lodgings? Give her a room and a bed? Dress her in silks?" Izak shifted in irritation. "Need I remind you, she attacked you just a minute ago? You should kill her and be done with it."

"She did not know what she was doing," Arak said, standing with Akasha in his arms. "I am certain of it."

"I am certain of it as well," a voice said. "Even we don't know the extent of her abilities yet." A white-haired man emerged from the reeds, his red, black, and white tunic identifying him as an elder in the Temple Beautiful.

"Mai-Ra." Izak shook his head and threw his arms up in the air. "This night cannot possibly improve any more than it has. What are you doing here?"

"I have come to collect what is lost." Mai-Ra motioned toward Akasha.

"You know you don't belong here." Izak held Arak back as he moved to hand the half-conscious girl over to Mai-Ra. "We have not decided what we are going to do with her. She was trespassing and we have the right to kill her." He looked down at the older man with a beautiful sneer. "And you as well."

"Earth Walker, you could try," Mai-Ra replied with a solemn bow.

"Don't tempt me," Izak glared.

Arak brushed his brother's hand off and placed the girl into Mai-Ra's arms. Mai-Ra examined her, frowning at her bruised neck.

"Is she reparable?" Arak was unable to hide the concern in his words, though he kept his face unreadable.

After a thoughtful stare at Arak, Mai-Ra nodded. "The Temple Beautiful is the best place for her. Healing the body is easily done. Healing the spirit is more difficult." He looked down at Akasha then back at Arak. "Maybe you should come with us. I never thought it possible before, but…with her abilities, we may yet be able to heal your soul…"

Izak hissed at the offer and Arak's full lips tightened into a very thin line. A palpable energy bent the air with such electricity Julie felt the hairs on her arm rise as it coursed through the yard between the three men. Even though the two brothers were agitated by his words, Mai-Ra remained calm and unyielding.

"Take her back to the temple," Arak said, stepping back to his brother's side. "Make sure she doesn't cross the boundary again. I will not spare her a second time."

"You show us kindness, Soul Traveler." Mai-Ra walked back to the reeds and stopped just before entering. "Izak," he called out without turning around. "Two of your groundlings are guests at the Temple Beautiful. They will be restored to health along with any others that cross the reeds." He disappeared into the tall grass within seconds.

Izak cursed into the night and turned to his brother. "Why did you stop me? I could be rid of that interloper once and for all. He has cost me some of my better progeny."

"On that count I do not begrudge him, brother. Your 'progeny' are repulsive. Why you create them is beyond me."

Izak, smiling for the first time that evening, puffed up his chest and strutted about the yard. "Because I am a god!" He shouted to the sky. "They worship the ground I walk on. They cower in my presence. Obey my every word."

"Leave the reeds and you would have any man, woman, and child behaving the same."

"Yes," Izak raised a finger, "but I have to *make* them by bending their will. My children do so of their own volition. It is so much more rewarding."

Arak shrugged his shoulders. "Suit yourself. I have made it no secret to you brother, if one crosses my path I will kill it."

"And I shall just make another." Izak placed a hand on Arak's shoulder.

Arak shook his head. "If they had a sense of refinement or civility, maybe I could understand your obsession with them, but they are no better than the animals we keep."

"Peace, brother, I will show you their usefulness." Izak closed his eyes.

Julie heard rustling throughout the reeds as about twenty people emerged, many unclothed, some in rags, all of them dirty and unkempt.

"My children," Izak addressed them. "For you—" he pointed to the deceased body. They rushed forward, with fangs bared, and swarmed as a group upon the corpse.

Arak turned away in disgust.

"Where are you going, brother?"

"To the house...I do not feel like going out this evening."

"Pout if you must, but I shall not give them up!" Izak called after him, fury penetrating each word. "I keep them because I *like* them. Just as you spared the life of that girl because you *like* her."

Arak stopped at his brother's taunt.

"Answer me, Arak. Why *do* you like her so much?"

Arak did not turn around, but Julie heard his soft words clearly. "I like her because she is the first person I have met that in spite of who I am and no matter what I do, she loves me." He entered the house and closed the door, leaving Izak standing stunned.

"That is not true, brother." Julie was surprised by the weight of emotion in Izak's words as tears welled in his eyes. "I love you." Julie couldn't tear her eyes away from his face. She had no idea the Earth Walker could love anyone.

Pain searing through her wrist tugged her attention from Izak to the hand that had a death-grip on her arm, pulling her to her feet.

♀

"What are you doing?" a raspy voice uttered. Julie looked up from her arm into Erik's icy stare.

They stood in the back bedroom, the ancient city no longer visible. He had removed her hand from his face, her other hand still clutched the cane. She had been so immersed in the vision it took her a moment to orient herself to reality.

"I...I...I," she stammered.

"Something is different." He rumbled.

Her mind swam with the information she had yet to absorb. Julie had to remind herself why she was in this predicament to start with: She had wanted to heal Erik.

"What have you done to me?" he shook her.

She looked at Erik's face, marred and unchanged. "Nothing, I've done nothing." She couldn't hide the regret in her voice.

He let go, stepping away with a wary look. "Why do you have the cane then, Juliana?"

Unsettled by his reaction, she tossed the cane onto the bed, raising her empty hands into the air. "I only thought..." she paused, not sure how to explain herself.

"You thought what?" he prompted.

286 · LAURIE L. BOLANOS

She sighed, dropping her hands. "I'm not going to mince words. Erik, you mentioned you wished your face was normal. I thought that maybe I could use the cane to heal your face."

She watched him breathe in her reply while studying her face, holding his emotions at bay. She wished that for once, she could figure out what he was thinking.

He touched his face. "That's not what happened did it?"

She shook her head, unwilling to elaborate.

Lowering his head, he looked her directly in the eyes. "Tell me."

The words echoed inside her head, compelling her to tell him though she tried to resist.

"Vision," she murmured, wondering why she couldn't stop herself from speaking. "I saw a vision of a girl." Julie stepped away from Erik until her back was against the wall.

"That is not the sum of what took place," he said as he inched closer to her.

"If you know already then why are you asking me?" She tried to stall him, uncomfortable by her inability to resist him. She wasn't sure what his reaction might be if he found out she had seen a vision about Izak and his brother.

"I want to hear it from your lips." Erik lifted her face, staring at her mouth then he allowed his fingers to encircle her throat. Not as a threat, but as an intimate claim.

"Oh," she barely breathed out. She could feel he was different. He towered over her, making her feel vulnerable. And as she looked into his eyes, she felt she would have to do whatever he asked of her. She felt intimidated and thrilled by his mere presence. His aura, unseen by her eyes, radiated with a power that enveloped her.

Julie trembled at his touch and from the possessiveness in his gaze. She was torn between giving him the information he wanted and begging him to ravage her with his mouth. When had she become that woman, the one who didn't know her own mind?

She had thought using the cane had been a good idea at the time, but what had she done? Erik *had* changed. He reminded her of Izak and his brother, Arak—even though he still bore scars on his face, he was fiercely beautiful. The kind of beautiful that should be feared.

CHAPTER FORTY-ONE

Erik released Juliana's neck, stepping back when he saw fear in her eyes, fear of him. It jarred him to the core. *Not from her*! He never wanted to make her feel that way. He turned away, unable to look into her eyes.

Drawing breath, he willed the powerful sensation coursing through him reined into submission. And in seconds, he felt the presence of the energy surrounding him surge within and go dormant...not gone, but biding its time for Erik's command to once again reveal itself.

"Forgive me." He faced her. "I know you meant no harm."

She gave a little sigh, staring at him with questions in her eyes. He wanted to say more to reassure her, but could not. Instead, he cradled the back of her head with his hand and kissed her...his hold careful, but unbreakable.

He increased the pressure of his kiss until her lips parted and he tasted her on his tongue and breathed the scent of her into his lungs. He felt Juliana's arms slide around his neck. Her body melted into his, making every cell in his body alert as again, he felt the simmering of the unnamed energy building inside him, joining in partnership with his arousal. He almost growled with the pleasure of the combination.

Her pliant body and fervent kisses fueled him further as he pinned her curvy frame against the wall. He claimed her, marking her as his. Christine had been the dream of what he wanted, but Juliana was the reality. His heart beat furiously at the realization—he wanted her and only her. And he told her that by his deep kisses.

You are mine.

She pulled back for breath, staring into his face, her golden eyes filled with passion and confusion. He released his hold on her, chilled to the core, realizing the unfathomable truth: Of all the women in the world, she was the very one he could never keep. She didn't belong to this time, she didn't belong to this place, and although his soul said the opposite, neither did she belong to him.

"Erik." Juliana breathed out his name. "You said you'd never kiss me again." She placed her hand on his chest and the warmth of it stirred him. "I am so glad you changed your mind."

He envisioned their bodies entwined, exploring each other with the raw passion that hovered behind her visage and which he was sure shone plainly upon his own face. It would be so easy to give in to his desires and hers. He brushed away a stray curl away from her face and resisted the urge to place his hands on her. For if he were to start again, he feared he would not stop.

"I want you, Erik," she murmured.

Another surge of desire pierced his heart at the invitation. He had never heard those words spoken from any person during the entirety of his existence. And behind the words, he felt something else...Juliana's love, unspoken. Something he certainly didn't deserve nor was he worthy of although, he craved it beyond imagining.

Oh wretched God!

What agony was this? What foul trick had been played upon him? Nothing, but what he had done to himself. He had brought her here. He had created this unholy mess and only he could remedy it. The only good and decent thing he could do would be to let Juliana go even though the last of his humanity would go with her.

He hoped that one day, by the very action of pushing her away, she would realize that it was his only means of showing her he loved her back, without words. Erik drew in a deep breath.

He loved her.

He studied Naomi's face, seeing Juliana's essence beneath the surface. He loved her.

Without thinking, he pulled her to him in a crushing embrace, one which she returned with equal measure. He kissed the top of her head as they stood there in silence, drinking in the warmth of each other.

He knew what he must do. Resolve made him stand straighter. He had to leave Juliana to ensure Naomi's protection upon her return. He needed to finish the herbs and ready himself to send Juliana home. What he could not do for Juliana, he would do for Naomi...loving a part of what would become Juliana one day. With stoic firmness, he released his hold on her.

"You know that I cannot."

Hurt rippled across her face. "Why? Is it Christine?" Juliana's lip trembled. "She doesn't want you. She doesn't love you. You have to give up this obsession."

"That is my concern not yours." He hated himself for his cold response and the tears that welled in her eyes. He forced himself to look at the pain on her face, speaking low. "I no longer require your assistance with my situation, but I am a man of my word. You will attend the ball as promised. Afterwards, you will go home."

"And," she said, frustration choking her words. "I suppose I don't have a say in this?"

"No, you do not." He left the room and collected his coat, Juliana at his heels.

"You can't just dismiss me like an unwanted child," she said to his back. "Please." She grabbed his arm in a desperate hold. "I'm truly sorry for whatever I did to you. I only meant to do something good. Don't punish me for my ignorance."

He shrugged into his coat and stilled at her plea. What could she be saying to him? That being sent home was a punishment? Since Juliana had opened her eyes weeks ago, all she wanted was to go home. Now that he offered the chance, she didn't seem to want to leave anymore. Could it be she wanted to stay here? With him?

As much as he wanted to believe it, he could not. He could not afford to hope for the possibility that she would want to be with him by choice. She had to be speaking from a sense of guilt or other motives he had yet to ascertain. Maybe some other ill-advised idea of dealing with the de Marignys. No, as he had decided, it must stand. He would send her back.

He must, for he could not bear having her here without truly being able to have her. That was an agony even he could not endure. So, with all the indifference he could muster he responded.

"It is not meant as a punishment, Juliana. We both knew this was the plan all along. Now, I have some business to attend to before the ball. I will leave you in the Krause sisters' capable hands while I am away."

Unable to meet his eyes, Juliana spoke. "How will I be able to reach you if I need you?"

"You won't. I will be out of the city."

"For how long?"

"As long as necessary," he replied, relishing the cold anger that mixed with the new-found strength within him. Whatever changes the crystal had made within him, it had opened the floodgates of his emotions. He resonated with the vibrancy of each feeling. First, his love superseded all others, but now...

He was angry. Life had been unfair to him since birth. He had been denied all manner of happiness, forced to create his own by deceit, which always left him less than satisfied. He had been cheated in this life and it was time once again to wreak a little justice on those who squandered their more fortunate lots in this world. It was time to wipe the slate clean. He would kill Joe B and make his way to Naomi's cousins.

Their deaths by his hands would pave the way for a brighter future for Naomi. He glanced at Juliana. She did not know this was who he was, a murderer of men. If she were to truly see him, know his heart in this matter, she would have no qualms about going home.

If she knew that to him, life for some was expendable, especially for the undeserving. Judge, juror, and executioner...he claimed as his right. He had always felt he was above those who lived in the world, separate and apart. He felt it more keenly now than ever before as if it was also his purpose and not shoved upon him by his differences.

He gave her a grim smile as he returned to the bedroom and grabbed the cane off the bed, while Juliana hovered behind him.

"I shall take this with me so there are no more attempts to be...helpful."

Juliana raised her chin in defiance. "You don't have to worry about me trying to help anymore."

Erik acknowledged her with a nod. The more she felt disdain for him, the easier it would be to let her go. He could not leave the house soon enough. Juliana did not know it, but he was about to secure her future as well as her present.

As he stepped into the chill of the night, he heard her soft voice carry.

"I'll be here...waiting for you."

"If only..." he whispered in reply.

♀

Erik stood motionless in the dirt road and in the darkness, studied the rotted country house of the people who had raised Naomi. Clouds covered the moon, but Erik's eyesight was keen, sharper than normal. The cane warmed under his hand as he concentrated. Even from this distance, the crystal allowed him to hear the even breathing of two sleeping people; the female, slept to the back of the house, the male, towards the front.

He snorted.

Neither would be an issue; both were heavily inebriated, cheap whiskey by the smell of it. Where would the fun be in that? No struggle, no begging for their lives. The thrill of this extermination would be non-existent except for the satisfaction of scratching it off his list of things to do.

As he strode toward the porch, he heard a grunt and thud from inside the house. He paused, listening. *What now?* He heard the soft release of bed springs and yet there was no sound of the woman walking the floors. Closing his eyes and sensing more deeply by using the crystal, he realized there was another presence in the house he had not perceived before…

Damn it all to hell!

Erik ran the final yards to the house and kicked in the front door to find the man, Eugene, who had raised Naomi with a heavy hand, lying prone on the floor, his head twisted so that it faced up at Erik with vacant eyes and lolling tongue.

Looking up from the mangled body further inside the shotgun house, Erik fumed. There Izak held the woman, Cora, as if she were a limp ragdoll, his mouth firmly clasped at her neck. Izak released his hold on the near-dead woman and stepped over her body, wiping his mouth with the back of his hand and walking toward Erik, his eyes gleaming iridescent green.

"For you," Izak said, with a flourish of his arm. His face was flushed with the pleasure of the kill. The pleasure he had stolen once again from Erik.

Erik clenched his fists, the cane falling to the floor. With anger so profound, his eyes glazed over with fury as a roll of thunder boomed outside. He flew at Izak in a primal rage with no forethought as to a plan of attack, driven by pure instinct.

Izak dodged each blow. He anticipated Erik's every move with alarming accuracy, which infuriated Erik all the more. Erik howled in frustration and another peal of thunder rumbled overhead as heavy drops of rain splatted onto the cedar-planked roof.

Erik could feel the power flowing from inside of himself, uncontrolled. He battled with Izak fiercely, but no matter what he tried, they were equally matched. They combated without success for what seemed like hours. Until, spent with exhaustion, Erik staggered back.

"Are we quite finished?" Izak bent over, catching his breath. Erik nodded. They both recuperated in silence as the rain petered out and stopped.

"Why are you here?" Erik finally voiced.

"Our connection has strengthened, Erik. Your need for revenge has become my need…your desire, mine." He nodded toward the inert crystal-topped cane. "Something has changed in you. You could not have fought with me as you did tonight unless…"

"Unless?" Erik tensed.

Izak stared into Erik's eyes, searching. "Unless you remember."

CHAPTER FORTY-TWO

A deep ache gnawed at Erik, as if just by Izak's words, something of importance wanted to push forward and be named, but it eluded him. "Remember what?"

"If you have to ask, then it is evident that you do not know." Izak approached Erik and looked deep within his eyes. "Even so, what is undeniable is that you have forged a connection with the crystal."

"I have done no such thing." Erik pictured Juliana's hand on his face. She had opened the door to something...*What in the hell did she do to him*?

"Extraordinary!" Izak tipped his head to the side, considering Erik's denial. "You refuse to acknowledge that you are different even though you must feel the changes within you. Your dexterity, your strength, your emotions...all are amplified."

Erik remained silent, refusing to encourage the Earth Walker, but he could not ignore the rising fear and excitement he felt at the truth of it.

"Such anger...so beautiful. I was almost spellbound by it...almost." Izak spoke with hushed reverence as he crossed his arms. "The changeable weather is too certain a sign, Erik. I always wished to command the elements, but that was never one of my gifts."

Erik turned his back on Izak and walked to the open doorway, the air still heavy with the recent moisture of the rain. "Are you suggesting that I made it storm?"

Erik stiffened at Izak's warm breath on the back of his neck.

"I am not *suggesting* anything. I am telling you that you did." Izak sidled past Erik onto the damp porch and gazed up into the calm darkness. "My brother possesses the ability to manipulate the weather."

"Brother?" Erik breathed—*more secrets*. "I have an uncle?"

Izak ignored him, staring into the vast blackness. "Except," he continued, "he had control over his emotions. The weather is driven by your emotions, Erik. Control your emotions and you will control the outcome." Izak turned to face Erik. "My brother and I would climb the highest point overlooking our city and he would make it rain. The colors were extraordinary."

Erik could sense the weight of Izak's memory and realized that their moment on the slate roof just days ago was an important gesture on Izak's part.

"I could teach you." Izak offered.

"What?"

"I could teach you to use your emotions to conjure the elements. Think of the benefit to mastering this gift, Erik," Izak said in earnest. "Imagine raining a hailstorm down on the head of your enemy in battle."

Erik looked around as he stepped out into the barren yard. "What enemies pursue me that I should have need to rain hail upon their heads? I think not."

Izak roared with laughter, patting Erik on the back. "Stubborn as ever—"

Erik shrugged Izak's hand away, frowning. He only wanted to eliminate one enemy at this moment: The elusive Joseph Batiste. Erik had sought him out first. For several days he had followed leads and scoured the area, but he had not been able to locate him. Joe B's trail had gone cold as if he had just disappeared off the face of the earth.

"Yes," Izak idly straightened his rumpled clothes. "I, too, was unable to find the man."

"Enough! Get out of my head!" Erik raised his hands in the air. Thunder boomed shaking the thin walls of the country shack behind him. His blood boiled with the reminder of how he had difficulty hiding his thoughts from Izak.

"If you dislike it so much, stop me. Close your mind. Exercise control." Izak gazed at him with arrogance, unfazed by Erik's outburst. "Let me teach you."

"Never!" Erik growled; a bolt of lightning split the darkness and struck the rotting roof in an explosion of sparks. A fire came to life, feeding on the old shingles. "Look what you have made me do! Just leave."

Izak said not a word, but smiled as the light from the flames consuming the house flickered eerily on his face. Erik saw etched in Izak's expression and emanating from Izak's very essence—pride, pride in Erik's destructiveness. Erik was never going to dissuade Izak from shadowing him. Erik stormed off toward the road, frustrated. Even though this was the country, the neighbors would eventually smell the smoke and come to investigate.

Erik turned around one last time at the edge of the property; a part of him could not help but rejoice in the destruction of the hellhole that was once Naomi's home. To his surprise, instead of finding Izak following him, he saw Izak striding straight into the flames of the burning house, the fire arching away from his approach. And, as the Earth Walker disappeared into the inferno, a shadow yelped and scuttled from under the house across the yard to hide inside a large, Hydrangea bush.

Izak emerged from the house, cane in hand as Erik walked past him to follow after the unknown entity. Erik focused his attention on the crystal as he passed by Izak. It might have been better for all concerned had the thing been destroyed in the fire.

Reaching the bush, Erik spread the branches apart and peered inside. Crouched down, looking up at him with large brown eyes sat a trembling coonhound. A strange feeling flooded over him as he stared at the animal. Surely, it could not be.

With his gaze, he willed the animal to calmness and picked her up, holding her close. He stroked her back, telling her by his touch how wonderful she was. Bijou—he owed this dog a debt—she had been willing to sacrifice her life for Naomi, *for his Juliana*. She licked his hand in affirmation. Although he was miles away from Juliana, Bijou brought his thoughts close to her.

Ah, Juliana. Erik's heart ached for her and the life he wished he could have.

"What have we here?" Izak stood nearby, taunting as his eyes perused over Erik and the dog in his arms. "Being sentimental are we? Why do you leave room for all of these emotions in your heart? You are so much more than this, Erik. When will you realize that you *can* have everything you long for?"

"I am not you." Erik turned his back to Izak once again and strode toward the road.

"Joseph Batiste has not disappeared, but you will not find him—," Izak called after him.

With a side glance to Izak, Erik stopped. "What do you mean?"

"If he is hidden from us, he is most likely with Marie. You know I cannot interfere in this matter. Apparently, you are not allowed as well. Not yet, anyway. Go home, Erik. Your opportunity will come soon enough."

"Why do you even care?" It made no sense to Erik that Izak was so keenly invested in him. This Earth Walker never seemed to do anything that wasn't of some benefit to himself.

"In time, you will have all the answers you seek. As for me, I will be around. I have nothing but time." Izak bowed then rubbed his hand over the crystal, a bright light seared the darkness, blinding Erik. As the light dissipated, Izak was gone, leaving Erik alone as he had asked.

♀

Although days had passed, Julie could not put Erik from her mind. She relived every moment with him, every word, and every touch—analyzing all she had done while here in 1898. She thought about all the lonely nights that awaited her if she returned home. Erik had become to feel like family to her.

She twirled into the living room, thinking about all the nights she had spent with Erik learning how to dance. She thought of his attentiveness, listening to her opinions even when he disagreed with them. He cooked for her and worried about her well-being. She knew he cared for her and she felt that there was almost nothing he wouldn't do for her, if she asked, except…let her stay.

Had she failed during this opportunity to experience her past? Julie wrapped her arms around herself, but the gesture provided little comfort from the flash of guilt that heated her face. How could she have even considered breaking up Christine and Raoul's marriage? She had almost ruined things for everyone. Now if she could only be certain of the true purpose for being here.

Maybe her purpose was to stay and be Naomi.

Julie thought about all the upheaval in her life; the affair, the emotional turmoil of the divorce, and her parents' death. That was not a life she would wish for herself. And, her only friend, James, was a relationship born of two broken people trying to fix themselves. There wasn't anything for her to go back to really. Once she had thought maybe Heath would be reason enough…meeting him had made her less guarded where her heart was concerned. But, trying to understand her own journey made her realize that just maybe, Heath's only purpose was to do just that—soften her heart to allow someone else inside.

For the first time in a long time, her path became a little clearer. Instead of going through the motions of life, she wanted to grab hold and not let go. There was nothing for her back home. She wanted to stay here…with Erik.

Julie leaned over the piano and touched the keys, thinking of Erik's hands flying over them producing such beautiful music. It would be so nice when he returns if he would teach her how to play. She missed him.

But something quickened inside of her, something whispered that her time was wrapping up. She prayed that making the decision to stay would change the internal whispering, but she could not be sure whether just choosing to stay would be enough. And what would be the point if Erik did not want her here?

Julie sighed. If that was the case, she'd be lost in either life.

She wished more than ever she knew what Erik thought. He had told her she had to go back, but his kiss said the opposite. *Stay*, she felt his soul speak softly. He left her confused and uncertain. He would pull her close only to push her away.

She held the curtain back from the drafty window. The day was drab. The sky had been overcast for days and the dirt street mucky from the previous day's rain. The small view from her window reflected back to her how she felt, unclear and plain messy.

A carriage rumbled past, splattering mud onto the brick sidewalk, and the sound of it muffled a fainter sound coming from the back of the house that Juliana hadn't noticed until the carriage was further down the street. Curious, she listened. It came from the back door.

She let the curtain go and headed toward the kitchen where the rattling persisted. She knew it wasn't the Krause sisters since they were at the French Market. She stood at the far end of the kitchen, staring at the door. The doorknob wasn't moving, but every few seconds, the bottom corner of the door edged forward and the rattle she had heard now sounded more like scratching.

Without glass panes to check outside, she opened the solid door a crack and before she could even look, a brown nose shot through followed by a round body, pushing the door open all the way. Julie gasped. She would recognize that dog anywhere.

Bijou! She was alive! Julie knelt down and smothered the dog with hugs and was rewarded with warm dog kisses in return.

With Naomi's memory of Bijou biting Joe B to defend her and recalling the sickening yelp from Bijou when Joe B threw her off, she grabbed the dog and held her tight, overwhelmed with gratitude. Both she and Naomi had thought that Bijou had died that awful day.

But...how did Bijou find her way here? Perplexed, Julie peered out the open doorway into the courtyard. Her heart raced and she smiled, breathless.

Erik was home.

He stood there, watching the happy reunion in silence.

Her soul leaped in joyful recognition as if pushing its way out of her body in an attempt to be near him. She stood up on shaking legs. She hesitated to speak, fearing he would leave again if she were to say the wrong thing. Yet she dared not keep quiet. She did not want him to get the impression that she did not want him here.

"Hello." Her voice sounded foreign to her own ears.

"Hello," Erik replied as he advanced toward the house.

Relief flooded within her. He was coming inside.

"Thank you for bringing Bijou home to me."

He paused for a moment. "I did not bring her home for you. I brought her here for Naomi."

"Oh." Her soul retreated back within her by the sting of his words. "I'm sure she will appreciate having Bijou."

"That is my hope," Erik replied as he walked into the house.

Julie closed the door and took a deep breath before turning around. "So, I suppose this means you still intend for me to go back from 'whence I came.'"

He kept his distance, but had the decency to look her straight in the eyes. "That is the plan."

She felt her lips tighten into a thin line, but did not reply to him. At least, not out loud.

Inside, one resolve beat in time to her heart.

Not if I can help it.

CHAPTER FORTY-THREE

Erik found it curious that instead of pursuing the subject further, Juliana shut the door.

"I really didn't like the way we left things. Can we forget the unpleasantness and start over?" Her voice resonated in the room and he realized how much he had missed hearing her speak.

"Wouldn't this make it the second time we've 'started over,' Juliana?" Erik ran his hand through his hair. As much as he wanted their last week to be a peaceful one, what he really needed to do was drive a wedge between them, to make it easier for both of them when she left.

She smiled up at him while showering Bijou with attention, scratching behind her ears. "As far as I know, there are no limits on starting over."

Starting over could have its own reward as it needn't be on a good foot. "Yes, you are right," he said after mulling over her request. "It's been a long journey. Let me freshen up and then I will tell you what I have been about since my departure."

"I can't wait to hear all about it," Juliana said, looking pleased as she grabbed a stale biscuit as a treat and gestured for Bijou to follow her. "I'll wait for you in the sitting room."

Erik leaned over the sink and splashed cold water on his face, wondering whether telling Juliana exactly what he had been up to was indeed the prudent course of action. Once he said the words to Juliana, there would be no taking them back. He was a murderer—black-hearted, unredeemable. But he was tired...tired of secrets and lies. He wanted her to know.

He dried his face with his handkerchief. When he replaced it in his vest pocket, his fingers brushed against the small vial of liquid he had placed there this morning. It was possible that when Juliana learned of his true identity, she would want nothing more to do with him and insist on leaving, and her liquid salvation was closer than she knew.

Today might be his last with her. Erik's heart dropped at the thought, sending a pain searing through his chest. She might very well leave hating him, while he continued loving her.

And he could delay it no longer.

"So," he said as he entered the sitting room. "Shall I start at the beginning?" He sat opposite Juliana while Bijou sprawled out on the floor between them, munching on the hard biscuit.

"No. Start with Bijou. How did you find her?" Juliana's eyes shone.

"She made her presence known to me when she escaped from the burning house she lived under."

"What?" Juliana sat up straighter. "Where was she living? Was the house abandoned?" She glanced down at the scraggy dog.

Erik sat back in his chair, clasping his hands. "I found her living on the property of Naomi's cousins. I don't think they took care of Bijou at all judging by her appearance. Juliana, I think she was waiting for Naomi to come back." He paused, wanting to hold on a little longer to her good opinion of him before he shattered it into pieces. "The house burned down with the occupants inside."

Mixed emotions flickered in her eyes as she processed the words. Juliana dropped her hand from over her mouth. "I know I should feel some loss at their passing, but I don't. From what I have seen, from what Naomi has shown me, they were hateful people, but no one deserves to burn to death no matter how cruel they are. How did this happen?" She looked at him with uncertainty.

He sighed, not willing to mince words any longer. "I did not go to retrieve Bijou. Finding her was an added bonus. I went to Marksville to kill Eugene and Cora."

Juliana sat in stunned silence. She blinked her eyes a few times before speaking. "I'm not sure I heard you right. Did you just say you went to Marksville to kill Eugene and Cora? Because," her voice shook. "I could have sworn that was what you said."

Without moving a muscle or offering apology, Erik confirmed it. "I did. However, if it is some consolation to you, they did not burn to death."

"If they did not die in the fire, how did you kill them?" Her words were measured, not revealing any of the true emotions he had seen earlier in her eyes, and her unwavering stare seared through him.

And for some reason he could not fathom, Erik could no longer bear her intrusive gaze. He stood up and crossed the room, keeping his back to her. "I didn't," he breathed out in part relief and part regret.

"I am confused." Her skirt rustled as she moved in her chair, but Erik willed her with his mind not to stand. She muffled a small cough. "Are you telling me that by some happy coincidence, they happened to both die on the day you intended to kill them?"

Erik closed his eyes, waiting for the octave change in her beautiful voice. She did not disappoint.

"And why—please explain to me—what would possess you to go kill them in the first place?"

Erik turned around. He was who he was and he would not pretend otherwise.

"I had every right to kill them. They didn't deserve to live."

Juliana stood, gesturing wildly. "Are you insane? You just don't go around killing people because *you* think they deserve to die! What were you thinking?"

Irritated, he reached her in less than three strides, grabbed her by the arm, and pulled her to him. Bijou jumped to her feet, whining in confusion, looking between them. Erik loosed his grip and eased her dress down her shoulder to reveal the edge of one of many raised scars that covered her back. "I was thinking of Naomi. I was thinking of this."

He knew it was a mistake the minute he touched her. He broke out in a sweat as he battled the voice of his heart beating: *mine, mine, mine.* He forced himself to tear his gaze away from her and then willed his hands from her luscious skin.

Not mine, he reminded himself as he put distance between them. Reaching the window, he pressed his hot forehead against its coolness, but in vain.

How could he ever bear to send her home?

♀

Julie's breath caught in her chest at the primal look that crossed Erik's face before he stepped away. She placed her hand over her arm where his touch lingered, burning against her skin. She wanted to throw sensibility out the window and reach for his touch again, so she also stepped back a few paces.

What could she say about the scars on her back, clear existence of her mistreatment? He had made his point, but their sins still didn't warrant death.

"What Cora and Eugene did to Naomi was heartless and inhuman. I agree. And even as I bear the scars from their hateful actions," she hesitated, adjusting her blouse back in place. "I can't say that what they did justifies their death."

Erik turned his back to the window, facing her again, his face flushed. "The point is moot, Juliana, since, in fact, I did not have the pleasure of killing them."

But you wanted to, she thought, feeling dread at the pit of her stomach. "Yeah, about that—"

"Izak killed them before I had the chance."

Somehow that did not make her feel better.

"And do not inquire as to the manner for I will not disclose the details." A muscle in his jaw twitched. Julie could imagine just how gruesome their demise had been since she had seen firsthand how frightening Izak could be.

Julie rubbed her hand over her face. Didn't Erik know anything about the concept of if you don't know it, it can't hurt you? Now she would have to deal with wrapping her mind around this unfathomable emotional bombshell he had just dropped on her.

"I am not done, Juliana."

Julie lifted her head and swallowed. Erik's mouth was tight, and the seriousness of his tone made her nervous. "There's more?"

Erik pulled out a thin rope from his pocket and pulled it taut between his hands. "Before you leave, I'm going to find Alphonse Batiste, put this around his neck, and squeeze until his eyes bulge and I hear the last gasp of his breath. He is going to pay for raping Naomi."

A flashback of that horrible experience flared up in Julie's mind. And in that moment, rage spread through her in agreement that Joe B should suffer for what Naomi had been made to endure. Part of her wanted to hide in the shadow of Erik's protection as he stood to defend her honor, but the other part of her cringed by his willingness to kill.

The look on his face chilled her. She had never seen such cold hatred from him before, not even in regard to Izak. And she suspected as Erik twisted the rope tighter and tighter that using it was not something new to him as his hands held it with a familiarity that spoke volumes. Before she could find her ability to speak, he continued.

"And when I am done with him," Erik said, his voice cold as steel as he rolled up the rope then placed it back into his pocket. "Marie Laveau is next."

Julie shook her head, trying to understand his logic. "Why Marie? What has she done to me that you feel she deserves to die as well?"

"Don't limit this to yourself, Juliana. I have Naomi to consider once you are gone. She is not strong as you are. She needs protection, my protection. Marie has her own agenda for Naomi and I assure you, it is not directed toward Naomi's welfare." His face uncharacteristically pale, he leaned forward. "They must die to ensure Naomi's safety. There is no other way."

A little of her tension dissipated with his explanation. Erik took a deep breath and pushed a lock of hair out of his face with a shaky hand, his face still pale. It seemed as if Erik felt he had no other recourse open to him. She held hope that meant she could make him reconsider his idea if she could offer a resolution. "Can't you just relocate and move Naomi somewhere else?"

His mouth twisted into a sad smile. "They will never give up that easily. People like that, people who feel they are owed, they don't just walk away. Take my word for it, I know. They will always be a danger to her. I will not have Naomi go through life always looking over her shoulder, living in fear. It stops here. It stops now. She will come back to a life without worry. It is the least I can do for her."

How could she make him see there had to be other alternatives? "This plan doesn't feel right, Erik." Julie paced the floor, trying to think of a way to persuade him. "I don't think Naomi would want you to kill anyone for her. I know you don't like Izak, but couldn't you consult him? Maybe he could do some kind of mumbo jumbo to their minds?"

He shook his head the second she mentioned the Earth Walker. "Izak is *not* an option. I want nothing to do with him."

"But—"

"This is not a negotiation. It is going to happen. I just want you to know that Naomi is coming back to a good life. I want you to know that I love her enough to make that happen."

Julie's breath caught in her throat. *He loved Naomi*? And all this time she'd thought…

Julie believed he felt something for *her* not Naomi. Her hope of staying with him crumbled and she lost the ability to breathe just as if he had punched her in the chest with his fist instead of his words. She had been certain that they had shared a connection, but all along, he had always been attracted to Naomi. How could she have been so wrong?

Wait. Wait a minute. He was willing to swap Naomi to live his life with another woman. When she first met Erik, he loved Christine, *not* Naomi. She pulsed with anger. Did this man have any idea of what loving someone really meant? She blinked back the tears threatening to fill her eyes.

"You love her?" Julie shook with contempt and hurt. "You have no concept of what love is, Erik. This…this is madness not love."

Erik looked up in surprise at her outburst. "I want her to be happy. I love her," he insisted, a fine line of sweat beading on his forehead.

A bitter taste flooded her mouth as his words sank in deeper and that it was not she whom he loved. Julie clutched a hand to her chest not sure how to calm her racing heart. She forced herself to steel her feet on the floor, fighting her desire to flee. She would not leave without having the last word.

Julie averted her eyes so he wouldn't see the pain in them. "I beg to differ. Loving someone doesn't mean you'd kill for them, Erik. Loving someone, truly loving someone, means you'd die for them." She ran out of the room with Bijou on her heels, grabbed her tignon, and wrapped it around her head, determined not to go back in there if he called out to her.

But he did not call to her.

Her fingers made quick work of the material. She reached for the doorknob and turned. It was then she heard him say her name, ever so softly. Bijou lifted her ears at his voice and ambled back into the sitting room.

She stood taller, feeling good for a moment that she would ignore him, until she heard a thud. She debated whether she should go check on him or leave, but not for long. She couldn't leave. Damn it! Even with all that had transpired, she could not quell her love for him.

She sighed and turned around. "Erik, if this is just a ploy—"

The chair Erik had been sitting in was tipped over and Erik lay on the floor, Bijou licking his hand. She rushed to him and turned him toward her. Smoothing the hair from his face, she could feel the heat from his skin. He burned with fever.

♀

Juliana's cool hands on Erik's skin felt as if an angel had reached down from heaven to soothe him from hell's flames. He had been feeling worn, but it had never occurred to him that he could be ill even though Izak had warned him to be careful days ago, on that morning he watched the rain spiral into color.

"We do not want your body to succumb to some unpleasant illness. Unlike mine, it is not immortal."

Until now, he had felt invincible.

The ache in his joints and muscles made him feel as if he were dying. He didn't even have the strength to writhe in the agony that consumed him. His body shook with coldness. Juliana placed a blanket over him.

"There's no way I can move you by myself. Erik, I have to go get help," Juliana said, concern in her voice.

Using all his strength, he grabbed her arm. "No. Don't leave this house."

She pried his fingers off without effort. "I have to go. I need to get you to bed and you need a doctor."

"I forbid it," he barely said the words.

He felt Juliana's lips brush against his forehead in a sweet kiss then her skirt whipped the air by his face as she stood. "When has that ever stopped me?"

CHAPTER FORTY-FOUR

Julie ran out of the room and grabbed her purse, searching it in the hopes that she had enough money for a carriage. If she had to walk the muddy streets, screaming for help, so be it. She had to do something. Erik's forehead had felt so very hot. For a temperature to take down a grown man like that, it had to be high. Her trembling hands found a gold piece in the folds of a handkerchief.

That should be enough to cover any expenses.

Before she could turn the knob and fly outside, the front door opened. Julie cried in relief as Bea bustled through the doorway carrying packages, with Agnes right behind her fussing about the price of corn. Julie hugged the woman, packages and all.

"Thank God, you're both home!" Her eyes welled with tears. "I need your help. Erik is sick." She tugged Bea toward the sitting room.

"Not so fast." Bea stooped and placed the packages on the floor, leaning her ear toward Julie. "Now, what's the problem?" Julie gasped in a breath, realizing her mistake. They knew Erik as Monsieur David de la Croix.

"Monsieur de la Croix is sick. A doctor needs to be called immediately and I need help getting him into bed."

"I'll summon the doctor," Agnes, said turning on the step, back onto the sidewalk.

"Let's see what we have, dear," Bea said, shuffling forward.

Hurry up. Julie clasped her hands together. People died of the simplest things in the nineteenth century...an infected tooth, a mosquito bite, even a scratch.

Bea grunted as she knelt next to Erik, nudging a hovering Bijou out of the way to feel his wrist. The woman's forehead wrinkled in concern. "Get me a bowl of cool water and a wash cloth, Naomi. We need to tame this fever."

She *knew* to do that. Why wasn't that the first thing she had done? Julie rushed toward the kitchen, but stopped short at the rich timbre of a man's voice.

"It appears you have a problem with which I can assist you." She spun around to find Izak in the hallway. Agnes stood by his side assisting him out of his coat.

"It was a lucky coincidence that I ran into Monsieur Ulloa," Agnes said, taking his hat.

"He says he is a doctor."

Julie froze, ice invading her spine. She stared into Izak's face while he appraised her with a serious gaze. Anyone else would see a handsome man with startling green eyes. Only she knew the dangerous being he could be. And Agnes had invited him inside.

Julie jumped at Bea's yell. "Naomi, what's taking so long? Hurry with that water!" Julie tore her gaze from Izak toward the sitting room. Erik needed her, but she couldn't trust Izak alone with him or the Krause sisters.

"I am only here to help," Izak said, as if reading her thoughts. "By all means, don't let me stop you. Fetch the water."

She hesitated, not convinced.

Raising a long-fingered hand, Izak crossed his heart. "I promise to do no harm to anyone in this home."

That would have to be good enough. Julie turned her back to him, rushing toward the kitchen.

She grabbed the first bowl she could find. Her hands shook as she filled it with water. Izak was capable of terrible things, but could he also make Erik better?

The last time he was here, he almost killed her. The memory of his savage rage flashed before her eyes, and she fumbled, almost dropping the bowl. That didn't matter. It wasn't about her right now. It was about Erik.

As far as she knew, antibiotics weren't being used yet. There wasn't even Tylenol or Aleve to help. Didn't they use to bleed people for illnesses? She didn't know whether she could put her faith in "modern medicine." Erik's best chance of recovery might just be Izak.

Carrying the bowl with both hands, a small towel tossed over one arm, she stole a glance at Izak as she walked into the sitting room and placed the items on top of the Jester's cabinet. Izak circled around Erik, his nostrils flaring as he inhaled the air with each breath Erik released. Bijou watched with a low growl in her throat.

"Might I make a suggestion?" Izak said to Agnes as he rolled up the sleeves of his shirt.

Agnes' eyes grew large.

"Ready the Master's bed."

Agnes gave a mute nod and left the room.

"Bea, is it?" Izak spoke not bothering to look at the woman he had just addressed.

Struggling to rise from her vigil next to Erik, Bea shot a nervous look at Julie. "Yes, sir." As Bea stumbled forward, Izak was by her side, assisting her to her feet in one smooth movement. Bijou scampered out of the way with hackles raised.

"You should make willow-bark tea to relieve the fever."

"Yes, sir, right away," she said with a quick curtsey, leaving the room.

Izak bent over Erik, but Bijou stood between them, growling

Julie started forward. "What are you going to do?"

"I am not going to let him lie on the floor like a common dog," Izak said coldly as he stared hard at Bijou. The soft ticking mantle clock was the only sound in the room until Bijou broke eye contact with Izak, whining. She backed away with her tail between her legs and plopped in the corner, promptly falling asleep.

Then Izak bent over and swept Erik's six foot-tall muscled frame easily into his arms and strode down the hall. Julie grabbed the water and towel, following behind them. Izak placed Erik gently onto the turned-down bed.

The Earth Walker's tenderness surprised Julie. His face softened and his eyes betrayed his feelings. Julie had seen that expression once before in the vision the crystal had shown her...in the moment Izak confessed his love for his brother, Arak.

Julie placed her bowl and towel down on the bedside table. Erik groaned in delirium and turned on his side. Reflexively, she jumped back as Erik vomited on the floor, a minute amount splashing on her shoes. Julie turned her head, trying not to gag from the sickly smell or from the consistency of the regurgitated mess that lie at her feet.

"Oh dear," Agnes said with a hand to her mouth as she walked in. "I'll just clean that up, shall I?"

Grateful, Julie turned away and was quickly escorted out of the room by a firm hand to her elbow. "Don't touch me," Julie ordered Izak, trying to wrestle free.

"We need to discuss Monsieur de la Croix's condition," he said loud enough for Agnes to hear. In the privacy of the living room, Izak released his hold on her.

"What is wrong with him?" Julie spun to face him.

"He has been infected with a very nasty strain of virus." Izak grabbed a bottle of whiskey from the credenza, ripped the top off with his teeth and drank deeply. After swallowing half of the bottle, he sat down. If this Earth Walker needed a drink, the news could not be good.

"A virus," she stuttered.

"Yes, one that has caused a collection of fluid to build in his lungs." Izak pulled a long drink again.

Oh, no. Julie cringed. *He has pneumonia.*

"Fluid swimming with a virulent bacteria," Izak continued, grimacing.

"How do you know this?"

Izak stared at her without answering. Of course, she should have just accepted that it was perfectly reasonable for someone to *smell* a diagnosis.

"Okay, okay," Julie said, pacing the floor. "What can you do to help him?" she asked, point-blank.

Izak tapped the nearly empty bottle on the edge of the chair. "I cannot cure him."

"What?" Julie's felt her heart bursting in her chest. No! Izak was her only hope.

"I cannot cure him," he said, standing up. "But I can make sure he survives it."

Julie leaned against the wall, weak with relief. "How? How can you make that happen?"

"I can take some of the illness into myself," he said, his green eyes darkened.

Julie pictured Izak waving the cane over Erik's body, pulling out the infection. "With the crystal?"

Izak's face erupted in a caustic smile, a few teeth longer and sharper than the others. "No, guess again."

She gasped, unable to tear her eyes away from his mouth. She stepped back, shaking her head in resolute refusal. "No...no...there must be some other way."

"There is no other way." Izak moved toward her.

"Ma'am," Bea called out. "Monsieur de la Croix is ready for Monsieur Ulloa."

"Thank you, Bea," Julie answered, grateful for the interruption.

"You have a decision to make, Juliana. But before you do," Izak said, striding past her with disdain. "Clean your filthy shoes."

♀

There was no time to clean her shoes. Julie's fingers nimbly untied her laces. She shucked them off her feet and ran to Erik's room. Erik was tucked in bed, a blanket up to his neck and a wet cloth resting on his forehead. Izak stood at the window, his back to her. Her pulse slowed. Izak hadn't touched Erik.

She sat on the bed and removed the cloth from Erik's forehead. She dipped it in the cool water, wrung it out, and dabbed his hot skin. What should she do? He needed help, but how could she allow Izak to bite him? Would he become an Earth Walker? Would he become a puppet like Niall? Would he forgive her?

"Wouldn't being your son provide Erik with a better constitution? If given time, couldn't his body fight this virus on its own?"

"It is because of our family link that he still survives." Izak turned around.

"What do you mean by that?" Julie asked while rolling the blanket down so she could put cool compresses on his neck and chest. Erik was dressed only in a long-sleeved shirt. Agnes or Bea must have removed his soiled jacket and vest. She began to unbutton his shirt. As she did, her eyes followed the scarred and puckered skin that covered his right neck and spiraled down his chest and side. Her heart ached at how he must have suffered. How he suffered now.

"The virus has been in his system for some time." Izak looked down on Erik's still body. "Any other man would have succumbed to it days ago. His heart rate is elevated and increasing. The bacteria is multiplying in his lungs. He needs me. You must say yes."

Julie struggled to remove the sweat-drenched shirt, fumbling because of her tear-filled eyes.

"Allow me." Izak raised Erik to a sitting position to make it possible for Julie to remove the shirt.

"I am curious. Why do you need my permission?"

"There is a barrier between Erik and myself. I cannot interfere without consent. He is unable to speak for himself and you are his wife..."

She finagled one arm from the sleeve and started on the other when Erik stirred. It seemed to take him great effort to just open his eyes.

"Erik," she said gently. "You are very sick. Try not to move, okay?"

As if her words didn't register, he turned his head until he laid eyes on Izak. And, even wracked with fever, he stiffened, trying to rise.

"Out...of...my...house," he managed to utter, veins bulging in his neck with anger. Julie shuddered as he rolled his head back to her. "You...let...him...in?" he breathed out the question.

"Erik, please." Julie tried to placate him. "Izak is here to help."

"Out," he repeated.

"Enough of this," Izak muttered as his eyes swirled iridescent green. "Sleep."

Erik went limp.

Izak closed the door to the bedroom. "You have a decision to make."

For all the misgivings Julie held about allowing Izak to help, she had more about not letting him. "Do it," she said, her voice wavering. She moved from Erik's side.

Agonizing minutes passed as Izak gazed down on Erik before sitting on the bed next to him. Julie started second-guessing her decision. She could always say no. But then Izak lifted Erik into his arms–slowly and deliberately, holding him close to his chest like a lover. Captive, Julie could not look away.

Izak loosed his grip enough to turn Erik's unscarred neck toward the wall, baring the skin. Julie cried out when she saw the gleaming white of Izak's elongated teeth just before they sank into Erik. She gripped her stomach, feeling sick. Erik moaned as Izak continued to hold him captive in this unnatural embrace.

Julie watched in silence, her chest tightening. How much longer could she endure this?

Just when she thought she couldn't stand another minute watching, Izak lowered Erik to the bed and stood. Julie gasped. His beautiful features were drawn and his green eyes dulled. Moving faster than a normal human being, but slower than he was usually capable of, Izak rushed to the window and threw it open, retching onto the alley.

Erik remained sleeping, his breathing slow and even and his coloring less pale. Even to her untrained eye, he appeared remarkably improved. She touched his forehead. It was cool.

Izak shook as he vomited one last time. "Only for him," he whispered, eyes closed, gripping the sill with white-knuckled fingers.

Julie was captivated by Izak's raw visage and dumbfounded by his honesty. There were cracks in the Earth Walker's armor, a vulnerability. Izak loved Erik. That meant she and Izak had something in common.

"Thank you," she said.

Izak pushed himself off the window frame, spared Erik a tender glance, and left.

Julie followed him into the hallway, but Izak was much too fast. He was already gone, draperies still moving from the air stirred by his departure.

She stood for a minute, listening to the Krause sisters bustle in the kitchen. She breathed in the scent of the willow-bark tea and let out a trembling breath. Peace settled over her, replacing the fear that had latched on to her heart. She didn't have to worry any longer. Erik would get better.

As she returned to his bedroom, she came to a dead stop.

Against the wall she noticed Izak's cane.

She looked around the empty room, making sure that she and Erik, still asleep in bed, were alone.

They were.

So, her eyes darted back to the cane, *why was it glowing?*

CHAPTER FORTY-FIVE

Erik clawed his way to consciousness. Being incapacitated was not an option. He had to protect Juliana and his home from Izak. Every attempt he made to wake was rebuffed by darkness and silence. Breathing in deeply, he searched for the strand of the energy that had made itself his companion. Pulling on its strength, he willed himself awake.

He opened his eyes to a blinding light, so bright he was forced to shade his eyes with one hand. Blinking to clear his vision, he turned around in disbelief. The darkened room and soft bed were no longer there. He stood on stone surrounded by stark white buildings. Their walls were embedded with metals and crystals, an artistry lost to time.

Men and woman in tunics of varying colors passed him on the street, heading to a bustling market square in the distance. Erik looked down. He wore the same such clothing, down to the thin sandals on his feet.

Though he did not recognize anything, this place felt familiar–the smooth, sun-warmed stone, the salty air, the distant waves crashing against a nearby seawall. These were not hallucinations from a sick bed.

Erik flexed his muscles, reveling in the fluidity and strength of his body. The unnamed energy he had called upon coursed through him in waves, so his body hummed with its vibration. He smiled. He had not felt this good in a long time. Not since...

He could not recall. There had never been a time in his life his body felt so powerful. Yet he was certain to his bones that he recognized the feeling.

He turned toward the market again and strode in that direction. It would be the best place to make his inquiries. On the way, he caught hold of a small lad to ask him where they were, but the child looked up at him with saucer-sized eyes, pulled free from his hand, and ran in the opposite direction. Erik squinted in disgust. He had forgotten his appearance could be frightening. He had covered his scars with wax and paste before he had gotten sick, but had no way of knowing whether the mask was still in place.

The street was lined with buildings of smooth stone that had open glassless windows. No glass. What could he use as a mirror? Farther down the road, the last building before the market square had large cuts of a flat metal embedded in its walls. At the wall, he looked into the reflective metal. Another man stared back at him, similar and familiar, and yet different. Erik creased his brow. A stricken look appeared on the handsome face.

What was the meaning of this?

A muscle twitched at the jaw line as Erik clenched his teeth. He touched the right side of his face and as he did, the reflection's hand did the same to skin that was flawless. This face was not scarred...so why did the boy...

A trumpet sounded and the merchants packed their wares and closed their carts. More people gathered in the square as the sound of drumbeats came closer. A little girl ran past him, calling to another that lagged behind. "Don't tarry, Havi! We don't want to be late for the Scapular of the Lamiak." Erik gave the reflection one more stare before pushing through the throng of people that had already gathered. Would the celebration hold answers for him?

Rows back from the street, Erik could just make out the tips of colorful flags turning the corner. The crowd blocked his view, the tall people standing shoulder to shoulder. A kind of longing stirred in his gut with each tap of the drum that carried toward them. He needed to see the procession. Erik slid his hands between the two men in front of him and forced them apart then backwards in one sweeping motion.

"By the stars!" the burly one yelled with fists raised. Erik postured in kind, power coursing inside of him with each heartbeat. The man's companion grabbed his friend's arm. "No, Kiliz. Look closely. He has changed again. It is the one from the Sekhat-Aztlan."

Kiliz lowered his fists. "A thousand apologies."

"Accepted," Erik said, hearing his voice for the first time. It was as rich and smooth as a fine cognac. He turned back as the trumpet sounded again.

Kiliz and his friend urged people out of the way to let Erik pass to the front. As each person turned to look at him, recognition flashed in their eyes and they moved without complaint. Who was he that people feared a beautiful man as much as a scarred one? Just as he reached the street, the flag bearers marched past with the drummer not far behind them.

"I thought you were not coming." A pleasant feminine voice spoke in his head.

Erik scanned the crowd for the speaker.

"*Why wouldn't I?*" Erik asked, trying to coax information from the woman as he sought to determine the source of the voice.

In the procession, a beautiful woman approached in step to the drumbeat with her retinue behind her. She wore a sheer form-fitting dress that hugged her upper torso and flared around her legs. Her fiery hair was piled on top of her head in an intricate arrangement and delicately held in place by a coral hairpiece.

"*It is beyond me why you make the choices that you do,*" the voice interrupted, laughing. "*If you have changed your mind about this, have you changed your mind on other matters?*" He could hear the hope in her voice.

"*Which matters?*" Erik asked, watching the oncoming celebrants. The people following the woman were not her retinue, but clerics. They walked with their hands clasped in front of them, holding flowers that resembled water lilies. Sheer veils covered their heads and trailed down their white tunics.

"*Must I say it? You know exactly what I speak of.*" She sounded exasperated.

As the red-haired priestess drew closer, Erik saw that she wore a scapular with long multi-colored ribbons attached to the back that curled and arched in the air as if alive. They looked like seaweed dancing in the waves.

"*Tell me,*" he commanded without turning his eyes from the captivating display.

The crowd cheered as the procession reached the square.

"*Very well,*" came the resigned reply.

The priestess turned her head, looked directly at him with bright, amber eyes, and raised an eyebrow. "*Will you sign the contract?*" she stressed his name so it sounded as if she said "Arak." not "Erik."

"*Contract?*" he asked, caught off-guard. This woman knew him. "*What contract?*"

At his question, her back stiffened and she turned her head forward.

Erik pushed his way through the people, keeping with her. "*What contract?*"

"*Do not toy with me. You know I do not like it.*" came the clipped reply as she walked onward.

He called out to her with his thoughts, but she did not respond, nor did she give him so much as a second glance. Erik tried to step into the procession to grab hold of her, but an invisible barrier prevented him. In desperation, he yelled to her inside of his head, "*Stop!*"

The crowd became silent, the procession ceased, and the priestess stumbled to a halt. The force of her sudden stop dislodged her hairpin. It shattered into pieces around her feet. Her hair tumbled down to her waist and the ribbons fell still.

The hushed crowd was nothing in comparison to the stillness inside of Erik. Stunned, he realized he had done this. With a single thought, he had silenced the crowd and stopped the procession.

The unnamed priestess slowly lifted her arms skyward. As she did, the ribbons and her hair rose as well. She moved forward again and they trailed behind her as if alive and flowing in water. The crowd roared with approval as the entire procession started once again.

Attempting to get to the priestess was useless. Erik pressed onward. He would get to the end of the procession route and confront her there. He moved to the outskirts of the crowd and quickly forged ahead. The line of people ended in front of an ornate building.

On the apex of the structure, stood a pyramid-shaped crystal and diamonds, rubies, sapphires, and emeralds were inlaid in the exterior stonework of the walls. Carved into the stone above the entrance were the words "Temple Beautiful." Within the pavilion in front of the stories-high building, stood an assembly of men dressed in tunics of red, black, and white.

The faint sound of harmonious notes filled the air as the men chanted softly. The closer he got to the men, the harder it was to move forward. The wordless song affected him like a spring releasing its tight coil. And suddenly, Erik saw colors twirling and mixing amongst the music.

How was this possible? The last time he had witnessed colors produced by sound was through Izak's assistance. Erik searched the crowd for the Earth Walker, but he was not there. As the priests continued to sing, the crystal on top of the temple glowed. The brighter it became, the stronger the power inside of Erik coursed.

The priestess arrived and turned to face the crowd. The singing stopped.

The sudden silence held a residual hum of energy. The clerics raised their hands to the sky and released the lily-like flowers into the air to swirl around the high priestess, as she rose, levitating above the multitude.

She hovered in the air just before rays of light radiated from the crystal on the temple and surrounded her with an intensifying glow. Arching her back, she extended her hands behind her while looking upward. All the while her hair and the ribbons flowed and the flowers swirled.

Then the priestess sang. One note. Pure and light. Erik stared, spell-bound, as he saw a gold hue twirl into the air along with her voice.

The uplifting vibration abruptly ended along with the note. The woman arched further back before bending forward with an explosion of light from the crystal, obstructing her from view. Flowers soared forward into the crowd of spectators who eagerly grabbed them up as keepsakes. When the light dissipated, the priestess was gone.

The clerics and priests turned and entered the temple single file. The procession had ended. A few people milled around, but most had walked away already.

Erik strode toward the temple, assuming the priestess was inside. A small man dressed in the same red, black, and white tunic stopped him before he could walk through the entrance.

"You may not enter." The man's voice was firm, though his face was lined with kindness.

"I must enter. I need to speak with–" Erik pushed forward, but found himself unable to do so. The priest held him back with a raised hand that emanated with a powerful energy.

"To enter, you must sign the contract. Akasha has explained this to you."

Akasha. That must be the priestess.

"If I might speak with her?" Erik tried polite humility.

The priest lowered his hand. "You know you may not, Arak."

There was his name again in the same heavy accent. These people knew him. Maybe the priest had the answers? Though he'd much prefer to get them from the woman.

"Mai-Ra?" A young girl peeked her head out. "You are needed in the sanctuary."

Mai-Ra stared at Erik a second before turning his back and walking inside the temple with the girl, but not before he waved his hand sealing the doorless entrance with a light barrier. Erik reached out to test it, but his hand could not come within a foot of the energy.

How would he get to either one of them now?

A male cleric walked through the barrier and raised his head toward Erik, speaking to him without missing a step. "Go to the back of the temple."

Erik rounded the last corner to find Akasha waiting for him, her expression indiscernible. She wore a simple white tunic now, and her hair hung loosely down her back.

"If you were to explain it to me again, I might be willing to sign the contract." Holding out an olive branch to her might get her reveal the answers he sought without having to ask. Without hesitation, she rushed into his arms and embraced him.

"I will explain it as many times as I need to." She breathed into his chest.

He found himself holding her tightly in response, smelling the sweet citrus scent in her hair.

She pulled back, looking into his eyes. "I cannot tell you how happy I was to see you among the people. But, why must you play with my emotions so when you know how much this means to me?" She didn't let him answer the question as she continued, grabbing hold of his forearms. "I will be with you the entire time. You will not have to go through this alone."

"Remove your hands from my brother," a familiar voice thundered. "Arak, you will not do this."

Izak stormed toward them. What was he doing here? Did he say brother?

Akasha tugged his arms to get his attention. "Do not listen to him, Arak," she pleaded. Erik stepped closer to her. He wanted to know about the contract. He wanted to know this woman.

"Arak," Izak growled, his eyes swirling iridescent green.

"Arak," Akasha whispered, sending comfort through her hands.

"Erik." A feminine voice called from a great distance.

"Trust me," Akasha promised.

An uncontrollable shaking overtook him and he stepped away from Akasha and backed further away from Izak. He closed his eyes, pulling from the energy to quell the tremors.

"Wake up." The unidentified woman's voice ordered.

Erik shook even more.

"I swear to God, Erik. Open your eyes." A hand slapped across his face. Instinctively, Erik grabbed it.

Juliana sat on the side of his bed in the darkened room, a waning glow behind her. He slackened his grip on her wrist and let it go. He rubbed his hand over his face, feeling familiar puckered skin.

Had Izak orchestrated this? Had he just seen a real memory through the eyes of Izak's brother? And if so, what was he meant to learn from it? Erik pushed himself up in bed with less effort than before and looked around the room. Was Izak still here?

Juliana's forehead creased in concern. "Erik, say something."

CHAPTER FORTY-SIX

"Where is Izak?" Erik flipped the covers back, placing his feet on the floor.

"He left about an hour ago," Juliana replied, scooting out of his way. She could tell by Erik's agility that Izak had removed most of the illness. "How are you feeling?"

"Much better." He tilted his head from side to side, rubbing his neck. The puncture holes had healed within seconds of Izak releasing him. Could Erik sense that he had been bitten?

"Where are my clothes?" He stood, broad-shouldered, looking down at his bare chest.

Julie soaked in the sight of his sculpted arms and toned abs. She wanted to trace her fingers along the masculine lines of muscle. Instead, she retrieved a clean shirt from his closet.

"Here," she said, holding the garment at arm's length. Their fingers brushed during the exchange. Julie longed to lace her fingers with his, but instead she tucked her hand into the folds of her skirt, resisting the urge to touch him.

"Thank you," he replied. When he was half-way through buttoning his shirt, he paused with a grim expression. "Why?" he asked. "Why did you disregard my wishes?"

"Erik–" She let her voice trail, feeling a spreading ache in her chest at his cold reproach. She didn't know where to begin.

"Why did you let Izak in this house when I expressly forbid it?" The scar on his face turned a darker red, but his expression betrayed nothing.

"*I* did not." Julie answered, lifting her chin. "Agnes invited him inside." Guilt ate at the edge of her conscience. If Agnes had not let Izak in, Julie would have done so herself. And she alone shouldered the responsibility of what had followed after.

Julie buttoned the rest of his shirt without meeting his eyes. "Well, if you're upset about that, you're definitely not going to like what I'm about to tell you next."

"Worse than Izak being in my house?" Erik leveled his reprimanding gaze at her. "He could have decimated this entire household without blinking an eye."

"Believe me, I was concerned, at least for Bea and Agnes. Remember how he tried to hurt me, but couldn't? I was pretty sure I would be safe. And, after today, I know he would never hurt you." Izak had upheld his promise to do no harm and Julie had seen the affection Izak felt for Erik.

"*Now* you know he would never hurt me? You're right," Erik said as he paced the floor. "I'm not going to like this."

"You have to understand, under any other circumstances, I would never have said yes, but...you were so ill...I was afraid." Julie put the palm of her hand on his chest, forcing him to stop. Erik's eyes trailed up her arm to her face and her heartbeat faltered. "I couldn't lose you," she confessed with a catch in her voice. He didn't know just how much he had come to mean to her.

He nodded. She dropped her hand.

"I gave Izak permission to–" Julie squared her shoulders. She knew Erik would be furious, but it had been necessary and she would not apologize for it. "Izak bit you in order to draw out the illness. It was the only way I could be certain you would not die."

Silence loomed between them as Erik touched his neck. He stared at her without blinking. "It must have been a difficult decision, but you did what needed to be done. If I were in your position, I might have done the same."

Julie gaped unable to digest his lack of reaction. "Did you understand what I just said? Izak. Bit. You." Erik did not respond. "He held you...he sucked...he drank..." she felt nauseated thinking about it. Watching the Sci-Fi channel and vampire movies could not have prepared her for the real thing. It was intimate and emotional and just plain made her skin crawl.

Erik drew a shuddered breath, his mouth twisting. "No need to elaborate, Juliana. I understood you perfectly."

"But–but–you're not angry with me?"

"No," he said, sitting down on the edge of the bed, rubbing his forehead with the heel of his hands.

She had expected some kind of heated reaction. This quiet acquiescence made no sense to her. "That's it? You accept my explanation?"

"Let it go, Juliana," he said gruffly, lifting his head commanding her to obey him with eyes that swirled iridescent blue.

"Jesus, Mary, and Joseph," she cried out, taking a step back. "Your eyes."

Erik moved past her to the dresser mirror, swearing under his breath.

Julie stood still, feeling shocked by his unnatural ability. Now she had her answer. The crystal *had* done something to him, or Izak had. At this point, she didn't know which.

When he turned around, his eyes were tranquil blue once again. "Juliana, I don't know why that happened. It's not something I did on purpose." He closed the space between them. "After Izak bid me sleep, I went somewhere–another place and time."

"It *was* the crystal," Julie mumbled, thinking about her own vision of another place with the red-haired little girl, Izak, and...

"Are you listening to me?" Erik tilted her face upward with a finger. "Izak once told me that what is happening now was set into motion centuries ago. He said there were many players in this game. I think...I believe there is someone yet to reveal themselves. Izak has a brother."

"Arak," Julie blurted out.

An array of expressions chased each other subtly across Erik's face in the moment that followed her admission. "I think it's time that you told me about what you saw the night you tried to heal me."

He did not use his powers of persuasion. Instead, he asked her of her own volition, making her feel valued. Whatever caution had held Julie back from disclosing the event in the first place evaporated and the story gushed out: the Sekhat-Aztlan, Akasha, Mai-Ra, and Izak and his brother, Arak, who was a Soul Traveler, changing soulless bodies like clothing. Erik's eyes glittered with interest.

"Tell me exactly how Arak moved from body to body. I need to know everything you can recall about him. Any details at all that might help us figure out what kind of danger he might present."

"Arak drew power from a nearby crystal. Then the body he was in fell to the ground and next thing I knew, he was in the other body." She wasn't sure how being a womanizer could be threatening, but she told Erik about the women of the city and Sybelle and the strong attachment Arak had for Akasha.

"So, it comes down to this," Erik said, looking as if he had placed the last puzzle piece to a particularly unpleasant picture.

"What? Comes down to what?" Julie's skin prickled at the tone of his voice.

"The first time you met Izak, he gave you a message along with the invitation to the ball. He said 'all the players will be in play.' I think this Masquerade ball will reveal the answers behind everything these past few weeks. I also think there is a strong possibility Arak will be there."

"Does this mean we aren't going to go now?"

"On the contrary," Erik answered.

"Really? No reservations at all?" Julie caught her breath in disbelief.

"Izak is powerful. Arak could be more so. Who knows what he is capable of? And unlike Izak, maybe he is not precluded from causing harm. So, don't misread me. I am deeply concerned. My initial reaction is to keep you home and safe. But, I also know I am ready to confront all of this–put it behind us as soon as possible." Erik took her hand into his own, rubbing across her skin with his thumb. Julie stared at their point of connection as warm tingles shot up her arm to her core while her heart began to beat an excited rhythm in her chest.

"Naomi is not strong enough to face this with me. It can only be you. I am not worried about what might happen to me. I am concerned for you. Knowing what we might be dealing with, are you still willing to accompany me?" Erik rolled his shoulders, giving her a frank stare. "I promise I will not allow you to be harmed. Izak and Arak are not the only powerful ones."

She nodded, feeling energy roll off him and settle around her, enveloping her with his promise. "You know I want to be there. I'm not afraid."

"And after, that very night, you will go home."

She winced inwardly at his words. God, he confused her. He'd touched her, kissed her, appeared to have feelings for her by his protectiveness and concern and yet, he never took anything further. In the end, he never said *stay*. And as he looked at her, waiting for her answer, she knew in that heartbreaking moment he would never say any of the words she longed to hear.

"Okay," she agreed, feeling the blood drain from her face as Erik stopped rubbing her hand and firmly gripped it in a handshake, sealing the deal.

♀

Speaking of sending Juliana home made Erik remember the finished potion. Where was the vial? "Where are the rest of my clothes?"

"Bea took them to wash. Why?" Juliana gave him a curious look.

"I had something important in one of my vest pockets," he said, feeling the urgency to find it. He had only made that one vial of tincture. If it was lost, he would have to start all over again and that would take time.

"Oh," Julie said as faint frown lines appeared between her eyebrows. "I thought we could use the privacy when you woke up, so I sent the Krause sisters home. They took Bijou with them as well as your clothes. Maybe Bea emptied your pockets before she left?"

"Let's hope so," he mumbled under his breath as he searched the house. It could be anywhere.

"Your tea has gone cold. I'll just reheat it for you," Juliana called out from the kitchen. "If you tell me what you're looking for, I can check in here."

"No need," he breathed out, allowing the words to carry to the kitchen as he triumphantly held the little brown vial he had found under one of the sitting room chairs. It must have fallen out when he had collapsed. He pocketed it, unwilling to disclose its existence to Juliana just yet.

Erik rubbed the phantom ache in his neck. Spotting an almost empty whiskey bottle, he poured a dash of liquid into his hand and splashed it onto his neck. The alcohol might remove any remnants that Izak left behind. He felt defiled and repulsed at the idea that Izak had connected with him in that way, but he couldn't blame Juliana.

She needed him alive. Without him, she'd have no way of getting back home. And there were only a couple of days left before the ball. The preparation between now and then would be crucial for both of them. He needed to make a few changes to ensure their success.

Pulling a chair up to the writing desk, Erik pulled out a sheet of paper and addressed it to Francesca Lorio's Dress Shop. He needed to alter the costume he had commissioned for Juliana. With a flourish of his hand, he sketched out a new design. No more Marie Antoinette. She would be going to the ball as a queen from another dynasty.

Including a hefty sum would ensure its delivery to him in twenty-four hours. He smiled as he finished the picture. He would make a few additions to the dress once it arrived. In order to make his personal alterations, there was something he was going to need first. And the object he required leaned against the wall in his bedroom. He retrieved the cane.

Erik recalled how Arak had stopped the procession with a thought. He placed his hand over the copper prongs that held the crystal in place. *Release*, he commanded. He felt energy emanate from his hand and the copper softened, enabling him to pry the crystal free and pocket it. The cane was of no further use to him, so he chucked it into the closet.

He heard a muffled sob.

"Juliana?"

"I'm almost done. I thought I'd toast some bread with the tea," she called out from the kitchen. "I'll bring it to you as soon as I'm finished. I'm still learning my way around a wood-burning oven."

Again he heard the anguished cry. This time he realized it was not a sound, but an internal trembling, a feeling of sadness that was not his own. Sensed emotions that belonged to another.

Arak, Izak's voice uttered. Another wave of loss and emptiness crashed over Erik along with a stark realization. The bond that Izak had claimed to have with Erik–feeling his strongest emotions and knowing his deepest desires–had evolved.

"Hmmm..." Erik breathed out, wondering why Izak carried such a weight of sadness as he built a mental wall to block the unwanted rush of emotions. It seemed the very connection that Izak used to upstage Erik at every opportunity ran both ways.

Erik smiled triumphantly. He would not hesitate to use this link to his own advantage.

CHAPTER FORTY-SEVEN

Julie tossed and turned in her bed, finding it difficult to get comfortable. The last couple of days had passed in a blur of activity. Yesterday, she had been ambushed by a slew of seamstresses for re-measurements. Their busy hands had draped pieces of white linen and gold silk over her, pinning them as they conversed animatedly in Italian.

Julie and Erik had originally agreed that Marie Antoinette was the logical choice for a masquerade costume. The oversized wig and powdered skin would prevent anyone from noticing that Julie was a woman of color. So why the sudden change now? And who was she to be?

More curious still, he had brought gold dust and a quart of gardenia-scented lard with instructions to mix it thoroughly and leave it to set overnight. She made guesses about her new persona over the din of activity, but Erik would not confirm or deny any of them. Later that night as Erik twirled her about the room for their last dance practice, Julie tried again to wheedle the information out of him.

"You will just have to wait," he had told her with an amused smile as he pulled her closer to him without missing a step. She had breathed in his scent and basked in the warmth of him, hardly believing she had so little time left.

Today, Erik had only made a brief appearance, claiming he was working on the accessories for the costume himself. Between the dressmakers and the Krause sisters, she and Erik had not spent a moment alone.

She had stayed up most of the previous night thinking about the suspicions Erik had about Arak. Tonight her mind was still alive with questions. Izak said the players would be at the ball.

But who were the players? Arak? Erik? Herself? Izak? Marie?

If Erik could sneak Julie past the New Orleans upper echelon, there was no reason to think that Marie wouldn't wear a mask of her own and attend. Julie squished her pillow into a ball and tried to get more comfortable. If need be, she could stand her ground with Marie, but she hoped that wouldn't be necessary. She wasn't scared of Marie. She just didn't want to cause more problems for Naomi.

"Arak," she mused out loud. Was it really possible that he would show up? Would there be a battle between Izak and Arak? Julie turned on her back, stretching her legs. *Nah...that would never happen.* Izak loved his brother as much as he loved his son.

Something else niggled at her, keeping her awake. Erik thought that all the unanswered questions they had would be revealed at the ball. Julie stared at the shadows on the ceiling in her darkened room and sighed. It would be nice if this past-life experience would tie up neatly like a beautifully wrapped present. But it wouldn't.

At least that was what her gut told her.

Julie let out a shaky breath as she got out of the bed and paced the room. There would be no sleep for her tonight either. As important as this ball seemed to be for resolving their questions, a thread of anxiety had wound itself around her heart with the knowledge that the ball also signified the end of her time here. Having to walk away from this life, leaving Erik, tore her apart.

She and Erik were in this mess together. They were partners and it wasn't right for her to leave him by himself to deal with any problems that might arise from tonight. She stopped short when her eyes caught sight of the rumpled tignon on her dresser. It glared at her as a stark reminder that this life didn't truly want her. That tignon belonged to someone else as did the dresser it lay on. This was Naomi's time, not hers. Who was she to want to deprive Naomi of the experience?

She gingerly folded the tignon, placing it neatly down. Next to the tignon lay the handcrafted gemstones that Erik had gifted to Naomi what seemed so long ago. Julie touched each one, pausing when she touched the butterfly. How ironic! She clasped it tightly in her hand. The metamorphosis a caterpillar must endure was no less grueling than hers.

She had changed.

Although she shouldn't want to stay, she did. It was this realization that contributed to her lack of sleep and the reason why any food she tried to eat tasted of ash. Her appetite had disappeared after her handshake with Erik, the one that whispered to her soul she was cosmically bound by her promise.

Why did she resist letting go of this life? Why did her heart feel as if it were breaking? She couldn't imagine things any differently, but giving Erik up felt like the ultimate sacrifice and so unfair!

She let out a grunt of frustration and shook her fist in the air, forgetting about the brooch until she heard it hit the floor flush between two of the wood slats. Julie tried in vain to pry it loose, but it was lodged tight. She plopped on the floor in defeat, staring at the lost treasure and felt the agony of her impending loss more keenly.

In resignation, she turned her head toward the window, looking at the shades of night as early dawn stretched its fingers into the darkness. Her last day had arrived and there was nothing she could do to stop it. Julie wiped a hot tear from her face. She would have to be brave enough to face it. Her love for Erik pounded through her heart. He depended on her, and she would not let him down.

♀

Erik set the last chipped piece of crystal into the delicate threads of gold and copper on the headdress for Juliana. It was perfection. He sat back to admire his work.

Brilliant.

His glance wandered to the finished costume on the dress mannequin, then to the finely decorated matching mask. An old satisfaction burned in him as the items screamed of his touch.

This is mine. It belongs to me. In turn, Juliana wearing his masterpieces, would make her his as well. At least for one night.

He looked past his handiwork to the window and saw the streaks of dawn pushing away the darkness. His only for one night.

This night.

He fought back the desire to demand she stay. No, he could not ask it of her. He would not. She belonged to another life. She deserved her own future, even if he wanted her to stay so badly he ached.

He tired of bending the will of others to get what he wanted. For once, just once, he wanted to be loved freely for himself. In time it was possible that Naomi would do just that. He would have to content himself with that hope. Only it wouldn't be the same. One soul. Two very different people.

Erik shook the thoughts from his head. He would do his duty by Naomi. However, he couldn't shake the dream he'd had of Juliana a couple of weeks ago, a faceless man dragging her from a ballroom of merry revelers and he helpless to save her. Was it a premonition of Arak? The very man whose identity would be indiscernible until one could figure out which body he inhabited? Erik wasn't going to take any chances. It was time to test his theory. He stood, silently willing it to work. Staring at the completed costume, he breathed out, "Protect."

The intricately beaded bodice, overskirt, and headdress began to glow as the small chipped pieces of crystal that he had taken from Izak's cane and had sewn into the dress flared to life.

Relief coursed through him. No matter where she was tonight, with a word he could keep her safe. That was all that mattered.

Erik rubbed a hand over his weary eyes.

He still had much to do and so little time to do it. He had to dismantle the torture chamber as he had no further need of it. But before that, he had something of greater importance to tend to. Sitting down, he pulled the magnifying glass over his work table. He emptied the small bag that had sat untouched for weeks and held the silver bracelet in his hand, removing the charm and discarding the blonde woven hair.

♀

Julie sat at the table once again unable to eat but a few bites of her meal. Agnes walked past, glancing at the untouched plate.

"Too excited about the ball to eat?" she asked. Julie nodded. That was as good a reason as any. Bea glowed in Julie's direction, causing her stomach to flutter. She knew Bea most likely thought her lack of appetite was due to pregnancy. *So not the case!* One would have to do more than kiss for *that* to happen.

"No worries. If you can't eat now, you might work up an appetite dancing. They'll have a refreshment room with tea, coffee, lemonade and most likely biscuits, cakes, and bon bons. Maybe even cold tongue sandwiches," Agnes said with excitement.

Ewww! Julie's stomach clenched at the thought of cold tongue anything. Bea left to answer a knock at the door.

"And at midnight," Agnes continued. "There is a sit-down feast."

If all went according to plan, she wouldn't even be here at midnight.

"Naomi, come see," Bea called.

Julie caught sight of Bea's back as the woman walked into the sitting room. "What is it?" she asked, looking at the large box Bea had set down.

"It is your costume."

"Really?" Julie ran to the box, feeling excited for the first time in a couple of days. She lifted the lid, revealing the gold half-mask that would leave only her lips and jaw visible.

Bea and Agnes nodded, humming in approval. Next, was an elaborate gold headdress. Were those diamonds stitched into the design? The jewels were pretty, but nothing compared with the dress.

"Ah..." all three women breathed out in unison as Julie pulled it out of the box. Julie couldn't believe the white and gold dress had been created from the silk bolts that were draped on her two days ago. The top was a corded corset bodice-type thing that cinched at the waist with yards of skirt spilling out from underneath it. Intricate gold threading and beadwork–more diamond-like gems–adorned the bodice and continued down onto the skirt more sparingly.

Julie hugged the dress to her. Erik's hand was so evident in the small touches.

He had told her she would be a queen from another dynasty and he did not disappoint. She looked down at the dress. You couldn't get more Victorian-Egyptian than this. She was going to the masquerade ball as a nineteenth century Cleopatra.

"There's something else in the box," Bea told Julie.

Julie lay the dress across the loveseat and removed the smaller boxes that had been hidden under the extravagant costume. She opened the larger of the two to find a broad-collared gold necklace that would surround her whole neck and cover most of her shoulders and chest. It was stunning. The smaller box contained a gold bracelet that wrapped around her forearm like a snake.

"You are going to be the most beautiful woman there!" Agnes smiled. Bea agreed reverently smoothing the dress. Julie smiled back at the women. If she weren't, she'd certainly feel as if she were, thanks to Erik.

"Now, let's get you ready for that ball." Bea nudged her toward the bathroom.

While Julie had been bathing, a note had arrived from Erik with instructions to apply the gold-flecked lard over any skin that would still be exposed once in her costume. She started with a small spot on her arm and her cinnamon skin turned a beautiful, shimmering gold. Julie had to hand it to Erik. He was a master of disguises. No one would ever guess it was she.

Within minutes the thin layer began to become firm, not tight or cracked, but in a way that made her skin look smooth and elegant. She looked up into the mirror to see her own haunted eyes shimmering with tears. She didn't know what she faced tonight, but she knew she didn't face it alone. What she did know was that this was to be the end. It would be terribly hard to say goodbye.

Julie dabbed her eyes at the sound of a tap on her door and applied more gold over the tear-streak on her face. "Yes," she called out as Bea and Agnes came in carrying the dress and accessories.

"Bless my soul!" Agnes stared at her. "Your skin is gold."

Julie smiled at her reaction. "Looks pretty, doesn't it?"

"I'd say exotic," Bea chimed in, tilting her head.

"I supposed it does," Julie agreed.

"Monsieur de la Croix will be here shortly. It is time to get you dressed."

Yes, Julie thought. *Time stops for no one.*

♀

Erik straightened the jacket on his black dress suit and adjusted the gold silk sash at his waist. He looked at his marred face in the mirror. It didn't matter anymore how he looked as he could alter others' perceptions at will. He could freely walk the streets without judgment now. He no longer needed to hide in shadows, creeping in the darkness of the world. He could be a son of the day. He could have everything he ever wanted, except for what he wanted the most: Juliana. And he deserved not to have her as his punishment for taking what he wanted all of his life without regard to anyone.

He slid the jackal half-mask over his face. Who better to be than Anubis, Egyptian god of the dead? After tonight, once he sent Juliana away, he wouldn't be truly living anyhow. But Juliana...she had a lot to live for and he would make sure she returned to her time to have a most wonderful life.

Erik's breath hung in the air as he called out for a cab. He couldn't wait to see Juliana. Tonight would be spectacular for her, even if he had to kill someone to make it so.

CHAPTER FORTY-EIGHT

From the moment Juliana's stepped into the room, Erik saw nothing else. As he had done many times for the Ottoman Sultan Abdulhamid II, he bowed low before her, but for Juliana, it was in genuine supplication. He honored her beauty. And he honored his own genius. For without him, this resplendent creature would not exist. Without saying a word, he secured her cape around her, offered her his arm, and escorted her to the carriage.

Leaning back against his seat, he tried to control his racing pulse. He found himself captivated by the rise and fall of the ornate necklace upon the tantalizing swell of the soft gilded skin above her bodice. And with each of her breaths, the instructions he had wanted to discuss before the ball dissipated from his mind. He wanted to savor in this memory of Juliana with slow sips. It was hard to believe that in mere hours, he would be bereft of her.

The lush padded seat provided no comfort during the agonizingly short ride to the hotel. Neither spoke. Neither's gaze left the other. Erik wondered what was going on inside that clever mind of hers. Was she excited about her first ball? Was she anxious about what might await them there? Was she anticipating her transition home, back to her time?

Juliana's kohl-lined eyes never wavered from behind her golden mask. Erik could sense her trust in him. Her belief in him. He knew full well that her life and her very soul were truly in his hands. She was safe with him. If anyone tried to harm her, it would mean their death.

He easily hid his feelings for her from behind his own mask. But his control did falter. For a split second, had she looked closely, his eyes would have told her he wanted to throw caution to the wind, damn the plan. *Stay. Stay with me.*

Instead, he remained silent. For her greater good, he told himself.

The carriage lurched to a halt in front of the Commercial Hotel and Erik descended the steps, holding a hand out to Juliana to assist her down to the sidewalk. He paid the aged coachman handsomely to wait directly across the street. Juliana gave Erik a questioning look.

"If we need to make a hasty retreat," he explained. What she did not know was if trouble ensued, he would stay and hold the enemy at bay, whomever that might be.

"Oh." She nodded without question.

Once inside the hotel, he escorted her to the reception committee's table where he presented their tickets. "Monsieur de la Croix and guest," a pleasant woman read his name from the ticket for her comrades who checked his name on the list. "Please raise your mask."

"Pardon?" he asked.

"We wouldn't want to let any unwelcome guests inside." The plump woman and her friends smiled and nodded at each other. "I need to confirm your identity since we have met before, I can verify that it is you."

"Madam, we have never met."

"Oh, but we have!" The woman's eyes lit up. "I'm Jane Tyler. James Gallier is my second cousin once removed. You sat in his box at the French Opera House." She cleared her throat at his lack of response. "For Berlioz's "Damnation de Faust"."

"Ah, yes," he said as he raised his mask, vaguely remembering the woman. That night he had been watching Christine. She sat in the third row, center stage. It seemed liked a lifetime ago.

"Welcome, Monsieur, to our masquerade!" Jane trilled with a flourish of her hand. Erik replaced his mask. "We have a photographer present to take your picture if you should wish to commemorate the evening. They will be mailed to you in a few weeks' time if you choose to do so."

Juliana touched his hand and whispered. "Yes, let's. It will be something to remember me by."

Erik nodded. Little did she know he did not need a photograph to remember her. For every line, every expression, and every movement, he had already committed to memory.

Jane's eyes admiringly swept over the elaborate Egyptian dress Juliana wore. "You need not lift *your* mask, my dear. It is entertaining for those in attendance to guess as to who is who. The entire party will unmask and declare themselves at midnight when the supper room opens. If you have need for drink or snacks before then, the refreshment room is just over there." She gestured to an open door where a serving maid stood.

"Thank you," Juliana answered, looking at the refreshment room then glancing at Erik. He knew she would not be eating anything tonight. Neither of them had an appetite and both would be gone before midnight.

Erik put his hand to the small of Juliana's back, ushering her toward the photographer and the cloak room. No time like the present to confront what awaited them.

♀

Juliana still had spots before her eyes from taking the picture as she handed the attendant her cloak.

"Ready?" Erik smiled at her, offering his arm once again. She accepted it with gratitude.

Closer to the ballroom, she saw flashes of jewels and twirling figures dressed in brilliant colors. She stopped short. In other circumstances, she would worry about remembering the dances or whether she would make a fool of herself. Tonight, she couldn't give a flying flip about what these people thought. Her heart clenched. There was so little time left before she would have to say goodbye to Erik forever.

"I won't let any harm come to you," Erik whispered in her ear, mistaking her pause. She believed his promise with every fiber of her very being. He just couldn't see that it killed her to leave him.

"I know," she said, walking with him through the open double doors.

Gas light sconces flickered against the burgundy walls, adding a soft richness to the color. There were large potted ficus in the corners and flanking the multiple open French doors that led to a courtyard. The contrast of the green shrubbery made a charming background as the colorful revelers moved about the room.

The attendees dazzled in marvelous costumes. Julie counted three variations of Greek women, a flamenco dancer, shepherdesses, queens, a geisha and an Italian peasant woman. These were not store-bought costumes, but hand-sewn, stunning Victorian versions. And nothing that she had seen so far compared with her beautiful gown.

She received a lot of backward glances from men and women alike. A man dressed as George Washington made a slight bow as he passed by her. A group of women whispered in the corner while staring her way. It was far too late to become a wallflower now even if she wanted to. Besides, a bashful Rapunzel partially hidden behind one of the potted plants already held the position.

Across the room a pianist, cellist, two violinists, and a cornetist finished playing a lively but unfamiliar tune, then transitioned into a waltz that she recognized.

"I believe they are playing our song. Let us give them something to talk about, shall we?" Erik asked her.

He led her to the dance floor, pulling her close to his chest. She placed her hand on his shoulder as he put his strong right arm around her waist and pressed her to him until every curve in her body shivered by the contact. And then they danced as if they were one. Nothing felt more natural than to go where he went and move as he moved.

If Julie could get any closer to him, she would. Was it possible to absorb him and allow his essence to flow through her and truly make them one? He continued bending her body to and fro with the music, whirling her effortlessly around the dance floor. His masked face revealed a fierce gleam in his eyes. Was he also filled with intense rapture as she was?

She kept her face upturned to his, holding his gaze as they turned about the room over and over. No other dancers existed. No party guests. No impending doom. No goodbyes to come. There was only this moment.

Then the music ended.

Her reverie broke, and Erik led her away from the dance floor. He pulled a small bag from his vest and handed it to her.

He spoke quickly. "I have sewn a pocket into the folds of your skirt. Place the bag in there."

Julie moved her skirt and found the cleverly disguised pocket, placing the bag inside as Erik had requested.

"I meant to give that to you before we entered the ballroom," he said with a smile that unnerved her as he leaned in closer to her. "But I was distracted." He reached out and touched a strand of hair that had escaped her headdress and tucked it away. She trembled at the intimate gesture.

"If we become separated for any reason, make your way to my house on St. Charles. In the bag you will find the oil you need and something of yours that ties you to your home. Put it on and follow the directions I have written."

She nodded, wishing the night would not end and she would never need the bag or its contents.

"If all goes well, I will claim another dance with you before the night ends. Then I will take you to my home and oversee the ritual myself, but until then be alert. I am only a call away if you should need me and I will be watching you the entire night. Now we must be generous with our time and dance with others." He looked past her. "An eager partner approaches as we speak." He bowed and turned. For her, the room darkened when he walked away.

She swallowed and nodded as a masked Revolutionary War soldier asked her to dance. She felt mismatched and uncomfortable in his arms as they joined the other dancers. The soldier made small talk, attempting to guess her identity. She politely answered, not really paying attention. Her eyes followed Erik as he crossed the room, stopped at the potted plant, and bowed to the shy Rapunzel, who blushed at his words.

Julie nearly burst with pride at his kindness to the skittish girl. She was sure her heart grew five times larger with Erik's gesture. She watched them dance. He was gentle and kind. Respectful and tender. The girl beamed. If there really were such a thing, Erik had just earned a gold star in his heavenly crown.

She turned her attention back to the soldier, who was a fair dancer in his own right once she was able to get used to his style. They swirled past another masked couple. The man was dressed in a suit with a blue sash–a small horn hung from his side–Julie guessed he was Little Boy Blue. And although the woman did not hold a curved cane, she was most definitely Little Bo Peep. As they crossed behind the couple, Julie saw the man touch the woman's curled tresses. She stiffened when she heard him speak in a thick French accent.

"Your hair is as smooth as silk."

She could not tear her eyes away from the pair as she impatiently danced around the room with the soldier, waiting until they got closer to the couple again. She could hear their conversation as she twirled nearer.

"How will you be able to tell me apart from the other Bo Peep?" the woman asked, also with a French accent. Julie scanned the room and saw the other Bo Peep costumer, but twisted her head back as the man answered.

"By your mesmerizing eyes, of course," he purred.

Julie shivered as a cold sensation shot down her spine. Raoul and Christine.

"Is there anything wrong?" the soldier asked.

"No." Julie said with forced cheer while her heart sank into the pit of her stomach. Two of the possible players were here. The soldier continued on with his conversation not knowing her world as she knew it might be changed forever.

Her desperate search for Erik ended when she saw him dancing with Rapunzel near the ballroom entrance. She stared at him, willing him to look her way. At that moment, he glanced at her, frowning at the look on her face. She pointed toward Christine and Raoul, mouthing their names in the hopes that he could lip-read. He followed the direction of her finger and his face hardened in recognition. Neither of them could relax now.

The song ended and the soldier, spilling compliments along the way, escorted her from the dance floor. Before she could thank the gentleman for the dance, she was surrounded by other masked men. As a reveler dressed as Napoleon asked her to dance, Erik stepped forward with his arm extended to her.

"I believe you need a bit of fresh air."

She grabbed hold of him as if her life depended on it. She leaned into him, breathing in the comfort of his presence as he maneuvered them outside into the courtyard.

"Have you seen anyone else besides the de Marignys?"

She shook her head. "Have you?"

"No, not as yet." Erik's eyes narrowed and he took a protective step closer to her. "I may have spoken too soon."

Julie followed his darkened gaze to a tall man walking across the dance floor, the dancers parting out of his way as he headed straight toward them. His black silk mask made his green eyes a focal point even more so than his brilliant smile. He wore a loose white tunic and thin-soled sandals, just as he had eons ago.

Izak had arrived.

CHAPTER FORTY-NINE

"How charming," Izak said, raking his eyes over Juliana and Erik's Egyptian attire. Erik noticed with satisfaction that Izak lingered over the crystals sewn into Juliana's costume and headdress. Izak's lips smirked before turning into his signature smile. "Such intricate tailoring. Tell me, did the stars weep as you sewed?"

"Small talk does not become you." Erik dismissed Izak with irritation. Juliana raised her eyebrows, but remained silent during the exchange and Erik willed her to remain so. "What do you want? Why are you here?"

"Ungracious as ever." Izak clasped Erik's shoulder, looking pleased. His smiled faded as Erik shrugged his hand off. "You knew I would be here. *I* am the one who sent *you* the invitation. And I want a front row seat for tonight's events."

Izak closed the space between them, staring into his eyes. Erik refused to step back.

"You look well." Izak inhaled deeply, making Erik feel as if Izak tried to breathe in his very essence. "In fact, you seem considerably better than the time I last saw you." A flicker of emotion crossed his face. Was that concern Erik saw there?

"Yes, about that." Erik cleared his throat. "Thank you for your assistance. Juliana told me I might have succumbed to the illness if not for you. It seems I owe you my life."

"A debt you can never repay," Izak replied.

"I never intended to," Erik said.

"Touché." Izak grinned. "So," he said. "Anubis, is it? Imitation is the sincerest form of flattery. He would be pleased indeed."

Before Erik blinked, Izak had moved beside Juliana and spoke in her ear.

"Cleopatra herself was not as beautiful as you are this evening." The hair on Erik's neck stood as Izak raised Juliana's hand to his mouth and kissed it. Juliana yanked her hand back.

"And who might you be this evening, Izak?" Erik knew the answer before the words left his mouth. He had recognized the cut and flow of the tunic as soon as he saw it, having seen through Arak's eyes the very same tunic.

"I have come as myself." Izak said as he touched the flowing material. "But," he added with a wink. "You know how easy it is to make people see what they want to see. That is until they realize the truth too late."

A chill swept over Erik at Izak's words. Edgar Allan Poe had written about such an eerily similar theme. Death masquerading as Death. Front row seats be damned. Izak was most definitely a player in whatever game unfolded if not the mastermind behind it.

Izak waved a hand toward the dancers in the ballroom. "The masqueraders see me in a fine gentleman's suit with a domino mask."

"Indeed. Just as they see me without my scars." What did Izak really want?

As if he'd read Erik's mind, Izak said, "You are right. We should not waste time with small talk. We are not commoners. Have you seen the de Marignys?"

"Yes. Are they supposed to concern me?" Erik raised an eyebrow.

"Perhaps not," Izak answered. "Were you also aware that Arak is here?"

Juliana gasped and Erik's muscles tightened on pure alert. "No," he answered. "Does he intend to cause trouble?"

Izak's eyes sparkled and Erik distinctly felt Izak's hope that Arak would. "I do not think my brother knows his own mind."

"Could you reason with him?"

"Oh, I assure you. I have tried to reason with him for centuries. Alas, he makes his own decisions contrary to my wishes."

"Will you, at the very least, point him out to me?"

"Tsk, tsk," Izak answered while waving a long finger in the air. "Now where would the fun be in that? I think not. However, I can promise that I will not allow him to harm Juliana if I may have a dance with her."

"No. Absolutely not," Erik growled with uneasiness.

"I will go." Juliana stepped forward.

Erik turned toward her, astounded. "No."

She pulled him aside, whispering in his ear. "Don't you see? I will be safe with Izak while you figure out which man is Arak."

"I don't like it, Juliana."

"You don't have to like it. Just find out which man in there is Arak."

Erik jumped as Izak whispered in his other ear. "The safety measures you have in place will work," he said, eyeing the crystalline chips studding Juliana's dress. "Should you need to use them."

"Very well," Erik conceded, wary. As Izak led Juliana to the ballroom dance floor the wariness left and his gut instead burned with jealousy.

♀

Izak was a proficient dancer and Julie found it easy to follow his lead as they entered the dance already in progress.

"You truly outshine everyone here, Juliana," Izak said, his voice lacking sincerity.

"Izak, you can stop with the false compliments. Why did you want to get me alone? What do you want?"

"You are a clever girl." Izak smiled. "I can see why Erik loves you."

"Loves me?" Julie repeated, astounded.

"Any fool can see that he does." The weight he gave the words suggested that she was worse than a fool for not having known. Julie scanned the ballroom for Erik. He walked purposefully through the room, stopping to converse with groups of people. Her heart glowed. She had hoped, but had never allowed herself to believe that he considered her more than a well-cared for friend.

"I believe Erik is in danger." Izak invaded her thoughts with the urgent statement.

"What?" she whipped her head back toward him. She felt a surge of imminence through Izak's touch. "What do you mean? What kind of danger? We have to tell him." She tried to pull away from Izak, but he held firm.

"Hear me out, Juliana. It can be avoided. Arak will walk away and there will be no trouble if you were to do something."

"Arak intends to harm Erik? What can I do to stop it? I would do anything." She meant it. If she could protect Erik from danger, she would do it.

"Leave. Tonight."

She grunted. All-knowing Izak didn't have a clue. "That's not going to be a problem. I am leaving tonight. You won't see or hear from me again."

"It is not as simple as that. You must both leave. You and Naomi. If you love Erik even a little, you will do this."

"What do you mean both of us? I wouldn't even begin to know how to do that."

"I do," Izak said as they swirled past Erik. Julie caught his eye and they stared at each other until she could no longer do so, her heart ached. He loved her. If only she could hear it from his own lips. She could stay. Believing he didn't love her was the reason she had been willing to leave...until now. Now his safety relied on her leaving.

A calmness settled over her with her resolve to protect Erik. "What do I have to do?"

"Marie Laveau is waiting outside in a carriage. You must go to her and you must leave without telling Erik, or he would never allow you to go. She will send your spirit back and keep Naomi hidden from Erik. Naomi will be cared for, and all will be as it should be."

With each word, Julie felt a pang of nausea. She wanted Erik safe and happy, but not at the expense of her past life's safety and happiness. She wouldn't do that to herself and Erik would not want her to. In fact, he had made her promise not to. Besides, this seemed to play suspiciously into Marie and Izak's favor. Was Erik even in danger at all? Was this a trap?

"There must be another way," Julie said, challenging Izak by looking directly into his eyes. They didn't swirl. They remained a clear green.

Izak clenched his jaw before answering. "There was a time I once loved a woman. Sometimes sacrifices are necessary and unfortunately, neither of us would make any sacrifices." His eyes glazed with a far-away look. "It did not end well. Believe me when I say there is no other way. Erik's future depends on it. This is not the time to be so concerned with your own."

She cast her eyes downward. "I cannot."

"You are a selfish woman, Juliana." Izak's voice dripped with poison as he enunciated each word.

"I will talk to Erik. He will find another way."

"There is no other way," Izak repeated. "And he must not know. He would fight you every step of the way. What is your answer?"

"I can't!" She gasped under the conflict that weighted her heart.

Cold fury rolled over Izak's face, but he spoke with restrained calm. "Then let the game begin." He tossed her away from him and stormed through the throng of people without a backward glance.

Julie found herself in the arms of an unknown masked man. He righted her and made sure she was steady on her feet. The masked man glared in the direction of Izak's retreating back.

"No gentleman would treat a woman in such a manner!" he said in an outraged French accent. He made to go after Izak, but fearing for his safety, Julie held on to his arm.

"Sir, it is not worth the trouble. I am fine. I merely stumbled on the hem of my skirt." She got a better look at the stranger. He wore a blue sash with a small horn hanging from it. Raoul.

Raoul stood, staring at her. "Do I know you?"

Julie evaded his question. "How could I possibly answer that? We are all masked."

He smiled. "Quite true." He moved a step closer. "Has anyone told you that you have the most mesmerizing eyes?"

She smiled back at him in spite of herself. "I have been told that on occasion."

"It is true," he said with an appreciative glance. Julie would have been thrilled at one time to see Raoul look at her in that way, but now she just wanted to get to Erik and tell him what had just happened with Izak. "Thank you for saving my modesty, but..."

"Dance with me," Raoul interrupted her.

"I really...can't," Julie found herself being guided to the dance floor even as she spoke.

"You are a splendid dancer," Raoul complimented her.

"Thank you, but I–" Julie stopped when Erik danced by with Christine.

Christine's Bo Peep skirt flowed about her ankles as they spun in the dance and she smiled at something he said. They made a very charming couple and Julie wanted to knock Christine's pretty little head off.

"I do know you," Raoul spoke near her ear, startling her.

"You do?" she replied.

"Yes, I do. It has been a while since I have seen you, Naomi."

Julie stumbled, causing them to swerve toward the right. "How did you notice?"

"I have always noticed you," he said seductively, pulling her closer. Julie stiffened, but he didn't seem to be aware. "I have noticed your smile. I have noticed the sway of your hips when you walk. Believe me, Naomi, I have noticed you."

"But you never gave any indication–"

"I held back for the sake of my son, but as you can see, my wife's heart lies elsewhere." He directed his gaze to Erik and Christine. "I am not sure the child even belongs to me."

Julie shook her head. No, this was not right. None of this was right. She looked at Erik dancing with Christine. He looked so happy. Did Izak lie about Erik loving her?

Raoul expertly turned Julie about the room bringing her closer and closer to the French doors that led to the courtyard.

"Run away with me, Naomi."

Her disbelief prevented her from answering Raoul's plea.

Julie thought about Simon and Monika. She had wanted revenge once, but not anymore. She had loved Simon once, but not anymore. She was in love with Erik and wanted his happiness. If Christine made him happy, Julie wouldn't stand in his way, but neither could she stand by and watch him fulfill his desire without having her heart break. She was going home and she would trust Erik to make sure Naomi would be cared for.

He repeated himself more urgently. "Run away with me, Naomi."

"No. I will not run away with you. I do not love you. My heart belongs to someone else."

"That is a shame," he said, his French accent gone. He tilted his head inadvertently revealing two puncture marks on his neck.

Julie froze in horror.

"It would have been easier had you come willingly." He yanked her out into the courtyard. "But it matters not how you leave just as long as you do."

CHAPTER FIFTY

Erik interrupted conversations, bumped into people, and extended his thoughts around the room, trying to sense Arak's presence. He was certain that having experienced a moment in Arak's life, he would be able to connect with the imprint it had left behind on him, no matter which body Arak inhabited now. But all his efforts were for naught. Arak was undetectable. Was Izak even telling the truth about Arak being at the ball?

As he danced with Juliana again, he held her closer than necessary. Even though he trusted that the crystals in the dress could protect her with but a word, he felt more relaxed having her in his arms, far away from the Earth Walker and his brother.

Juliana's silence troubled him. She spoke her mind so easily. Normally, he couldn't stop her from talking. What did Izak say to her to unsettle her so? Her movements were stiff and her usual animated demeanor was unreadable, so unlike herself.

Why had Izak been so eager to dance with Juliana? What agenda did Izak harbor? Erik started forging a new agenda of his own, a change of plans.

Ever since Juliana had used the cane to try to heal his face, and more so after Erik spent time in Arak's skin, he had felt empowered by the energy that surged through him. He was changing, becoming more alive. More present. And with this dawning awareness, somewhere deep inside of him, a voice rustled, telling him he was capable of making his dreams a reality. And the voice was his own.

"The air feels charged with energy tonight," he whispered in Juliana's ear.

She pulled back, eyebrows raised. "Oh? How so?"

"Look down," he said without taking his eyes off her.

A slow smile pulled at her lips as she saw the gems on her dress glowing. "You sewed the crystal into my dress and you have mastered its use with mere thought."

"Yes." He searched her uplifted eyes. "And soon, just as Izak doesn't require the crystal, I will also master my abilities without it."

"You seem very confident about this," she said, staring intently without revealing her thoughts.

"I am."

Erik waltzed her to a less crowded section. For all of his confidence, his heart skipped a few beats before he spoke again.

"Juliana, I want you to stay."

Her forehead creased and she opened her mouth to speak, but before she could get a word in, he continued. "I think I can bind you here permanently. And just as I can hide my true face from being seen, I know I can make you undetectable. We can fake our deaths. I've done it before. Then we can travel the world, together. Just say the word. We'll leave now. Izak and Arak be damned."

Her look of pity caught him by surprise. "You might be able to hide us from the common people, but never Izak. There is no disguise that could ever hide you from him. Besides, why would I want to do that?" She smiled coldly. "Everything that means anything to me is at home. There is nothing here for me. No," she paused. "I think not. I'll be leaving."

Hurt shot through him at her unexpected response. Did he mean nothing to her? "That isn't—" he started to say.

"It is not up for discussion," she said, turning her head away from him, inadvertently revealing two puncture marks in her neck. At the sight, the illusion of Juliana faded away, crumbling away like glittering dust only Erik could see. And now, he found that he had been dancing with Christine all along, duped by a master manipulator.

"Izak," he spat out.

Christine's head swiveled back with Izak's lazy smile on her face. "Ah...now what gave me away?"

Erik discreetly dragged her from the dance floor to a corner of the room. "I thought you were not able to interfere without being asked," Erik seethed.

Izak shrugged Christine's shoulders. "Am I interfering? From where I stand, it is Christine with whom you are conversing. I, in fact, am not even in this room."

"Why? Why are you doing this?" *And why couldn't I sense anything?* Erik's heart raced. "Where is Juliana? I will kill you if you have laid a hand on her."

"That's the spirit!" Christine slapped Erik on the back. "Only you would want to try to kill someone who cannot die."

"I'll find a way," Erik promised.

Ignoring his threat, Christine shook her head. "You do realize I could not let her stay."

"You have no say in this." Erik clenched his fists, resisting the desire to punch the condescending look off Christine's face.

"She will ruin everything if she does," Izak explained with a flick of Christine's hand. "It is in her nature to do so."

"That is not for you to determine. It is her decision to make," Erik snarled.

"Not any longer," Izak sang out eerily with Christine's voice. "You are too late." With her eyes rolling upward, Christine stumbled forward and collapsed to the ground. A blur of people swarmed to her assistance. A man shouted for the crowd to step back and give her air; Erik had already abandoned her to search the room. Juliana was in trouble.

Juliana! He called out to her with his mind. *Where are you?*

♀

The thick hedge surrounding the edge of the courtyard snagged and ripped at Julie's dress as Raoul pulled her through it. Or rather, whoever made Raoul pull her through it. The bite marks on Raoul's neck reeked of Izak, but only Arak could switch bodies–albeit soulless bodies–but maybe his abilities evolved to enable him to inhabit the souled as well.

She didn't care who it was. She wanted to escape. As she struggled, her headdress tumbled away. The grip on her arm only tightened, and no matter how loud she hollered, her voice sounded muffled. The loud music and the chatter from the ball was also dampened. No one would hear her. She was on her own.

To her surprise, she didn't feel much fear for herself. Instead concern for Erik overwhelmed her. How would he feel if he found her injured, or worse, dead? Knowing he wasn't there to protect her when she needed him most, and her not being able to reassure him that it wasn't his fault.

Raoul stopped dragging her once they entered the side alley. She stopped yelling and tried to communicate with him. "Are you going to kill me?"

"Now why would I want to kill you?" The person inside of Raoul answered. "You would just find another way to come back, and I do not want to have to deal with you any longer than I have to. I am sending you away. Losing you will become the incentive Erik needs to embrace his destiny."

He thrust her forward, and she found herself face to face with Marie Laveau. The whites of the Voodoo queen's eyes seemed to absorb the light of the moon and glowed eerily. Marie gripped her shoulder firmly, and Julie jumped.

"The first time we met, I made you an offer." Marie dug her fingers into Julie's skin as she turned her around. "This fine gentleman insists that you take me up on it now."

Raoul staggered backward, blinking his eyes, placing a hand on his neck.

"Not that man." Marie raised a long finger toward the end of the alley. "That one."

Izak stood at the mouth of the alleyway. In an eye blink, he was arm's length from them.

"Naomi," Raoul cried in alarm as he tried to put himself between Julie and Izak.

"Wretched little man," Izak said, picking Raoul up by the neck with one hand. Raoul's feet dangled in the air as he struggled to breathe, Izak's fingers slowly crushing his throat. "What is it about a woman's honor they treasure so highly?" Izak murmured.

"Let him go!" Juliana pushed forward, but Marie's steely hands held her back. "Izak, please," she begged. "Don't hurt him."

"But that is the thing is it not, Juliana. You ask me to have mercy, but you have no difficulty hurting people when it suits you. This very man, in fact." Izak spoke to Raoul, loosening his grip to allow him brief access to air. "She was intent on destroying your marriage. Did you know that?"

Raoul continued to gasp, uselessly pulling at Izak's hand, while his tear-filled eyes darted toward Julie.

"I'm so sorry." She cried out the words quickly as she reached out an arm to him. "It was a thought that I never acted on. I wouldn't have done it. It was wrong and I figured that out." Marie pulled Julie to the far end of the alley where a covered carriage waited. Julie turned to Izak, resisting Marie. "Please, please let him go."

"It is a little too late for that." Izak shifted his swirling eyes her way, his grip tightening. Raoul's face mottled under the dim light from the corner streetlamp.

Marie continued to pull. Izak squeezed harder. Raoul grunted. Julie didn't know when she started to hyperventilate, but caught in Marie's unyielding grip, Julie found it difficult to breathe. Thick unnamable emotions swirled in her gut as Izak continued to speak.

"Everyone has a history, Juliana. Your blood is rich with memories. You say you love? We both know you fail those you love. Perhaps your parents would be alive today if you had been home."

"Leave my parents out of this," she said with little conviction as she watched Izak loosen his grasp, allowing Raoul another moment to gasp for air.

"Raoul and Christine. Simon and Monika. You insinuate yourself into relationships that you were never meant to be a part of. You are the mistake in every equation. You were never meant to be here. Do everyone a favor, Juliana. Erase yourself."

"Never," Julie answered. The sound of thunder rolled around them and a calmness settled over her. She felt as if she had just been tested and passed.

"Come, child," Marie coaxed, casting a wary look toward Izak.

Julie felt the hair on her arms start to rise. The air in the alley bent as it would under the low pressure of a storm. A voice spoke in her mind. A beloved voice.

Juliana, where are you? Her eyes welled with tears of relief. She didn't know how it was possible that he could speak with her, but her heart rejoiced and she found strength.

Erik! I'm here! I'm here! She visualized the alleyway in her mind with Izak, Marie, and Raoul.

I'm coming. He sent a pulse of reassurance that poured through her.

"You're wrong." Julie attempted to stall Izak. She shook Marie's hand off her and faced Izak directly. "I'm not a mistake. I have a purpose."

"I do not care about your purpose," Izak said with disdain. "Go with Marie now or people will start dying, beginning with Raoul. After I am done with him, I will kill one person a minute. How many innocent people must die for you, Juliana? And if that will not convince you, I promise you this: I will kill Erik. I gave him his life and I will take it from him before I allow his association with you to continue. I have endured enough."

She saw it all as he spoke. Raoul's neck snapping. Izak grabbing a stranger from the street, ripping his throat open, and breaking the neck of the woman who was with him. Erik stepping out from the hedge into the alley. Izak twisting Erik's head around, howling as he did. Erik's body falling in a heap on the flagstone street.

"No." She shook the painful images from her head. Horror enveloped her as she saw the tailored trouser leg of Erik's suit emerge from the hedge.

"No!" she yelled. And time slowed. The gems on her dress glowed, pulling light from the streetlamp. A warm current of electric energy pulsed from them, sending a wave through the alley.

Izak let Raoul fall to the ground as he lifted into the air, a look of surprise on his face. Marie yelped next to her as she also rose. Then time sped up again as they were both flung to opposite ends of the alley and Erik fully materialized from the courtyard.

"Juliana," he called to her, abruptly stopping as he took in the three unconscious bodies on the ground and the dimming light of the crystals on her dress.

She ran into his outstretched arms, returning his tight squeeze with a trembling embrace.

"What happened here?" he asked as he smoothed her hair.

"What do you mean?"

He cupped her face with his warm hands. "Who did this? Who stopped Izak and Marie?"

"I thought you did."

His brow creased in concern and he dropped his hands from her face. "It wasn't me."

"Then who?" Her voice quivered.

"Now is not the time to worry over that. We need to get you away from here." He took hold of her hand and ran with her.

As they passed Izak's still body, Erik pitched forward, nearly taking Julie with him as he slammed to the ground. Julie stopped.

"Not so fast," Izak snarled, his hand clenched around Erik's ankle. Erik raised his head. Even in the dark alley, Julie could see his blue eyes swirl with anger and fear.

"Run, Juliana," he said urgently. "Run!"

CHAPTER FIFTY-ONE

Once the train of Juliana's dress disappeared around the corner of the hotel, Erik twisted and kicked Izak in the face. Izak released his ankle, and both men jumped to their feet. A trickle of blood dripped from Izak's nose.

"Not so invincible after all," Erik taunted.

"If you prick me, do I not bleed?" Izak calmly wiped his nose with the back of his hand, smearing the blood on his face. "And if you wrong me, shall I not revenge?"

Erik charged.

Izak countered with an arm block.

As they sparred, Erik opened the link between himself and Izak, anticipating Izak's every move. They fought with equal measure. Each blow blocked by the other, the ongoing fight was at a stalemate.

When Raoul roused and staggered to his feet, Erik allowed Izak the upper hand, keeping Izak's attention focused upon himself so Raoul could leave unnoticed. Air exploded from Erik's lungs as Izak slammed him against a brick wall.

"I do not want to hurt you, but if pushed to it, I will," Izak grunted.

Raoul disappeared through the hedge. Erik shoved Izak away, but Izak gripped his arm and both of them fell, rolling on the flagstone street. Erik landed on top. He slammed Izak's head against the stone ground, repeatedly.

"I don't want to hurt you either," Erik said through gritted teeth each time he smashed Izak's head. "I want you dead."

Izak laughed, planting his hands on Erik's chest, thrusting him off. "That is not going to happen." He stood, feet anchored apart. "Let me remind you that I am not breakable as you are. I would tread very carefully."

Erik bristled at Izak's warning, throwing a well-aimed punch that Izak easily swatted away. He threw another punch that Izak caught with his hand.

"You are getting stronger, but you are not strong enough, little man." When Izak released Erik's hand, it dawned on him that Izak had been playing with him all along. Izak stared at Erik with swirling eyes, then dismissively turned away.

As Izak turned, a loud bang reverberated in the small alley. Izak stopped short. Smoke hung in the air as the badly bruised Raoul stood with a gun in his outstretched hands. More men filed out from behind the hedge, holding candlesticks or brandishing knives. They entered the alley grimly blocking the exit with weapons at the ready.

Izak turned toward Erik, ripping his shirt open to reveal a gaping bloody wound. In fascination, Erik stared as the wound healed before his eyes.

"Stay where you are," Raoul yelled at Izak's back while he reloaded the pistol.

Izak buttoned his shirt over the healed bullet wound while keeping his eyes on Erik, speaking inside of his head. *You see, I cannot die.* Then Izak turned toward the growing crowd of gathering men. He showed mental images to Erik of the carnage he could inflict on the mortals.

Not worth my time. He tossed a grin Erik's way, leaving in a whirlwind just as Raoul pulled the trigger. The second shot whizzed past Erik's face and entered the brick wall behind him. Multiple gasps hung in the alleyway; the men's faces crinkled in confusion. Izak was gone. After a few moments, the foolish men, feeling empowered by their numbers, followed Izak while Raoul stayed behind.

"Monsieur de la Croix, are you injured?" Raoul asked him.

"No."

Raoul surveyed the alley. Erik followed his gaze to Marie Laveau who still lay unconscious on the ground. Raoul ran to Marie's side, placing his face near her chest. "She's alive."

Erik could not have cared less whether the Voodoo Queen had survived. She had some type of arrangement with Izak even though Izak had sworn not to involve her in their affairs. He turned away. "Let the women tend to her."

Raoul stood, speaking hoarsely. "I've not seen a man that has strength such as that nor the speed to outrun a bullet. My aim was true, yet he did not fall. What manner of man does not die?"

"That was no man," Erik muttered to himself, wondering where Izak had gone. Had he figured out that Juliana had fled to the St. Charles house instead of the Creole cottage?

"You and I will have to give a full account of tonight's events. There will be an inquiry."

"There will be no inquiry for me," Erik said, harnessing his inner energy, bending Raoul's mind. "I was never here."

♀

Julie held her tears until the carriage stopped at Erik's St. Charles house and she was safely inside. She shook with adrenalin and fear unable to wipe away the image of Erik yelling for her to run as he lay on the ground...she prayed to God that he was okay.

As she stood in the foyer, the unleveled floors glowed in the warm light of the gas wall sconces. She imagined Erik lighting them before leaving to pick her up for the ball, and the thought comforted her. Still, it felt strange being in this house again. She had not been back since the day she left.

Amazing how one month could change a person. Amazing that a month could feel like a lifetime. There was a saying she remembered hearing once: Don't cry because it's over. Smile because it happened. She was doing both.

Julie walked down the narrow hallway, following the lighted path created by Erik. He had left the hidden doorways open, and it didn't take long to reach the suite of rooms in which she had awakened earlier. It was only fitting that she leave from the same place she had arrived.

The room was just as she had left it. Everything was as she remembered: blue walls, mahogany bed, the open French doors to the faux courtyard, and the piano in the corner.

The fireplace roared with life. Julie shivered despite the warmth. The room seemed inviting, as if it waited for happy occupants to arrive and enjoy its ambiance. This was no happy occasion for her. She was leaving a place that felt like home and she was leaving a man that she wanted more than he would ever know.

The time had come to let go of this life and the man who would never say he wanted her to stay. She removed the snake bracelet and heavy necklace, placing them on the dresser. She struggled to remove the heavy material of the beautiful costume she wore. It took some finagling, but she was able to extricate herself once she loosened the corset.

Wearing only a simple shift, Julie folded the gown as best she could and, looking at it longingly, placed it on one of the chairs facing the fireplace. The crystals caught the light of the fire and turned amber against the white and gold silk.

Erik had put so much time and effort into having the dress made and adding his special touch to it that she knew he had to care about her. She thought about the time spent in his company, the hours they had spent talking and dancing. She would never forget the kisses they had shared. But in the end, he would never admit to feeling anything for her and she didn't know why. Staring at the dress and thinking about what she was giving up made her eyes tear, so she looked away.

It was then that she noticed the small bundle of sweet grass on the mantle. She remembered Star telling her to make sure she burned the sweet grass. She remembered lighting it on a plate, putting it in the bathroom with the window open to diffuse the smell, and yet the fragrance of it still had filled her home. That must be why it was here. She must need to use it again. But it would all be in the Erik's instructions. She'd forgotten that she had them.

Julie retrieved the bag Erik had given her from the dress pocket. The first item she pulled out was a small walnut-colored bottle filled with liquid. No surprise there. Behind it was a folded piece of paper. She opened it and saw Erik's scribble-scratch handwriting.

Put the sweet grass in the fire. Put the oil on your hands, feet, chest, and forehead. Take handkerchief on the bedside table infused with sleeping draft. Breathe it. Lie on the bed and let it take effect. Then leave the rest to me.

Simple enough. Been there. Pretty much done that. Her hand holding the bag still felt heavy. She tilted the bag until a familiar object spilled out into her palm. She'd recognize it anywhere.

The silver balls with the silver charm. It was Jenny Lind's bracelet, a present from her lover, Frederic Chopin, with their entwined blonde hair on the face of the charm. The precious gift that was lost for a century until Julie discovered it in her house during renovations. The bracelet that Heath had been so interested in. The bracelet that had given her a view of her past. This was the something that Erik wanted her to have.

She flipped the charm over, expecting to see woven blonde strands. Her hands stilled in surprise, her heart beating wildly against her chest.

The blonde hair was gone. In its place, honey-colored and black woven strands of hair mingled together in an intricate pattern.

A hot tear rolled down her face as she lovingly touched the charm. She and Heath had wondered why the hair color had changed. Now she understood. Erik had replaced the lovers' hair with their own.

It was her love story.

Hers and Erik's.

It was his way of showing her how he felt. Erik must be crazy if he thought she'd walk away from their relationship so easily now that she knew the truth. She was staying and would make her relationship with Erik work, or die trying.

♀

Erik quickly dealt with every man in Raoul's posse. One by one, as they ran up and down the street looking for Izak, he changed their memories. There wasn't time to waste. Juliana was alone, and he had no idea where Izak had gone.

Once done, he ran down the alley to the front of the hotel where the horses and carriages waited for their fares. The drivers conversed together under a streetlamp, smoking, and sipping from their flasks while they bided their time. All were oblivious to his presence as he approached the nearest coach. He raised his hand toward the horse's harnesses, visualizing the leather straps falling.

"Release," he commanded.

The harnesses fell to the ground. Erik swung onto the horse's bare back and dug his knees into its side, urging the animal to gallop.

"Hey!" One of the coachmen yelled, running behind him. "Stop! Stop! That's my horse!"

Erik ignored his calls.

"Help! Stop thief!" The man's shouts faded in the distance.

Besides the danger Juliana might face from Izak, Erik was disturbed that he still had no clue who had caused that burst of energy in alleyway. Arak might have his fingers in this after all. If he did, his actions seemed to be those of assistance. Unless Arak freed Juliana to have her for himself. The thought maddened him, and Erik gave a quick jab of his heel.

Faster, he told the mare.

The animal snorted, her legs stretching farther, picking up speed. At the sound of the police whistles behind him, Erik veered the horse to the right, narrowly avoiding a drunk man that had ambled into the road.

They flew past building after building in the French Quarter, crossed Canal Street, and entered onto St. Charles Avenue. His feeling of urgency increased the closer he got to his house. He couldn't get to Juliana quickly enough.

There was no time to stop the riled-up animal, so Erik focused his energy on every muscle in his body. He swung his leg over the horse's back and jumped to the ground as the horse careered past the front of his large home. He landed easily on his feet, pushed the iron gate open, and ran to the porch. The front door was ajar. Had someone followed Juliana inside?

He entered the foyer, his heart pounding. Nothing seemed amiss. The house was silent except for the sound of his own ragged breathing. He headed straight to Juliana's room.

As he entered her quarters, he stopped, cold fear spreading through him. Juliana's dress lay draped on a chair. Her bed was undisturbed, though the bundle of sweet grass he had set aside now lay on the floor. The room was empty.

CHAPTER FIFTY-TWO

Julie fought the urge to rush from the house to search for Erik. It was agonizing to wait for him. And her thoughts ran wild. Was he still in the alley? Had he killed Izak or was he fighting for his life? Had Arak appeared?

Leaving wouldn't do her any good. Erik could be anywhere by now. And if she left, Erik would be angry that she put herself at risk. She had to trust that Erik would come as he had said he would.

Only, she couldn't let go of that feeling, the compelling need to be with him. Her heart thrummed. In her mind, she kept hearing Harry tell Sally, "When you realize you want to spend the rest of your life with somebody, you want the rest of your life to start as soon as possible." Erik couldn't get there fast enough for her.

She had to do something to quiet her mind as she waited. Looking down, she saw her chest and arms were still covered with the gold paint. And glimpsing herself in the hand-held mirror Erik had left on the dresser, she saw that the kohl that had once lined her eyes now ran down her gold face in streaks from her tears. She was a frightful mess.

The heated Italian tile on the bathroom floor kept her warm as she placed the water basin under the bathtub faucet and filled it with water. She had just finished scrubbing her face clean when she thought she heard a sound come from the bedroom. She paused to listen. Only silence replied so she resumed drying her face. Until she heard another sound.

It was unmistakable this time. A heavy deep-voiced sigh reached her ears. Her heart sped up and the towel fell from her hands. A man was in the house.

Please let it be Erik, her heart cried.

She stood in the frame of the bathroom doorway. Relief flooded through her trembling body when she saw Erik, shoulders sagging, staring at the empty bed. She understood at once. He expected her to be asleep in the bed. And she wasn't there.

"Erik." She ventured into the room.

At the call of his name, Erik's eyes sought hers, capturing her gaze with an unnerving look, one that wrapped itself tightly around her and squeezed. She gasped from the intensity of it. He reached her in less than three strides, enveloping her in a powerful embrace and Julie lost herself in the rawness of his grasp.

"I am so glad you are here," she whispered, clutching him just as tightly.

♀

Erik did not trust himself to speak with his emotions cresting so close to the surface, so he held Juliana in silence. He savored the feel of her body pressed safely against him and inhaled the sweet fragrance of her as he crushed her closer. What would he have done if something had happened to her? He would never have forgiven himself for underestimating Izak.

Reluctantly, he released her. "You're still awake." Why had she delayed the ritual? He did not know, but he thanked the Universe he still had the opportunity to tell her how he felt.

"About that—" Juliana said as she smoothed his rumpled jacket.

He stopped her. "I want you to stay."

"I want to stay," she finished at the same time.

"You do?" their voices echoed each other. And they laughed.

He loved her laugh.

Craving reassurance, he gently twisted a lock of her hair in his fingers, searching her face for a telltale sign of this change of heart. "This is an interesting development."

"It certainly is," she replied, studying him in return. "And a very fine discussion for the ride home." She grabbed his hand, lacing her fingers through his. "Take me home, Erik."

Her words warmed his heart. Home. A place he had never had until now. It awed him that her concept of home meant being with him.

"Gladly," he said, the corners of his mouth twitching as he noticed she was dressed in only a shift. He tugged at the thin material. "Let's get you dressed first." Juliana blushed, and Erik decided it was a good look for her.

"I forgot. I was washing off the paint." He didn't resist as she pulled him to the bathroom. "Help me get the rest off before I put the dress back on." She grabbed the wet towel and held it out to him.

Her boldness captivated him. He had never experienced the intimacy of bathing a woman before. And it brought back the memory of seeing Juliana bathing herself, re-stirring the desire for her he had tried to keep at bay.

Taking the towel from her, he dipped it in the basin and made a gentle stroke down her arm. The paint washed off easily, revealing a strip of her cinnamon skin. He dipped the rag again, wiping all the gold away from that arm.

Juliana raised her chin as he started on her neck and chest. The golden water trickled down onto the shift, soaking it to her skin and partially revealing her breasts. Erik's pulse raced at the sight of her nipples peeking through the thin wet, cotton.

Without thinking, he glided his fingertips over her skin, stroking her bare arm up to the soft hollow of her shoulder then to the softer rise of a full breast, leaving streaks of gold in his wake. The temperature in the bathroom began to rise.

Erik removed his jacket and rolled up his shirt sleeves, then resumed bathing her, not bothering to be careful, drenching the shift until everything underneath was visible. Juliana's lingering, heavy-lidded stare fueled him on long after the gold paint had been washed off.

By the time he finished, her skin glistened with beads of water. Erik's gut tightened as he relished the beauty of the lines and curves of her body. There was no mistaking the silent expectations in her gaze as she peeled the wet shift off and dropped it to the floor. She offered an invitation he would not refuse. He pulled her to him, claiming her lips.

Juliana leaned into him, returning his kiss with equal fervor. Her ragged breathing only served to heighten his desire. He released her, staring into her passion-filled eyes then down to her lips, swollen from his kisses. There was nothing to hold him back anymore. She was his.

He recaptured her lips again, more demanding this time while he explored her naked skin with his hands. He growled inwardly as her body arched at his touch as if she were a living instrument he had been born to play. He could feel Juliana's desperate want as her body moved against him. Then, to his surprise, Juliana pushed him against the wall.

"This can't happen with so much between us." Her voice came out breathy as she unbuttoned his shirt.

He wasted no time helping her to remove it. Once free, he cradled the nape of her neck and pulled her to him again with deep kisses. Juliana ignited every fiber of his body with her eager touch.

Her nimble fingers released him from the constraints of his trousers. After they fell to the floor, he quickly kicked them out of the way, along with his shoes. With nothing between them any longer, Erik fought against the intense heat and pressure of his desire as it churned liquid fire, ready to deploy and difficult to contain.

Fueled by the dormant sexuality of his body now roaring with life, he lifted her up and she wrapped her legs around his waist. He turned around and used the wall as leverage, staring into her eyes as he entered her. Skin to skin, she was his.

As they moved together, over and over he coaxed sensual sounds from her. Erik inhaled her long surrendering moans, sucking in every breath as if it were his last. His blood burned hotter as passion possessed his mind and soul–building, building, building into a blinding crescendo of pleasure. At the same moment, he heard Juliana cry out his name as she held on to him, breathless.

Erik felt he could conquer the world. He crushed Juliana close and carried her triumphantly to the bed, gently setting her down. Climbing in beside her, he scooped her back into his arms and fitted himself against her curvy warmth. Her body felt so good against his. He could hold her like this for the rest of his life if she would let him. He craved her in every imaginable way.

"I've wanted that for a long time," Juliana confessed with a hitch in her voice.

His desire for her had been building for quite some time as well. Their coupling was more than he could have imagined, but for some reason he could not say the words back to her.

Instead, he stroked her arm. "I want to marry you, Juliana."

She turned half-way around, smiling, her left hand raised to show him the wedding band. "Technically, we already are."

"Naomi may be a part of your history, but she is not you." He leaned over and kissed her parted lips, hoping she could sense all the emotions he couldn't voice. "Marry me, Juliana."

She twisted completely around to face him, searching his eyes. Could she see how much he wanted her? How he would never force her to love him, but oh how much he wished she did?

"I want nothing more." She buried her face in his chest as she clung to him.

"As soon as possible," he commanded, holding her tightly.

"Yes," she agreed as she pulled back to look at him.

"We'll stay here until tomorrow evening. Then we'll leave at dusk and catch the priest after the last All Soul's Day mass. I'll make a generous donation to the church. He will not refuse us. And if he does at first, I will...persuade him." Erik thought of how easily he had manipulated the minds of men in the alleyway without the use of absinthe. Like it or not, he was Izak's blood and he would use his developing powers to his advantage.

358 · LAURIE L. BOLANOS

He paused, relief washing over him as he realized that at no moment during their lovemaking had he felt even a stirring of power. It was just him and Juliana and the rawness of their uninfluenced desires. She really was his and willingly so.

"Okay...but don't you think I'm going to stick out like a sore thumb in my costume? I have nothing else to wear."

"There are still a few dresses in the closet." They would travel light and buy whatever they needed when they arrived at their destination. "As soon as we are married, I want to be on our way to Europe."

Juliana's forehead creased. "Do you think that will keep Izak from us?"

"No, but if we can stay a few steps ahead of him, I'll be happy for now." At some point, he would be able to mask their trail or at least finally be strong enough to defeat his father.

"And Arak?"

Erik rolled onto his back, head cradled in his hands, staring at the ceiling. Izak said that Arak was at the ball, but Erik had not sensed him there. And undeniably, something extraordinary happened in that alleyway, something that could not be explained. Was it Arak? If so, his actions had been of help.

Finally, he answered her. "I am not convinced we have something to worry about with Arak. If he even exists."

♀

Julie had no idea how many times they had made love. They had spent a good portion of the night and early morning together in bed. She propped her head up in her hand and watched Erik sleep with a peaceful expression on his face. Then she took in the rest of his sleeping form. The way his naked body had settled intrigued her–all long limbs and interesting angles. As she stared at him, she relived the past few hours.

The tenderness in his hands and his mouth as he pleasured and caressed her. Erik deep inside her. How he confessed over and over again his need of her. And the last time they tumbled into oblivion together, she treasured hearing her name on his lips.

As she watched Erik sleep, her love grew so big, bright, and beautiful that it took up all the room in her heart. And it didn't matter that neither of them had yet to say those precious words–I love you. The feeling wrapped itself around her and she felt well-loved.

Julie eased herself from the bed without disturbing him and freshened up. She was starving and knew that when Erik woke, he'd be hungry, too. Wouldn't it be nice if she could surprise him with breakfast in bed?

Don't wake up, she thought at him as she gathered her underclothing from next to the fireplace. The cotton shift had dried, but would not be enough to keep her warm in the drafty house. Julie also slipped into Erik's jacket and pulled it tight, smelling his scent on the fabric. She smiled as it felt as though Erik's presence went with her to the kitchen instead of lying there asleep on the bed.

Don't wake up, she wished harder as she looked back at him. He turned over, breathing deeply. Satisfied he was still asleep, she tiptoed from the room. On her way out, she couldn't help brush her hand across her beautiful silk dress. It was amazing how prettily the stones sparkled in the dim light of the dying fire.

CHAPTER FIFTY-THREE

In the dim light, Julie rummaged through the barren kitchen, shaking her head. All she could find were a couple of eggs and some bread that was questionable. Typical for a bachelor's house.

She located a knife and cut the mold from the edges of the loaf. Now, how would she prepare this meal? She didn't know how to get a wood stove started and there wasn't a toaster handy. She had a lot to learn now since she had decided to stay in 1898.

She smiled, doing a happy jig. She was staying!

Not starting the stove wasn't an obstacle; she did have an active fire blazing in the fireplace of their bedroom. She shivered with pleasure of the intimacy of her last thought. *Their bedroom.*

The eggs could be scrambled and the bread toasted. She grabbed utensils, butter, the bread and eggs, and two plates, placing them all inside a pan to carry to the bedroom. All she needed was some spices for flavor and she'd be in business, a rustic breakfast for her man. She found a tin of ground pepper and was about to put it in the pan when from the kitchen alley, she heard what sounded like the cry of a baby animal; the wail of persistent whimpering mixed with high-pitched screams.

Julie went to the kitchen side door and looked out the small inset panes. She grimaced. Dawn had not broken yet and a heavy fog pressed down, making visibility too poor for her to see. But the desperation in the escalating cries pulled at her heartstrings, compelling her to go check anyway.

When she cracked open the kitchen door, the chilled air took her breath away. She looked at her bare feet, dreading having to step on the cold stone outside. The cries were close by, just a few feet away. She steeled herself against the shock of the frigid weather and ran on tiptoes into the fog.

Shivering, she dropped to her knees once she reached the source of the sound. As she leaned forward, she could see a puppy caught in a tangle of string. One leg was pulled in an awkward angle as the puppy struggled to free itself.

"Poor boo boo," Julie cooed to the frantic animal while she attempted to free it with fingers that were quickly becoming stiff. It quieted down once she had released its leg. "What are you doing out here, little baby?" she asked the puppy as she cuddled it under Erik's jacket close to her chest.

She stood up, sighing. This puppy was coming inside with her. She couldn't leave it out here alone in the cold. She and Erik would just have to figure something out before they left. Bijou would probably love to have a little companion. As she turned to walk back to the house, a muscled arm grabbed her from behind, lifting her off the ground. A large hand covered her mouth and a portion of her nose, making it difficult to breathe.

Julie instinctively brought her arms up to force the man's hand away, dropping the puppy as she did. It yelped and scampered under the house. Fear coursed through her veins from her wildly beating heart as the man dragged her past the open kitchen door toward the rear of the property.

Her eyes locked on the door to the kitchen. If she could get inside, she would be safe. If she could scream, Erik would be there in an instant. She could only manage a muffled grunt against the pressure of the hand on her face. The further back they went, the farther away the kitchen door became and with it, her chance of freedom. Her heart sank with every step and her soul cried out in desperation...*Erik, wake up.*

The assailant was more powerful than she, but it didn't stop her from trying to wriggle free. His clammy hand slipped from her nose and with each desperate inhale, she smelled alcohol, dirt, and sweat. The combination was unsettling and familiar.

The man breathed into her ear, sending chills down her spine. "You're a good hider, Mimi. But I don't gives up that easy. Mamzelle told me where you'd be and I knowed the puppy would bring you outside."

Julie stiffened with dread. Few people called her by that name. And although he whispered, she recognized his voice. She arched, tilting her head back to look directly into Joe B's small, blood-shot eyes.

He stopped dragging her for a moment. "We got unfinished business, we do. Shame to you, Mimi, for whoring yourself to this man when you belongs to me."

Alarm bells rang in her head, shooting adrenalin through her, replacing the fear. She was sure he would have killed Naomi had Old

Hortense not stepped in last time. And Julie had no reason to believe he would not kill her now.

Oh, hell, no! her mind screamed.

She had something to live for and had no intention of dying today. She became a wildcat in his arms, but he held firm as he forcibly dragged her with him, kicking and fighting through the backyard to the carriage house.

She slipped an arm free and elbowed Joe B in the ribs just as they were across the threshold. He yowled in anger, grabbing her arm, bending it until it snapped. Excruciating pain unlike anything she had felt before enveloped her as she screamed into his hand, tears flowed down her face.

He released her.

Just as she sucked in a breath to scream, he punched her in the face. The force sent her reeling to the ground, bright dots replacing her vision. On one hand and both knees, she crawled, her left arm held protectively to her chest, not sure of what direction she was going. Any direction was good as long as it was away from Joe B.

The right side of her face throbbed and she felt it swelling. Shooting pains shot up her arm, limiting her ability to move. As she made slow progress getting away, she heard Joe B unbuckling his belt.

Not again.

Even if she could muster a scream right now, Erik would never hear her from inside the carriage house. She closed her eyes, voicing in her mind, *Erik...Erik...Erik*, and with his name she sent the unspoken plea of help just as she was knocked down flat from a belt across her back. She fell on top of her broken arm, sending a wave of pain and nausea through her. This time her screams echoed off the walls of the empty carriage house.

♀

Erik woke from a deep, dreamless sleep with an uneasy sensation pressing on him. He reached out for Juliana, but the bed was empty, her side cold. He quelled the immediate concern he felt, realizing she was probably in the bathroom. He yawned and stretched his pleasantly sore muscles then slipped on his trousers.

"Good morning," he said, giving his most charming smile as he sauntered into the empty bathroom, his smile fading as he realized he was alone. "Juliana!" Erik called out as he left the room in search of her. That woman would be the death of him yet.

The hallway was cold. Erik followed the draft to the kitchen, observing the pan and food along with the open kitchen door. And in that moment he heard her voice in his mind saying his name over and over. The cadence of her voice chilled him. Something was terribly wrong.

Erik stood taller, felt stronger. The powerful energy inside of him soared to life as he flew out of the house. He could sense Juliana nearby and he smelled her fear. And he recognized the smell of the man with her, Joe B.

Erik's muscles moved in seamless motion. His bare feet scarcely touched the hard, icy ground as he ran toward the carriage house. He didn't feel the frigid cold on his bare chest as heat pulsed out of him. He only knew the urgent need to protect Juliana. When he heard her scream, his vision turned red and his feet no longer touched the ground at all.

"You belongs to me," Joe B said, raising his arm, a knife in his hand.

Erik saw Joe B's broad back just inside the doorway and leapt, grabbing hold of his raised arm, yelling. "You're wrong. She's mine!"

Both men tumbled to the ground, missing Juliana by inches. The knife scuttled across the dirt floor in the melee. They rolled and jumped to their feet, facing each other.

"Run, Juliana!" Erik commanded, without looking at her. Filled with hate and disgust, he charged Joe B, clasping his hand around the larger man's neck and lifting him up with little effort as Izak had once done to him.

Power and hate enveloped him as the blows Joe B rained down on him felt like mere wasp stings. Energy surged through Erik and around him. He reveled in the feeling, knowing he could destroy Joe B without breaking a sweat. Yet something felt wrong.

He could feel Juliana behind him even though he had told her to leave. *Hard-headed woman*! He twisted around to demand again that she get to safety when he caught sight of her; swollen face, bloody nose, and broken arm. His heart plummeted as she slowly, painfully inched her way toward the door of the carriage house.

Rage as he had never known before burst from him at her injured state. Without a thought, he crushed Joe B's windpipe and threw him across the room with such force that when he hit the back wall, he left a life-size indention before falling to the floor like a ragdoll.

Erik rushed to Juliana and lifted her up into his arms, cradling her as if she were a fragile china doll. "It's over, it's over," he repeated, rocking and soothing her.

"I'm so sorry," she groaned, tears of pain in her eyes.

"For what?" His voice cracked.

"I knew not to leave the house, but I went outside anyway."

"If I had been awake..." Guilt hit Erik square in the gut. "No, had I killed Joe B when I had wanted, none of this would have happened at all." The fault was his entirely. He hugged Juliana close to his chest and started toward the house.

Erik made a mental list with each step. He would tend her wounds, bind her arm, get her warm, and then make sure he had indeed killed Joe B. If not, he would finish the job. No need to dispose of the body. It could rot in the carriage house since he and Juliana would be long gone before anyone smelled him.

*Well, well, well...*Izak's voice penetrated Erik's mind. *Juliana does not look too good.*

Erik stopped walking and stiffened.

"What's wrong?" Juliana whispered.

"Izak is here," he whispered back. "Show yourself," he yelled to Izak.

"Look up," Izak replied out loud.

Erik raised his head to see Izak perched on the roof, smiling down at them.

"Can you walk?" Erik spoke in Juliana's ear.

"I think so," she answered.

Erik gently put her down and steadied her while she found her footing. "I will hold him off for as long as possible. I want you to get in the house and lock the door."

Juliana hobbled next to him, looking up in defiance. "Do you think a locked door will keep Izak out? If you are taking a stand, we stand together."

Izak jumped down, landing lightly. "You do realize I can hear you? Had you followed my plan, none of this unfortunate business would have happened," he said as he walked toward them.

Erik moved Juliana behind him.

Izak raised his hands in surrender. "There is no need to fight, Erik. I have just come to collect Joe B and I will be on my way."

"You!" Erik cursed. "You sent him here!"

Izak waived a finger in protest. "Not I. I had a different plan, remember? It was Marie who loosed him upon you." His face crinkled in a half-smirk. "She really does not want you to be happy, does she? I wonder why that is?" he asked.

"No reason I have ever given her," Erik fumed, knowing that one more person would die by his hands today before he left New Orleans.

"That is an argument for another day. Now, I know Joe B was here." He looked at the shivering Juliana. "I can see his handiwork. Just point me in his direction and I will be on my way."

"If it is truly your business to retrieve Joe B, you will find his dead body in the carriage house. Take him and leave us in peace."

Izak creased his brow, frowning, and then breathed in deeply. A slow smile crept across his face. "You are wrong about that. Injured, not dead. It is a good thing he still lives. Joe B has something very precious to me."

The wheels in Erik's mind clicked. "All this time...the reason I could never find Joe B is because you masked him from me. You never wanted me to find him."

Izak nodded. "He has my protection."

"He is an animal!" Erik moved forward, wanting to slam a fist in Izak's face. Juliana placed a shaking hand on his arm to stop him.

"It's not worth it," she pleaded.

"You think him an animal?" Izak raised an eyebrow. "How interesting."

"I do," Erik said coldly. He could not let Joe B live. The man was like a deranged beast that needed to be put down for its own good. But he would only have moments, seconds, to reach Joe B and finish him off before Izak stopped him.

"I cannot allow you to do that, Erik." Izak gave him a warning look, undoubtedly having been privy to Erik's thoughts.

"What? Allow what?" Juliana asked looking back and forth between them.

"Get in the house, Juliana," Erik said through clenched teeth as he turned on his heel, sprinting toward the carriage house, Izak a hair's breadth behind him.

CHAPTER FIFTY-FOUR

Izak slammed Erik to the ground feet from the carriage house and kept him pinned there. Erik cursed. The sole of Joe B's shoe was visible through the door. He had been so close.

"Put your concerns aside for a moment," Izak grunted, attempting to keep Erik down. "Joe B does not need to die. I will keep him away from you and Juliana."

"Not need to die!" Erik repeated with a snarl. "He defiled Naomi and attempted to murder Juliana. I assure you, I am not interested in his longevity."

"As a gesture of goodwill, I am going to get up and let you go. I promise Joe B will not cause any further harm. You shall never lay eyes on him again." Izak loosened his hold on Erik and stood.

Erik stood as well, slapping the dirt from his pants. "Your promises are empty. Your words are meaningless." He turned, but Izak grabbed his upper arms, forcing him to turn back around.

Erik tried to pull away. Izak countered by tugging him back, gripping tighter. Erik could not free his arms. The more Erik tried, Izak dug in deeper, causing pain to shoot up to his shoulders, infuriating him. He channeled his energy and focused directly into Izak's eyes. "You *will* let me go."

"I *will* not. I can do this all day," Izak warned, as his eyes swirled green in response. He stared back at Erik with a fine sheen of sweat breaking out on his forehead as the heated exchange continued to pulse, encasing them in a ring of energy, dampening out the world around them.

"Release me," Erik demanded again, concentrating.

Izak smirked. "Not in this lifetime."

"Why the sudden interest in Joe B? What could he possibly matter to you?" Erik twisted his arms in an unsuccessful attempt to free himself.

Izak inched his face closer as if to speak. The answer lay unspoken inside Izak's swirling eyes, but Erik could not penetrate Izak's mind to know his thoughts and Izak spoke not a word in response.

"Must I remind you that we are blood? I have the right to know why you deny me my vengeance."

"Damnation, Erik!" Izak cursed, exasperated. "I am bound to silence by the contract. No one wants you to know the answers more than I." Erik opened his mouth to retort when he and Izak, still grappling the other, flew sideways to the ground, pushed out of the pocket of energy they had created by a greater energy.

Stunned, he looked up and saw Juliana now stood where they had been. She was bent over by Joe B's blow to her stomach, his fist still in contact with her mid-section. Terror pierced Erik's heart when Joe B pulled his arm back. His hand glistening with blood.

Juliana looked at Erik, wide-eyed.

Consumed with rage and fear, Erik surged from the ground, grabbing Joe B's head, twisting it. The sound of his spine snapping echoed in the yard and Joe B's body folded in on itself as Erik landed on his feet. On the edge of his vision, Juliana collapsed.

"No!" Both men yelled.

Moving faster than an eye blink, Erik caught Juliana before she hit the ground. At the same moment, Izak caught Joe B's lifeless body.

Erik carefully avoided knocking the steel handle of Joe B's knife protruding from her abdomen. Juliana struggled to breathe and with each spasm, blood gushed around the blade. Her cotton shift turned red, the stain spreading with obscene speed.

She looked down at her stomach and gingerly touched the handle. "He stabbed me?"

As he smoothed her hair out of her face, Erik's eyes burned with tears he struggled to hold back. "Yes, Love, but he will never hurt you again. I promise." Erik followed Juliana's gaze to Izak. He held Joe B, studying the man's face, turning it left and right.

"Was it worth it?" Erik snarled, as he gently held Juliana to him. Bright red blood soaked into his trousers.

Not finding anything of interest, Izak discarded Joe B's body with disdain. He rose, casting his eyes down just before facing Erik, a trace of remorse on his face. "When we first met, I told you that these events had been set in motion a long time ago. I told you that this was uncharted territory. I could not know what the ramifications would be if Joe B were to die. His death was a chance I could not take. Although, you seem to have gotten away with killing him."

Erik turned away in disgust.

He gazed at Juliana. Her skin was pale, her breathing shallow, and blood continued to ooze out around the knife.

Her wound was mortal.

Pain crushed Erik's heart and weighed down on him like a heavy blanket. Just when he had given in to loving Juliana, he would lose her, their happiness stolen by the sharp stab of a blade.

The weapon taunted him from where it nestled. His instinct was to yank the murderous blade from her body, but he feared the blood would gush out faster.

"It hurts," Juliana gasped.

Erik tried to pull from his energy to heal her. He placed a shaky hand over her stomach, blinking rapidly to clear his vision. Nothing happened. His composure was scattered, disrupted by emotions that prevented him from even easing her pain.

He never felt more human.

♀

Julie's fingers fumbled around the cold steel that stuck out of her stomach. She had to touch it again. She could not process the fact that she had been stabbed. Surely it was a dream, but dreams did not feel like this. It hurt like hell every time she breathed.

When her muscles expanded, they pulled on her torn insides, burning and stinging. Blood flowed through her fingers as she instinctively kept her hands over the wound. Growing numbness pervaded her lower extremities; Julie knew she was dying.

She looked up at Erik's stricken face, managing a shaky smile. She would take a knife for him again and again without question even knowing she would die a thousand deaths.

She could do nothing to remove the anguish from his eyes. Nothing except to tell him how she felt. Juliana touched a bloody hand to his cheek. "I love you," she said, her voice weak.

He covered her hand with one of his own; the muscles in his face drawn tight. "Everything is going to be fine. I'm going to fix this," he said firmly.

Julie blinked, wishing she didn't have to say the words. "You can't fix this." She could see his mind searching for an answer, sorting through scenario after scenario.

Then he turned toward Izak, still standing nearby.

"Heal her," he ordered.

"That is beyond my abilities," Izak replied.

"You healed Erik." Julie clung to the hope that Izak might be her salvation.

Izak pursed his lips. "I removed an invading illness from his body, but I cannot heal the damage that has been done to yours. What I can offer you would be a life more horrible than you could imagine. And for Erik's sake, I would not."

"I would rather have her than not at all! What is this offer?" Erik demanded.

Izak kneeled next to Erik. "You would hate me worse for it. It shall not be spoken of but..." his voice trailed off as he looked at Julie.

Julie shivered under his gaze. She remembered the horrible people Izak created. They had feasted on the soulless body Arak had discarded. That was not an option.

"But what?" Erik prompted him.

"There is something we can do while there is still time."

"Name it." Erik grabbed hold of Izak.

"We can send Juliana back."

"No," Erik shook his head, speaking softly without conviction.

"I cannot believe I am saying this," Izak muttered. "If you do this, you have a chance of seeing her again. We can try to bring her back later, but if she perishes in this body, her soul will be irretrievable."

Yes, Julie thought, the idea warming her weakened body. The first thing she would do when she returned to her old life would be to find Star. Star might know how to open another portal. At least she would have the hope of seeing Erik again one day.

Struggling for her every breath, she gasped. "You must let me go, Erik. It is our only chance."

Still on his knees, Erik rocked her in his arms in an embrace that felt like a goodbye. He leaned over her, resting his forehead on hers, their tears mingling. "I could not bear to go on living without knowing that you have life. There isn't much choice, is there?"

"No," she gurgled, coughing. Erik lifted his head and gazed at her face, seemingly memorizing it.

"What do I need to do?" she asked Izak.

"You need not do anything. Let us handle it." He placed a hand on Erik's shoulder. "Peace," he uttered. Erik's facial muscles relaxed, his shoulders sinking. Izak took Erik's free hand. Erik resisted Izak's touch at first until their hands moved directly over Julie's feet.

"The oil..." Julie muttered weakly.

"We don't need it," Izak said. "Erik never needed it."

Penetrating heat emanated from their hands. Pleasure mixed with pain as she could again feel sensations in her once-numb legs. Izak continued to direct Erik's hands over her body, moving toward her head. He murmured in a strange tongue, and Erik joined in. When they reached her chest, Erik hesitated and looked at her. Something inside of Julie stirred under his longing gaze.

I know you–his eyes said. *As no one has ever known you and I love you.*

"I will find you," Erik promised her. He shoved Izak's hand away and placed both of his over her forehead. She felt the air shift minutely around her and then her world went black.

As before, her hearing was the last to go. Tumbling deep within herself, she heard Erik's bone-chilling cry of agony and her heart joined in his loss. He continued with a string of blasphemies and expletives wrapped in heart-wrenching sobs. Then even his voice faded into the silence of the blackness.

♀

Erik bent over Juliana's lifeless body, his fists at his sides. How long had he remained that way? Time no longer had any meaning. No more cries would pass his lips. He was tired and spent. What he felt now was too deep for tears, his loss too great. His life would never be the same again.

Then Juliana stirred.

Panic and joy jolted him. She had returned to him. Why? Her return could not be good. He lifted her in his arms. "Juliana," he said.

Beguiling golden eyes peered up in confusion. Lines of wisdom no longer graced her face. "David? What...?" she managed to ask.

This wasn't Juliana. He swallowed his guilt. "I'm so sorry, Naomi."

"I'm so cold. Why am I so cold?" Naomi asked.

"You're dying." He wouldn't lie to her. He owed her that. "I promised you a life of happiness. I promised you so much and I failed you. Forgive me."

She moved her lips to speak, but no sound emerged. Naomi shuddered in his arms, attempting to breathe, only managing a few shallow gasps. Blood trickled from her mouth, then her trembling stopped. So did her breathing.

It was over.

Naomi was gone and with her, Juliana all over again. She was an innocent soul, an earlier life of Juliana who had been caught up in the web he had created. Erik gently released her and stood, facing Izak, who silently watched him.

Erik had no words to say to the man who gave him life. The man who contributed to Juliana's death and left him in anguish. A man who could not die, at least not by mortal means. But Erik had just lost the last of his humanity. So, he reached out his hands and willed the life from Izak.

Erik drank him in, pulling energy from the Earth Walker. Izak didn't try to stop him, but remained as he was with a small smile on his pale face. Even from this distance, Erik could see Izak's green eyes becoming dull. Energy surged and flowed from Izak, strengthening Erik by the second and depleting Izak.

Heat and power pulsed through Erik's skin, his veins, and his life blood, overwhelming his senses. He saw clearly and heard distinctly. Through his bare feet he could feel the vibration of the earth's core.

His desire to kill the Earth Walker kept him pulling energy until Erik felt as though he would burst out of his own skin. Unable to withstand any more, he stopped abruptly, staggering as if he had imbibed beyond his limit.

Erik crashed to his knees, howling. The energy had heightened everything, including his emotions. His agony washed over him anew. He wanted to rip a hole in the world so that everyone could partake in his suffering.

As he howled, the sky darkened and the wind blew, lifting leaves from the ground, swirling them around him. And with each cry, the pain dissipated, replaced by anger. He wanted Juliana back. He wanted her back now.

Erik lifted her lifeless body up and held it protectively to him, shooting Izak a look, daring him to interfere. Izak leaned weakly against the backyard brick wall as Erik walked past him into the alleyway of his house.

"Erik, where are you going?" Izak uttered as he passed.

Erik ignored him and continued on.

Normally, the working class people would be trudging their way to the menial jobs that allowed them to put food on their tables, but the streets were still empty. The fog had dissipated under a heavy cover of darkness that had descended on the city.

A storm moved in and the people of New Orleans watched the signs, cautious of impending floods. But this was no ordinary storm. It was the result of a broken heart.

"You cannot traipse around the city holding a corpse in your arms." Izak stumbled across the front yard after Erik.

"I don't intend to."

As Erik neared the street, the solitary clopping of hooves rang out. A lone carriage pulled up sans driver; Erik had willed the nearest horse within range of his thoughts to come. He gently settled Juliana's body on the covered seat, then he jumped on board.

"Where are you going, Erik?" Izak demanded weakly.

"You're not in a position to question my actions." Erik snapped the reigns, and started off. *But if you must know*, Erik broke through Izak's mind. *I'm going to the lake front. I think a visit to our Voodoo*

Queen is in order. Someone needs to teach her that she is not immune to the spiritual price of her actions.

CHAPTER FIFTY-FIVE

Marie.

Erik's thoughts were linear as he drove the horse onward.

Marie Laveau.

He saw and thought of nothing else. Instead of angular buildings, Erik saw her fiercely beautiful face and insincere smile. Instead of carriage wheels, he heard the clinking of her bracelets. Instead of live oak limbs bending in the wind, he saw the sway of her tall form.

The trek on the uneven streets caused Juliana's body to shift on the seat behind him, driving him to the brink of madness. He grit his teeth to prevent himself from releasing his pain in another howl as a roll of thunder broke overhead and echoed around him in response to the emotions he refused to express.

He did not need to debate with himself where to take Juliana: Marie's Creole cottage or the Maison Blanche. The moment Erik had thought of Marie, he could sense that she was at the latter. Her presence called to him as if a beacon. Maybe she even waited for him? Prepared. It didn't matter.

His will would be done this day.

The carriage continued onward, almost of its own accord; animal and buggy moving in synchronicity with his desire to destroy Marie Laveau. Erik imagined wicked scenarios in his mind. Torture beyond her wildest imagination. Physical pain that breached endurance. Though tempted to do so, he would not rip her to shreds as his heart had been. Nothing he could do to her would compare to the pain that he suffered from losing Juliana. At best, he would savor his revenge slowly.

He would give Marie hope and then tear it away, allowing her to know what despair felt like. So, being the consummate gentleman, he would extend to her an offer. A choice, albeit an impossible ultimatum. Bring Juliana back to life or die.

Erik relished the thought of being the vehicle of Marie's demise, but not before he showed her what she had taken from him. Not before she knew how her meddling had ruined his life. Not before she trembled in fear. Not before she knew *her* life was the price she had to pay for the life she stole.

As he neared the shore, the wind pelted him with a salty mist and tossed his dampened hair across his face. The brackish lake churned, stirring waves closer inland. The rain had yet to fall though the clouds weighed heavy. A bolt of lightning lit the sky, revealing a portion of the stark white brothel within the shadow of Erik's darkness made manifest.

He pulled the carriage up short and jumped down, tying up the horse. He strode toward the house, but stopped shy of the wide porch, refusing to step foot on it. "Marie," he commanded, sending his voice through the closed door into the house so that it vibrated the very walls. "Come out."

Seconds later, Marie stepped onto the porch. The faint light from the entryway wrapped her body in a soft glow, casting a long shadow toward him. She gazed into in the blackness of what should be morning and then looked at Erik. "What you seek is not here," she replied, jutting her chin in the air.

"And how would you know what I seek?" Erik narrowed his eyes, stepping closer.

Marie jangled her bracelets with a nervous twitch of her hand and four large men stepped from inside the house and stood behind her, flexing their muscles. Erik almost smiled. Let her feel a false sense of security. As if anyone or anything could stop him now.

"Again, I say to you, what you seek is not here. Joe B left long before morn and I know not where he is."

This time he did smile, a calculating one. "Is he the reason you believe I have bestowed a visit on you? Not the case, I assure you. But to put your mind at ease, before we discuss my business, let me enlighten you as to his whereabouts, dear lady.

"Joe B has relocated to an environment more suitable to his nature. In fact, I played no small part in his departure." Erik bowed in false modesty. "And I absolutely must take credit where credit is due." He leveled a stare at her. "I sent him to hell just after he stabbed Juliana."

Marie shifted in unease at the news, her mouth twitching. "How fares the girl?"

"How fares the girl?" he snarled, taking one more step closer so that the light of the porch illuminated him. Marie recoiled as he revealed his blood-drenched trousers and skin. Her forehead remained in a slight crease, but her face no longer registered any expression.

Her silence stirred his fury. "Have you nothing to say, queen?"

She clenched her fists tightly at her side, refusing to answer. Behind her mask of indifference, Erik saw a trace of fear.

"Shall I show you how the girl fares?" Erik started forward, his hatred surging in a palpable wave before him. Marie extended her arms out, opening her hands, releasing an odorless powder.

With a mere thought, Erik willed the particles inert.

Marie's mouth opened as she stared at the powder suspended in mid-fall between them. Erik gestured sharply, sending the fine particles flying back to the four men behind Marie. One by one they fell as they inhaled the quick-acting sleeping concoction.

Before Marie had time to react, Erik ripped the tignon off her head and dragged her from the porch by her hair. She clawed and scratched at him in terror the entire way to the carriage and her resistance stirred a deep-seated pleasure in his gut.

He shoved her head inside the carriage so that her face was next to Juliana's body. "You can see she does not fare well. How much did Joe B pay you to tell him where she was?"

She twisted as best as she could to face him. "I do not charge my own people for help, but I'd not have told him if I'd known he'd harm the girl."

"Lies!" He yanked her back from the carriage, knocking her head against the side. "You never wanted me to have her. You always had some scheme to take her from me."

"Tis true," she said, spitting blood from her mouth. "I didn't want her with you, but I would not have harmed her. I told Joe B where she could be found because I thought he loved her."

"I loved her! Me!" Erik shook Marie then tossed her to the ground, pressing her down with an invisible barrier so that she would be unable to rise.

He paced before her. "Joe B was obsessed with her. He never loved her. Because you chose to send Joe B to her, she is dead. And I hold you personally responsible."

Marie struggled to lift her head with stubborn resistance in her eyes. "I could say the same for you."

"What did you say?" Erik leaned toward her, daring her to repeat herself.

The Voodoo Queen squared her shoulders while on her hands and knees. "Maybe it was *your* choices that brought us to this moment. I warned you that you would have to pay a spiritual price for your actions."

Furious, Erik raised his hand and Marie rose into the air. "I have paid my price and soon enough you will pay yours." With a flick of his wrist, he tossed her across the yard, her body landing close to the shoreline. Erik gathered Juliana into his arms, walked to where Marie had fallen, and gently laid Juliana down before the Voodoo Queen.

Marie sucked in her breath as she got a better look at Juliana's bruised and battered body, the knife still buried deep within her. The eyes that rose to meet Erik's were dark and filled with doom. Erik released the heavy weight that bore down on Marie, allowing her to sit.

"Have faith, Mamzelle. There is hope for you yet." When Marie did not speak, Erik knelt down before her. "You can save yourself. It shouldn't be too difficult for you, the mighty Voodoo Queen. Summon your Loas. Pray to your gods. Do what you must to heal this body. Call Juliana back to me, and you will be redeemed."

Marie slumped forward as though Erik still crushed her. "I cannot raise the dead. How can I bring her back? Where would she go? If I were to try to bring her back, her soul would drift with no body to inhabit."

"That is exactly what I told him," Izak said from a few yards away, sending his voice into the wind. Erik refused to acknowledge Izak, instead curled his hands into fists.

The Earth Walker would not let him have even this moment. Erik wished down to his soul he had burned Izak to ashes even if it had meant his own destruction. He put a barrier up between them to keep Izak at a distance.

Marie's face lit up when she saw Izak. "I hid Joe B as you had asked," she addressed him. "I kept him distracted. Tell him that I only did as you requested."

Erik turned his head to see Izak's response.

"It is as you say," Izak answered solemnly, easily stepping through the invisible barrier.

"Do not interfere in this, Izak," Erik threatened.

Izak gazed at Erik while continuing to speak to Marie. "However, I do not recall asking you to send Joe B after Juliana." He turned, bestowing a cruel smile on her. "Erik, I have no intention of interfering. The world is your stage, so to speak. Do with her as you wish."

Marie inched backward.

"Halt!" Izak raised a hand and Marie froze.

Erik stood, fuming. "I said to leave it to me."

"I will," Izak assured him. "I have questions for her." He walked over to her and grabbed her chin, forcing her to stand. "Why did you want to keep Naomi from Erik? Why could you not leave well enough alone?"

"I don't know," she answered, trembling. "I was consumed by my thoughts. I couldn't dismiss Erik from my mind. And I couldn't abide his happiness."

"Fascinating," Izak murmured, releasing her. He moved away to sit on top of the lake's breakwater rocks. "I am blocked from portions of her mind, but she tells the truth."

"Are you *quite* finished?" Erik asked.

"Quite. Carry on." Izak's brilliant smile eerily lit the darkness.

Erik faced Marie. "Will you do as I ask?"

Marie's eyes darted to Izak.

"Don't look at him. Will you do as I ask?"

Returning her gaze to Erik, she spoke, her lips trembling. "What you ask is impossible. It cannot be done."

Erik let the silence sit for what seemed an eternity. He stared out into the crashing waves and marveled at the power of nature and his own power of manipulating it. He was the moon and the water genuflected in his presence, backed away, and genuflected again and again.

Without lifting his gaze from the water, he walked forward, grabbing Marie by the hair, dragging her behind him. He was not a cold, thoughtless killer. He was a man bent on revenge.

Marie struggled against him again. She would not go easily. She cried out at the immersion into the frigid lake water. Erik felt not the coldness of the night nor the sting of the water. He burned hot from the inside. He continued out, not stopping until he was waist deep. He buried his bare feet into the sand, anchoring himself. He righted Marie to a standing position and held her in a lover's embrace, gazing into her eyes.

"Don't kill me," she begged through chattering teeth. "We would make good allies. I could be an asset to you." He ignored her suggestion and said the words he had prepared.

"Marie Laveau, for crimes committed against myself and Juliana, you have forfeited your life." Without allowing another word to come from her wicked mouth, he plunged her beneath the water. She clawed at his arms. As he held her there, a peace settled over him and the troubled clouds obstructing the dark sky dissipated, allowing him to clearly see the stars. Staring at their shimmering light, he decided death was not good enough for Marie. He would brand her as God had branded Cain.

He raised her up from the water. Marie coughed and sputtered, gasping for precious air. He looked down at her dispassionately. She would pay. Pay for an eternity.

He tried placing his hand on her forehead. She turned her head away in fear. "Be still," he ordered and she became ram-rod straight.

He molded his hand to her forehead. "Marie Laveau, I swear to you, that as long as there are stars in the heaven, you will not find rest until you have remedied your part in Juliana's death." He removed his hand and where it once rested, a bright crimson mark remained. A single tear rolled down Marie's face right before he pushed her under the waves again.

The swells stilled as Erik calmed inside. He could see through the placid water. Could see Marie's face as the salty liquid filled her lungs. Could see as her eyes became dilated and vacant. He released her, observing her body motionlessly float farther out.

Erik turned from her and made his way to shore. His will had been done.

Now he would find a way to get Juliana back. He walked past Izak, signaling him to follow. If he had to collaborate with the Earth Walker to regain his lost love, so be it.

....

CHAPTER FIFTY-SIX

Sixteen months later, Oklahoma, March of 1900

Erik drummed his fingers on the table, irritated. The half-empty whiskey bottle that rested on the uneven wood overturned, spilling the remaining contents onto the floor. As Erik stewed, Izak waved a barmaid over to clean the mess.

Traveling through many states and many cities, he had sought out healers, mystics, and shamans in the hope of discovering a way to be reunited with Juliana. Her body, long-ago buried, was not a viable option. He needed ideas.

Their meandering cross-country journey had been based on Izak's "feelings." They were in *this* forsaken town because Izak had insisted he felt a bend of energy. And just as with all the previous times, this meeting proved to be fruitless. Wasting his time made Erik angry.

The last time Erik had become angry, a bolt of lightning erupted in a clear blue sky, striking the exterior of the house he had just left. The building caught fire, burning to the ground. The owner barely escaped with his life. On another failed attempt to seek information, he had produced a hailstorm on a hot summer night, breaking windows and destroying crops.

The sun-weathered man, features shaped by Native American ancestry, who sat across from them had no idea of the potential destruction he faced. His deep-set eyes did not recognize the building fury in Erik. Though recommended to Izak by intimidated townsfolk, this medicine man could offer no solution.

No answers.

Erik's anger sharpened his senses, the smell of unwashed body, sickly sweet tobacco, and whiskey assaulted him. He clenched his fists, trying to quell his rage, but he wasn't quick enough. The man raised a wrinkled hand to his nose, wiping. His eyes widened at the smear of blood on his skin; more blood trickled from his nostril.

"Let's go," Erik said, through clenched teeth, standing. He didn't want to kill the shaman, but if stayed a moment longer, he was certain he would.

Izak stood as well. "Where is the fun in that?"

"I am not here for your amusement," Erik answered, aggravated that Izak enjoyed the havoc. Unconcerned by the crowd of people that sat around them, Erik extended his arm toward Izak, releasing a burst of energy that sent him flying into the wall. Patrons at the bar stood, mumbling in confusion. He stiffened at Izak's laugh. If he didn't find a way to calm down, he might cause some natural disaster.

Erik knew Izak could never be trusted, but who would be more suited to assist him? Erik would do whatever was necessary to see Juliana again even if that meant relying on Izak and his irritating ways.

Erik stepped outside, sucking in the fresh air. He pulled a small patch of fabric cut from Juliana's tignon out of his coat pocket and held it to his nose, savoring the faint essence of Juliana's scent that lingered. It helped him to focus, reminding him of his purpose and stirring the bittersweet feelings of love and pain.

He still lived with the pain of Juliana's absence every day. Every hour. Every minute. From the moment he had released her soul from Naomi's body, she had been lost to him. Every time he extended his consciousness to seek her out, he found only silence. Blackness.

For months, he reached out for her in his sleep only to feel the coldness of an empty bed. He had started the habit of sleeping with her clothing next to him, the remnants of her scent providing comfort until it no longer remained. All he had left was the small piece of her tignon, the scent nearly gone.

He blinked back the rush of emotions that always followed when he thought of her death. He needed Juliana back. One night with her would never be enough. He could not fail.

Someone knocked Erik forward, and he dropped the small piece of Juliana's tignon. His heart froze as he saw the precious item flutter to the ground. He swiftly retrieved it. Glaring, he raised his hand to smite the unfortunate offender who had bumped him.

"A thousand pardons," the man apologized in a decidedly Southern accent.

He was fresh-faced with the energy of a soul not weighed down by life. Erik lowered his hand in amazement. A white glow, the man's aura, surrounded him. This was the first time Erik had seen someone's aura.

"No harm done," Erik answered, watching as the stranger loped away in the direction of the train station. Izak sidled up next to Erik, staring after the young man. The curiosity on Izak's face suggested that he too saw the bright aura.

"Come," Erik said, slapping Izak's back, feeling encouraged by the new development. "We're going on a trip."

Erik boarded the train and strode down the aisle, looking into each compartment until he found the shining man. With a hand to Izak's chest, he held him at bay before sliding the door open. "Do not interfere."

"As you wish." Izak bowed his head, allowing Erik to go first.

Erik stepped into the privacy car and sat on the padded bench across from the shining man just as the locomotive's horn rent the air and the car jolted forward. Izak sat beside him.

"Good day, gentlemen," the man said as they sat down. "I apologize again for my clumsiness. I'm Edgar." He grabbed Izak's hand and shook it. "Edgar Cayce," he said, shaking Erik's hand next. Aside from the glow, there was nothing extraordinary about him, no power in Edgar's touch.

"Where are our manners?" Izak raised an eyebrow at Erik. "I am Izak Ulloa and this sullen-looking fellow is Erik."

"Nice to meet you," Edgar said, loosening his collar and tie. "Where do your travels take you on this fine day?"

Erik squinted as he stared at Edgar. If he looked at just the right angle, the light that surrounded the man shimmered.

"We are just traveling this fine country. And you, Edgar? Where are you headed?" Izak asked.

"I am on my way home from a work meeting. I sell insurance for Woodman of the World. Would either of you gentlemen be in need of a policy, perhaps?" he asked with a hopeful lilt to his voice.

Izak waived him off as Erik shook his head. "We have no need."

"Just as well." Edgar sighed, looking back and forth between Erik and Izak. "My journey has been a long one, and I am bone tired. I'd like to catch a few winks if it wouldn't bother you fine gentlemen too much."

"Be our guest." Izak gestured with a smile.

Edgar removed his shoes, tucking them under the seat next to his suitcase. He looked around the room as if getting his bearings, then turned so that his head faced south. Stretching out on the bench, Edgar rested his hands over his chest and closed his eyes. He began to snore softly within minutes and his aura dimmed.

Erik turned on Izak. "Did you put him to sleep?"

Izak bristled. "Had I wanted him to sleep, it would have been done the second I commanded. I thought *you* had sent him the suggestion since it took so long."

Resisting the urge to punch Izak, Erik gritted his teeth instead before speaking. "Have you ever seen anyone glow like that before?"

"It has been a very long time, but yes."

"Well?" Erik prodded.

Izak stared across at the man. "When we shook hands, I felt nothing. As if he were a clean slate without a history of any kind or..." Izak shook his head. "I don't know," he said.

"Can't you just go over there and smell him or something?" Erik asked with an impatient wave of his hand. "Any sense you can get from him might give us a solution to bring Juliana back to me."

And I would want that why? Erik clearly heard Izak's thought in his mind and felt the truth behind it. And knew it wasn't something he was supposed to hear. Erik froze as all the pieces of their fruitless chase began to come together.

Izak had lied.

The Earth Walker had never intended to help him, but rather to manipulate him with the false impression of assistance. Erik pushed deeper into Izak's feelings, encountering a thread of fear and longing.

Izak wanted a companion. He was lonely. Lonelier than any human could endure. Instead of anger, this revelation stirred something foreign in Erik as he experienced Izak's deepest emotions.

Compassion.

Erik knew what it felt like to be alone.

Edgar cleared his throat, and Erik turned away from Izak. Edgar's aura had become intense sparks of light shimmering; all the while he remained, to all outward appearances, asleep.

Erik startled when Edgar spoke.

"Here we have the bodies of two inquiring entities, Izak and Erik Ulloa." The sleeping man spoke in a monotone voice unlike the pleasant Southern drawl he had earlier. "The entities present with certain problems and questions that will be answered as befits the entities' understanding and the task of interpretation before them."

Raising his brow, Erik caught Izak's eye. *What is this dog and pony show?*

Izak shrugged his shoulders then leaned toward the sleeping speaker. "Who are you?"

"You have before you the soul essence within a human experience. The name is not of importance."

"Can you tell me how to bring Juliana back?" Erik didn't hesitate to ask, believing that this might be the answers the soul essence meant.

"Hold on," Izak said, cautiously, one hand held up. "We do not know with whom we are dealing."

Edgar sighed. "As to the question presented, we see the physical mind attempting to gain from the subconscious knowledge of conditions pertaining to that which is paramount in the physical mind. Relating them to that condition regarding the entity Juliana."

"Do not speak to It anymore." Izak jumped from his seat to kneel next to Edgar. Izak placed his hand over the center of Edgar's forehead. Erik could see an exchange of light passing between them. "Reveal yourself!" he commanded.

"The entity should remain unnamed." Edgar struggled, groaning. "The contract unraveled yields revelations of proportions not previously allowed."

"Reveal yourself," Izak commanded again, grunting from the effort. The being's life force inside of Edgar shot outward. Izak flew backward, and Erik's back slammed against the wall.

"As you wish it, Earth Walker." Edgar sat up, opening his eyes as his life force receded back into his body. The soft-spoken, enunciated words sent a chill through Erik.

"It cannot be," Izak shook his head in disbelief.

"It can and it is," Edgar answered, folding his hands in his lap and leveling a stare at Izak,

Izak stood, snarling as he backed away from him. "How?"

"You never really understood the complexity of life outside your own world, Izak. To explain now would be a waste of our time. You must simply accept it."

"Why are you here?" Izak asked, staring daggers. Edgar turned and looked at Erik. Izak stepped between them. "You stay away from him. Haven't you done enough damage?"

Edgar smiled. "No, not I. Between you and him, your energies have bent the natural course. I have come to set things right and guide him back to the greater design."

"Don't speak as if I am not here," Erik growled.

"Several pardons," Edgar answered with a nod of his head. "But you are becoming too powerful for your own good, your *human* good. Your brother gave you access to your soul-power at your birth when he provided your body for this incarnation. The power that mostly lies dormant, yet is strong enough to manipulate the contract."

"I have a brother?" Erik leaned into his seat, piercing Izak with a stare. "Why didn't you tell me?"

Izak did not answer, his face stony. Edgar spoke instead. "Much has been kept from you in order for you to complete the tasks agreed upon. Izak's silence was sealed when the contract was signed. It was your choice, and he cannot be blamed."

"My choice?" Erik threw his hands in the air. None of this man's ramblings made sense.

"Free will," Edgar answered. He looked out the window for a moment at the scenery flying past as if to gather his thoughts. He turned back to Erik. "Take this individual." He motioned to himself. "My consciousness has a limited time here with you. When we finish speaking today, I will withdraw, and the veil will shadow my memories as I continue to live the life of this man, Edgar. He has come to waken other souls in their sojourns to a higher awareness of their purpose in the world. It is my choice to be that voice for others. But I shall not remember who I am or whence I come from. You, Erik, you are waking up to your true self, and therein lies the problem."

"What is he talking about?" Erik asked Izak. "I can make neither heads nor tails of it. And how does this information bring Juliana back to me?"

Izak crossed his arms, directing his answer to Edgar. "Am I allowed to explain the contract to him?"

Edgar templed his fingers. "How can you explain what you don't fully comprehend yourself? You were offered the same opportunity and refused."

Izak sneered. "I understand the basic principle."

Edgar closed his eyes in consideration. "Every soul born is given a name. Most souls, for the benefit of learning and growth, agree to incarnate into human existence in order to achieve a set of goals. Each life they live is rich with memories and experiences that sometimes leak through into a future life. Such leakage is a normal occurrence, especially if a lesson needs to be learned from the past.

"But none ever remember their soul-self. To remember would defeat the purpose. It's cheating. If you sit for an exam at school with all the answers provided, you learn nothing. The problem is, in your case, Erik, you have only ever lived one life. One very long life until now. Your original self is waking. And that is why I am here."

"And who are you, exactly?" Erik asked. Izak turned away, but not before Erik saw the grim lines on his face.

"You have no knowledge of my truest self, but we were acquainted in one of my lives. Before you started this life, you signed a binding soul-contract in the Temple Beautiful. The contract was witnessed by a high priest. I was that high priest. I am Mai-Ra."

"No." Erik refused to believe Mai-Ra's words even though they evoked the memory of a beautiful red-haired priestess asking him to sign.

Izak sat next to Erik, placing his hand on Erik's shoulder; an act that Erik would normally find annoying instead felt comforting. "He is speaking the truth."

Mai-Ra continued. "You are an original soul. And Izak is your brother. You, my friend, are the only known Soul Traveler. *You* are Arak Ulloa."

CHAPTER FIFTY-SEVEN

Erik grabbed his head with both hands, finding the truth difficult to believe. Izak was his brother, and yet...

"It is not a lie. In a sense, I am your father, Arak." Izak removed his hand from Erik's shoulder. "My seed created the body you inhabit. It is what you and I have always done throughout time. The bodies I create are soulless vessels made for you. Only I did not know...I did not know you would take up residence in this one. It was not planned."

Mai-Ra interrupted. "You were to have been born to human parents in this life. You were supposed to experience the love of a mother and a father. Be raised with many siblings. Become a brick-layer as your human father before you. Marry and have children of your own. You were supposed to know a good, well-lived life. Izak and your mother changed all of that with one choice, Arak."

"Stop calling me that," Erik snapped as he stood up and paced the small compartment.

Izak shook his head, frowning. "I told you not to sign the contract, brother. You refused to listen to me."

"The contract re-wrote itself." Mai-Ra continued, ignoring both of them. "Instead, you embraced the lessons of rejection, fear, hate, vengeance, and cruelty. The darkest parts of humanity took residence in your heart. You were born with many qualities to your benefit. You are inventive, creative, and influential. Yet you took these qualities and used them against others for most of your life.

"You agreed to enter Earth's school to purify your soul with experiences. To be a thief, to be stolen from. To suffer loss, to cause loss to others. To love and be loved. And you did not come here alone."

Erik stopped pacing, the thrumming of his heart beat against his ribs. "Not alone?"

"Sit," Mai-Ra, motioned to the spot next to Izak.

Erik sank onto the bench.

"There have been occasions when a highly evolved soul volunteers to incarnate, and one beautiful soul did—such a little thing, so bright and eager, filled with love and light. All of which she directed to you. I believe her soul-purpose has been to be your healer. She was born strong enough to help an original soul."

Erik thought about the lovely red-haired priestess. The one who kept asking Arak to sign a contract. "Akasha?"

Mai-Ra nodded. "Yes, she signed your contract hours before you did. She joins you in this agreement. Her body rests in the Temple Beautiful, not far from yours as both of your souls participate in the process of your cleansing and purification. She is experiencing humanity with you every step of the way."

Erik could hardly catch his breath at the thought. "Juliana?"

"Yes, Akasha is Juliana," Mai-Ra confirmed.

Erik turned on Izak. "You knew! That's why you hated her."

"Yes, I saw the cellular memories in her blood." Izak stared coldly at Erik. "Should I care for the woman who took my brother from me?"

Erik tried to absorb the ribbons of information dangled at him. "And Naomi?"

"The contract re-wrote itself when Izak lay with your mother. Akasha had wanted to be the first to greet you. However, instead of the loving mother she had hoped to be, you were met with one who showed you indifference. Akasha's first incarnation was Ellendora, your mother."

"What!" Izak hollered at the revelation, jumping up and hissing in disgust. "How could I not have known? I did not sense anything." His face paled. "I am going to be ill."

"You had relations with Akasha?" Erik felt a thread of anger pulsing through him even though he understood it was Akasha in a different life. He couldn't prevent seeing the image of Juliana in his mind's eye and realizing the two were one.

"Well, she wasn't Akasha when I did. I would take it back if I could." Izak squinted with a shudder. "I feel so violated."

Erik threw a clenched fist at his brother, but Mai-Ra caught it in mid-swing. "Enough of this. We have not time for your squabbles."

Mai-Ra closed his eyes as if searching his mind. "When your mother's body gave out, Akasha was born again as Naomi. Her life here was difficult and the human she inhabited was emotionally frail. She could not be of much help to you in her weakened state. But as Juliana, she could bring out the best in you. And she has interacted with you without any conscious recollection of her true-self. In this one life of yours, Arak, she has already incarnated as three important connections to you. She works hard on your behalf while struggling with her own humanity."

The hair on Erik's arms rose as he listened to Mai-Ra.

"Your wish was to make this process as expedient as possible. In the Temple Beautiful lies your body with ten percent of your essence within, completely aware of your experiences. Seventy percent of your essence is within the body that sits before me, all memories hidden behind the veil of forgetfulness. The other twenty percent? Well, in extreme cases when there is the need for ultimate learning in a short duration, a soul has been allowed to live simultaneously as two different people."

A feeling of dread gripped Erik and his shoulders knotted with stress. "Who? Who else am I?"

Mai-Ra raised an eyebrow. "You mean who were you?"

Izak coughed and wouldn't return Erik's questioning gaze.

"Just tell me," Erik whispered, a foreboding feeling in the pit of his stomach.

"Joe B was the other life journey you took."

Erik recoiled. *How could that be?* If this was true, that meant that a part of himself killed Juliana. How was he supposed to live with that?

"The contract as it pertains to Joe B was to meet Naomi and be her friend. Both of you had difficult lives. You were supposed to support each other through the troubled times. You were to accept her friendship as it was, knowing it would never be more. Instead, you took what you wanted. This life became all about you. Although it was not the intended design, many valuable lessons were learned. No choice is ever wasted."

Izak interjected. "I tried to protect your soul, Arak. I did not know what would happen if Joe B died."

Mai-Ra spoke with a thoughtful look on his face. "I guess this is a fine example of being your own worst enemy."

"Where is the rest of my soul now?" Was he compromised by his soul being splintered into percentages?

"It waits for your next incarnation. You will need much strength as you will be born to two human parents as was first agreed upon. You will not have the benefit of your brother's inhuman contribution. The veil will remain in place. You will not remember yourself, Arak. But, you will retain the memories of this life. You will always retain your self-knowledge of being Erik through the remainder of your lifetimes. For you suffer the loss of Juliana deeply and will do so for generations to come in return for the lives you have taken callously in this sojourn. You must understand what you sow, you reap."

Erik's heart crushed in his chest. "So I shall never see Juliana again? As payment for my sins?"

"Did I say that?" Mai-Ra breathed out a patient sigh. "You must live through your lives and the intended lessons until you are born into the life and time that Juliana lives. Only your choices will determine that outcome.

"Have hope. Akasha will be with you in each life. Even now, at the moment of Naomi's death, she has already incarnated. A new-born babe making its way into the world. She could be male or female, a parent, a sibling, a friend, a co-worker, or an acquaintance, but rest-assured, she will be there with you the entire time until she moves on to the next life."

Erik was speechless. He was Arak. Juliana was Akasha. He rubbed the palms of his hands over his eyes until bright lights appeared. He could not deny the truth. But how? Why had he seen the past when he was meant to forget?

Even though Erik did not voice the question out loud, Mai-Ra replied. "Juliana was near the crystal-topped cane. It is an ancient stone from our city. Her humanity wanted to heal your outer scars. Her soul longs to heal your inner ones. Her higher self thought bringing you to the moment you chose to evolve might assist you on this journey. She roused you from your soul slumber."

"Now that he knows, can he break the contract?" The intensity of Izak's question vibrated between the men.

"Earth Walker," Mai-Ra spoke with tolerance. "The contract is binding and will remain in effect until it has been honored. How it unravels is entirely up to Arak."

"Stop calling me that!" Erik growled fiercely. "I don't know that life. How can I be someone I do not remember?"

"There is nothing standing in the way now." Izak leaned over, placed his hand behind Erik's head, and whispered, "Remember."

♀

Erik's vision tunneled and instead of the sunlit train compartment, he was inside his childhood home. He could sense Izak's presence behind him and feel Izak's hand on his head. Ellendora, his mother slept sprawled across a straw bed. Soiled, bloody linen lay in a pile on the floor and a baby whimpered in a crudely made bassinet in the corner of the one-room house.

The front door blew open off its hinges and Izak stood in the doorway, nostrils flaring. He looked first to the bloody remnants on the floor; glanced at Ellendora, who now sat up startled from her sleep, and then rested his gaze on the baby.

"A child?" Izak asked accusingly.

"A son." Ellendora's lips trembled.

"Why was this hidden from me?" he growled.

"How was I to tell you? You abandoned me long ago to parts unknown. Not a word or inquiry as to my health."

"I am taking the child." Izak strode toward the bassinet.

With almost unnatural speed for a woman in her weakened condition, Ellendora flew from the bed and nestled the baby protectively in her arms.

"Give me the child, Ellendora," Izak said with an impatient wave of his hand.

"No," she said, eyes flashing.

"Give. Me. The. Child," Izak commanded in a deep, resonating voice, his eyes swirling green, and elongated teeth bared.

Ellendora stared in horror, glancing back and forth between Izak and the baby. She handed the child to Izak and fled the house, tripping over a piece of splintered wood from the door on her way out. The baby screamed at the top of his lungs as Izak held him by one leg, upside-down.

"How did I not know about you?" Izak stared curiously at the screaming infant. "No matter, I cannot let you live. We cannot have a soulless human wandering around." Izak flipped the child around, his free hand going for its neck.

He won't be soulless for long.

Erik heard the words in his mind as did Izak, who froze.

Hello, brother, the voice said.

Erik held his breath for a moment as a swell of recollection surged in him. Standing behind the bassinet was the ethereal outline of Arak, the outline of himself.

Izak stood motionless, his jaw set as he stared at his brother, the baby still dangled in his outstretched hand. Brother to brother they remained stoic and silent, the strain of their feud spoke volumes in their eyes.

Izak broke away first, took the babe in his arms. "Sleep." The child's cries stopped. Izak walked forward and dropped the child into the bassinet.

Careful, Izak. I need that baby intact.

Izak crossed his arms.

This body calls to me as all your offspring do. The contract stipulated a human baby, but I want this body.

"Is that so?" Izak bit out. "I want you to go back to that Temple, get up, and walk out of there. I want my brother to return to me. It has been centuries for me without you. Give me those years back."

You can have me here and now.

"We both know it won't be you." Izak's eyes swirled in anger.

I cannot go back. I have to see this through.

"You will go through it alone."

You would forsake me, brother?

"As you have forsaken me, Arak." Izak pointed a trembling finger at him. "As you have forsaken me."

Arak's face rippled with resignation. *So be it.*

Erik watched in fascination as the full apparition of Arak seemingly entered the small body of the child. The baby stirred, opening eyes that radiated knowledge beyond its years. The child slowly turned its head and looked directly at Izak.

"Abomination!" Ellendora ran into the room with a wooden bowl brimming with a liquid that sloshed over its side. Izak's nostrils flared at the scent.

"No!" Izak grabbed the child, but not before some of the liquid splattered on the baby's face and chest. The child screamed in pain. The rest of the acid ate away at the bassinet where he once lay.

CHAPTER FIFTY-EIGHT

"Monster! Demon!" Ellendora screeched, flinging herself at Izak and the screaming babe he cradled in one arm. Without time to spare, Izak grabbed her by the throat.

"Cease." Her body stopped flailing.

"Sleep." She crumpled to the floor.

Izak tended to Arak. With light pouring from his hands, Izak pulled the remaining acid from the baby's skin, tossing it across the room. Had Izak not intervened, the body would not have survived such an assault. Where the acid had made contact, the skin was raw and blistered.

"There is nothing I can do to repair you or ease your pain except to let you sleep through the worst of it."

The baby looked deeply into Izak's eyes as he howled in pain.

"Mai-Ra explained to me what you are doing and I want you to know, before your memories fade, you will not see me again. This is your choice and yours alone. Once I walk out this house, I turn my back on you."

The baby grabbed one of Izak's finger's in his tiny hand, looked away, and cried.

"Sleep," Izak whispered with a hitch in his voice. The baby closed its eyes before a tear slipped down Izak's face, but as a silent astral observer per Izak's invitation, Erik saw.

Izak swaddled the baby in an old sackcloth and laid it in the straw bed. He turned back and lifted Ellendora off the floor and placed her on the bed as well.

"Wake," he commanded, anger in his swirling green eyes.

Ellendora's eyes fluttered open.

"You will forget all that has happened. You hate the child's father, and the child will remind you of him every day of his life. You will never do harm to this child, but you will not love him either. You will provide only for his most basic of needs."

Ellendora blinked.

"Do you understand?"

"Yes," she mumbled.

"Good." Izak nodded. "Sleep now." Ellendora closed her eyes.

Before leaving, Izak turned in the doorway, addressing the sleeping child. Erik heard Izak's pain when he spoke. "Now you will know what it has been like to be alone in need of a brother and without one."

As Izak removed his hand and the shabby room faded away, Erik gasped for air under the weight of Izak's intense hurt and resentment.

☥

The bright compartment and comforting sway of the train was a welcome reprieve from the cheerless scene Erik had just lived through. He had never understood how a mother could not love her son. How he had always longed for love, but felt he was not worthy of being loved by others. Now he began to understand the bleak existence of his life.

Had he known Izak had intentionally condemned him to such misery months earlier, he would have hated his brother. But he could not. Instead, his heart ached for Izak. He looked at Izak and saw vulnerability in his brother's eyes. Izak had felt betrayed and abandoned.

Erik could not recall his life with Izak, but he understood loneliness. All of Izak's misdeeds toward him were born from resentment and hurt. Try as he might, Erik could not remember why he had signed the contract or what events had led up to that decision. However, he knew his actions had caused centuries of hurt to the man who called himself his brother. A simmering swell of energy deep inside pricked his soul, urging him to make peace. Erik extended his hand toward his brother, placing it on his knee.

"Izak, forgive me for having left you. Clearly, I gave no thought to how you would feel. I cannot change what happened, but I see how my choices have affected you and for that, I am truly sorry."

Izak looked away. The train clacked forward and the three men swayed in silence on their seats. Finally, Izak cleared his throat. "So what now? What must be done to reunite Erik with Juliana?"

Mai-Ra's pleasure shone on young Edgar's face. "He will have to be born again, but the time is not right. There are still lessons yet to be learned in this life."

"So you cannot tell me when?" Erik interjected.

"You will know when the time is right, Soul Traveler."

Erik trembled in vague recognition at the title.

"You will feel the call of the body that awaits you." Mai-Ra clasped his hands in his lap. "To the soul, time is not linear. Past, present, and future are occurring simultaneously. If you were to meditate, you might sense the lives that are part of your soul's journey. But I warn you, a barrier has been set in place for knowing your life as Arak. Once your final body has drawn its last breath, you will wake in the Temple Beautiful to resume your original life, Arak. Use this time well."

"How will I feel this call?"

"You will not reincarnate in the same manner as other souls. You have the unique ability to travel from body to body as was your design from the moment of your creation. The plan...the lives you are to live...were chosen before you closed your eyes in the Temple. If you were to concentrate, you would be able to connect with them and prepare yourself for the journey."

Mai-Ra paused, tilting his head slightly as though he listened to words the brothers could not hear. "My time here is done. The message has been delivered. What you do with the knowledge you now possess is up to you, Erik."

"Wait!" Erik said urgently.

Mai-Ra lay down on the train bench and closed his eyes.

Erik shook him. "Wake up! I still have questions."

The monotone voice Erik had heard once before filled the room. "Here we have before us two male entities. Dialogue was exchanged for the allotted duration and no further questions are warranted. This essence will discontinue at this time."

Edgar began to softly snore.

"Leave him be. You will get nothing further from him, Erik."

Erik reluctantly sat back, digesting the events of the last hour. There was hope. That hope would be tested by days, months, years, and possibly decades of waiting, but in the end, he would see Juliana again. His heart filled with relief. He *was* going to see her again.

He slapped Izak on the back. "Come on, brother. I've got to prepare for the future. Let's go home." Erik stood up and headed for the door of their train compartment.

"Not just yet," Izak said.

"Why?"

Izak stood over the sleeping Edgar, his hand around his throat. "This man is not going to repeat *that* story to anyone." He added, under his breath, "Especially about how you were born." Before Erik could stop him, Izak spoke. "Speak no more."

Izak looked up at Erik, a smirk on his face. "My work here is done. Let's go, brother.

♀

Erik grunted as he moved about on his hands and knees, searching the bedroom floor of the St. Charles house for the small walnut bottle he had given to Juliana on Halloween. He had already located Juliana's bracelet and had placed it on the mantle.

"What are you doing?" Izak leaned against the door jamb, an eyebrow arched.

Erik sat back on his heels. "I believe the oil I made to send Juliana home is the very oil that brought her to me in the first place. I will separate the mixture from the oil since it is likely to get rancid. One day, she is going to buy my house and find that bottle. I have to bury it inside the floor of the Creole cottage for that to happen."

"Why are you trusting me with this information? I could easily remove it once you move on to your 'new life' and you'll be none the wiser."

"You could. But you won't."

"Oh, really? And what is to prevent me?"

Erik smirked. "I think you want to see how my soul journey turns out as much as I do."

"Irksome, but true." Izak conceded.

Erik resumed his search.

"It is curious to me that you chose this house to purchase," Izak said.

"Why is that?" Erik stood.

He ran a long-fingered hand against the mantel woodwork. "I built this house."

"You? You built this house?"

"Yes."

"The Devil's house?"

Izak bowed with a grin. "The one and only. Although the reports of my activities have been greatly exaggerated."

"Hmmm...." Erik stopped again, digesting Izak's admission. "I purchased this house because of the rumors that surrounded it and the privacy it would afford me, but I was drawn to it the moment I saw it."

Izak slowly paced the floor. "I tell you this now because I want you to know I am not wholly unsympathetic to your situation. I will never accept Akasha, but I understand your struggle because I loved a woman once, and I built this house for her."

Although astounded by Izak's confession, Erik refused to show it.

"I will not bore you with the details, but suffice it to say, our love was not meant to be...lasting. I left her, along with this house." Izak sat in one of the wing-back chairs by the fireplace and crossed his legs.

This Earth Walker could love a woman? His aloofness and disregard was just a mask? Erik remained silent, not daring to interrupt Izak as he expressed such intimate information about his past.

"Imagine my fascination when I found out that someone had bought the house I had abandoned over fifty years ago. I came back to the city and discovered it was you, grown up and devoid of your memories, masquerading as Monsieur David de la Croix.

"I had been so angry with you for choosing Akasha over me. I carried that grudge for centuries, not knowing when or if I would ever see you again. I only knew I was not going to help you ruin your life, your soul. Until there you were, standing next to the newly born infant I had created, the very thing I had tried to prevent. Seeing you again, I foolishly held out hope that you would change your mind. Yet still you refused my request to end this foolish sojourn. Again...you denied me.

"Did you know how careful I was not to get a female with child? Over countless centuries, only two women conceived. I killed the first child immediately after its birth. The second was the body you now inhabit.

"Once I saw you in New Orleans, I followed you, tapping into your thoughts and the thoughts of those around you. Of course, I was intrigued by the irony that you wanted to reconstruct my house to hold a woman captive. You had such big dreams, brother. I found I could no longer watch from a distance."

He watched Erik expectantly. Erik had followed the motion of Izak's foot as his heel clinked against something brown under the chair. Erik reached beneath Izak's legs and retrieved the small bottle, clasping it in his hand. He held it to his chest, relieved to have found the missing treasure.

"Have you heard a word that I have said to you?" Izak grumbled.

"Yes." Erik carefully deposited the bottle in his pocket, giving Izak his full attention. "I get the feeling I will have plenty of time for you to fill in my lost memories, if you are willing to help me...to serve as my brother while I continue this journey. Will you follow me from life to life and help me find Juliana?"

Izak hesitated. "Well, since I have not anything better to do, why not?"

"Thank you." Erik sat down in the wingback chair opposite Izak. "There is something bothering me on which I hope you can shed some light."

Izak raised his brows.

"Mai-Ra said that when I have completed and honored the contract, I will wake up in the temple and finish my life as Arak."

Izak pursed his lips as though the words were distasteful. "Erik, I can see where this is going..."

"Did I wake up?"

"Yes."

"And?"

"You were no longer the brother I once knew. And you tried to explain...everything...but I was not willing to hear it. You were different. You had changed and I blamed Akasha. However, centuries can wear away at a hardened heart. Watching you live this human existence is helping me to understand now what I could not then."

"Where..."

"Don't ask me anything more, Erik. You are not to know the past, remember?"

"Did I tell you about Juliana?"

"No." Izak breathed out, exasperated. He leaned forward, elbows on his knees and hands clasped. "Look at me." Izak whispered, searching Erik's face with regret. "Do not ask me anything further. I can only say...that you and I...we parted on very bad terms."

CHAPTER FIFTY-NINE

New Orleans, Louisiana, 1919

Erik skimmed a wrinkled hand over the patchy fur of the old dog sitting next to his chair. Bijou's daughter, Chanel, was as faithful a friend to him as her mother had been. She was his one and only companion at the Creole cottage. Memories of Juliana lived in his heart and mind, but they were not real and tangible as Chanel. He was glad not to be alone.

It had been years since Juliana was ripped from his life, yet he still held out hope that one day he would see her again. When that moment came and she asked him how his life had been, he wanted the account to be one that would make her proud. So in the intervening time, while he waited for the future to unfold, he supplied food to soup kitchens, donated money to the good charity society, and slipped coins into the hands of the homeless.

Unfortunately, good acts did not a good man make. He proved that fact to himself more than once. A long time past, on one evening when taking a long walk outside of the city, he had seen dirty-faced children walking home from the hot, overcrowded factories nearby. Out of curiosity, he peered through a cracked window pane and saw the floor manager, stick in hand, striking more than one child. His anger erupted, not just for the children, but for his own bitter childhood.

On this matter, he could not honor Juliana's wish for him to be a better man. The factory owner was lucky that Erik stopped short of making his stomach explode and only left him with a small bleeding ulcer that under Erik's hypnotic suggestion, acted up fiercely when anything less than kindness was shown to the small workers.

The floor manager, who had struck the child, was another story. The police had investigated his mysterious disappearance, but he was never heard from again. Erik smiled at the thought as he shifted more comfortably in his seat. He couldn't be expected to make a total change in one life.

As more years passed, Erik rarely felt like going out in public. And at the same time, Izak's visits became few and far between. First, Izak claimed he didn't have time to waste watching Erik become a do-gooder. Then he professed, much too loudly, that he could never settle in one place for too long. But Erik had distinctly felt Izak's unease at seeing him grow old.

Chanel nuzzled Erik's hand with her nose, requesting more rubs. Her presence really did comfort him. Especially since he began hearing the heartbeat. He had first noticed it a few months ago as a soft whooshing sound in his ears when he lay down to sleep. Now he could hear it all the time, strong and constant. The new life that he had been waiting for was drawing nigh.

Erik was troubled.

Not that he wasn't prepared to move on. His list of things to complete had been checked off long ago. He handcrafted a wooden box exactly as Juliana had described it to him, placed the walnut bottle along with all of his notes and his journal inside, and secured it under the floorboards.

He gave Izak primary stewardship over his corporation, his property, and monies. He could not relinquish all that he had achieved, especially if in his new lives he was without means. He was not beyond taking advantage of his brother's immortality. He had already experienced poverty, and he wanted to avoid that life again. Maybe it was cheating, but it was his choice. He didn't see how Juliana could find fault with that. Self-preservation was a natural instinct.

He had sent a ripple through the weakened connection between himself and Izak, so Izak would make his return to New Orleans. Once he vacated this body, someone would have to see to the remains. He wanted to be buried with Naomi. Everything had been prearranged, though he expected no one save Izak to attend the funeral.

His other requests of Izak were to return the lovers statue to Jean Lafitte's old blacksmith shop. Juliana had told him the statue was a connection she made with her past and future selves. Also, the bracelet...Izak would keep the precious jewelry safe until it could be given back to Juliana, so they could complete their love story.

Yes, he was prepared to move on, but what troubled him was the unknown.

He was supposed to be able to make a connection with this new life–have some idea who he was to become. He was supposed to know how to leave this body and to enter the next, and yet he still had no earthly idea.

400 · LAURIE L. BOLANOS

Erik's hip joint popped as he slowly crossed his legs. Chanel lifted her head at the noise, walked to the far side of the room, and plopped down.

"Don't worry girl, it's just my old bones," Erik soothed her.

Trying to meditate in the lotus position reminded him how much his body had aged. But he had had some mild success with meditation over the past week, so he wanted to try again. Each time he tried, he felt closer to his future body. The life was new, growing in its mother's womb.

Erik closed his eyes and started to concentrate. "*Om...Oom...,*" he chanted in time with the heartbeat, trying to clear his mind of all thoughts except for the growing life.

A snort jolted him just as he entered into an altered state.

"What *are* you doing? I leave you for a few months and you turn into a Tibetan monk. You look ridiculous."

The clip of Chanel's nails against the wood floor echoed in the room as she ambled toward their visitor for rubs. Erik kept his eyes closed, fighting back a smile. Izak was back. He never thought he'd be glad to hear his brother's voice. "I am meditating." He could hear Izak sink into the nearest chair.

"Really, Erik. You take this humanity entirely too seriously. I cannot believe that I am going to say this, but Juliana brought out the best in you. At least when she was here, you were on the verge of being your true self again."

Erik opened his eyes. "That side of me departed piece by piece after Juliana left."

"I know," Izak said while trying to satisfy Chanel's need for affection as she leaned into him. "What is wrong with this animal? Can she not be controlled?"

"What can I do? She loves you."

Izak leaned forward to pet Chanel some more, but not before Erik caught the satisfied look on his face. He was glad they had bonded. She needed a caretaker once he was gone.

"So what is all this nonsense about?" Izak waved at Erik.

"Oh." Erik uncrossed his legs and stood, holding on to furniture for support while he slowly straightened his legs. "I still don't know anything. I was attempting to connect with my future self."

Izak made an exasperated grunt. "This body-bending, mantra-humming nonsense is completely unnecessary. You keep thinking so small. I see I will have to help you *again*. You are fortunate my curiosity is piqued or I'd leave you to figure it out on your own, little human."

Erik ignored Izak's condescending quip. "If you are offering, I will not refuse your help. I haven't made the kind of progress I would like."

Izak motioned. "Come to me then."

Erik nudged a reluctant Chanel out of the way and sat on the floor in front of Izak's chair with his back against his brother's legs. Izak placed a hand behind his head. The heartbeat pounded and the room became dark, surrounded by a pulsing sensation.

Izak removed his hand, returning them to the Creole cottage. He grunted in disgust. "Are we inside a woman?"

"Yes," Erik said, excited at the oneness he had felt with the body. "Take me back."

Izak inhaled and placed his hand behind Erik's head again.

The room faded away, and Erik was again surrounded by warmth and a feeling of security. Weightless, he floated in fluid. There was an odd sensation around his mouth; he was sucking his thumb. Erik focused on using the body and removed the thumb.

Excuse me while I die of boredom, Izak interjected. *Are you done playing around with the baby?*

Give me a chance to get acclimated, Erik answered. *I am unsettled that I will be trapped in a developing child with all the knowledge of an adult and the inability to express myself. I would like to see how much I can control.*

You chose this, Erik, and you must live with the consequences. Figure out how you need to move on. I cannot say I care for the milieu.

He could not argue the point. This was his journey. As Arak, he had chosen this path and it was his to walk alone.

All right, all right, Erik conceded. Using Izak's strength, Erik pushed his mind outside of the baby, while still keeping a connection to the baby and his body in the Creole cottage. The room had a lacy bedspread and French art hanging on the crimson wall. A blonde woman with a rounded belly slept on the bed.

My mother, Erik thought.

No, Izak replied. *She is simply the vessel that grows your new life.*

Hmmm. Erik looked at her closely. She was no beauty, but she was not common either. Even though she appeared to be very young, she wore a wedding band. Mai-Ra said he was to experience a life with two loving parents. Maybe this one would be that life?

He pushed his consciousness out of the bedroom, and Izak mentally joined him. In the hallway, walking toward him, was a tall, dark-haired man in his early twenties. As the man passed by to peek in on the sleeping woman, Erik caught sight of familiar slate gray eyes and abruptly stopped.

Who is he? Izak asked.

"Philippe!" A woman called from elsewhere in the house.

"Shush, mother," he hissed on his way back. "Louisa is still asleep."

Oh, this can't be happening, Erik groaned. He had left his obsessions behind a long time ago. He had forgotten the little boy he had once called godson and that little boy's mother as well as her husband. All of whom were about to become his family.

This is poetic! Izak laughed once he had intercepted Erik's thoughts. *I think I will be staying in New Orleans for a while. I do not want to miss this priceless soul growth you've chosen for yourself.*

That doesn't surprise me, Erik mumbled while projecting himself farther into the house, leaving Izak behind. He found Philippe in the sitting room, his mother refilling his cup of tea.

Christine sat across from Philippe. Her gray-tinged chestnut hair was scooped into an elegant bun, and her once youthful face now reflected the maturity of her years. Erik watched in silence.

The voice.

The woman.

The obsession that changed his life forever. All drowned out and forgotten with his love for Juliana. Christine was still as beautiful as she once was and for a fleeting moment, Erik wondered if her voice would still captivate him.

"Not much longer now, son." Christine patted Philippe's knee.

"I'm worried about Louisa. Is it normal for her to rest so often? Maybe we should send for the doctor," Philippe mused.

Christine's flawless laugh filled the room. "If you were carrying around an extra person inside of you all day, you would be tired, too. It is completely expected for her to rest often, especially so late into her confinement. And I'll have you know that I did the same for you and your brothers."

Why was he to be a part of *this* family? And where was Juliana? She should be at least twenty now in her new life. Would she be his nanny or one of his uncles? It was going to be difficult to embrace this life without her in it. His heart fluttered. Was Juliana his mother, Louisa?

He soared back to the sleeping woman and hovered over her. He pulled on Izak's strength to poke about her unconscious mind, but felt nothing familiar. Louisa did not feel like his Juliana. Disappointment drained his energy. It was time to go for now.

He retreated back into the baby, settling inside for a moment to get used to the fit. The de Marignys did not know what they were in for with this child. If they knew he was at the helm, would they want him?

Oh, I would not worry about that, Izak interrupted.

And why is that?

While you've been flitting about the house gawking at Christine, I've been checking on a sense I had as we passed through this body.

A sense? Erik was skeptical. *Why didn't I sense something unusual?*

You were too busy playing pull the thumb from baby's mouth.

Just get to the point, Erik snapped in exasperation.

Well, the good news is I am here for you, brother. I am going to spend this entire life watching over you.

Thanks? Erik answered. Where was Izak going with this?

It's nothing. Izak mentally waved him off. *Would you care to know my reason?*

I tremble with anticipation.

First, I would not miss your reunion with these fine people. Izak hesitated as though he were sucking in breath he didn't require.

And the second reason would be? Erik prompted.

Izak removed his hand from Erik's head and the two of them were back at the Creole house, leaving the baby behind to continue to grow undisturbed.

"Congratulations, brother!" Izak slapped him on the back with a laugh. "You are going to be a girl."

♀

Erik tethered Chanel with a rope and closed the door behind him. After discovering the details of his next life, his evening routine included long walks. Walking helped him to sort his thoughts.

A girl. That was a hard idea to digest. What could he possibly accomplish being a female? It wasn't as if he was starting over with a blank slate. Not that he wanted to forget who he was, but he would be a man with a man's memories, desires, and wants, living inside of a female.

Izak was no help whatsoever. Anytime Erik tried to broach the subject and express his concerns, Izak brushed him off. In fact, Izak took great pleasure in the idea that he would be a girl and had bought bows and dolls to give to Erik once he was born, a gesture that totally infuriated him. He would deal with this complication on his own, as always.

Images of him dressed in frilly skirts and bows in his long, curly hair flashed in his mind, and Erik cringed. Could his situation get any worse? He stoically swallowed his distaste, sighing. If it meant one lifetime closer to Juliana, he would do whatever it took.

Erik wiped away the sweat that had beaded on his forehead. It had been a warm winter, and this night was no different. As he replaced the moistened handkerchief into his pocket, he stopped. The air had changed. It no longer carried the scent of jasmine, sweet olive, and the usual fragrances of the Quarter. Instead, it smelled of ash.

Smoke billowed down Toulouse Street. He released Chanel from her rope and shooed her home as he rushed toward the commotion. Shouts echoed down the street. Fire engine bells rang in the distance, but Erik could see angry flames consuming the roof of the French Opera house. The situation was a dangerous one. The fire could easily spread to the surrounding buildings.

He stood in front of the burning Greek Revival building he had admired on his arrival to New Orleans. He recalled watching Christine from the balcony box seat as she sat next to Raoul. How he had wanted her, had wanted to own her. It seemed so long ago. He was not that man anymore.

A woman jostled Erik as she ran past toward the opera house. "Henry! Henry!"

A line of men had formed a bucket brigade and threw water on the flames. The man at the end grabbed the woman.

"You can't go in there, ma'am."

"My husband! Henry!" she struggled and yelled.

"The building is not safe to enter. You must wait." The man held the woman back. She collapsed into his arms, breaking into tears.

As Erik stared into the flames, excitement spread through him, and his fingers and toes tingled. Every fiber of his being told him he could save Henry. He pulled out his handkerchief and wrapped it around his face, covering his mouth and nose. Ducking his head, he ran into the building unnoticed.

The heat was searing and invigorating. The ache of his aging body retreated. He felt powerful, dodging the flames with the graceful movements of a skilled dance partner, moving past the worst of the blaze to the smoke-filled interior. His hearing intensified as he strained to listen for Henry, who did not disappoint, emitting a dry cough.

He reached the incapacitated man, lifting him up, and slinging him over his shoulder. As Erik navigated the smoky interior, the smoke blackened. He could see nothing. Yet, his internal sense told him there was a large floor-to-ceiling window nearby. Walking fast with his hand along the wall, Erik stopped when his fingers touched warm glass.

He smashed it with his fist.

He tossed Henry through the opening. He lifted his leg to step through himself, but the fire and smoke disappeared. He floated in nothingness. His heart beat rapidly, and something compressed his body. The steady beat of another heart reverberated nearby, soothing him. He was surrounded by warmth. He could feel the presence of several people.

"Breathe, Louisa. It is almost time," said a muffled female voice as it penetrated through layers of skin and fluid.

He was about to be born. He imagined his adult body consumed by flames. Somehow he had pictured a different end for himself. *Get my body*, he thought to Izak unable to tell whether his brother had received his request.

He felt compressed again. It was not an altogether unpleasant sensation. As it reached the pinnacle of pressure, he found himself back in the burning building. Although smoke and flames filled the opera house, his vision was not affected.

Erik shivered at what he saw. His body sprawled against the wall. His handkerchief had fallen from his face, and soot darkened his nose and mouth. He had spent many years in that body, and gazing down upon himself disoriented him. Yet, being in spirit was wholly familiar, and for a split second, he remembered being a Soul Traveler.

"Brother."

Izak approached.

Izak, Erik nodded. *Don't let the body burn.*

"Never," Izak replied as he bent to retrieve it.

The body coughed, and Erik found himself inside of it once again. He lifted his head to gaze into Izak's eyes, safe in his brother's arms.

He thought of the baby and was simultaneously with both his brother and the infant.

He passed through the birth canal, and then someone vigorously rubbed his new body. He coughed.

As Erik, the cough was hoarse, and he couldn't draw air.

As the baby, it was watery and deep. He began to wail, grabbing air into his newly cleared lungs.

Dodging falling beams, Izak held him close and exited the opera house, the crowd oblivious to their movements.

The midwife wrapped him securely in a blanket and handed the newly born baby to Louisa. Even with blurry newborn vision, he could see her pretty blue eyes looking down at him. At the same time, Izak's green eyes stared into his as his brother grasped him tighter.

A feathery kiss on his forehead distracted him.

"We have been waiting for you, my precious girl." Louisa held him closer, rocking him.

"What shall we name her?" Philippe asked, leaning over him.

"Josephine, after my grandmother," Louisa replied.

Not such a bad name, Erik thought as he settled in the small body then focused his energy on his brother.

I am ready, Erik told Izak, about to relinquish his last hold on the life he had known for so long.

Izak blinked. *Peace, brother.*

Erik turned his head away from Izak and focused on the sky...dark and starry. He exhaled one last breath.

It was time to let go.

CHAPTER SIXTY

New Orleans, Louisiana, 2009

Julie woke to her first inkling of consciousness. She touched her face. Something was on her nose. Someone gently moved her hand away. She raised her hand to her face again, and again someone eased it back down.

"No more of that, Ms. François. You need to keep that oxygen on. If you try to take it off again, I'm going to tie your hands down," a woman fussed at her. Julie shuddered. She definitely didn't want her hands tied down.

Don't touch my face, she reminded herself as she became increasingly self-aware. A rhythmic whirring sound played in the background as she collected her thoughts.

Where am I?

Voices echoed in what must be a hallway.

"Dr. Rivera, I need you over here. Room 302 is responsive now."

A male voice cut in, a familiar voice. "How is she, doctor? Can I see her now?"

"Let me assess her, and then you can see her briefly. We still don't know what caused your friend to lose consciousness." That voice must be Dr. Rivera.

"My fiancée," the man corrected with a drawl.

Fiancée? No, that wasn't right. Was it?

A man's footsteps entered the room, and he stood beside her bed. He smelled of Old Spice and old coffee.

"Okay, Ms. François, I'm going to check a few things," Dr. Rivera said. A cold instrument rubbed against the sole of her foot, and her toes reflexively curled. Then sharp pricks played up and down both legs. She jerked her legs away from each stick.

"Very good," Dr. Rivera said, placing his hands in hers. "Now, squeeze as tightly as you can."

She concentrated, squeezing his hands as hard as she could. He let go. Someone pried her eyes open and assaulted them with a bright light.

"Pupils equal and reactive to light," he murmured. "Looks as if you are coming back to the land of the living, Ms. François. I'll be back to check you in another hour." To the nurse, he added, "call the lab and see whether the toxicology report is ready."

She heard both Dr. Rivera and the nurse leave the room.

Julie struggled to open her eyes as if her lids had five-pound weights on them. An IV machine stood next to the bed, softly whirring as it pushed the fluid into her veins. Her gaze followed the IV tube to the entry point in her hand.

"How is she, doc?" the eager deep-voiced man asked. "Will she be able to go home tonight?"

"We are waiting for her blood work to come back. If her health issues are drug-related, we need to ascertain whether she purposely caused herself harm. That will determine how long she will be here. In the meantime, she will be admitted for a couple of days at least. The nurse is working on getting her transferred to a room."

Julie blinked her eyes until they opened freely. Both side rails were raised on the hospital bed. She moved a hand to the tubing in her nose. *Oxygen.* Why was she in the hospital? Drug overdose? Not possible.

"Can I see her now?"

Julie looked at the pitcher sitting on the bedside table and a sudden thirst overtook her.

"Yes, but not for long."

Thanks, doc!"

She raised her eyes. A large man filled the doorway. She smiled when he gave her a gentle bear hug.

"Dawlin', you had us worried. I've been waiting so long to see you." He dropped his voice to a conspiratorial whisper. "The only reason they let me in is because I told them we are engaged." Typical James. She was ever so glad to see him.

"James," she rasped. "Please get me some water."

"Sure thing, Sweet Cheeks." He poured cold water into the plastic cup next to the pitcher and steadied her hand as she put it to her lips.

She gulped the water greedily until it was empty. "What am I doing here?"

"That's what they're trying to find out. Heath and I found you unconscious on the floor. We called 911. You've been at the hospital for several hours. Le-a and I have been beside ourselves with worry. She's baking up a storm to feed you when you get back home. Heath sent me a text. He went to look for Star. He thought she might have some answers."

Voodoo.

She turned her head away from James. She remembered. The vial. The sweet grass burning. The lit candles. The oil. The words.

Erik.

Remembering his cry of agony as he sent her back, she felt her heart crush inside of her chest and she lost her breath. She had to get out of here. Erik had promised to find a way to her. She had to look for him or find Star and see if there was a way she could return to Erik. She fumbled with the blanket.

"What are you doing, honey?" James asked with concern.

"I have to leave. I have to leave *now*." Her frantic words came out slurred. She pulled the oxygen tube from her nose and clumsily worked on the tape that secured the IV to her arm.

"Stop that," James said, moving her hands back. "Something happened to you, and you are not yourself. You must stay here."

"No, you don't understand." Julie's heart beat erratically. "I have to find Erik."

James frowned. "Who's Erik, Honey?"

"I don't have time to explain now," she answered, trying to extricate her hands from James' hold. Completely alert, she felt the adrenalin coursing through her veins along with the urgent call of her spirit to find Erik.

"You mustn't excite yourself. You need to rest. I'm going to call the doctor." James rose.

I'll tie your hands down, she heard the nurse's voice in her head.

"No." She tugged on James' shirt, pulling him back. She couldn't have her hands tied or the doctor called. She needed to leave. Maybe she could convince James to help her? "Please don't call the doctor. I wouldn't leave if I didn't have a good reason, James. I need your help."

"Yes, you do, Dawlin'. I'm gonna get you the best help possible," James said while pressing the call light. "I need help. She's trying to leave."

"No," Julie whispered, tears welling in her eyes. Erik needed her and she couldn't get to him. The nurse and two men dressed in scrubs entered the room. Julie saw a syringe in the nurse's hand.

"I'm going to give you a little something to relax, Ms. François. Just hold still a minute," the nurse said.

"No," Julie said, slipping out of the bed. The two men grabbed hold of her, keeping her in place. She struggled. "James," she pleaded with him, a hot tear falling down her cheek.

"I'm sorry, Dawlin'," he said, his forehead creased. "It will all be better in the morning. You'll see."

The nurse had already pushed the medicine through her IV and reapplied the tape. Julie felt its effect almost instantly.

"What did you give me?" she asked, fighting to keep her balance.

"Something to make you sleep," the nurse said as she and the two men got her back into bed. Julie didn't resist. The nurse placed a soft restraint around her wrists, tying them to the bed.

"Is that necessary?" James asked her.

"We don't want her hurting herself. Now, sir, visiting hours are over. You need to leave."

"I'll be back first thing in the morning. You hang in there, Dawlin'." Julie heard James say as he left the room. The nurse and the men followed. Alone in the room, Julie could hear the IV pump whirring. Heartbroken with the need to be with Erik, she closed her eyes, succumbing to the medicated sleep.

♀

Erik's gut twisted into knots of helplessness as he watched the ambulance pull away with Juliana inside. He had hoped to prevent Juliana from using the oil. His plan had been a simple one. Once he had located her, he would insinuate himself into her life. Befriend her. Get her to trust him.

Until Juliana remembered her past, she would not recognize him for who he was. Somehow, he would have coaxed her to let him gently pull Naomi's memories and hers to the surface. Let her remember her life with him without having to live it. He wanted to spare her from the worst experiences...Naomi's rape and her murder.

He clenched his fists. His timing had been way off, and he had missed his opportunity. He never knew exactly when on the timeline Juliana had used the oil. That had been the only variable. And now he was too late to stop it.

As the ambulance turned the corner, Juliana was already reliving the past. The worst part was the uncertainty. Had he and Izak truly sent her back that horrible morning? Did she survive the experience? Had he come this far only to find that she never wakes? Or would he have to watch her die all over again? Knowing he had no control over the situation and that he never really did, he clenched his hands tighter and tighter until his knuckles turned white

Her next-door neighbor got into a cab and headed the same direction as the ambulance. Erik decided not to follow suit. She would have a familiar friend with her. It could be hours, it could be days, or months before she woke, if she awoke at all. He couldn't sit idly on the sidelines. He needed answers.

He inhaled, feeling more frustrated as he smelled the mild scent of sweet grass that still hung in the air. What had Juliana told him? Star was the one who told her to rub the oil on her skin. Star was responsible for her trip to the past.

No.

The old Erik would have placed the blame on Star, but in truth, the blame lay with him. Her actions had been preordained. He should have stopped Juliana, but he had been too cautious and it may have cost them both.

Wispy hair, so-blonde-it-looked-white, caught his eye as a small-framed woman disappeared onto Bourbon Street. Shortly after he moved to the Quarter, he had met the infamous Star. Everyone who was anyone knew who she was, and Star's unique appearance wasn't hard to miss.

He had wanted to find her now to ask her questions and there she was up ahead, a serendipitous opportunity. Erik was grateful for his good luck. If it was luck. He couldn't help but wonder why was she just leaving from Juliana's street? Had she waited and anticipated this very outcome? After all, Star was the one who had explained to Juliana how to see her past.

A cold chill swept over him and the hair on his arms rose. He hadn't sensed anything amiss with Star before, but now, his gut told him something was not right. Erik strode after her, but when he got to Bourbon Street, she was nowhere to be seen among the Halloween crowd. He scoured the street, looking into alleyways, stores, bars, and restaurants. Eventually, out of the corner of his eye, he caught a fleeting glimpse of her again as she made her way to another street.

Star led him on a wild-goose chase, frustrating him further. He could do nothing...except not give up. Long ago, he had lost the unnatural abilities of Arak. All that remained was a very limited ability of persuasion. And that wouldn't do him any good. He trudged on with eyes narrowed. For as innocuous and innocent as Star had seemed, darkness shadowed her now.

He swore under his breath. Nothing he wanted came easy. He had to earn his way step by step the entire distance through this contracted sojourn. Why would he expect his reunion with Juliana to be any different? The Universe knew better. No matter what was thrown at him, he would never simply walk away.

Once the sun went down, he saw the top of Star's head more often through the thickening Halloween-costumed Quarter revelers, but just as he'd reach out to grab her, she was gone. His chest constricted with the futility of it all. Erik leaned against a storefront wall overcome by years of exhaustion, sliding down to sit with his face in his hands. So long he had waited and now he was being tested yet again. He took the moment to collect his thoughts. Where might a Voodoo practitioner go?

He knew that Star had no fixed location of business, but did palmistry and sold potions on the streets of the Quarter. Frustrated, he called out to the Universe, "A little help here!" expecting no reply. No sooner had he spoken the words than an image popped into his head. He saw a row of crypts, one in particular covered in X's with a small shrine in front.

"You've got to be kidding me," he mumbled as he stood.

It was Marie Laveau's tomb.

CHAPTER SIXTY-ONE

"Wake up," a voice commanded, reverberating inside of Julie's head.

Julie roused, opening her eyes as ordered.

A tall man stood by her bed. He wore jeans that clung to muscular legs, a YOLO t-shirt that embellished his well-defined chest, and a baseball cap that hid his face, but not his magnificent smile.

"Izak," she gasped, sitting up. "What...why...?" *What was he doing here?* Then she remembered everything that had transpired all over again.

He dismissed her with a wave of his hand. "I've come to retrieve you."

"How did you know I was here?"

Izak gave her a deadpan stare. "I suggest you get dressed. Let's not keep Erik waiting." Her heart skipped several beats at the sound of Erik's name while Izak removed her restraints and IV in less time than it took Julie to blink. Once freed, she went straight to the small closet, hoping her clothes were inside. Izak turned his back to her, giving her privacy.

She slipped into her jeans and pulled on her shirt. She could smell the scent of burnt sweet grass in the fabric as it slid over her face. It really happened. Everything really happened. She was home. She was in *her* life.

Her heart refused to settle down. She was going to see Erik. It had only been minutes for her since she had last seen him. It had been over a hundred years since he had seen her. Would he still feel the same?

She hesitated.

Was her enthusiasm clouding her judgment? This could be a trap. Izak was never one to be trustworthy. He always had ulterior motives; anything that served his purpose. Was he truly going to help her? But what choice did she have in the matter? He was her means to Erik.

One thought wormed its way inside her head. *Why hadn't Erik come for her himself?*

After she finished dressing, she realized she didn't have any shoes. She wasn't wearing any when she had collapsed. She gave a subtle cough to get Izak's attention. He turned, following her gaze down to her bare feet, toes wiggling.

"No matter." He hoisted her over his shoulder.

No one noticed them as they left the room–not one person in the hall, nor in the waiting room, nor in the elevator. He glided easily past the costumed tourists and locals, carrying her down dark street after dark street, masking their presence to those around them. It was still Halloween night. She had spent a month in the past while only hours passed in the present. As he strolled onward, his shoulder dug into her stomach and jostled her as he moved, making her nauseated.

"Please." She placed both hands on his shoulders. "Can we stop for a minute?"

He released her, looking down at her. "I thought your soul's primary intent would be to reunite with Erik as soon as possible. Why are we stopping?"

"I'm feeling a little sick." She smoothed her hair from her face. The nausea eased as she stood straight. She inhaled the humid night air, feeling better with each breath.

Izak leaned against the brick wall of the building next to them, crossing his arms. "Is this going to take long?"

She shook her head, taking deep breaths.

"So, what was it like to die?" Izak asked her.

Stunned, she raised an eyebrow. What a curious question to ask. "I don't know. I didn't die. One minute I was in Erik's arms and the next minute, I woke up in a hospital. There was no time in-between. Why do you ask?"

"Erik did not get off as easy. I hope you were worth every trial he had to endure."

Her stomach filled with dread and she became nauseated again. "What trials? What did he endure?"

His green eyes flicked over her. "You can ask him yourself."

"Let's go then." She started walking, heading toward home. She didn't care if the bottoms of her feet became dirtied. She would walk to Erik on her own. Step by step, her mind played havoc with her emotions as she imagined what might have happened to Erik.

Did he spend years and years trying to get to her? Had he defied aging? Or did he find a connection to her present as she had to the past through Naomi? Izak followed her, allowing her to take the lead until she stopped in front of her house. The windows were dark. Julie tossed Izak a questioning look.

"He is not in there." Izak said, closing his eyes, inhaling the air. "But he is close. Let's wait for him inside." Julie opened the door, it was unlocked. She entered the foyer and Izak entered just behind her.

"Be still," Izak ordered before she could turn on the lights.

Julie felt an invisible blanket wrap around her, preventing movement. It was not an altogether unpleasant feeling, but none-the-less, she glared at Izak. "I thought you couldn't come in uninvited?" she muttered.

"Erik invited me in a long time ago."

"What do you plan to do with me?"

"Nothing, you simple woman." Izak stepped back. "I just want you to understand what Erik has gone through for you. He has lived and died for you all these years. And I...I have been the one to watch him do so."

"What does that mean?"

"It means there was no quick or easy flash forward for Erik. He had to reincarnate over and over to find you again. He lived inferior lives to the life of perfection he was born into, such an unnecessary and messy business. I do not believe you are worthy of his sacrifice."

Juliana struggled against her invisible bonds to no avail. "Who is to measure my worthiness? You?" she snapped. "The only person who needs to find me worthy is Erik and I think his choices have spoken to his feelings. Now let me go! Take me to Erik!" Her anger sharpened her words, but as soon as Erik's name left her tongue, it sounded more like a plea.

"Free yourself." Izak circled her. "You started this...finish it."

"You have always blamed me! What have I ever done to you?" Julie yelled at him, mentally pushing at her restraints, creating bursts of light. She stilled, surprised by what she had done. "Jesus, Mary, and Joseph," she whispered as the lights faded.

Izak laughed at her shock. "It has been you all along. Wake up, Juliana," he commanded, placing two fingers on her forehead. "I said *wake up.*"

Pain shot through her brain. Fragmented images flooded her mind. She skipped down a flagstone street, her red hair flying into her face. She sat at a table studying gems. Standing in a courtyard balancing a ball of light in her hands. Crying over the crumpled body Arak once inhabited. Choking with Izak's hands at her throat. Mai-Ra creating healing light of restoration for her wounded neck. Love growing and growing for the Soul Walker and he loving her in return. She growing older and older and stronger and stronger. Her dedication ceremony as High Priestess. Aching to heal Arak's soul so that they could bond as equals. Signing the contract. Laying down to sleep in the temple. Being born.

Power surged in her.

"No more!" She freed one arm from his invisible shackles, knocking his hand away from her forehead. She sagged in her bonds, sweat beading on her brow. She was humbled by the remembrance of her life.

"I blame you, Akasha, because it is your fault. You have orchestrated this sojourn from beginning to end. Even now, interfering with power your human self doesn't know you possess. May I remind you of what you did in the alleyway the night of the masquerade ball when I tried to remove you from my brother's life?"

She pictured Izak and Marie suspended in mid-air and thrown to the ground. She was the one who had done that? Now she understood why Izak hated her so deeply. She had taken his brother from him, one life at a time as Erik's soul evolved. Juliana cried out as pain rippled through her. The pain turned to angry sparks of resentment then quickly spread through her soul as love. Izak's pain, resentment, and love for Arak.

Erik's soul vibrations were changing, and he and Izak would at some point not be able to connect with each other as they once had. If they even could any longer. The visions she had seen slipped away, unable to stay a part of her consciousness even though she grasped at them.

"Don't bother." Izak stopped her as if he were able to see her struggle. "It is beyond both of us. The contract does not allow you to retain your memories of that time just as it does not allow me to alter events."

Julie sighed. There was nothing she could say to Izak to ease the pain he felt. She looked up at him. "If you cannot alter events, then let me go and take me to Erik."

Izak's green eyes flicked over her. "Fear not, Juliana. He is on his way here. I release you." Izak breathed the last words over her, and the blanket fell.

"Thank you," she said, moving her arms and legs, testing their mobility.

"I do not want your thanks."

"Well, you have it all the same."

Izak cocked his head, listening.

Julie opened her eyes wide with excitement. "Is he coming?"

Izak blinked swirling green eyes at her. "No. I need to go to him. And you must wait here."

"I'm not waiting a minute more..." Julie ranted.
"Be still," Izak ordered. Her body froze.
Damn.
She was wrapped in the invisible blanket again.

CHAPTER SIXTY-TWO

Erik was two blocks away from Cemetery No.1 when even in the dim moonlight he could see Star push the gate open. He breathed his thanks to the Universe and ran after her. The normally locked gate was ajar. Erik walked inside. Marie's tomb was easy to spot. Several flickering candles cast shadows on the face of her resting place. And before it, Star stood with her back to him.

"Star." His voice echoed off the crypts, making it sound much louder than he had intended.

She turned to face him, strands of wispy hair falling over her face. Her small, delicate features drew themselves into a sad smile. "Erik."

Startled, Erik took a step back. "No one here knows me by that name."

She sashayed up to him, raising her face to meet his eyes. "I know."

"How do you know who I am?" Erik asked Star as she moved back to Marie's tomb.

"You shall know soon enough." She shifted from foot to foot with an unblinking stare. "It is almost All Souls' Day." She turned and made an X on the tomb before her, dropping the piece of chalk to the ground.

Erik grabbed her elbow and whirled her around. Her cryptic answer would not suffice. "What have you done to Juliana? Can it be reversed?"

"And how does one reverse destiny, hmm?"

"I want you to bring her back safely," Erik said, gripping her arm tighter, his anger mounting. "Now."

"Her destiny was my curse. Soon, we will both be free." Star easily slipped her small arm from his hand.

A chill settled over Erik. "You speak in riddles, woman."

Star turned toward the sound of the St. Louis Cathedral bells as their chimes carried in the air, striking midnight. November first, All Soul's day. When the bells ceased ringing, Star turned back to Erik.

"I have fulfilled my obligation to you."

"What obligation?" He tried to shake her, but she pulled away from him again.

Star began to twist inhumanly as if she were a snake shedding its skin. She grew taller, her shape changing. She grunted, leaned forward, and spoke.

"As long as there are stars in the heaven, you will not rest until you have remedied your part in Juliana's death."

Pale skin turned light brown, blonde hair turned black. Her hair wrapped itself up in a tignon that materialized out of thin air. Large hoop earrings swung from her ears and gold bracelets dangled on her wrists. She raised her head, staring into his eyes at equal height.

"Marie," he uttered.

"Well is this not a surprise, brother?"

Erik spun around to see Izak leisurely leaning against a tomb.

"I did not see this twist coming. Did you?" Izak asked him.

"Definitely not," Erik growled, turning back to Marie. "Marie—" he started.

She held up a hand. "Do you think Temple Beautiful is the only temple capable of soul cleansing?"

Izak stood next to Erik, his expression reflecting the same curiosity Erik felt. How did Marie know about the temple?

"Law of One are not the only practitioners, Arak. I myself sleep inside a Temple of Beliel, having a sojourn of my own. I want to revoke my contract. I never wanted to be a part of your soul growth in the first place. Against my own volition, I followed you into this ridiculous sojourn."

"I knew it." Izak smirked. "I knew there was something different about you when I could not break into your past."

"My past was hidden from me as well, but not anymore. Not since you cursed me as you took my life." She looked at Erik. "And there is no need to hide my past any longer."

Without the struggle he witnessed from Star, Marie's next transformation was much more subtle. The tignon unfurled and long hair spilled down her back. Her skin turned olive and her curvy figure was evident under her form-fitting tunic.

Erik didn't recognize her new persona.

"I know you," Izak said. "You're Sybelle, one of Arak's lovers."

She gave a regal nod.

"If I recall, you tore up Arak's face," Izak said with a hint of admiration.

"Yes, I did. And it set into motion many events that needn't have happened, Arak."

"Both of you stop calling me by that name," Erik ordered, not wanting to associate himself with the person he no longer knew.

She ignored him. "The day I struck you, you cursed me."

"It is our way. Human life is so easy to manipulate," Izak said. "And it would not pose a problem for Arak now had he not taken this unnecessary soul challenge. My brother and I lived outside humanity's karmic law. I still do."

"But he chose to walk in the human world as a human. And I followed, unfortunately." Sybelle sighed.

"We cannot change the past," Erik said. "I cannot undo what has been done. What can we do to break the second curse?"

"It broke the night you took my life, because you interrupted my sojourn. I have not reincarnated since. I have been energy made manifest every night until I could fulfill the brand you placed on me."

"How exactly did he curse you the first time?" Izak asked.

Sybelle faced Erik. "You rejected me–degraded me–for loving you. And you made sure I would never forget it. I hear your words even now. *'You will always yearn for me, knowing for the rest of your life with every beat of that wicked heart of yours that I will forget you the minute you walk away.'*"

Even though he could not remember speaking the words, they haunted Erik just the same. Who was he to curse a person to a life of unfulfilled yearning? As Arak, his wish could come into existence. Her very soul was forced to obey him. And although his curse was probably meaningless to him, it changed the course of her life. Once human, his own actions as Arak ultimately changed his human life as Erik.

"You were compelled to want him against your will," Izak said. "No wonder you could not leave Erik or Juliana alone."

Erik took a deep breath. "If it matters any, I regret my actions. I was conceited and cruel." He approached her and whispered in her ear. "If there is a chance you are wrong and my words still bond you to me when you wake, I set you free, Sybelle. I set you free." He stepped back.

A tear slid down her face. "Thank you."

Erik nodded.

"My debt to you has been paid," she addressed him. "As you have already paid the price for your actions by losing Juliana once. Spiritual consequences, remember? You cannot alter other people's lives without having it ripple through your own. Heed my words and maybe you won't have to lose her again."

Erik nodded. He yearned only for a simple life, and he had no intentions of being "that man" any more. "I need you to bring her back to me. Please, wake her up."

Sybelle creased her forehead, looking past Erik to Izak. "But she is already awake."

Erik raised his eyebrows at Izak, his heart soaring.

"What? That's why I am here...to get you. Juliana is waiting. Believe me, she is *not* going anywhere."

Erik faced Sybelle again. "I cannot thank you enough."

She nodded at his thanks. Then her silhouette morphed from solid to energy. Her form shimmered into a million brilliant little lights that hovered in a human shape briefly before soaring off into the night sky.

Izak placed an arm around Erik's shoulder as they both gazed at the stark darkness where Sybelle once stood. "No sense standing here any longer. Let's get you to your beloved."

Juliana, Erik's heart pounded her name.

♀

Julie heard footsteps approaching. Izak appeared, mumbled a few words, releasing her mouth and her body from the invisible bindings that had held her captive.

"Stop doing that!" She hissed, whirling on him. But he just smiled at her. Air brushed against her as Izak disappeared, moving faster than her eye could discern and leaving her quite alone.

"Hey!" she yelled after him, stomping. "You were supposed to take me to Erik!"

"Juliana?"

Hearing the familiar, rich-timbered voice, Julie trembled. Her breathing quickened, making her gasp. As she turned around, she could barely form the word, that one most beautiful word. "Erik?"

At first, she couldn't see anything but a shadow inside the darkened doorway. The shadow turned into a man as he silently approached, answering. "Yes, it is I."

Her jaw dropped, and tears welled in her eyes at seeing him. His face was no longer scarred. His tall, muscular build was years younger than the man she once knew, and he sported black hair in a buzz-cut. His skin was cafe-au-lait.

Heath.

Erik *was* Heath.

Heath *was* Erik.

She sobbed, flinging herself into arms that embraced her without hesitation. She laughed and cried, kissing his face only to hug him tightly again, so tightly as to not leave any space between them. If she could become a part of his very essence, she would. Being safe in his arms made her feel as if the world had righted itself and she were finally home.

"I cannot hold you close enough," he breathed into her ear, as he squeezed her even closer. "It has been a very long road back to you, Juliana.

"I can't imagine what you've been through," she said, pulling back to look up at him. She saw Erik's soul looking back at her through Heath's brown eyes.

"It was worth it," he said, placing his warm hand on her face.

She leaned into his palm, reveling at his touch. "Promise me that we will never be separated again."

"Never again," he reassured her, moving his hand from her face to pull her into an embrace again. "You don't know how hard it was to be around you and not tell you who I really was."

"I felt a connection when I first met you. I just didn't recognize it for what it was because I hadn't seen my past yet."

"I know," he said, then pulled back, concern creasing his eyes. "Are you okay? You didn't suffer any injury from me sending you back?"

"No, I'm okay," she said, smiling. "Better than okay."

"Yes," he said, inspecting her from head to toe, his gaze resting on her lips. "I can see."

The longing in his eyes prompted Julie to rise on her tip-toes and kiss him. At first, her kisses were soft and tender, almost chaste, in reverence of having something most precious returned to her, but his response kindled her passion. Their kisses deepened with mutual need, mutual passion, and mutual surrender. And with those kisses, she relived the moment they had made love, recalling every second, his scent, the weight of his body, the ardent look in his eyes.

She pulled away, breathless. "Erik–"

"I love hearing you say my name." He raised his face to the ceiling and sighed. "Say it again."

"Erik," she whispered for the love of saying it. "Tell me what happened after you and Izak sent me back. How did you find me again?"

A slow, reflective smile spread across his face. "More than a century has passed since I saw you last. The explanation is neither a short nor a simple one. And I intend tell you every detail, but not now...not yet. We have the rest of our lives to sort it all out." The truth of his words settled on her, calming her soul.

"Yes," she said, her heart thrumming. She pictured a future with Erik at her side. "We have the rest of our lives." She laced her fingers with his, tugging him toward the bedroom. "Let's start our future now."

He laughed at her eagerness and kissed her again. "There is one thing I'd like to do first." He dug into his pocket and pulled something out. Even in the shadowy darkness of the house, she could see the silver balls. It was her bracelet with Naomi's and Erik's hair entwined on the charm. Their bracelet. Their love story.

"How...," she started to ask. She had thrown it to the back of her closet.

"I retrieved it before the ambulance came. I thought I might need it to bring you back to me." He lifted her hand, encircled her wrist with the heirloom, and closed the clasp. "On this bracelet, we are bound together. Let's make it official, Juliana. Marry me."

"I will," she said, kissing him again. He swept her into his arms and kicked the front door shut, striding with her toward their bedroom.

"Now, let's start our lives together."

She nodded. Julie's heart beat with love for Erik.

She was his.

And he was hers.

CHAPTER SIXTY-THREE

···

Many years later...

Erik roused to half-awareness when the bed he slept in shook. Not yet able to open his eyes, he heard the whispered echo of Izak saying, *"This is your choice and yours alone. Once I walk out of this house, I turn my back on you."* He found it odd that he should recall his brother's words as he lingered in that mysterious realm between sleep and wakefulness. Instead of dwelling on the moment, he succumbed to the memories that flooded his mind when his unexpected soul remembrance began.

He was a young boy with a sackcloth over his face, feeling the emotions of his early life. Taunting. Suffering. Cruelty. Hunger. Then becoming Phantom and bewitching Christine. Charm. Deceit. Desire. Moving to New Orleans. His metamorphosis into the Prince of Conjurers. His nemesis Marie Laveau. Bringing home Naomi. Deception. Triumph. Conjuring Juliana. Meeting his brother, Izak. Letting go. Falling in love. Losing Juliana. Grief. Despair. Unwavering hope. Death. Life. Death. Life. Death.

Then the sweeter memories came, lingering longer for him to savor.

Heath's early years. Carefree. Privileged. Loving parents and siblings. Izak's constant support. High school. College. Eagerness. Buying the antique store, collecting and filling it with tangible pieces from all of his lives. Waiting for Juliana. He didn't dare check into her life for fear of changing their past or future. Wondering what his beloved even looked like. Anticipation.

Their reunion. Building a well-deserved life together. Traveling together. Loving each other. The day Juliana presented him with a positive pregnancy test. The birth of their firstborn, Aaron. Holding his son in his arms. Izak embracing the role of uncle. Unending joy. Warm, lazy New Orleans days. Another son, Isaac. Laughter and love. A daughter, Lilith Rose, his little princess. School days. Grown children. Marriages.

Gray hair. Walking hand in hand in Audubon Park. Grandchildren.

And the last memory before closing his eyes for an afternoon nap: a large family meal of fried oysters and shrimp. Hugs. Giggles. Silliness. Togetherness. Feeling like the luckiest man in the world. Juliana's lips on his forehead, kissing him as he drifted off to sleep.

Erik woke with a smile on his face. He stared lazily at the ceiling, reveling in his journey until the rumbling earth shook the bed. Eyes widening, he sat up, disoriented. New Orleans did not have earthquakes, and this was not his bedroom. A spray of dust rained on him from the disgruntled building as the earth shook again.

What was happening?

Confused, he glanced around the sparse room. Crystals embedded in the walls provided the soft light that allowed him to see. Panic rose in him. The beautiful bedroom Juliana had carefully decorated, including their four-poster bed, was gone. The room was bare save for the suspended bed he sat upon. To his right, an arched doorway flanked by stone pillars led to a hallway.

Erik lowered his bare feet to the cold flagstone floor. As he stood, the crystals shone blindingly, and a surge of energy flooded into him. When the light receded, he rose to his full height, power seeping from every pore of his body. He spread out his arms and stretched his fingers, feeling renewed and whole again, no longer the old man he had been this morning.

Another surge of power flowed through him with an intensity that made him cry out. The jolt awakened his mind, lifting the veil of forgetfulness, recovering and comingling his memories.

He had been released from the contract.

He flexed his muscles, reveling in his restoration. He was Arak once more.

A small man entered the chamber. "Soul Traveler, you have done well."

Arak smiled in recognition, embracing the priest. "Mai-Ra, where is Akasha?"

"Akasha went before you, and she shall return after you. It is not yet her time to wake."

He sucked in a breath. "Why am I here? Why did the contract end?"

"You have accomplished what the contract entailed, and your earthly body ceased to function. In the time period you just left, your family is laying your empty vessel to rest."

As Arak exhaled, his gut wrenched, tears stinging his eyes. He would never leave Juliana behind, *never*. "No, this is not what I want! Send me back!"

Mai-Ra folded his hands, responding patiently. "In your sojourn, Akasha succumbed to death before you over and over again, leaving you to feel the agony of deep loss, and now, it is her turn to experience the feeling. She will endure it and complete her part of the contract."

The room shook again, harder, forcing Mai-Ra to brace himself against the wall. Arak steeled himself, remaining upright.

"Mother Earth is unhappy with us. It is not safe here anymore," Mai-Ra said once the trembling stopped. "We are evacuating the temple and the city."

"What has happened?"

"The city is sinking into the great waters. Our outer rings and islets have already disappeared. We have combined our energy to delay the island's destruction, but we can only delay the inevitable. As we speak, the shores and outlying areas have crumbled. Soon, Atlantis will sink, leaving little to indicate it ever existed."

Arak sank down on the suspended bed, his throat constricting. His home for thousands of years was to be no more. "What caused this disaster? Why was it not prevented?"

"Nothing could have been done. The Earth has chosen to reclaim what is hers." Mai-Ra gently grabbed Arak's elbow, assisting him from the bed and directing him toward the hallway. "You must leave now."

Arak pulled his elbow from the priest's hand. "I am not leaving without Akasha. Where is she?"

"She is in her own chamber. What remains of her soul is asleep. Must I repeat that it is not time for her to wake? We will see to her safety."

Arak leveled his eyes at Mai-Ra. "I shall see to her safety," he said, hoarsely. "I will leave with her or not at all."

Mai-Ra sighed. "Until you are bound to her, Akasha is the responsibility of the Law of One."

Couldn't this wretched priest hear how his heart pounded? Couldn't he see the love that poured from his soul? Their sojourn...their contract was not for nothing. Akasha was his and he was hers. "We *are* bonded!"

Mai-Ra searched Arak's eyes, a tender smile spreading on his face. "And so you are. But she cannot be woken until she is released."

"What can I do to delay this destruction and keep her safe?"

Mai-Ra raised an eyebrow in speculation. "If you were to join your energy with our own, we might yet earn a long-enough reprieve. Our priests are in the antechamber of the sacred stone, harnessing energy to keep the land stable. Your power would enhance their strength."

"How? I have felt the energy of the stone, but Izak and I could never harness it." He remembered the day Akasha marched in the procession, calling on the energy of the crystal that sat on the pinnacle of the temple to send flowers into the crowd.

"It was not possible before because your soul vibrations did not match that of the crystal, but now they do. The Temple Beautiful was established for soul cleansing. You have been renewed."

Arak nodded, his soul resonating in the truth of the priest's words. "I will join you and do what I can. But first, let me see Akasha."

Mai-Ra motioned. "Follow me."

The temple was silent and empty. Their footsteps made no sound. They passed several chambers that resembled the one Arak had just left, all empty.

A severe tremor shook the ground once more, cracking the floor in a long, crazed line. Several stones fell from the wall to land at his feet. Arak waved his hand and with a thought cleared the path. There was nothing in life he couldn't have. Anything he wanted, he took. He and Izak had devoted their lives to selfishness. The world, and those in it, revolved around them.

No longer. His first concern was not to satisfy his own desires, but to help others. And one other in particular. Akasha had known who he could be all along. He had walked a mile, no...many lifetimes in many different shoes. He would never see life the same again.

Mai-Ra stopped, gesturing to the archway at the end of the hall. Arak ran to it and entered, the chamber's crystals brightening with his passing. Akasha's bed swayed from the tremors. Arak reached a hand out to one of the suspension cords and steadied it, gazing down on her. Her red hair splayed around her beautiful, expressionless face.

"I am here, beloved. I have not left you. All you need do is open your eyes," he whispered in her ear, watching her face for any indication that she had heard. Akasha remained motionless. He released a breath of disappointment and caressed the side of her face. "Come back to me soon."

He didn't want to leave her. He wanted his face to be the first she saw when she was released. He stopped under the archway and turned to look at her once more, with the silent wish that he could ensure there would be a city for her to wake up to.

"Arak!" his name reverberated through the empty temple.

Hope lit in Arak's soul. Izak was here. Together they could stave off the disaster until Akasha and the clerics had time to evacuate, he using the crystal's energy and Izak the darker Earth energy.

"Izak!" he called, running toward the sound, Mai-Ra following at his heels. Arak stumbled forward as the ground heaved. The walls writhed and quaked, advancing and receding.

"Arak, there is no time to waste. You must follow me." Mai-Ra caught up to him.

Arak stopped. "Do you not see? Izak could help us."

Mai-Ra shook his head, sadness in his eyes. "Your brother would seize the opportunity to get his hands on the stone to corrupt its purity."

Arak shook his head and continued to follow Izak's call. They were soul-bonded brothers. Izak would aid him in this quest. Just the idea of the challenge would intrigue him. There wasn't anything they wouldn't do for each other. That was how it had always been.

"Brother!" Arak was lifted off the ground in a strong embrace. Izak squeezed him tightly once more before releasing him. "I felt the moment you woke." Izak walked around him, appraising him, concerned. "They did not do anything to you? You are intact?"

Arak smiled grimly. "Brother, I am well. Your timing is impeccable."

"I have been trying for three months to break through their defenses to get to you." The Earth rumbled as if on cue. "Since the destruction commenced, their defenses are no longer in place. Let us get out of here before the whole infernal place collapses. Half the city is rubble. I was thinking we would go to Egypt. They would welcome us with open arms. What say you?"

"Arak has agreed to assist us," Mai-Ra said.

Izak's nostrils flared at the interruption, and his eyes grew dark when he saw the speaker emerge from the shadows. Before Arak could stop him, Izak raised his hand and sent Mai-Ra flying against the stone wall, holding him there.

"Stop," Arak ordered, his protective instincts rising.

Izak forced the air from Mai-Ra's lungs, suffocating him. "This interloper has interfered enough with us, Brother. I'm going to finish him off once and for all," Izak replied through gritted teeth.

The priest could not fight back. All the energy of the Law of One was being channeled into keeping the city from descending into the deep.

"Let him go, brother," Arak ordered again.

"No."

Arak stepped in front of the priest and released a pulse of energy to arrest Izak's attack. Mai-Ra slid to the floor, gasping for air.

"Move aside," Izak said, sending angry energy pulses back at Arak as they circled each other in a dance of wills. "How dare you defend this human."

Arak remained steady, holding Izak back even though it hurt him to challenge his brother.

Izak frowned as their energies continued to collide, squinting at the brightness. "Your energy is different."

"It's not just my energy. I, too, am different. Again, I ask you to stop. As my brother, will you stop?" Arak lessened the intensity of his assault.

"As your brother, is this the thanks I get? Keeping vigil day and night? Trying to penetrate this stronghold to remove you from this palace of deception? Three priests dared to stop me just now. I killed them all to get to you."

Mai-Ra wailed out in grief.

Arak was appalled. There was no need to slaughter the priests. And now there were three fewer people in the antechamber holding Atlantis together. "Why?"

Izak lowered his hand and Arak did the same, ceasing their combat. "You are my brother, and I love you. There is no one I would not kill for you."

Arak stared at his brother, fighting back tears. He understood that kind of love. It had been his way of life as well until Akasha. Even as Juliana, Akasha's wisdom reached his soul.

Loving someone doesn't mean you'd kill for them, Erik. Loving someone, truly loving someone, means you'd die for them.

And she proved it more than once so he could continue to live. Izak could not understand this kind of love. It would not make sense to him. Asking his brother for help would be pointless now. He had to let him go.

"I am staying. I am going to lend my energy to sustaining the city for as long as possible, so people can continue to evacuate."

"What do you owe these people, Arak?" Izak spit out. "Let them perish. It is nature's way."

"They deserve to live, and I am going to see to it that they do."

"At what cost? Your own life? Because that is what will happen, Arak. The Sekhat-Aztlan sank an hour ago along with your replacements. If this body dies, you have no recourse. You will be *lost*."

A chill swept over Arak. He looked at Mai-Ra who by his silence, confirmed Izak's words. It was Arak's choice to make. It was an easy one. Living without Akasha was not an option. He steeled himself. "I will take that chance."

"Fine." Izak's eyes blazed. "So be it." He flung his arms out in fury, pinning Arak against the wall. Before Arak could catch his breath to make things right between them, his brother was gone. He fell to his knees.

The earth shook again, longer and harder, the ground heaving into broken mounds. When it stopped, Arak stood, helping Mai-Ra to his feet. The priest nodded in gratitude, silently leading Arak deeper into the modest temple. A low hum emanated from the antechamber as they drew closer. Mai-Ra opened the golden double-doors, revealing an oval room with priests standing in a semi-circle around a closed copper door, meditating. The air wavered with the heat produced from their energy. Their tunics were soaked with sweat.

"Why are they not in contact with the sacred stone?" Arak asked. "They could produce so much more energy."

Mai-Ra folded his hands. "Not everyone can stand in the presence of the sacred stone."

Arak nodded, understanding. By their birthright, sons of Adam and Lilith, he and Izak were not subjugated to the laws of man. "But I can."

"Yes, you can," Mai-Ra confirmed.

Another round of violent tremors shook the temple. A stone pillar fell, knocking crystals from the wall, shattering them into small pieces. The fractured quartz reflected muted images to Arak, showing him a solution. "Has everyone evacuated the temple except for these few?"

The high priest nodded.

"Have you a means of escape?"

"We have a ship in the harbor."

Arak picked up the pieces of crystal and handed them to Mai-Ra. "Take the men and go to Akasha. Unanchor her bed then place these stones around her. Carry her out of here. I will hold the temple and the land steady until you are safely away."

"Are you sure this is what you want?" Mai-Ra searched his face.

Arak breathed deeply. "Yes." Did he want to die? No. Would he stay behind to save her? Yes.

He pushed through the men and opened the copper door, stepping inside the chamber. He looked up to the underside of Temple Beautiful's apex. The bottom of the crystal sat in the center. He could feel the untapped power inside of the faceted gem, and it took his breath away.

He did not have to turn around to know that the priests had left. He had sight of all he wanted to know as he gazed into the sacred stone. He could also see the surrounding land outside of the temple walls. And what he saw did not bode well for the priests' survival. The last evacuees of the city had just pushed off, and the sea was speckled with tiny boat after tiny boat. The larger boats were tiny dots farther out. Anchored to the pier, the temple boat rocked, threatening to break free.

With one hand raised to the sacred stone and the other directed toward the buckled floor, Arak blasted a hole in the flagstone. He could steady the land better if he was in contact with it. He stood on the small patch of bare earth and juggled energy between keeping land and temple intact. He fortified the area of the temple in which Akasha's chamber resided as well as the path to the exit and allowed the walls to crumble where not needed.

Water rushed forward to hungrily claim the portions of land the priests had tried to keep dry, drowning several people still huddled in their homes, refusing to leave. Arak protected a wide strip of earth that led to the ship and the pier, keeping it elevated and the churning water at bay. His muscles bulged with the effort, sweat beading on his forehead.

Akasha. His thoughts turned to her, and he watched Mai-Ra leading the priests who carried her. The glowing crystals kept her in her suspended sleep. The ground shook under his feet, and he saw the priests stumble, but none let go of Akasha. One hooded figure lagged behind. Arak sent a burst of energy to push the man forward. Time was running out.

The men made it out of the temple. Arak's relief was short-lived; he narrowly missed blocking a wave that would have swept them out to sea. He allowed the walls of the temple to fall around him, keeping only the pinnacle above him intact. Then he blasted a path through the collapsed stone. *Akasha. Akasha.* Her name beat in time with his heart. He could see the bright redness of her hair getting farther and farther away.

He tired. The sacred stone gave power and it took power away. The grueling task took its toll on him. He would not last much longer. His legs trembled under the strain of keeping the small patch of land above water.

The priests had tied ropes around Akasha's bed, and those already on board hoisted it onto the ship. The priests, one by one, climbed up a ladder then urged the hooded figure over the rail. It was almost time to let go. Almost.

Did he see movement? He daren't move his arms to wipe the sweat off his face. Yes. Akasha sat up, surrounded by the blinding light of the crystals. Mai-Ra finally followed the last priest onto the ship. And Arak filled his lungs with all the air he could hold and blew with all of his might, commanding the wind toward the ship, lifting its sail, and sending her away from the ill-fated island.

The small figure of a woman ran to the stern of the ship. With the last of his will, he pulled energy from the sacred stone and viewed from increasing distance her lovely face, her fear-filled amber eyes, her mouth forming his name, and her arms outstretched as the priests held her back from jumping overboard. Releasing the sacred stone, he stretched his arm to her in return, sending his love.

As he did, the water rushed in, and earth and stone bore down on him. Without strength to counter the elements, he sank into his grave without a struggle. Seeing Akasha safe filled his mind, and Arak smiled as he felt his soul release from his body. His beloved was the last image he saw with human eyes.

He drifted upward, weightless.

Arak had moved from body to spirit to body many times before and had always been a fully-formed entity. Now, he was pure energy, formless. His soul was dispersed over the earth, reaching into the expanse of space.

He was wind, stone, and water. He was rock, plant, insect, and animal. He was salt.

Akasha's tears.

He was on the boat next to her as she sobbed in Mai-Ra's embrace. Arak had no hand with which to sooth her. He was wood. He was metal. He was fiber. He was crystal. He was thought.

Arak, Akasha's soul cried. He was her pain personified.

Arak, someone else cried out for him. Miles away, he surrounded Izak. He was sand. He was fury. He was agony.

He sensed living beings. There was refuge; three soulless bodies hovered nearby.

He was knowledge. Izak had lied. He had saved these vessels for Arak. He wanted Arak to choose him...to choose life as it had always been. Arak longed to enter a body, but to take residence in one of these hosts would tie him to a brother and a life that no longer served him.

"Arak," Mai-Ra called to him.

He was back aboard the boat. "Arak," Mai-Ra spoke into the wind, removing the hood of the priest that stood next to him, a soulless priest. The priest that had lagged behind and needed assistance onto the ship.

Arak was memory. This soulless one was a secret offspring of Izak's. A baby born without a soul taken to the temple of the Law of One. A child raised and nurtured by Mai-Ra, unbeknownst to the other priests or Akasha. Arak heard Mai-Ra's projected thoughts into the Universe along with the hope that Arak listened.

Arak, you had to make your choice believing there was no salvation. It would not be a true sacrifice otherwise. You have done well. You have a home and a choice to make. He moved away from the motionless priest, leaving Arak to make his decision.

Arak vibrated joyfully. He was sunshine. He was air. And still, he was far-reaching.

Izak continued to howl, searching for Arak's presence, unable to sense him. Izak was not capable of knowing Arak in this new manifestation, but his brother was not ready to let him go. Arak pushed light into Izak's heavy density with words only the keenest ear could perceive. *We will meet again, brother.* Arak saw swirling green eyes, bright with tears, stare vacantly ahead as Izak's howling ceased.

He pulled his energy back without regret, directing his attention to the priest on the boat. The universe could not fit inside the confines of flesh and blood. Arak drew in upon himself, moving from the four corners of the earth, descending from space. He was spirit. He was form. He was a Soul Traveler.

Arak slipped inside the body, connecting with the brain, spinal cord, organs, muscles, and senses. Salty wind pelted his skin. The scent of briny sea filled his nostrils. He opened his eyes, seeing his beloved.

Arak's heart expanded. Akasha leaned against the stern of the ship, her long red hair whipped by the wind behind her. She faced the empty waterscape where Atlantis once thrived and he perished.

"Akasha," he projected his voice to her ear, striding toward her.

Akasha turned, wiping a tear from her reddened eyes. "Yes, priest?"

Akasha's pain, a palpable energy, forced him to stop at arm's length or be overcome by it. "Not priest, beloved," he choked on the words.

She blinked, truly looking at him. Her amber-eyes widened, reflecting the surprise etched on her face. And he waited in wretched suspense as she stood in silence.

"Arak?" she finally spoke, her eyes lit in hope and disbelief.

He nodded.

"Arak!" she sobbed, flinging herself into his open arms. He enveloped her into the curve of his body. She ran her hands over him as if to convince herself he was real. She pulled back, rising on her toes, smothering his face with kisses and tears. He kissed her greedily in return, savoring each one.

"Oh, Arak," she said, looking back at the churning waters of Atlantis. "Our home is gone."

"My home is where you are." He raised his hand. She placed her palm against his and they entwined their fingers.

Warm, compatible energy flowed between their palms. His heartbeat gathered speed and his breathing along with it. He craved her closeness in ways he could not express. Hands still clasped, he pulled her against him. He crushed her mouth in a deep kiss as she leaned into him leaving no space between them. And still, he yearned for more.

He groaned with need, driven to be closer still. And then he felt part of his soul release from the tight confines of his body, resonating into Akasha as her soul did the same, co-mingling. The persistent yearning dissipated as he truly became one with Akasha, feeling a completeness he could have only imagined in his wildest dream.

Joined to her, sharing their energies, he was no longer Phantom. He was not Prince of Conjurers. He relinquished his claim of Soul Traveler.

He was simply Arak.

Akasha's Beloved.

♫ AUTHOR'S NOTE ♫

I chose to follow Edgar Cayce's version of events as related to Atlantis as opposed to Plato's written account. Another tidbit you might be interested in for those of you not familiar with Edgar Cayce; he lost his voice for about a one year period. No one could determine the cause of his malady. At some point, it was suggested he see a hypnotist.

During this visit, Edgar performed his first reading. He diagnosed himself, prescribed a cure, and healed his vocal cords. I'm sure Izak was a little annoyed when he discovered Edgar had found his voice again. Maybe one day, you'll find out for yourself just how annoyed Izak was...

Thank you for taking the journey with me. I hope you enjoyed Prince of Conjurers.

❧ ABOUT THE AUTHOR ❧

Photo by Jack Chance

Laurie L. Bolanos lives below sea level in a small cottage on the edge of a city shaped like a bowl. When given the opportunity, she doesn't mind hopping a few states over to enjoy Gulf breezes and to dip her toes in the ocean. She likes to take long walks on the beach, sip on the occasional piña colada, and soak in the rays of the sun. No matter the venue, her preference is to be barefoot. However, she will bend to social expectations and don a pair of shoes when necessary.

She enjoys attending a monthly drumming circle where she was, in fact, told she has a "natural ability." Loving the vibrations of the drum, she has also invested time with tuning fork therapy, although she has not yet been certified in the craft.

Laurie comes from an Italian family and can prove it with her DNA results from 23andMe as she is 40.4% confirmed Italian. Other nationalities need not feel left out as she also has French, German, British, Irish, Iberian, Balkan, Sardinian, Scandinavian, Ashkenazi, Middle Eastern, West African, and Yakut, proving by her very existence that we are one world and should not be divided by race.

She started writing Prince of Conjurers in December of 2008 and plugged away at it until giving you the completed version you now hold in your hands. Although this is her debut novel, she insists that she has plenty more stories swirling around inside her mind, so keep an eye out for more titles in the future. Hopefully the next book won't take so long! If you want to contact Laurie, you can email her at *princeofconjurers@yahoo.com* and check out her website at *princeofconjurers.com* or at **Laurie L. Bolanos** on Facebook.